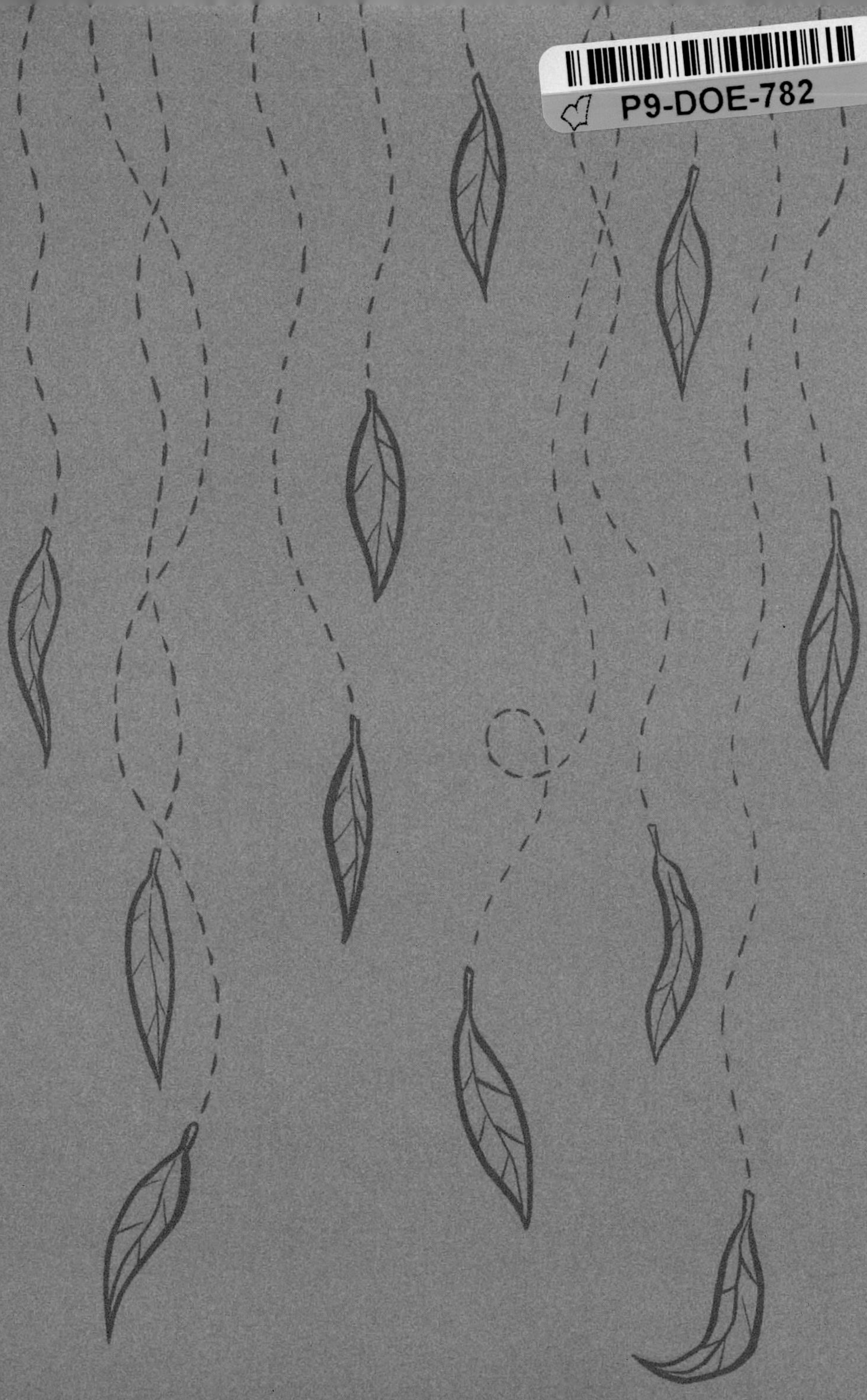

RAINA TELGEMEIER

DRAMA

WITH COLOR BY GURIHIRU

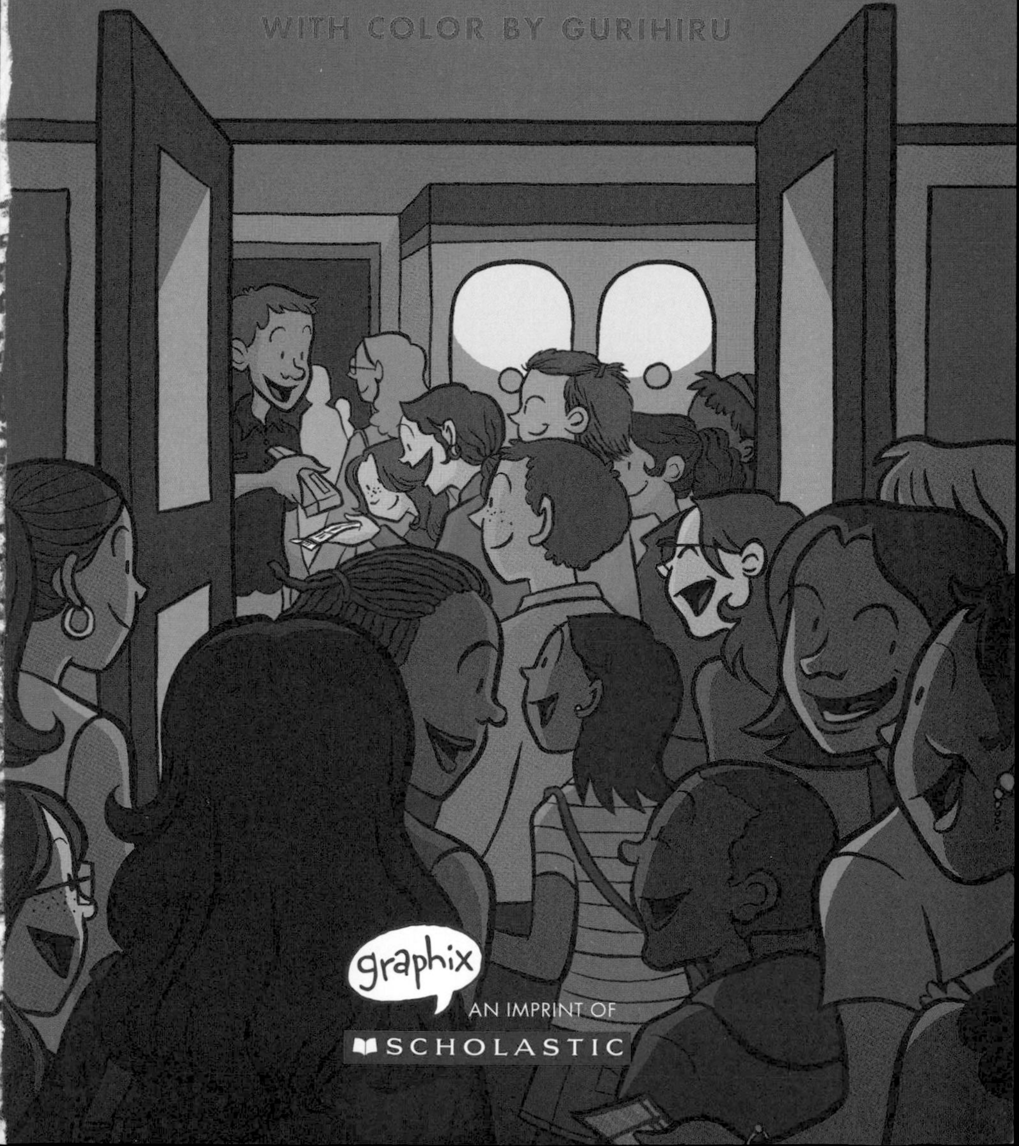

graphix
AN IMPRINT OF
SCHOLASTIC

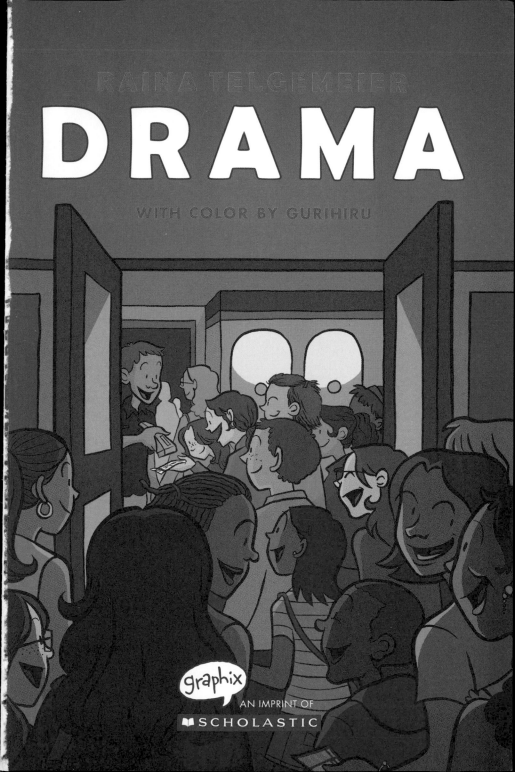

For Jake and Jeff, who continue to inspire me.

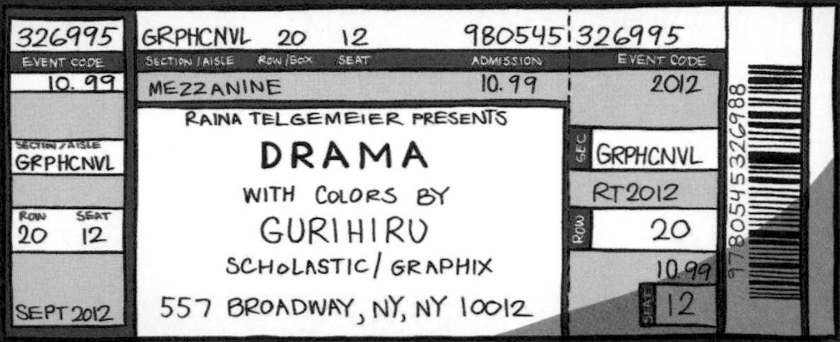
326995
EVENT CODE
10.99
SECTION/AISLE
GRPHCNVL
ROW SEAT
20 12
SEPT 2012
GRPHCNVL 20 12 980545 326995
SECTION/AISLE ROW/BOX SEAT ADMISSION EVENT CODE
MEZZANINE 10.99 2012
RAINA TELGEMEIER PRESENTS
DRAMA
WITH COLORS BY
GURIHIRU
SCHOLASTIC/GRAPHIX
557 BROADWAY, NY, NY 10012
SEC GRPHCNVL
RT2012
ROW 20
10.99
SEAT 12
9780545326988

Library of Congress Cataloging-in-Publication Data

Telgemeier, Raina.
Drama / Raina Telgemeier ; with color by Gurihiru. — 1st ed.
p. cm.
Summary: Callie rides an emotional roller coaster while serving on the stage crew for a middle school production of *Moon over Mississippi* as various relationships start and end, and others never quite get going.
ISBN 978-0-545-32698-8 (hardcover)
ISBN 978-0-545-32699-5 (paperback)
1. Graphic novels. [1. Graphic novels. 2. Theater—Fiction. 3. Interpersonal relations—Fiction. 4. Middle schools—Fiction. 5. Schools—Fiction.] I. Gurihiru. II. Title.
PZ7.7.T45Dr 2012
741.5'973—dc23
2011040748

25 24 23 22 21 20 19 21 22 23 24 25

First edition, September 2012
Edited by Cassandra Pelham
Lettering by John Green
Book design by Phil Falco
Creative Director: David Saylor
Printed in China 62

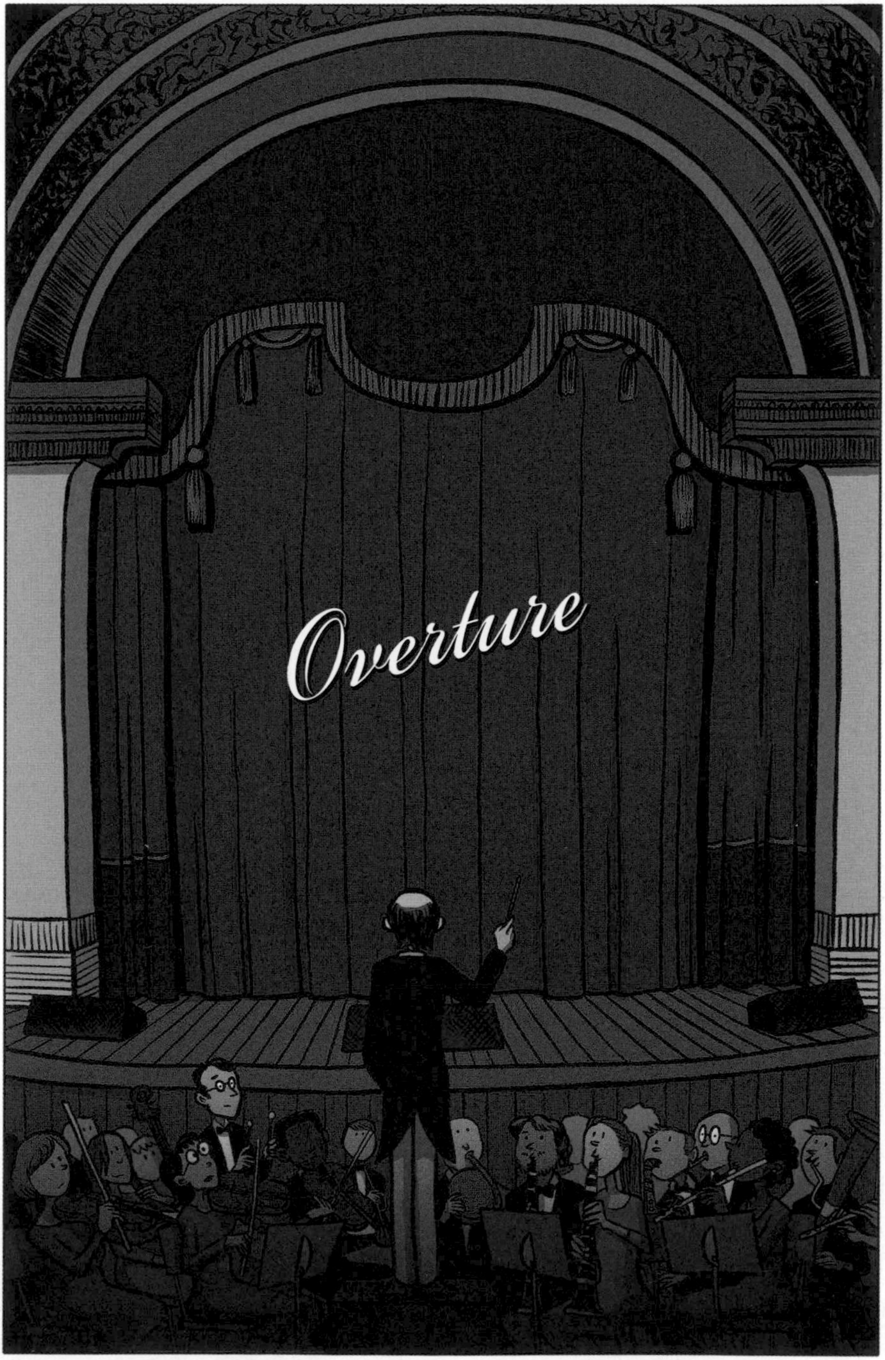
Overture

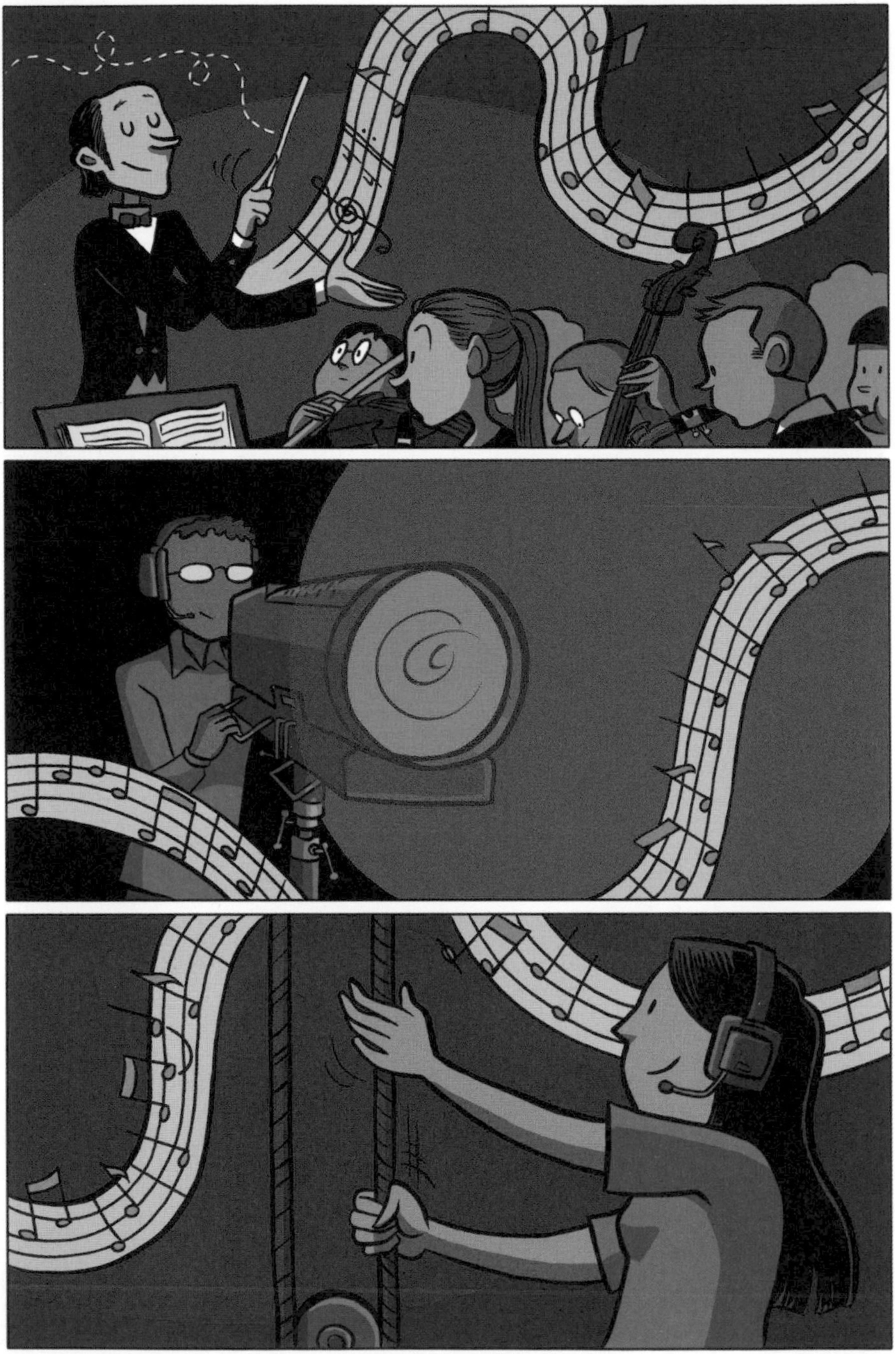

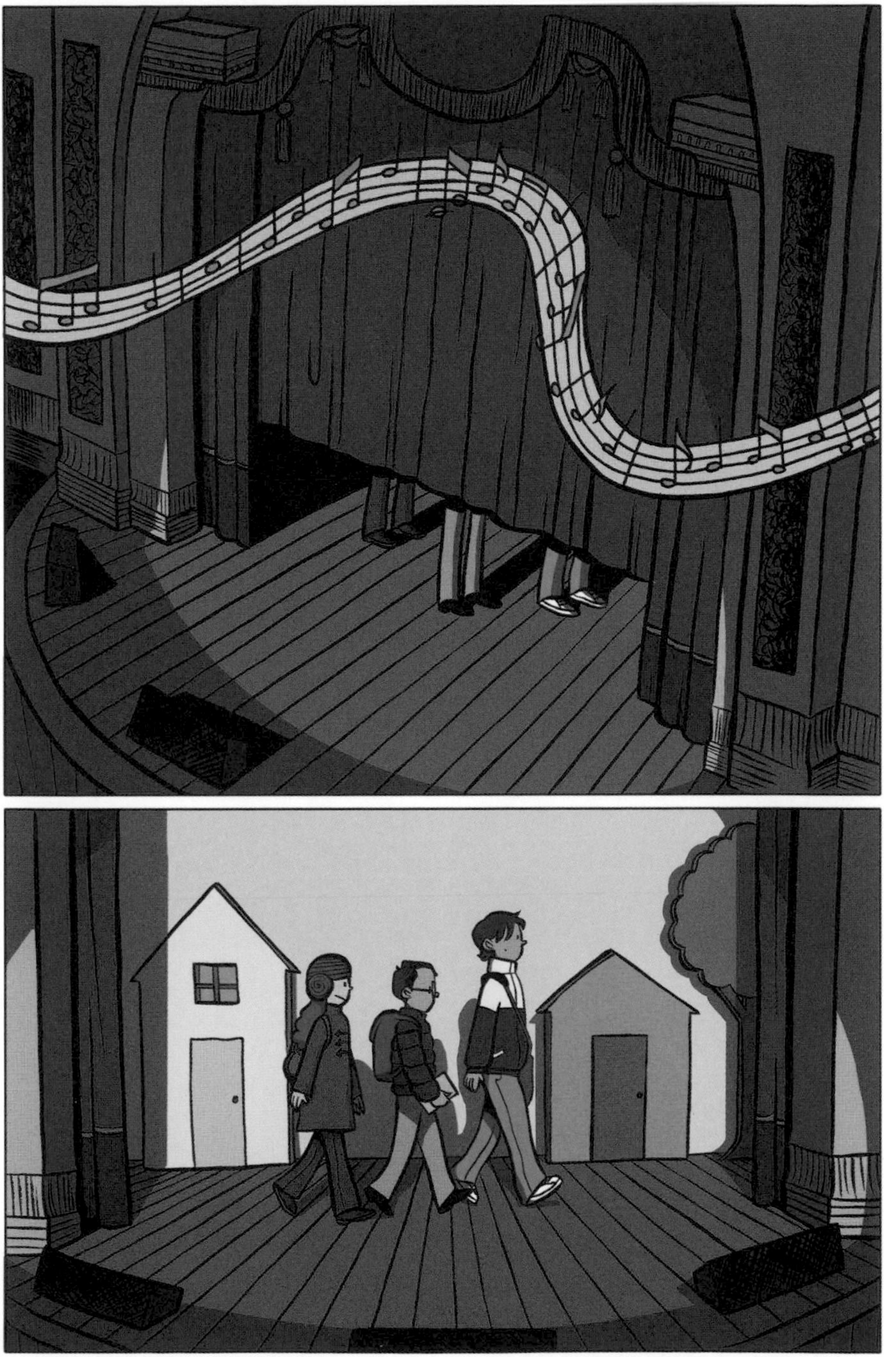

ACT I

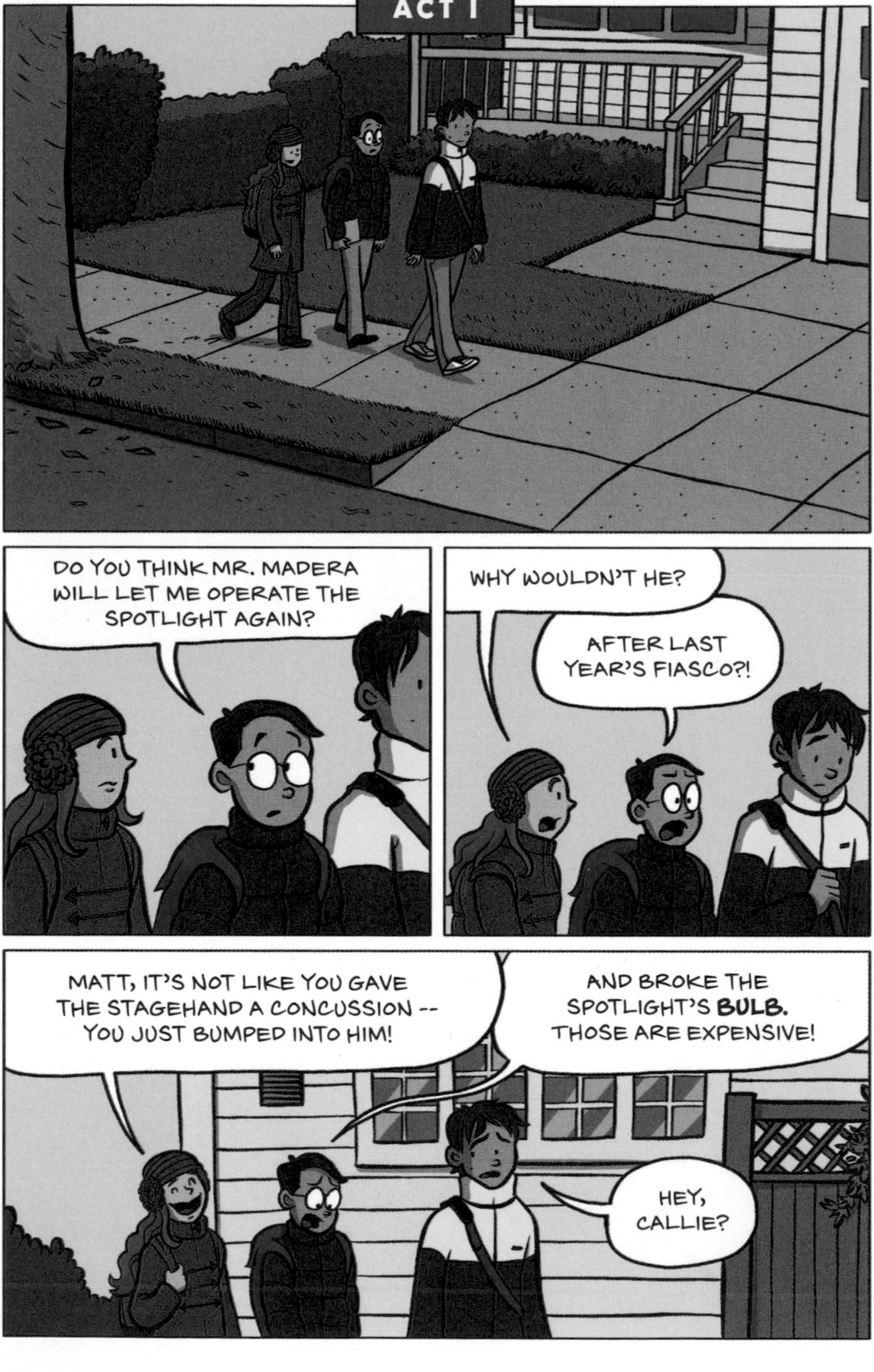
DO YOU THINK MR. MADERA WILL LET ME OPERATE THE SPOTLIGHT AGAIN?
WHY WOULDN'T HE?
AFTER LAST YEAR'S FIASCO?!
MATT, IT'S NOT LIKE YOU GAVE THE STAGEHAND A CONCUSSION -- YOU JUST BUMPED INTO HIM!
AND BROKE THE SPOTLIGHT'S **BULB.** THOSE ARE EXPENSIVE!
HEY, CALLIE?

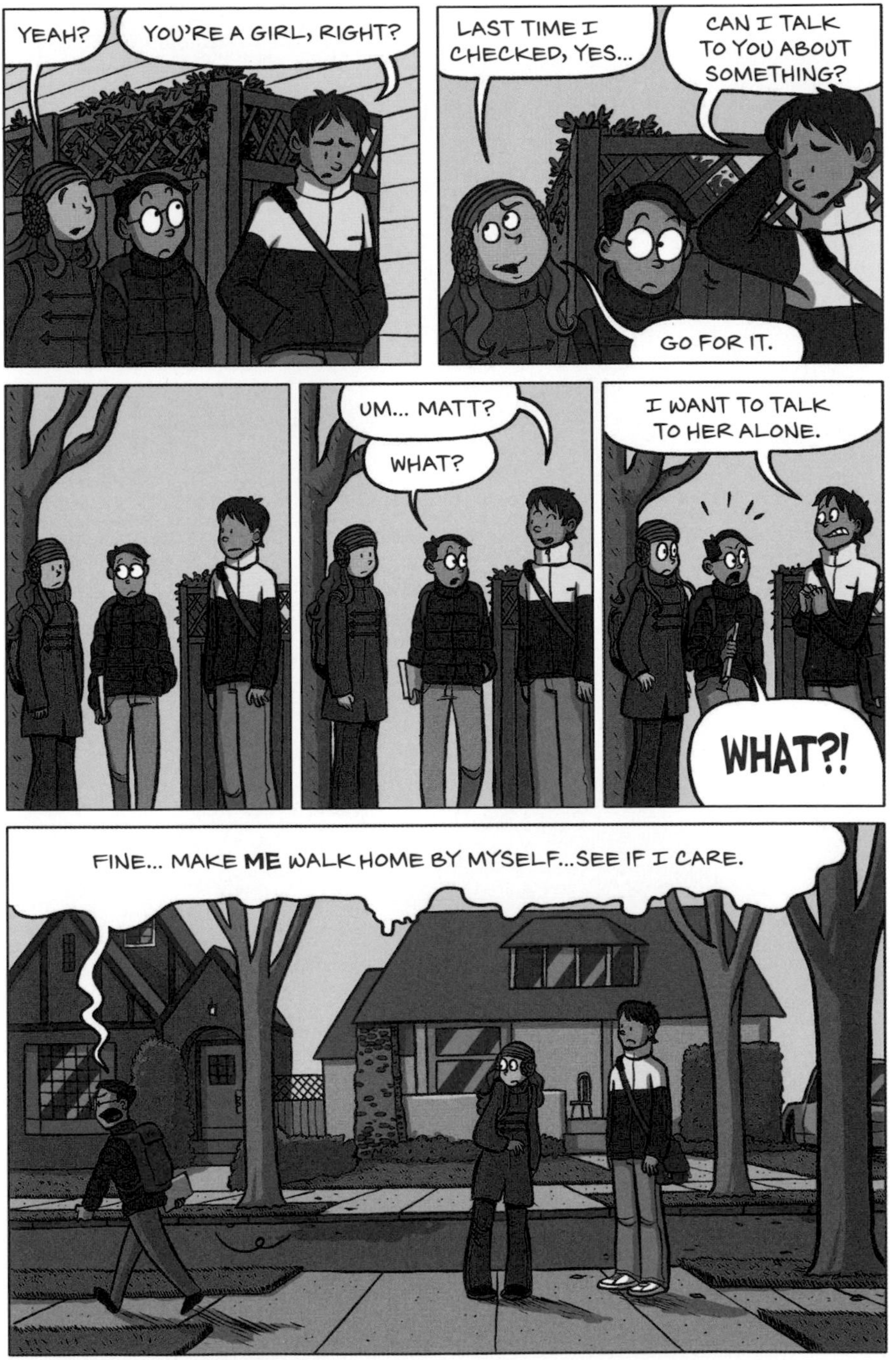
YEAH?
YOU'RE A GIRL, RIGHT?
LAST TIME I CHECKED, YES...
CAN I TALK TO YOU ABOUT SOMETHING?
GO FOR IT.
UM... MATT?
WHAT?
I WANT TO TALK TO HER ALONE.
WHAT?!
FINE... MAKE **ME** WALK HOME BY MYSELF...SEE IF I CARE.

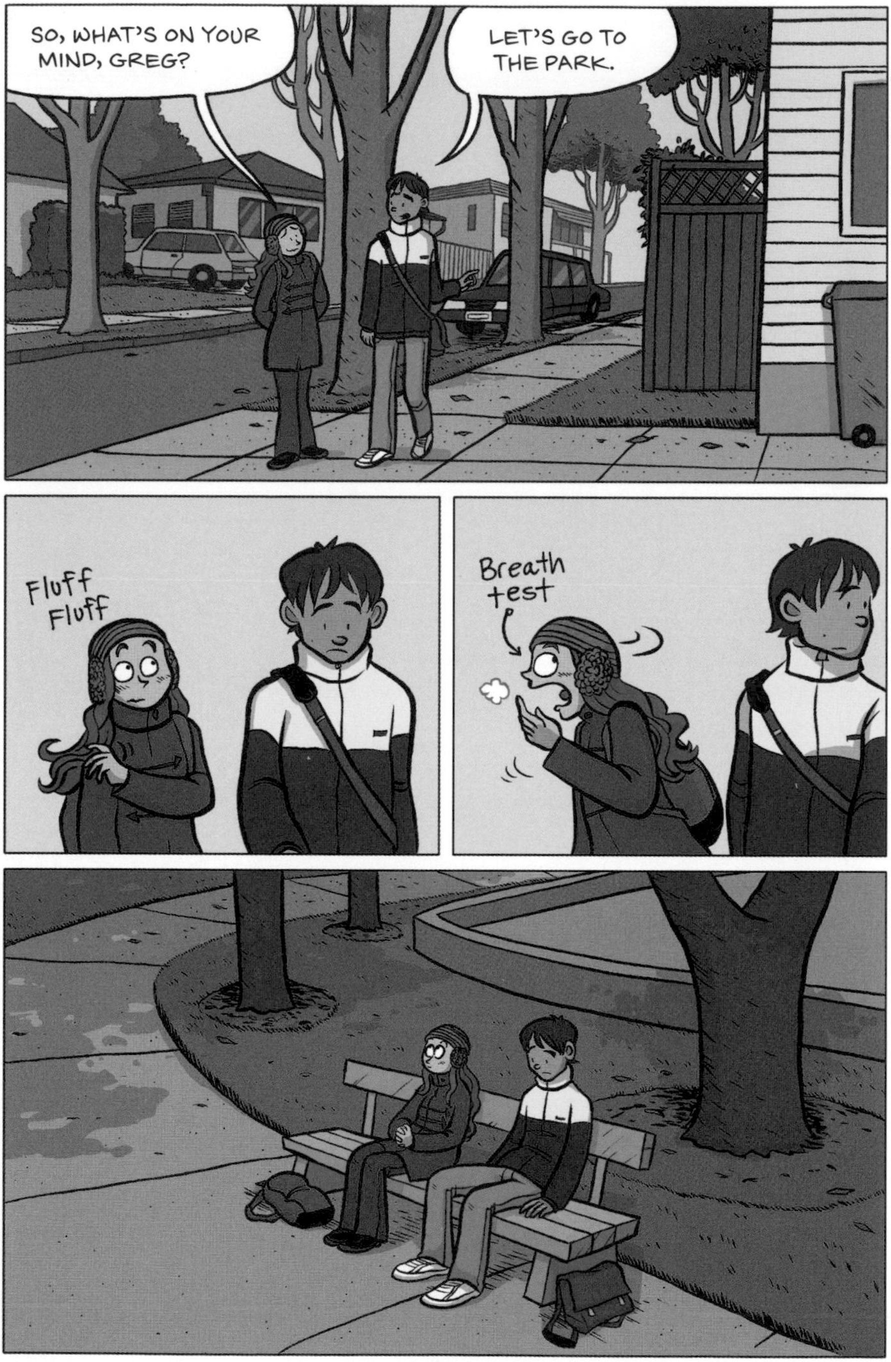
SO, WHAT'S ON YOUR MIND, GREG?
LET'S GO TO THE PARK.
Fluff Fluff
Breath test

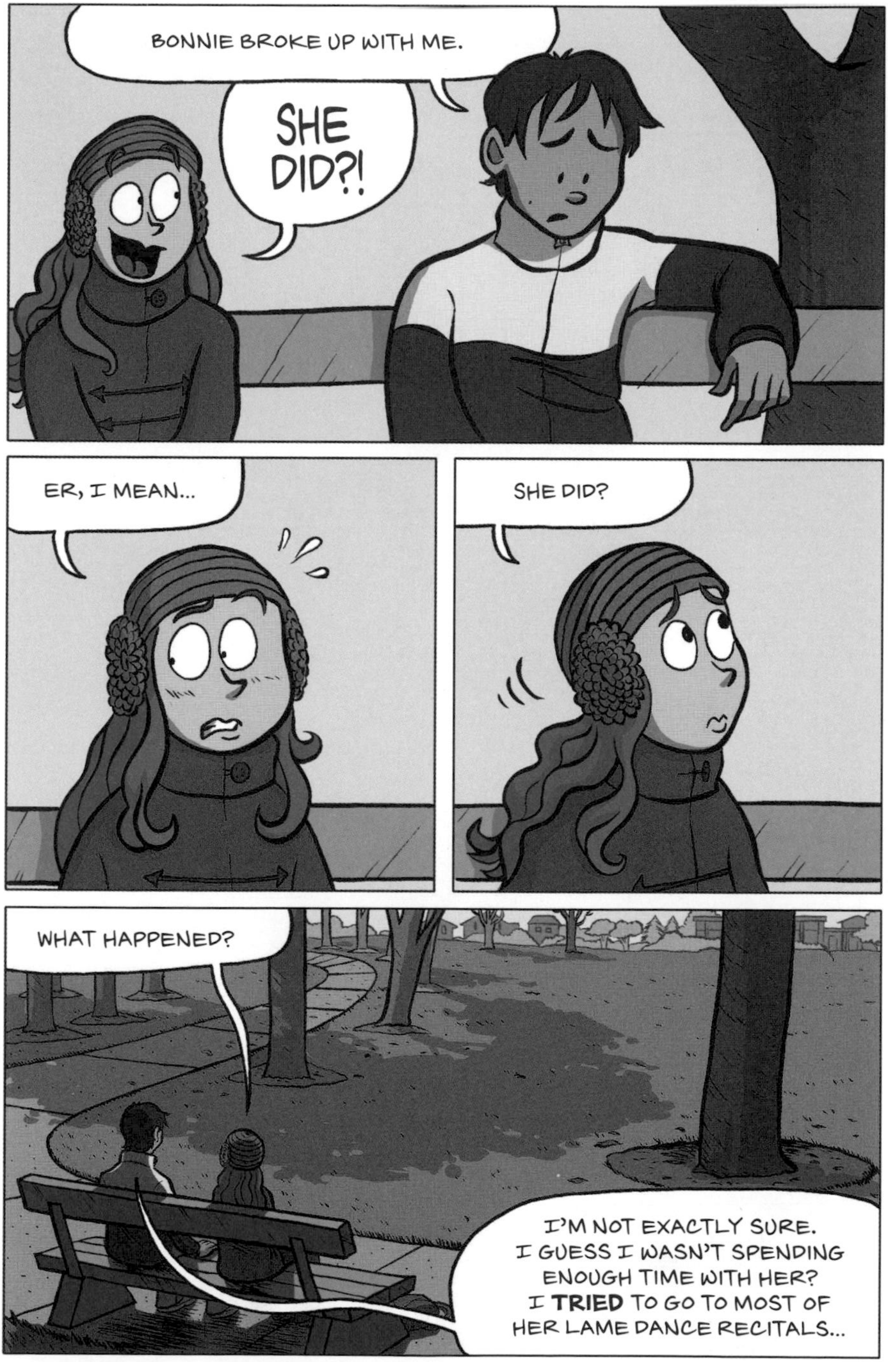
BONNIE BROKE UP WITH ME.
SHE DID?!
ER, I MEAN...
SHE DID?
WHAT HAPPENED?
I'M NOT EXACTLY SURE. I GUESS I WASN'T SPENDING ENOUGH TIME WITH HER? I **TRIED** TO GO TO MOST OF HER LAME DANCE RECITALS...

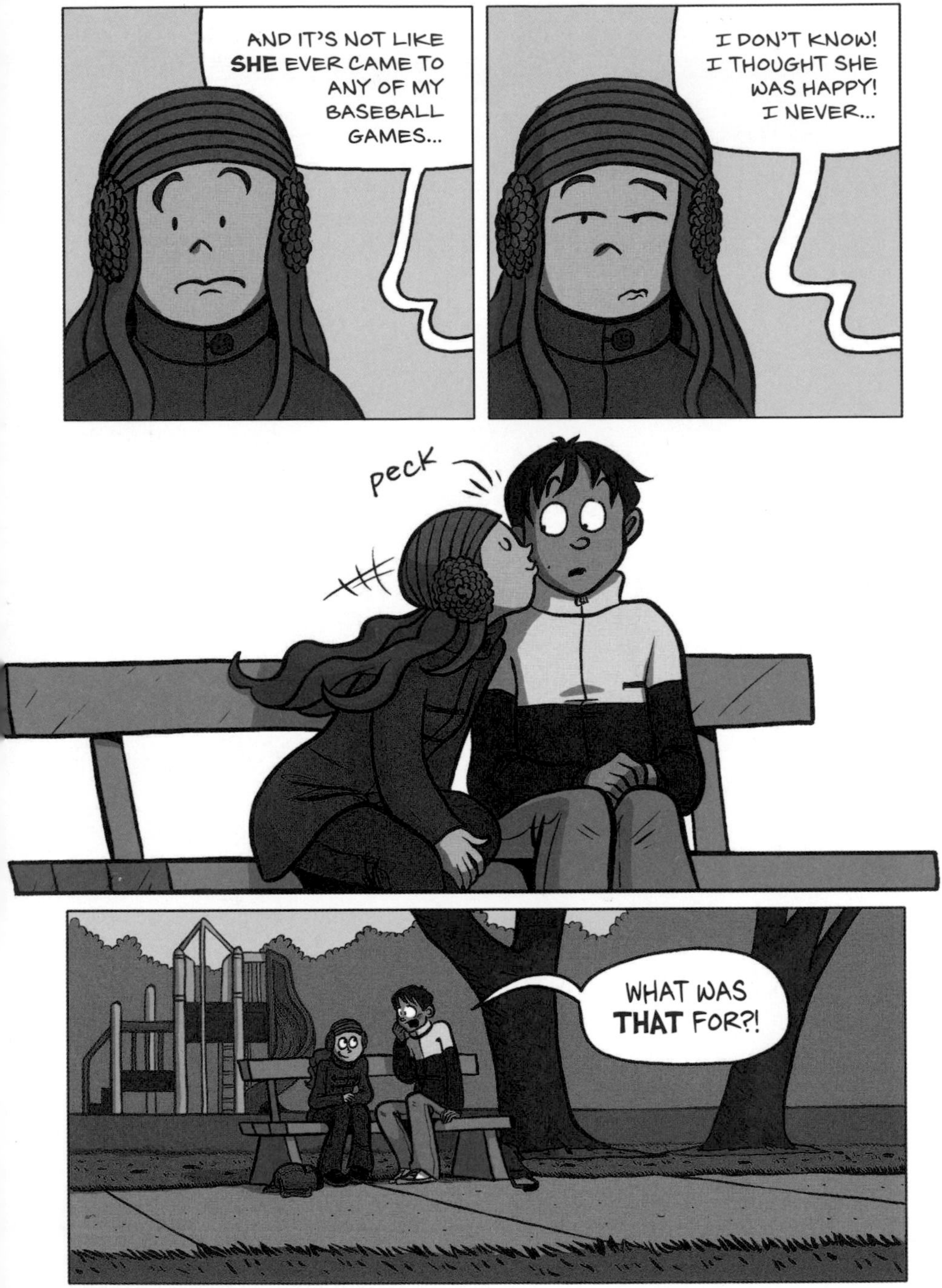
AND IT'S NOT LIKE SHE EVER CAME TO ANY OF MY BASEBALL GAMES...
I DON'T KNOW! I THOUGHT SHE WAS HAPPY! I NEVER...
peck
WHAT WAS THAT FOR?!

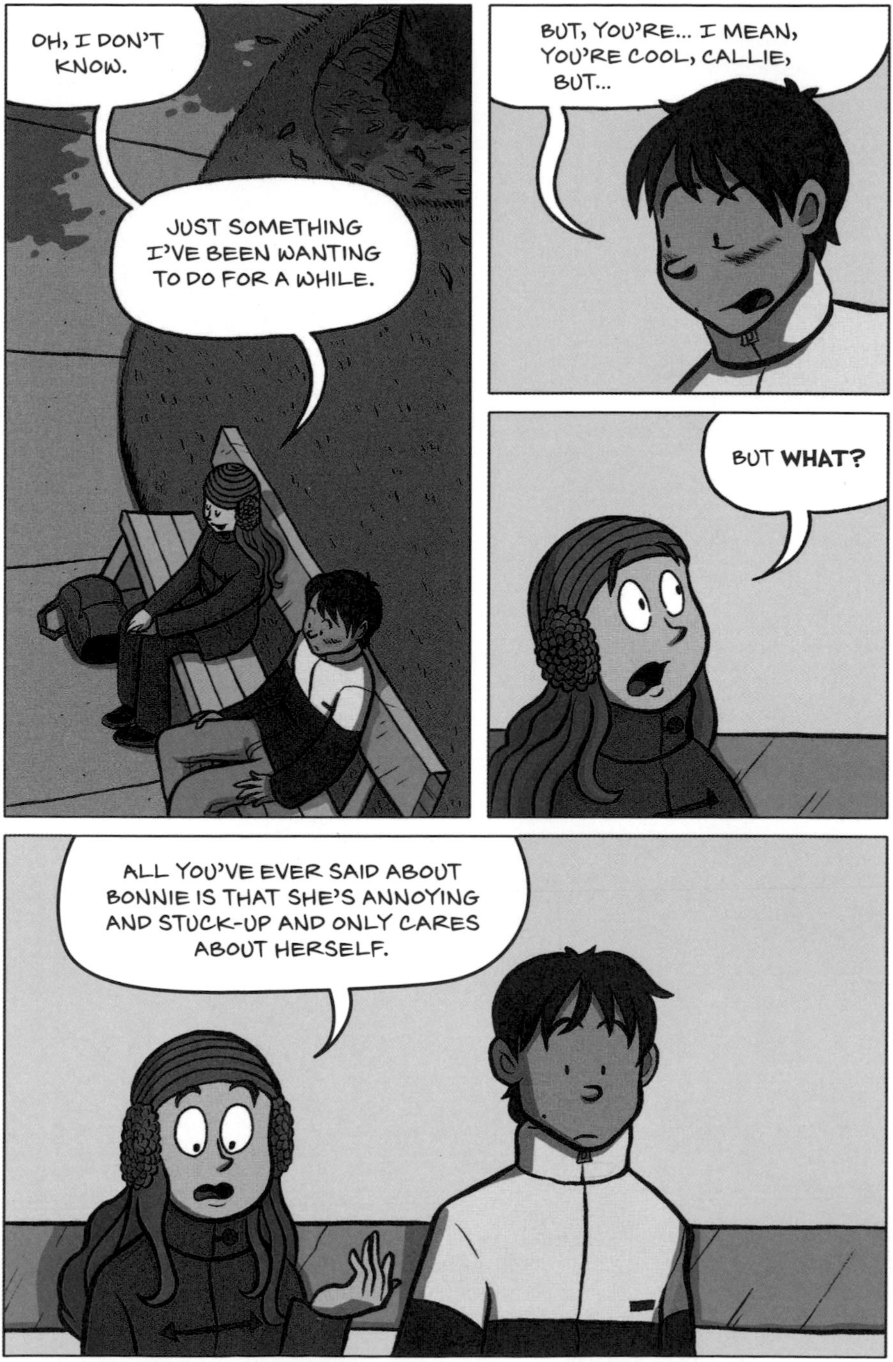
OH, I DON'T KNOW.
JUST SOMETHING I'VE BEEN WANTING TO DO FOR A WHILE.
BUT, YOU'RE... I MEAN, YOU'RE COOL, CALLIE, BUT...
BUT **WHAT?**
ALL YOU'VE EVER SAID ABOUT BONNIE IS THAT SHE'S ANNOYING AND STUCK-UP AND ONLY CARES ABOUT HERSELF.

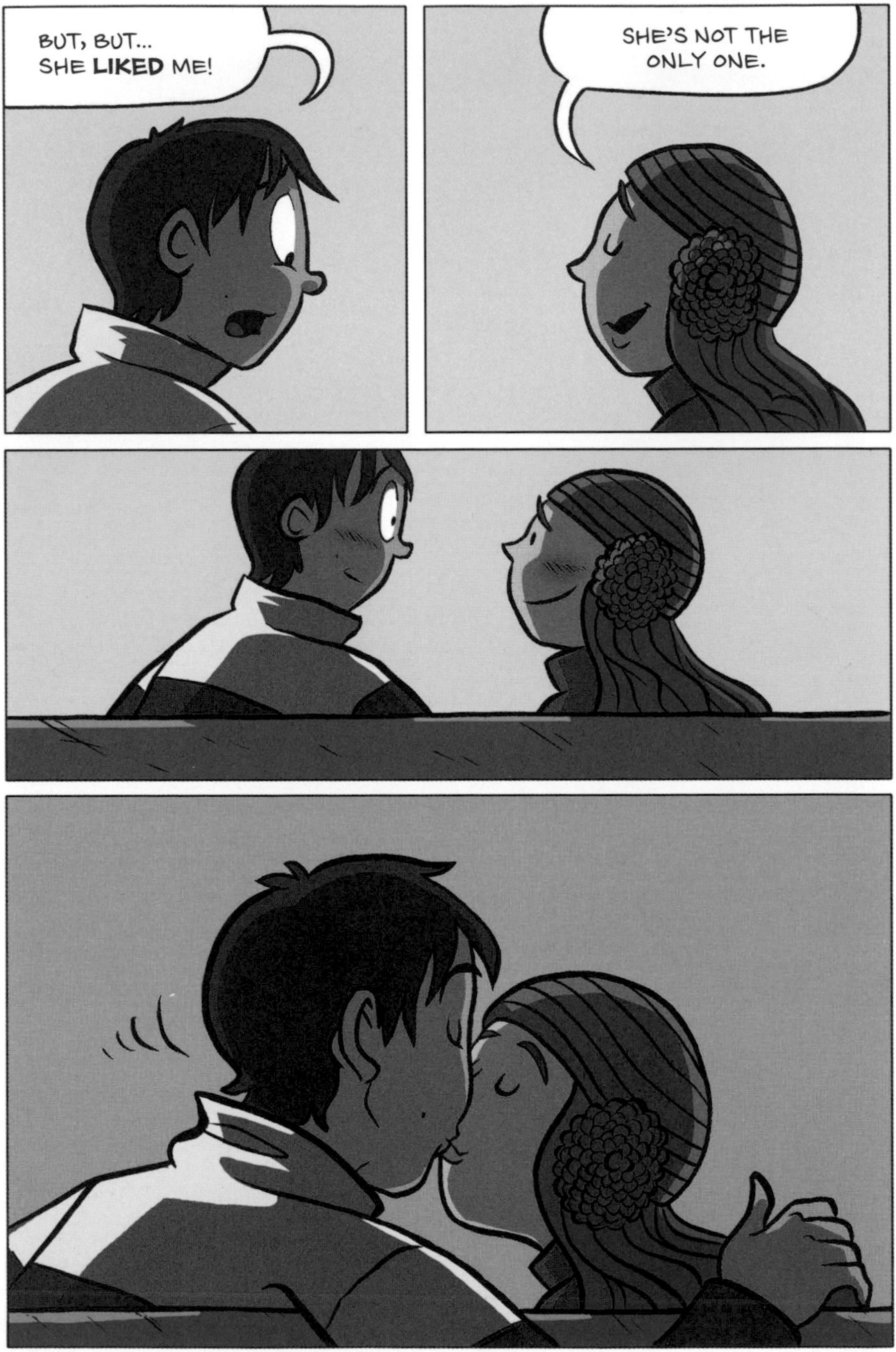
BUT, BUT...
SHE **LIKED** ME!
SHE'S NOT THE
ONLY ONE.

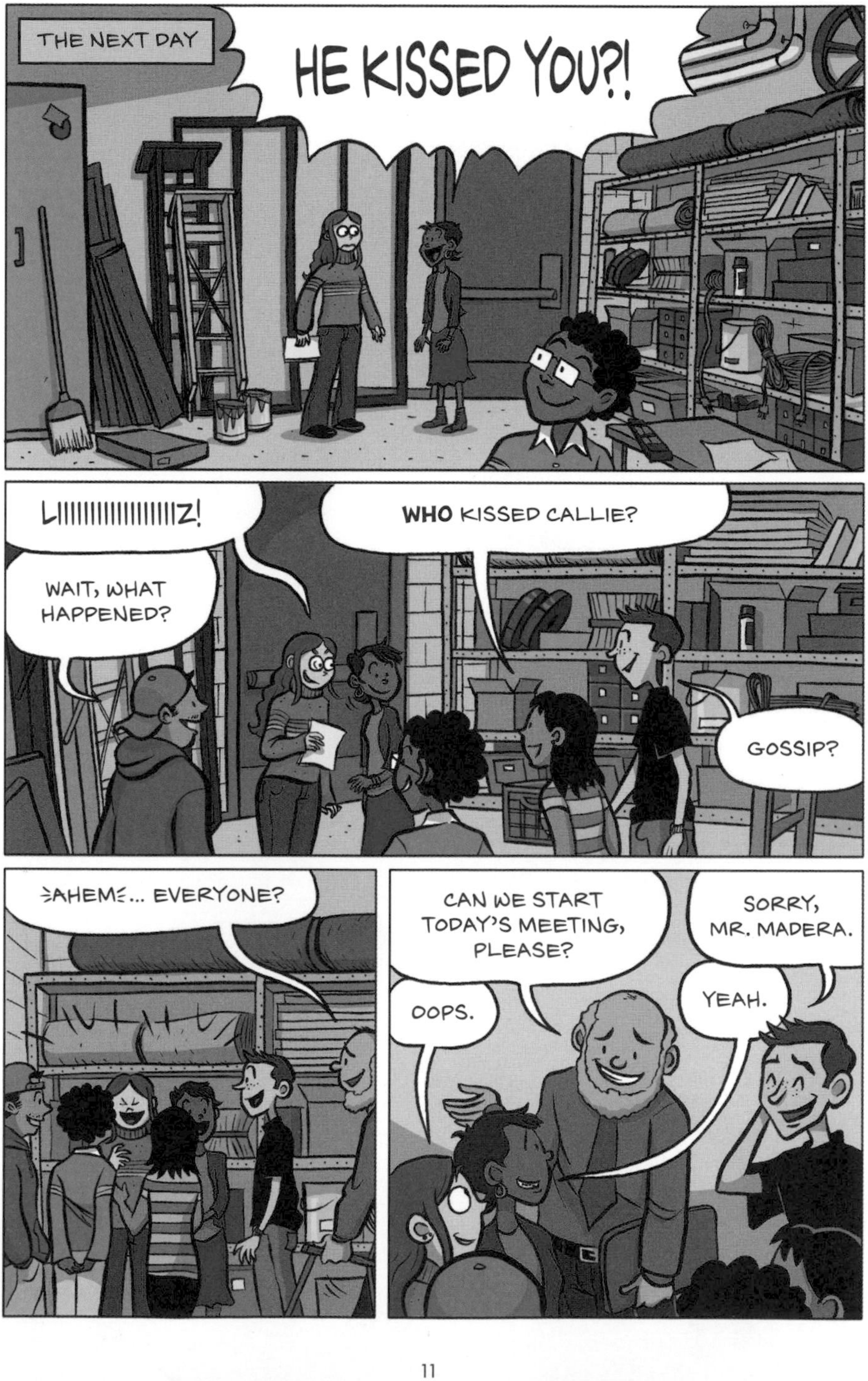
THE NEXT DAY
HE KISSED YOU?!
LIIIIIIIIIIIIIIIIZ!
WAIT, WHAT HAPPENED?
WHO KISSED CALLIE?
GOSSIP?
AHEM... EVERYONE?
CAN WE START TODAY'S MEETING, PLEASE?
OOPS.
SORRY, MR. MADERA.
YEAH.

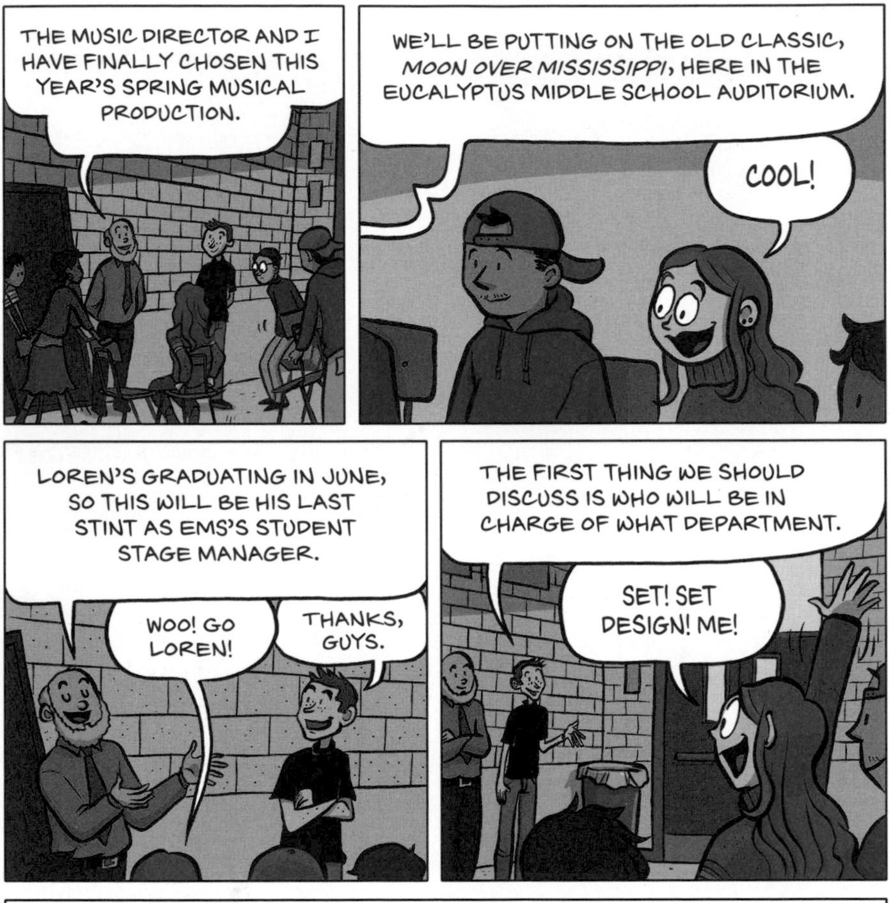
THE MUSIC DIRECTOR AND I HAVE FINALLY CHOSEN THIS YEAR'S SPRING MUSICAL PRODUCTION.
WE'LL BE PUTTING ON THE OLD CLASSIC, *MOON OVER MISSISSIPPI*, HERE IN THE EUCALYPTUS MIDDLE SCHOOL AUDITORIUM.
COOL!
LOREN'S GRADUATING IN JUNE, SO THIS WILL BE HIS LAST STINT AS EMS'S STUDENT STAGE MANAGER.
WOO! GO LOREN!
THANKS, GUYS.
THE FIRST THING WE SHOULD DISCUSS IS WHO WILL BE IN CHARGE OF WHAT DEPARTMENT.
SET! SET DESIGN! ME!
I'VE NEVER SEEN A LIVE PRODUCTION OF *MOON OVER MISSISSIPPI*, BUT I'VE GOT THE DELUXE EDITION CAST ALBUM, WHICH HAS A TON OF PHOTOS FROM THE ORIGINAL BROADWAY PRODUCTION, AND THEY BUILT THIS AMAZING --
OKAY, CALLIE, WE GET IT.

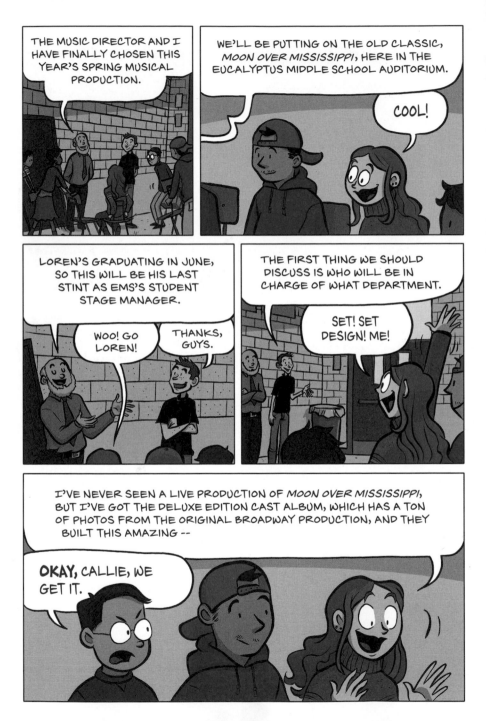

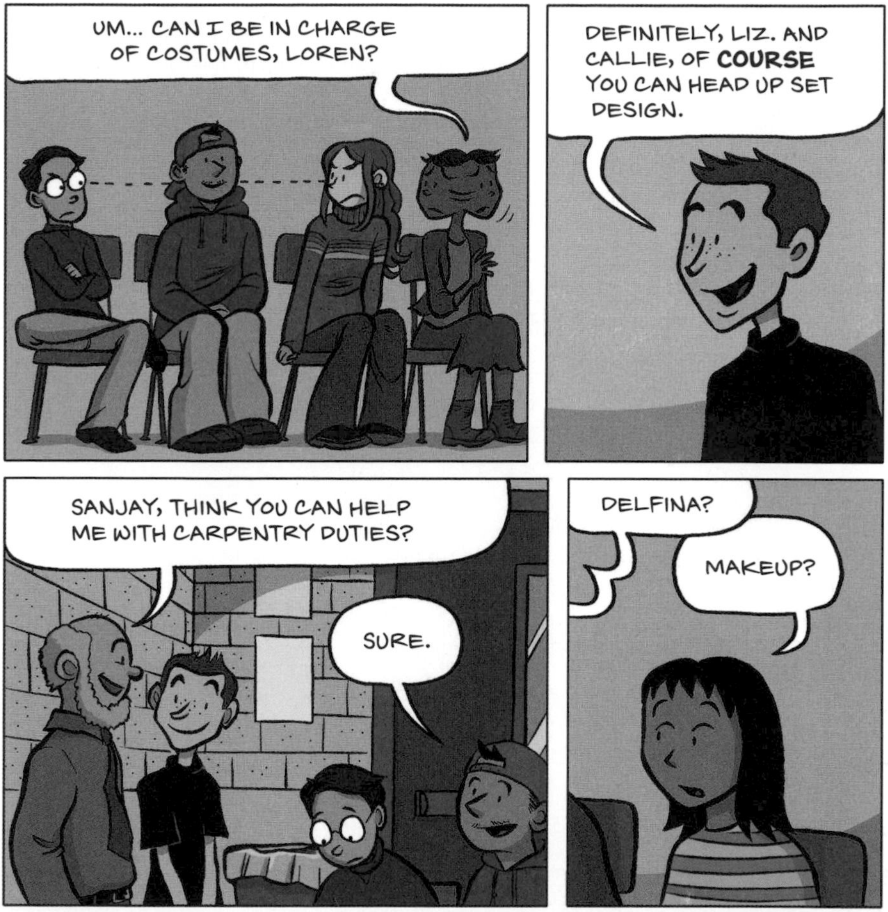
UM... CAN I BE IN CHARGE OF COSTUMES, LOREN?
DEFINITELY, LIZ. AND CALLIE, OF **COURSE** YOU CAN HEAD UP SET DESIGN.
SANJAY, THINK YOU CAN HELP ME WITH CARPENTRY DUTIES?
SURE.
DELFINA?
MAKEUP?
GOOD. MATT? WANT TO WORK THE LIGHTS AGAIN?
YOU MEAN YOU'LL LET ME??
ABSOLUTELY. MIRKO, DO YOU WANT TO BE THE SOUND BOOTH GUY?
COULD I?! WOW!

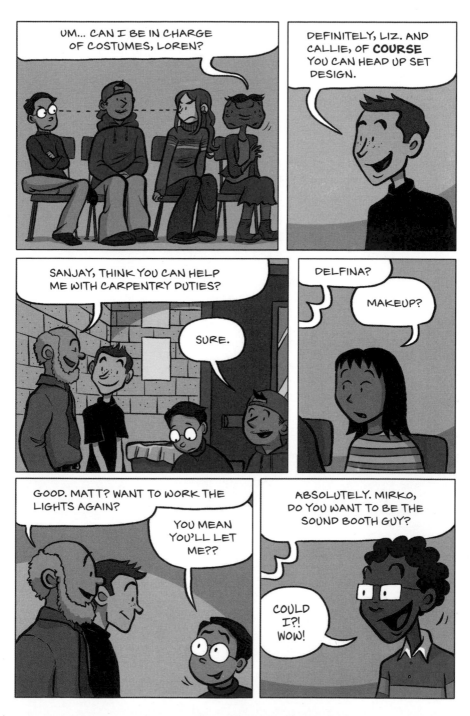

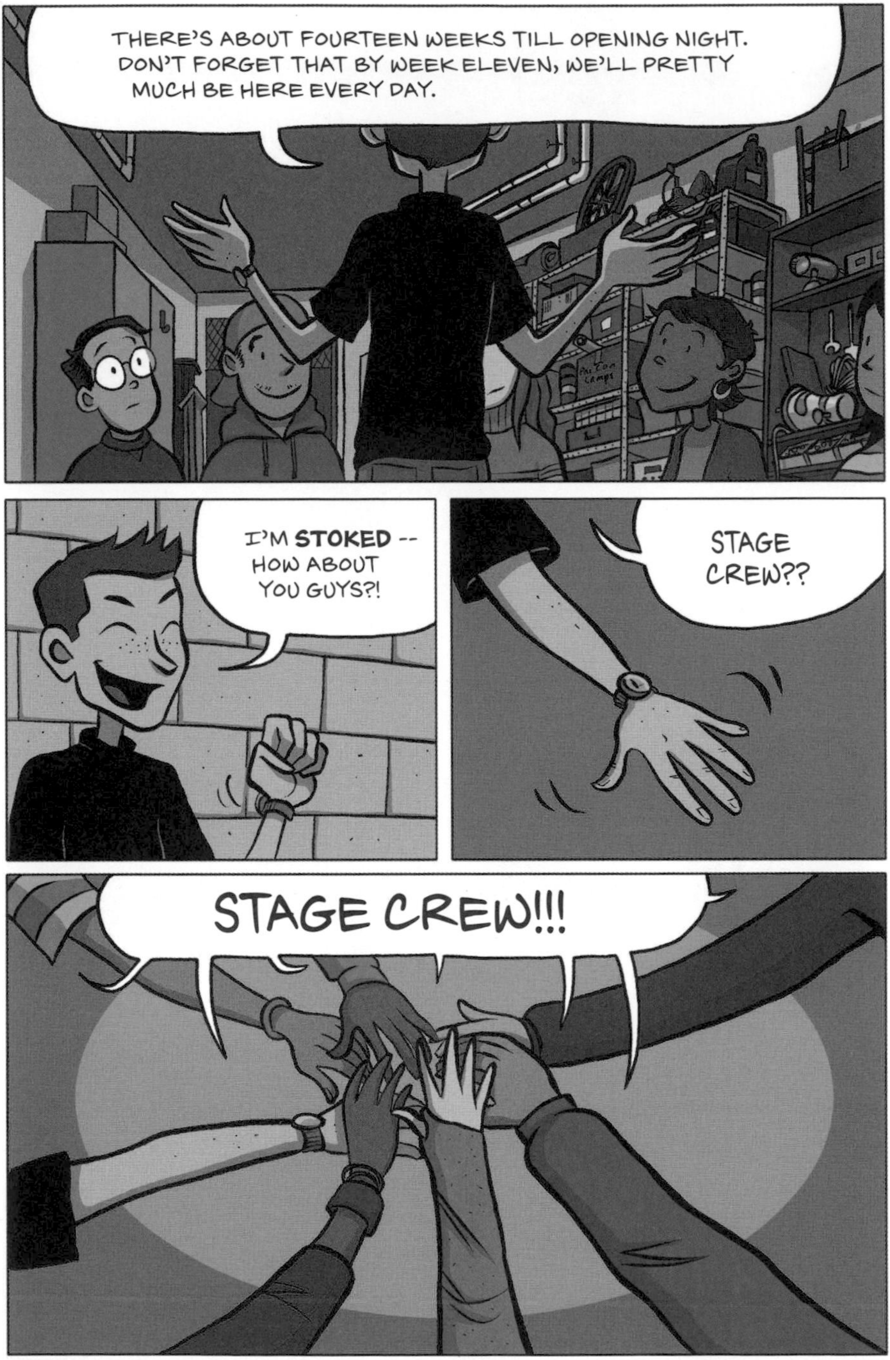
THERE'S ABOUT FOURTEEN WEEKS TILL OPENING NIGHT. DON'T FORGET THAT BY WEEK ELEVEN, WE'LL PRETTY MUCH BE HERE EVERY DAY.
I'M **STOKED** -- HOW ABOUT YOU GUYS?!
STAGE CREW??
STAGE CREW!!!

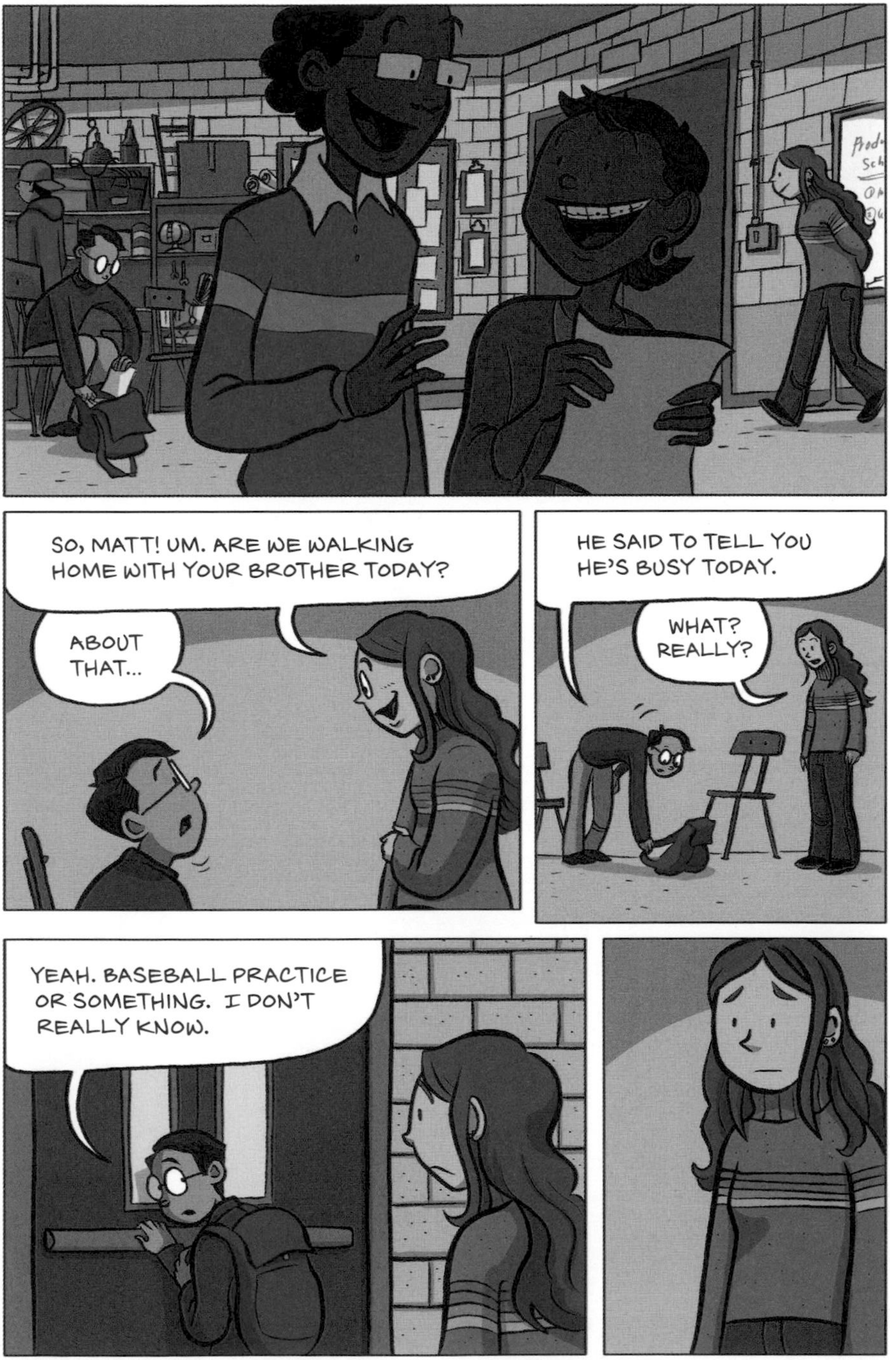
SO, MATT! UM. ARE WE WALKING HOME WITH YOUR BROTHER TODAY?
ABOUT THAT...
HE SAID TO TELL YOU HE'S BUSY TODAY.
WHAT? REALLY?
YEAH. BASEBALL PRACTICE OR SOMETHING. I DON'T REALLY KNOW.

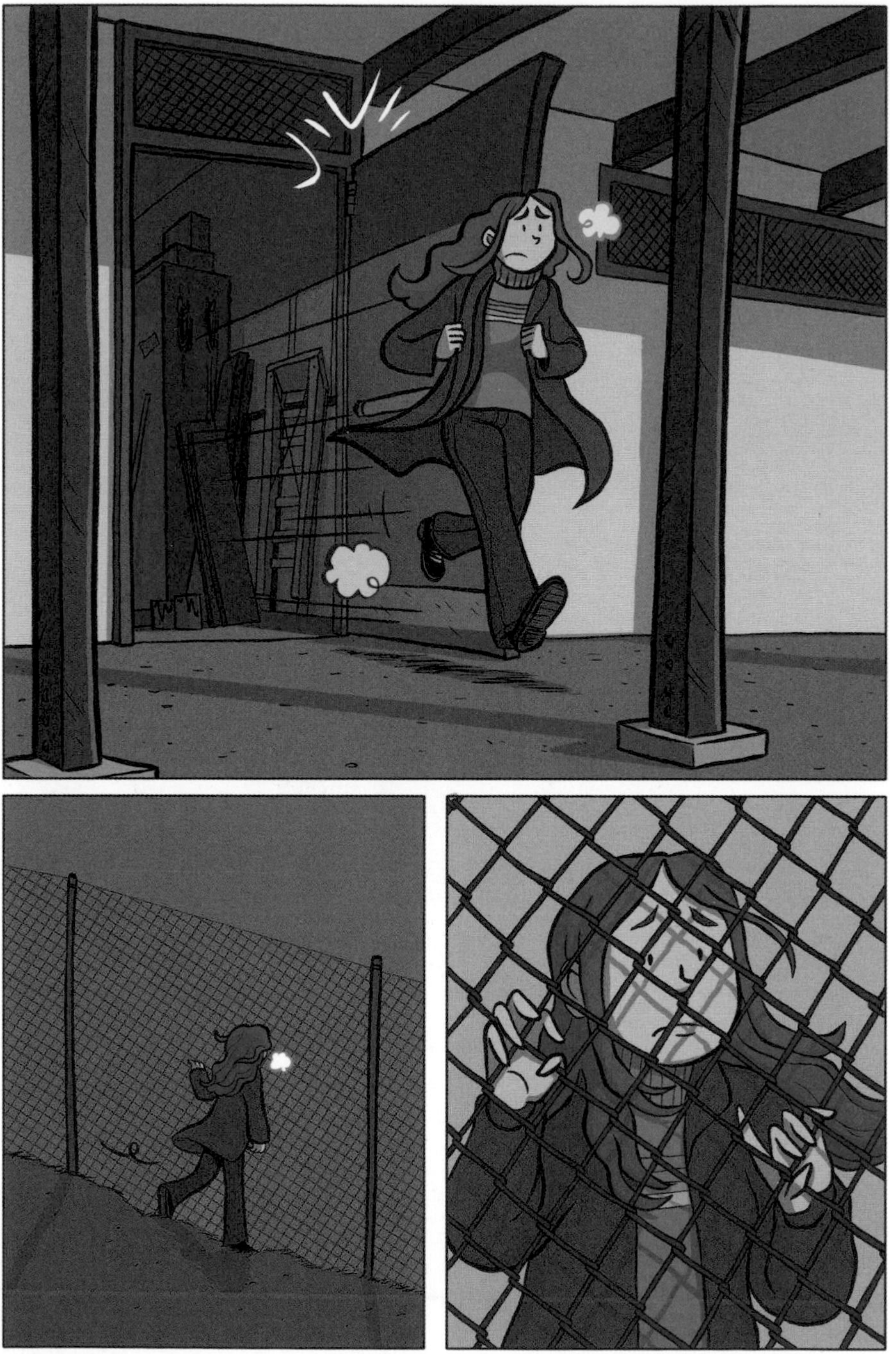

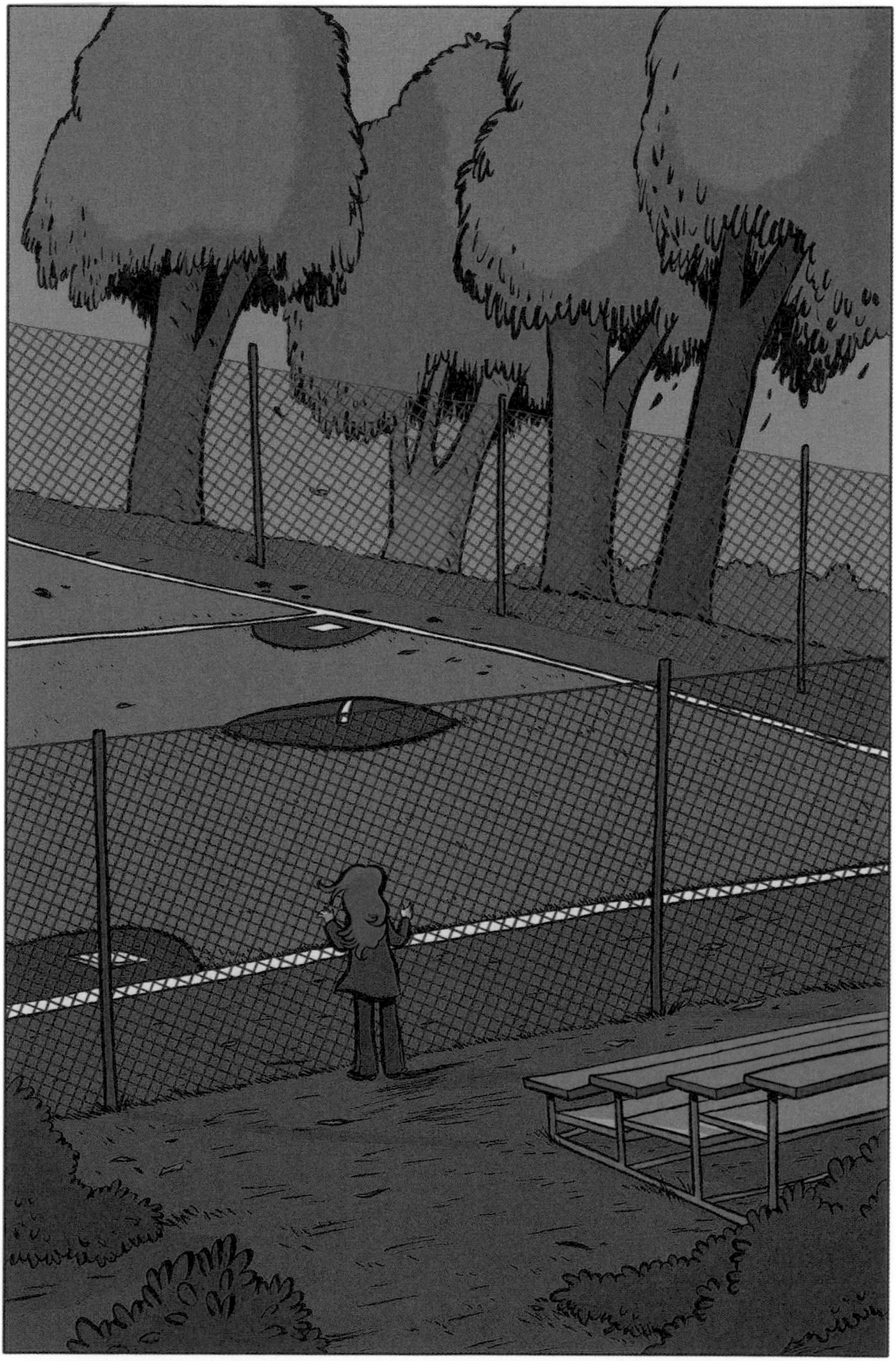

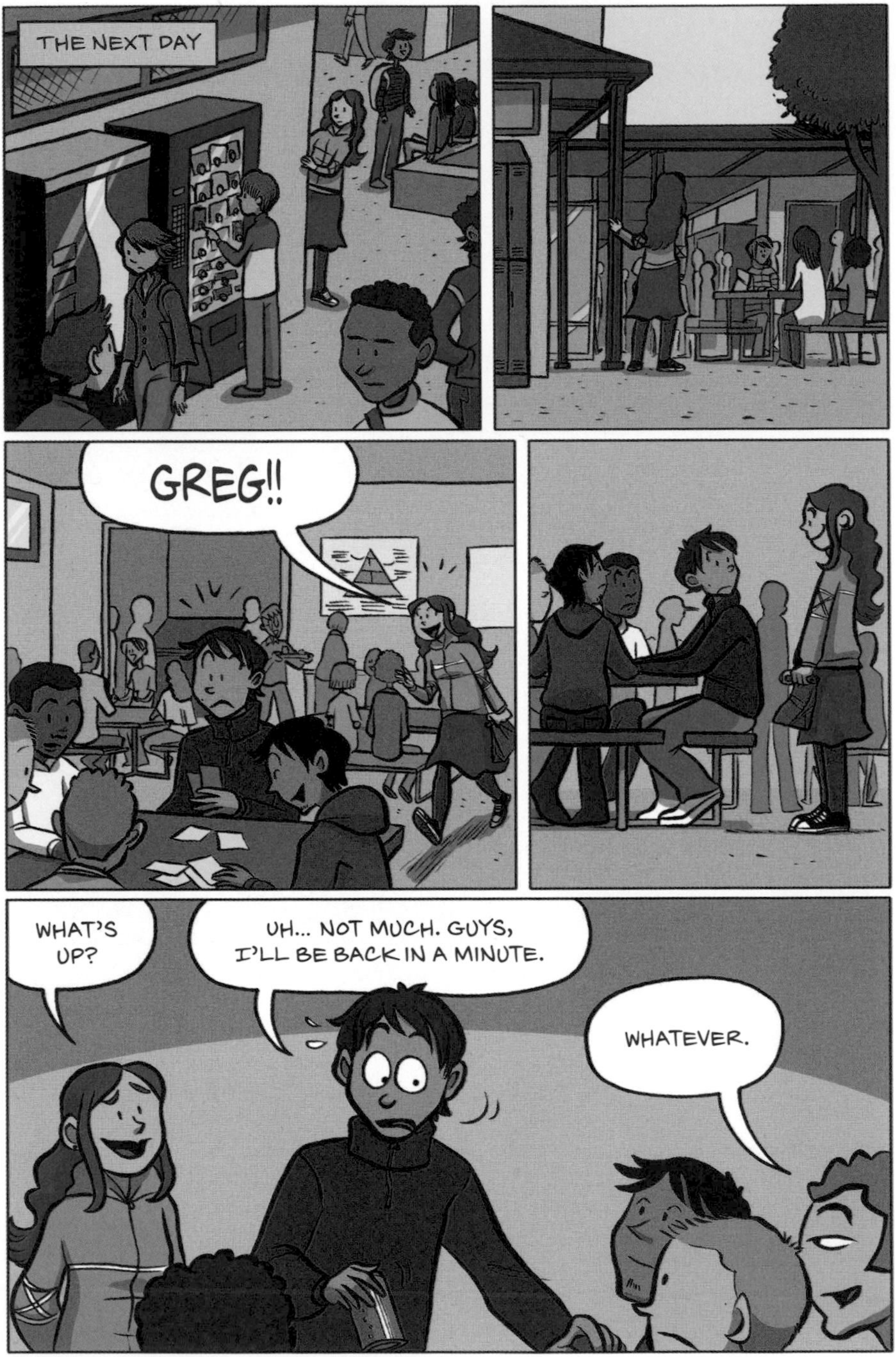
THE NEXT DAY
GREG!!
WHAT'S UP?
UH... NOT MUCH. GUYS, I'LL BE BACK IN A MINUTE.
WHATEVER.

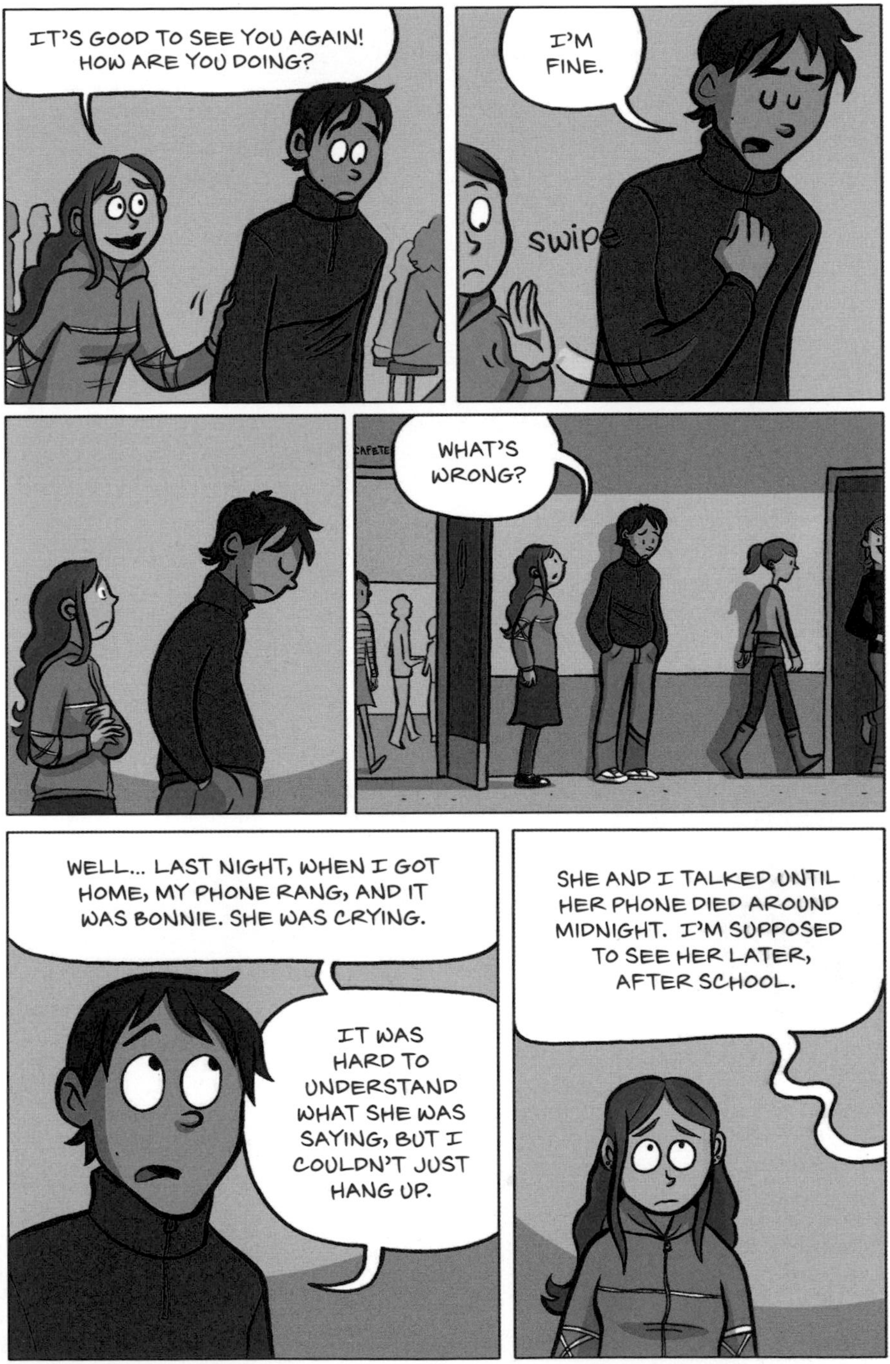
IT'S GOOD TO SEE YOU AGAIN! HOW ARE YOU DOING?
I'M FINE.
swipe
WHAT'S WRONG?
WELL... LAST NIGHT, WHEN I GOT HOME, MY PHONE RANG, AND IT WAS BONNIE. SHE WAS CRYING.
IT WAS HARD TO UNDERSTAND WHAT SHE WAS SAYING, BUT I COULDN'T JUST HANG UP.
SHE AND I TALKED UNTIL HER PHONE DIED AROUND MIDNIGHT. I'M SUPPOSED TO SEE HER LATER, AFTER SCHOOL.

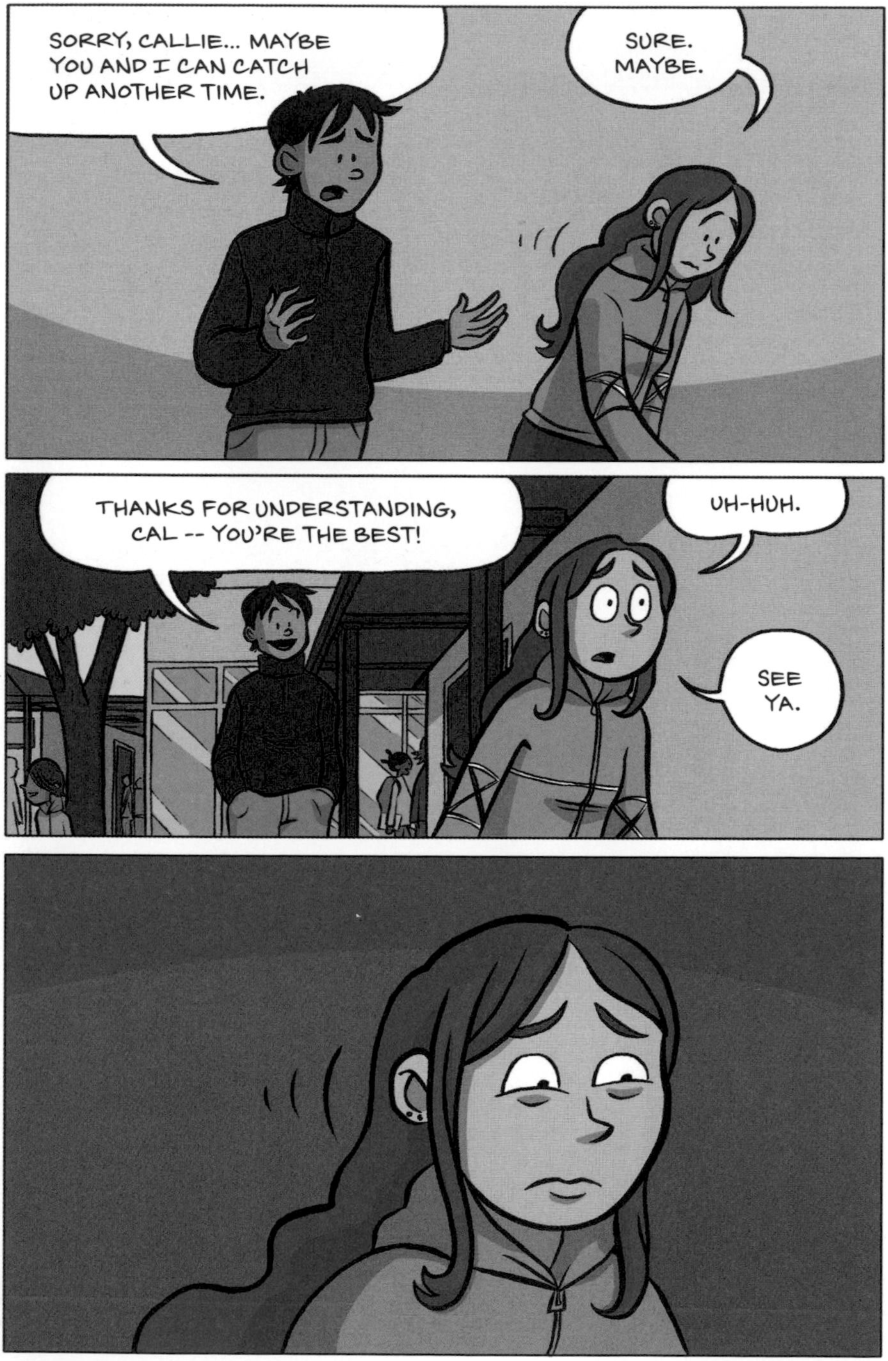
SORRY, CALLIE... MAYBE YOU AND I CAN CATCH UP ANOTHER TIME.
SURE. MAYBE.
THANKS FOR UNDERSTANDING, CAL -- YOU'RE THE BEST!
UH-HUH.
SEE YA.

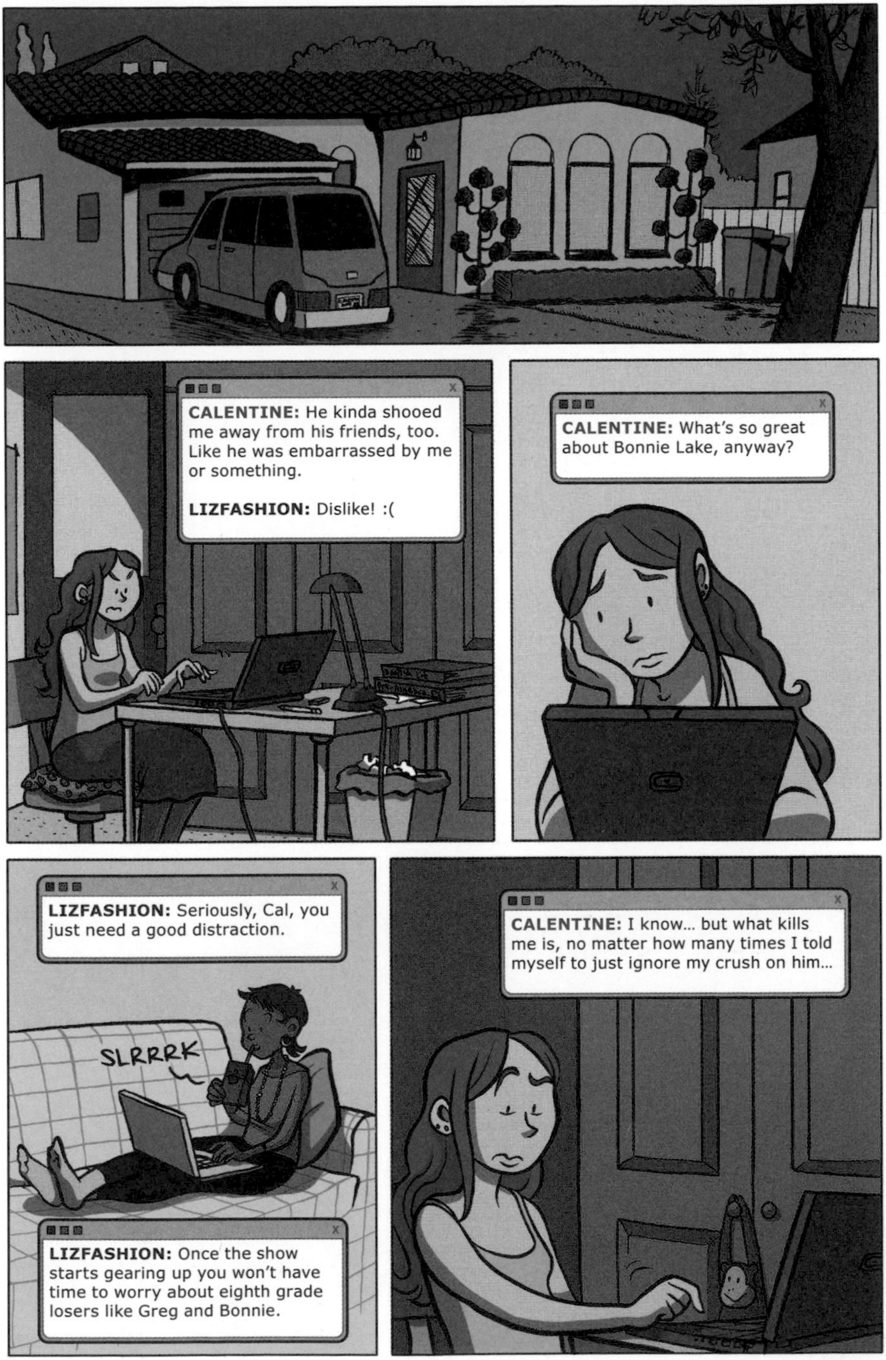
CALENTINE: He kinda shooed me away from his friends, too. Like he was embarrassed by me or something.
LIZFASHION: Dislike! :(
CALENTINE: What's so great about Bonnie Lake, anyway?
LIZFASHION: Seriously, Cal, you just need a good distraction.
SLRRRK
LIZFASHION: Once the show starts gearing up you won't have time to worry about eighth grade losers like Greg and Bonnie.
CALENTINE: I know... but what kills me is, no matter how many times I told myself to just ignore my crush on him...

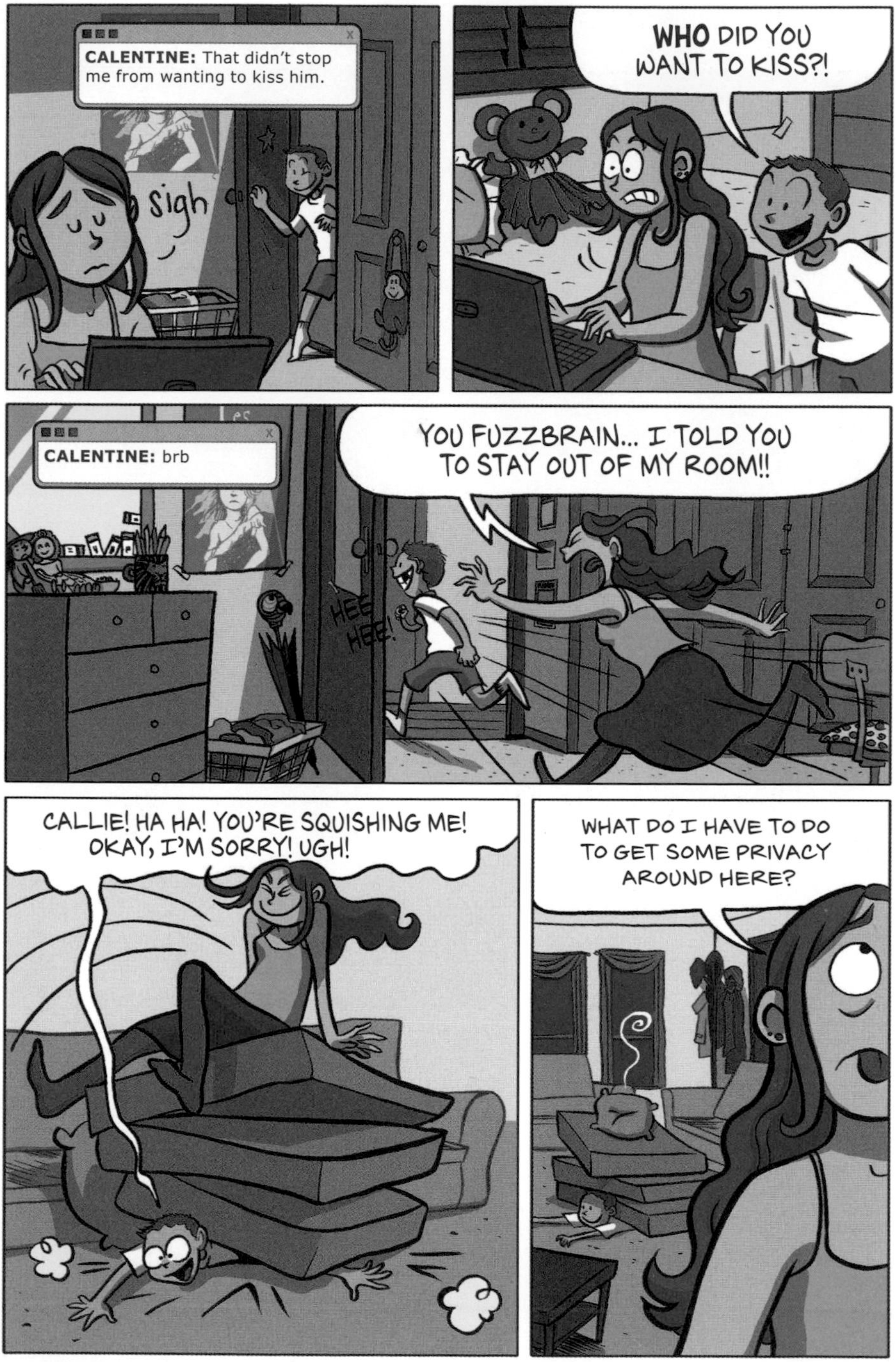
CALENTINE: That didn't stop me from wanting to kiss him.
sigh
WHO DID YOU WANT TO KISS?!
CALENTINE: brb
YOU FUZZBRAIN... I TOLD YOU TO STAY OUT OF MY ROOM!!
HEE HEE!
CALLIE! HA HA! YOU'RE SQUISHING ME! OKAY, I'M SORRY! UGH!
WHAT DO I HAVE TO DO TO GET SOME PRIVACY AROUND HERE?

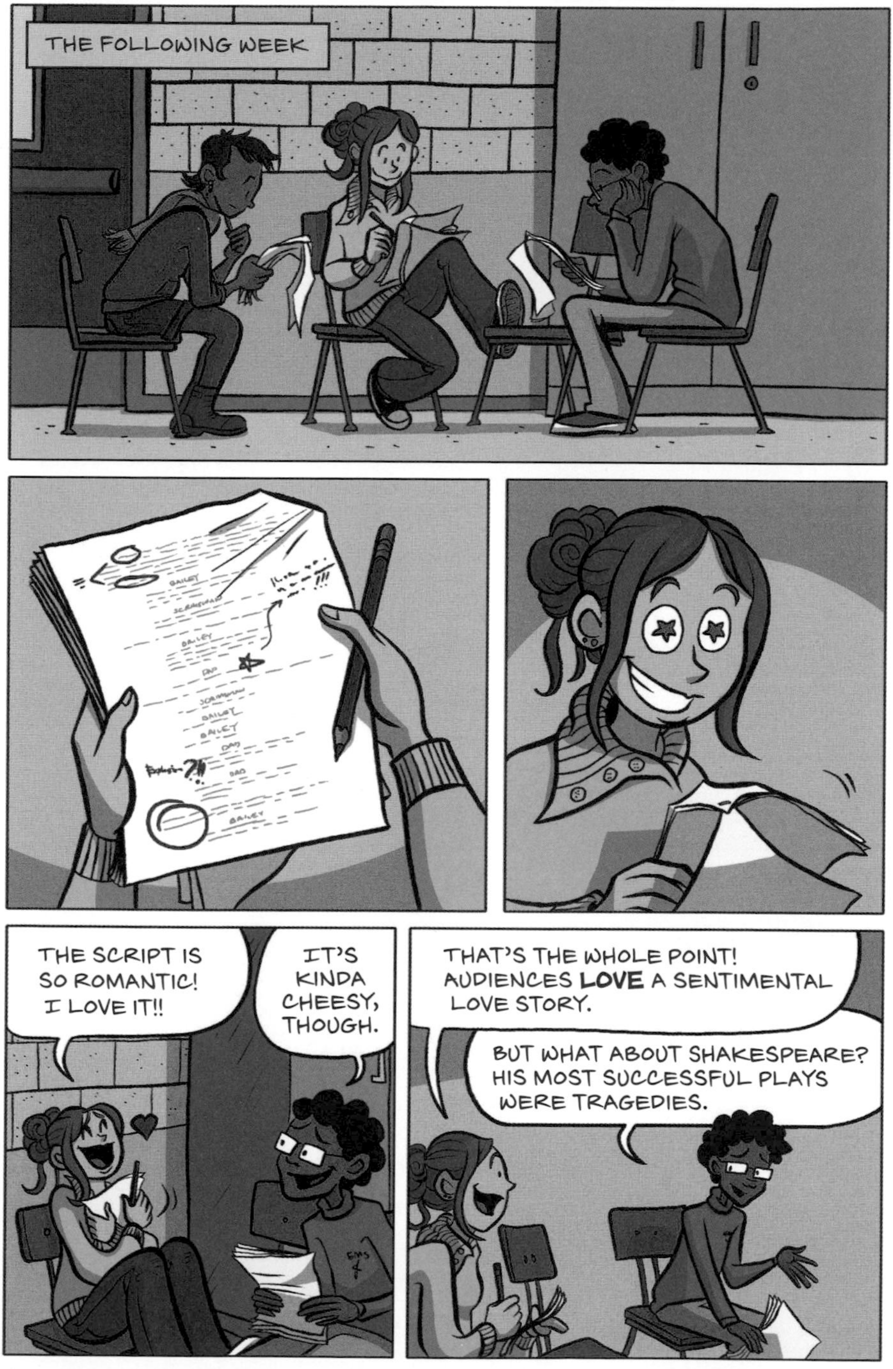
THE FOLLOWING WEEK
THE SCRIPT IS SO ROMANTIC! I LOVE IT!!
IT'S KINDA CHEESY, THOUGH.
THAT'S THE WHOLE POINT! AUDIENCES **LOVE** A SENTIMENTAL LOVE STORY.
BUT WHAT ABOUT SHAKESPEARE? HIS MOST SUCCESSFUL PLAYS WERE TRAGEDIES.

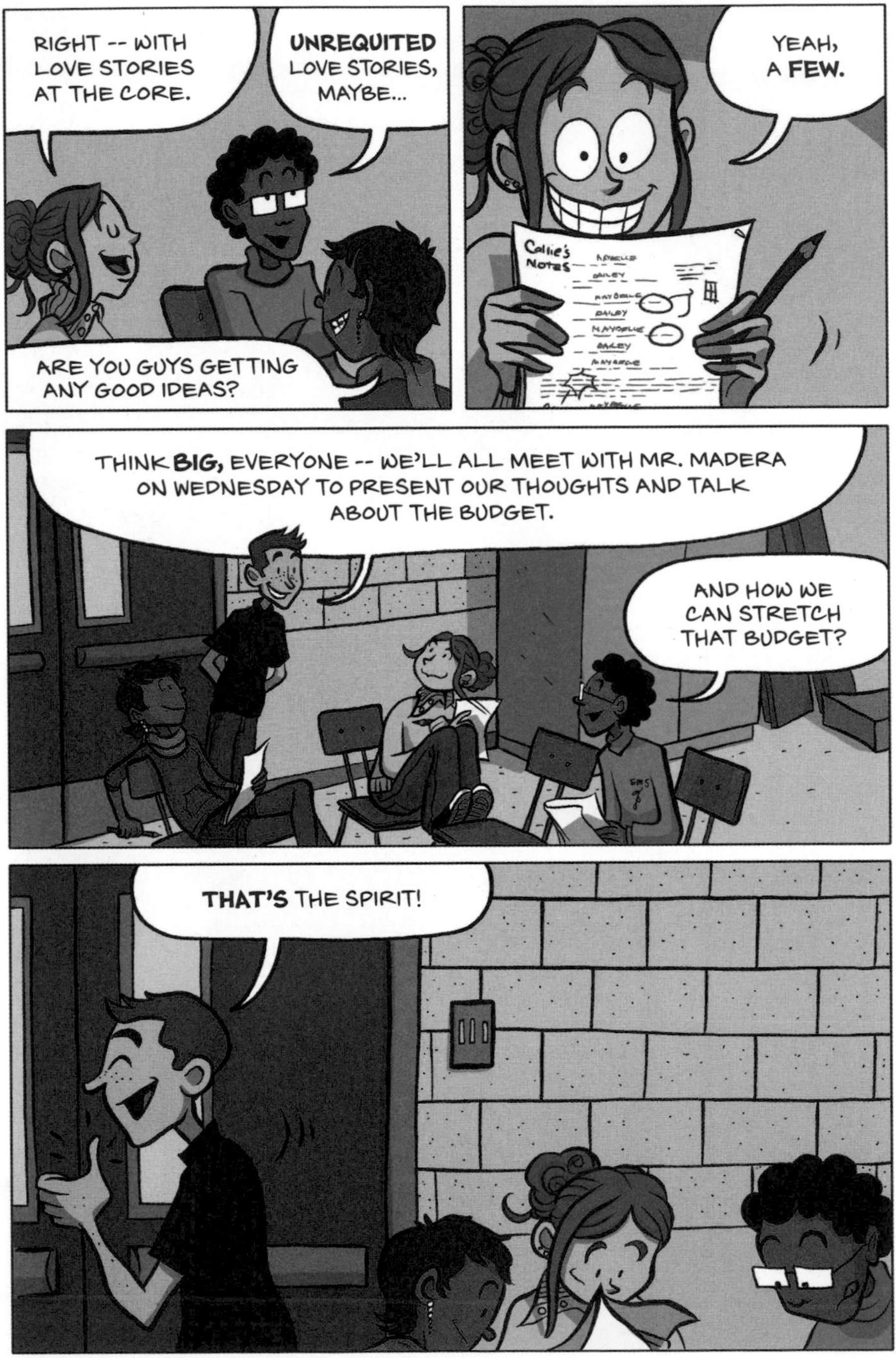
RIGHT -- WITH LOVE STORIES AT THE CORE.
UNREQUITED LOVE STORIES, MAYBE...
ARE YOU GUYS GETTING ANY GOOD IDEAS?
YEAH, A **FEW.**
Callie's Notes
THINK **BIG,** EVERYONE -- WE'LL ALL MEET WITH MR. MADERA ON WEDNESDAY TO PRESENT OUR THOUGHTS AND TALK ABOUT THE BUDGET.
AND HOW WE CAN STRETCH THAT BUDGET?
THAT'S THE SPIRIT!

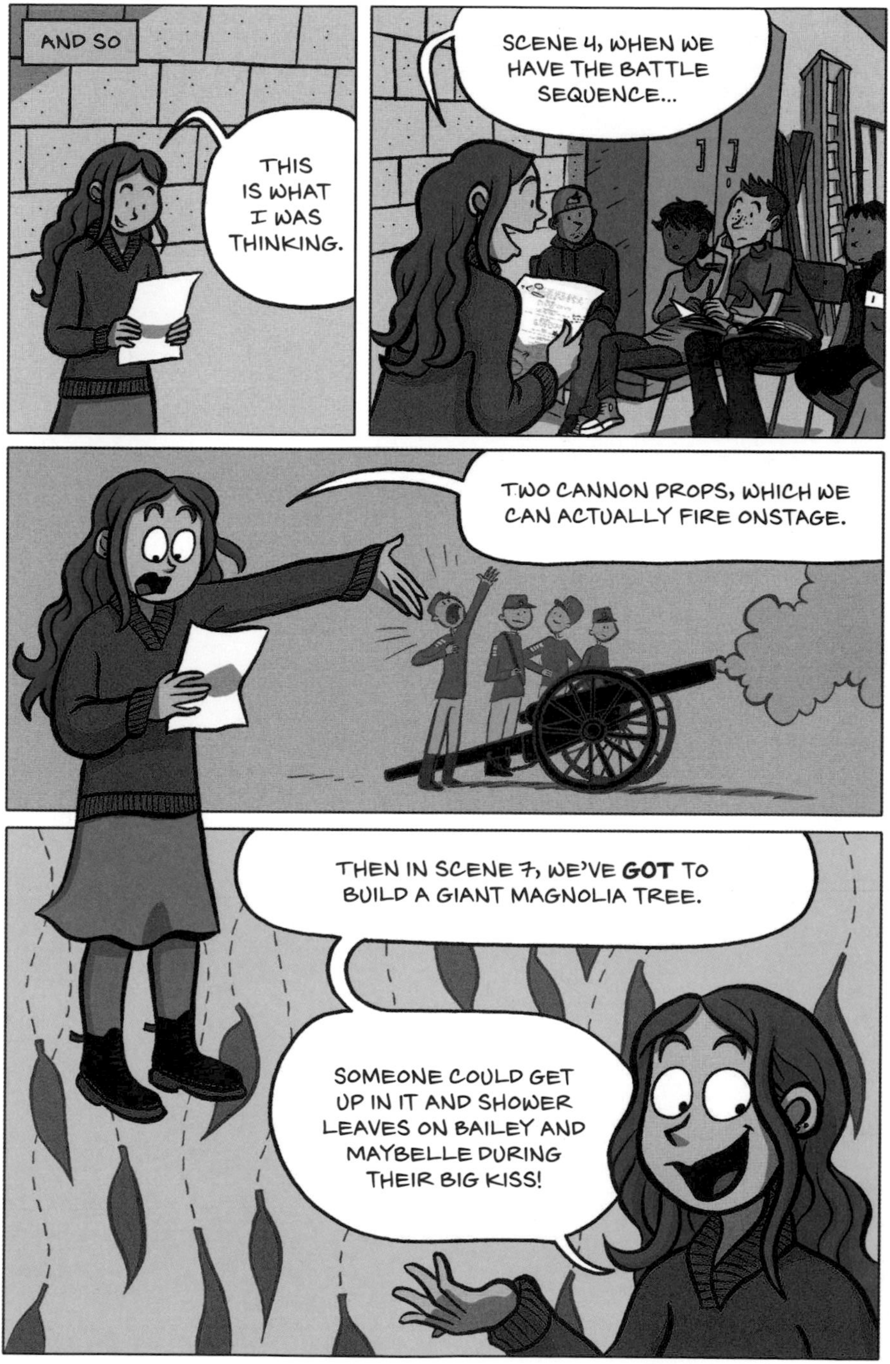
AND SO
THIS IS WHAT I WAS THINKING.
SCENE 4, WHEN WE HAVE THE BATTLE SEQUENCE...
TWO CANNON PROPS, WHICH WE CAN ACTUALLY FIRE ONSTAGE.
THEN IN SCENE 7, WE'VE **GOT** TO BUILD A GIANT MAGNOLIA TREE.
SOMEONE COULD GET UP IN IT AND SHOWER LEAVES ON BAILEY AND MAYBELLE DURING THEIR BIG KISS!

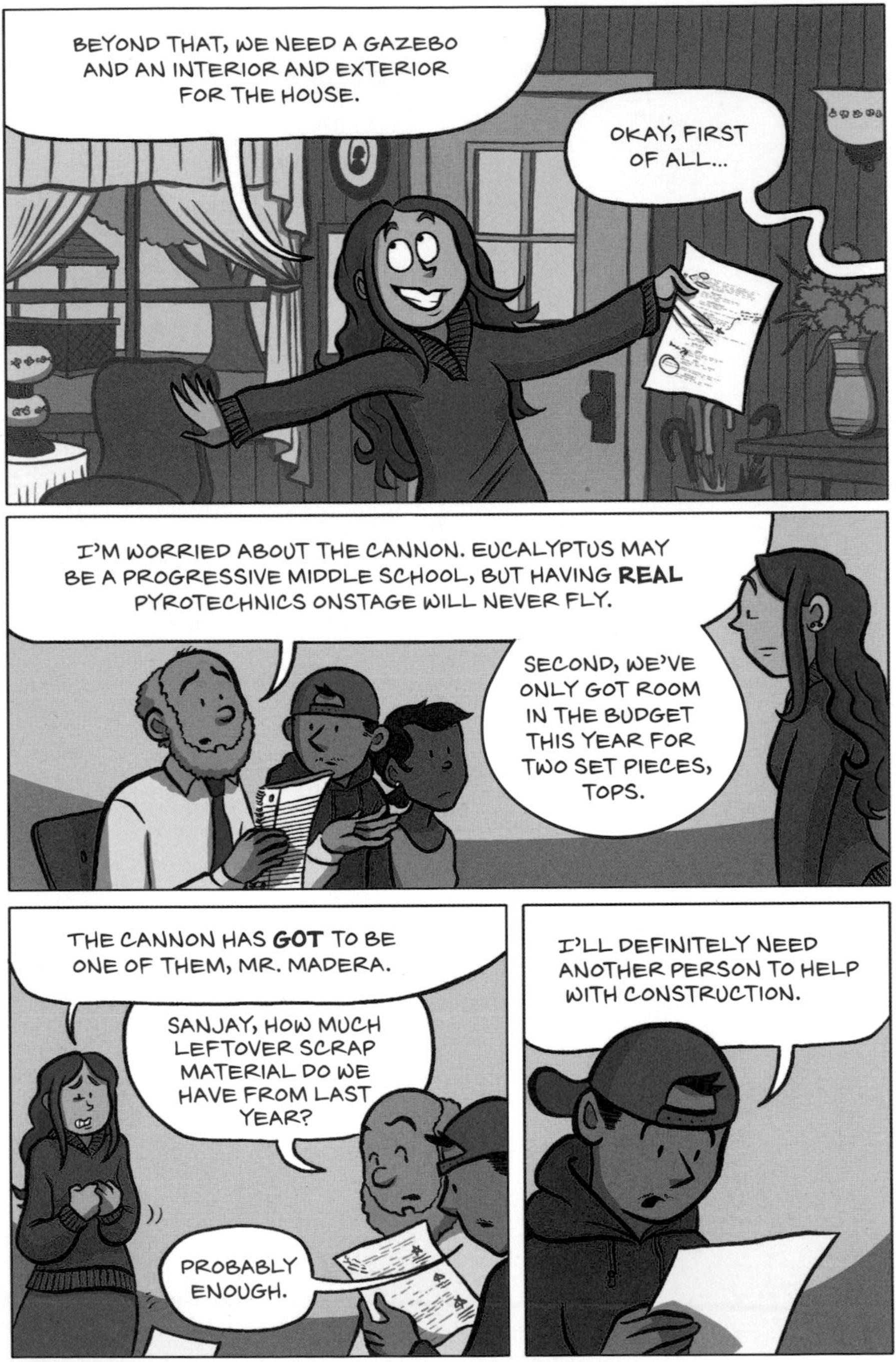
BEYOND THAT, WE NEED A GAZEBO AND AN INTERIOR AND EXTERIOR FOR THE HOUSE.
OKAY, FIRST OF ALL...
I'M WORRIED ABOUT THE CANNON. EUCALYPTUS MAY BE A PROGRESSIVE MIDDLE SCHOOL, BUT HAVING **REAL** PYROTECHNICS ONSTAGE WILL NEVER FLY.
SECOND, WE'VE ONLY GOT ROOM IN THE BUDGET THIS YEAR FOR TWO SET PIECES, TOPS.
THE CANNON HAS **GOT** TO BE ONE OF THEM, MR. MADERA.
SANJAY, HOW MUCH LEFTOVER SCRAP MATERIAL DO WE HAVE FROM LAST YEAR?
PROBABLY ENOUGH.
I'LL DEFINITELY NEED ANOTHER PERSON TO HELP WITH CONSTRUCTION.

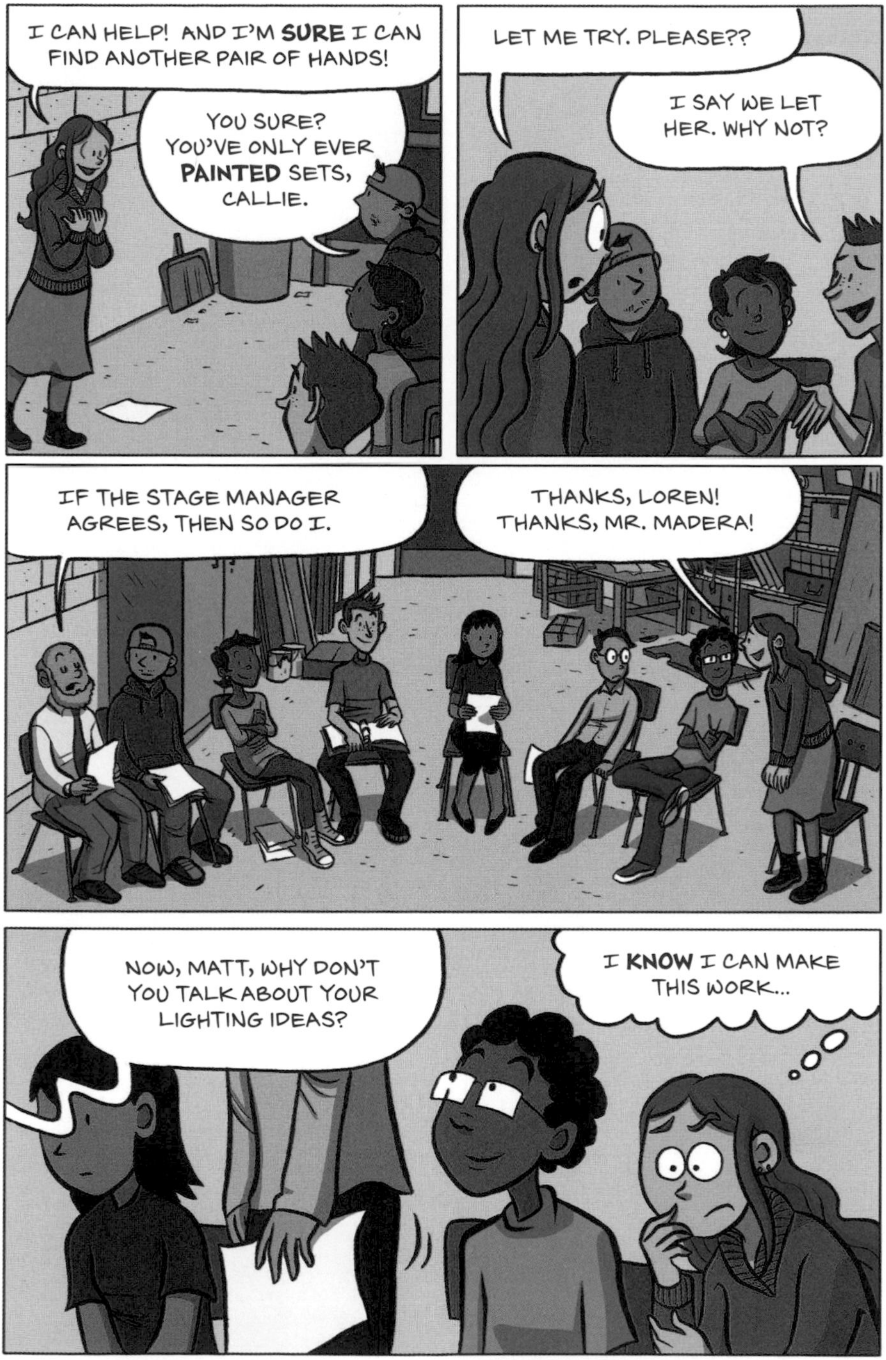
I CAN HELP! AND I'M **SURE** I CAN FIND ANOTHER PAIR OF HANDS!
YOU SURE? YOU'VE ONLY EVER **PAINTED** SETS, CALLIE.
LET ME TRY. PLEASE??
I SAY WE LET HER. WHY NOT?
IF THE STAGE MANAGER AGREES, THEN SO DO I.
THANKS, LOREN! THANKS, MR. MADERA!
NOW, MATT, WHY DON'T YOU TALK ABOUT YOUR LIGHTING IDEAS?
I **KNOW** I CAN MAKE THIS WORK...

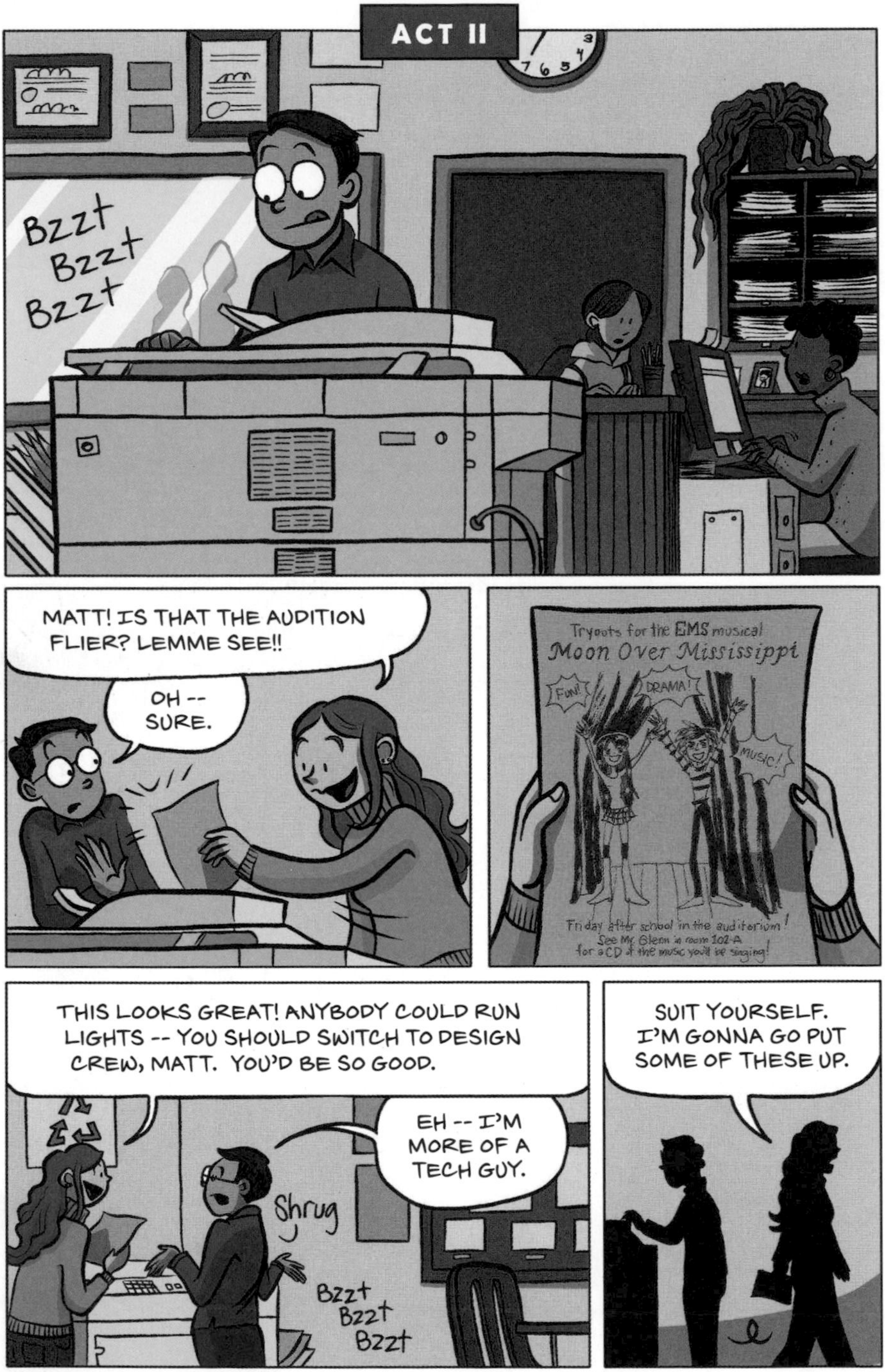
ACT II
Bzzt
Bzzt
Bzzt
MATT! IS THAT THE AUDITION FLIER? LEMME SEE!!
OH -- SURE.
Tryoots for the EMS musical
Moon Over Mississippi
FUN!
DRAMA!
MUSIC!
Friday after school in the auditorium!
See Mr. Glenn in room 102-A
for a CD of the music you'll be singing!
THIS LOOKS GREAT! ANYBODY COULD RUN LIGHTS -- YOU SHOULD SWITCH TO DESIGN CREW, MATT. YOU'D BE SO GOOD.
EH -- I'M MORE OF A TECH GUY.
Shrug
Bzzt
Bzzt
Bzzt
SUIT YOURSELF. I'M GONNA GO PUT SOME OF THESE UP.

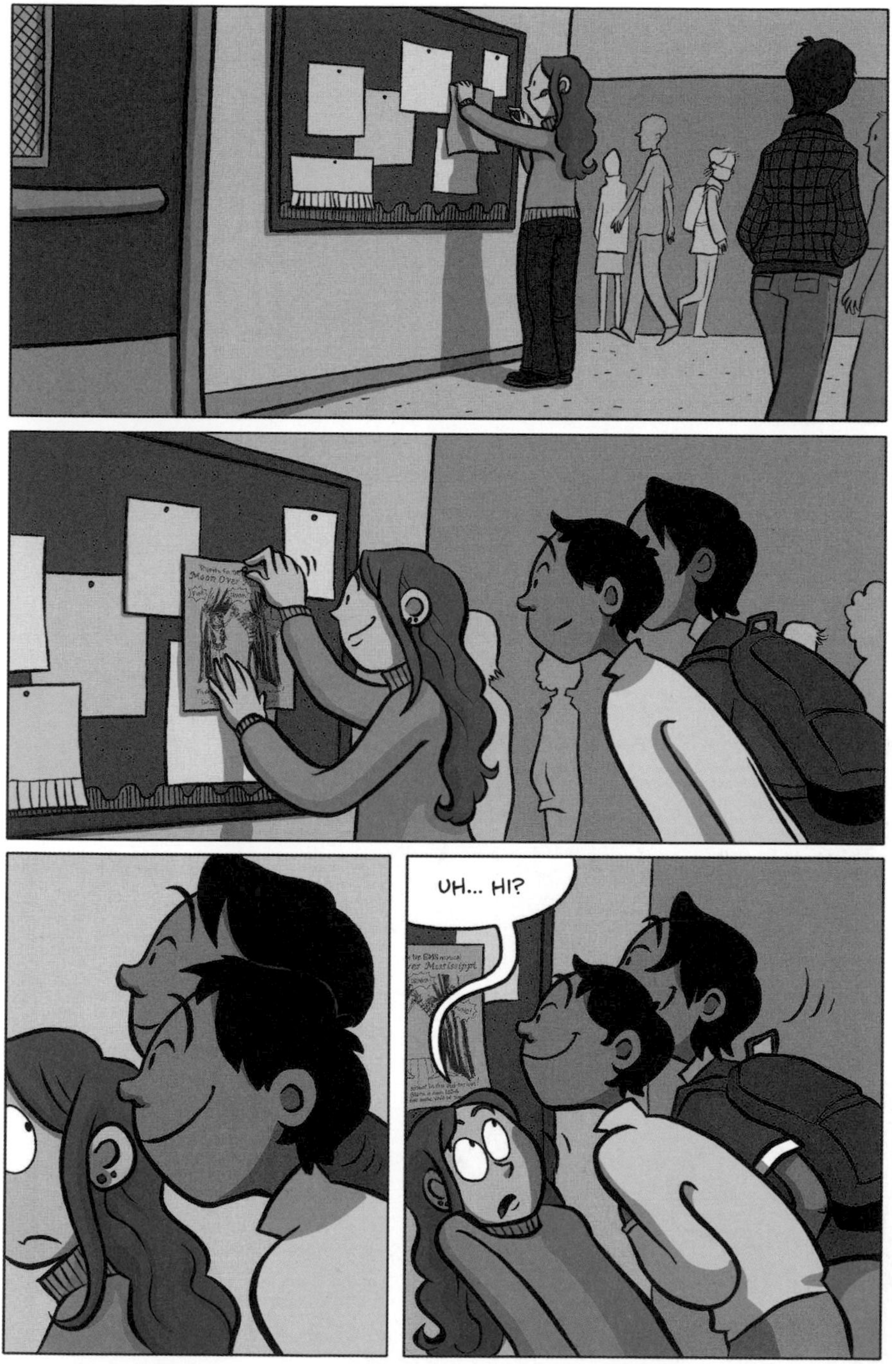
Moon Over
UH... HI?

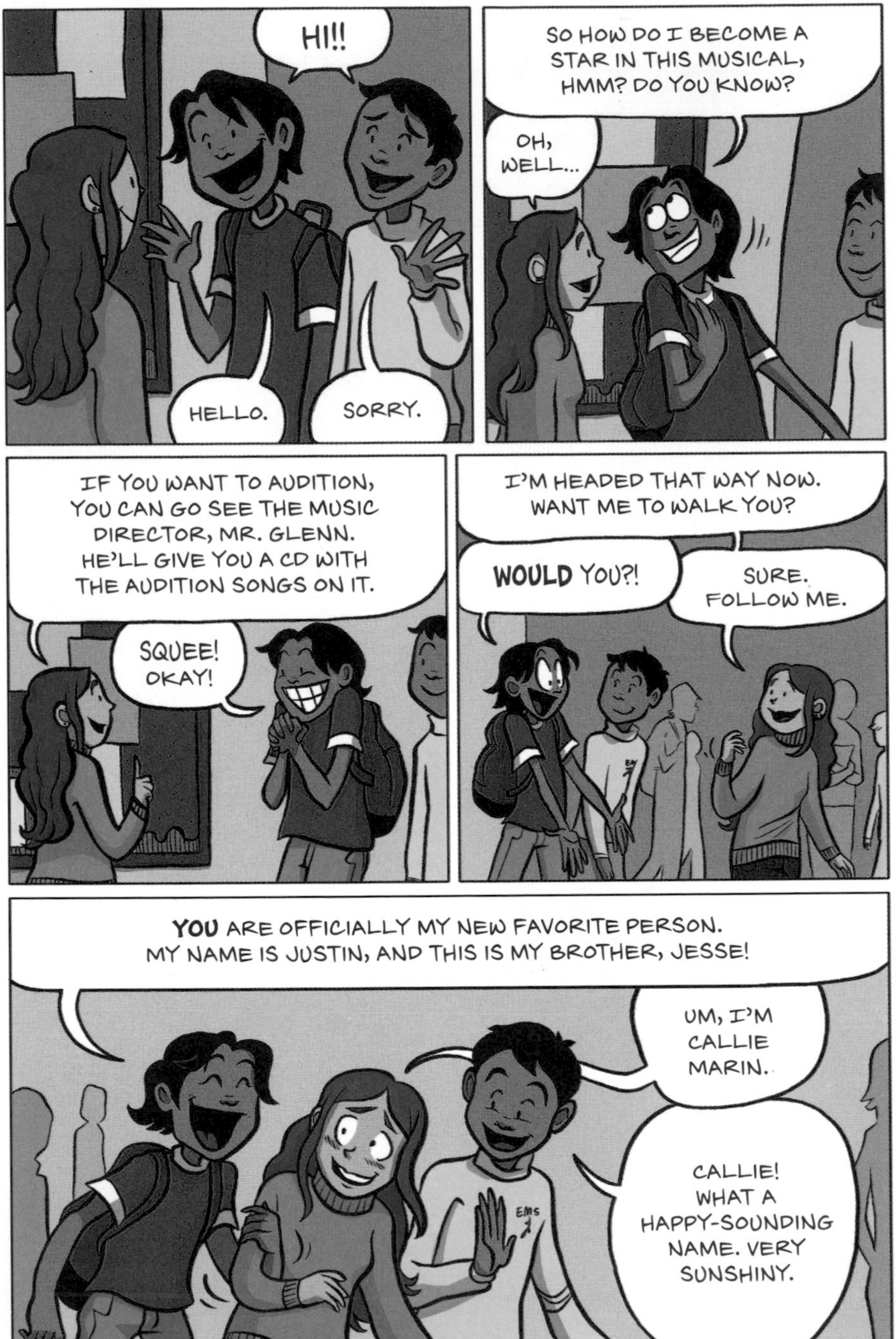
HI!!
HELLO.
SORRY.
SO HOW DO I BECOME A STAR IN THIS MUSICAL, HMM? DO YOU KNOW?
OH, WELL...
IF YOU WANT TO AUDITION, YOU CAN GO SEE THE MUSIC DIRECTOR, MR. GLENN. HE'LL GIVE YOU A CD WITH THE AUDITION SONGS ON IT.
SQUEE! OKAY!
I'M HEADED THAT WAY NOW. WANT ME TO WALK YOU?
WOULD YOU?!
SURE. FOLLOW ME.
YOU ARE OFFICIALLY MY NEW FAVORITE PERSON. MY NAME IS JUSTIN, AND THIS IS MY BROTHER, JESSE!
UM, I'M CALLIE MARIN.
CALLIE! WHAT A HAPPY-SOUNDING NAME. VERY SUNSHINY.

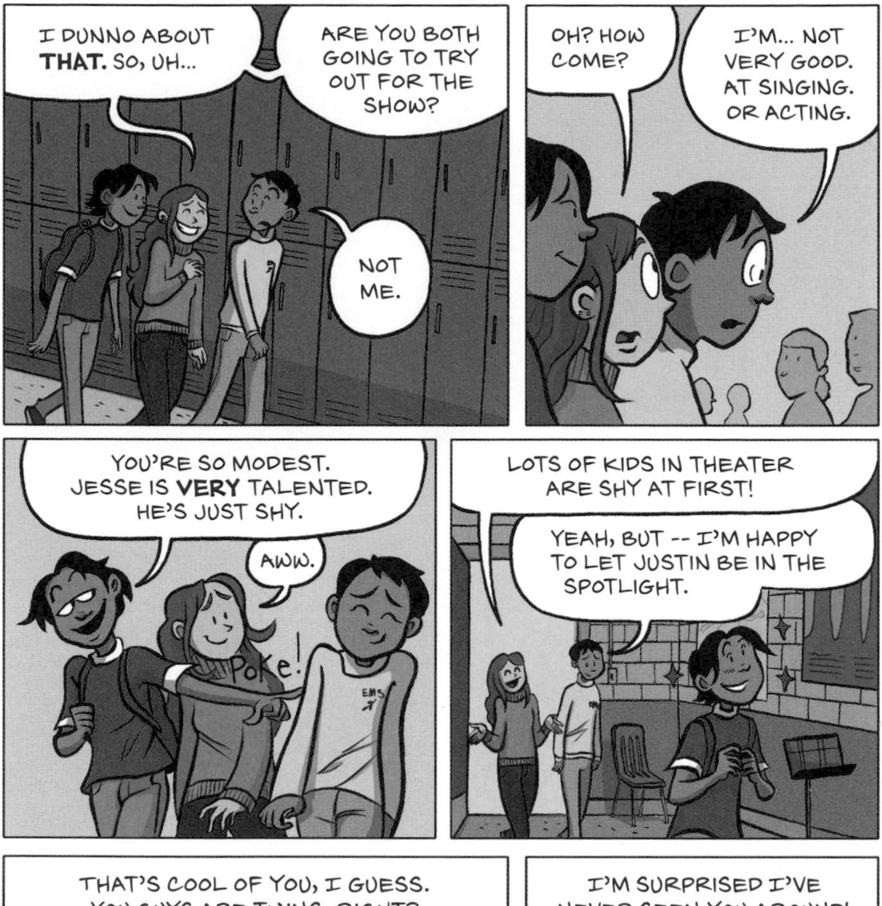
I DUNNO ABOUT **THAT.** SO, UH...
ARE YOU BOTH GOING TO TRY OUT FOR THE SHOW?
NOT ME.
OH? HOW COME?
I'M... NOT VERY GOOD. AT SINGING. OR ACTING.
YOU'RE SO MODEST. JESSE IS **VERY** TALENTED. HE'S JUST SHY.
AWW.
POKE!
EMS
LOTS OF KIDS IN THEATER ARE SHY AT FIRST!
YEAH, BUT -- I'M HAPPY TO LET JUSTIN BE IN THE SPOTLIGHT.
THAT'S COOL OF YOU, I GUESS. YOU GUYS ARE TWINS, RIGHT?
UH-HUH.
THE MUSIC MAN
I'M SURPRISED I'VE NEVER SEEN YOU AROUND!
WE SPEND A **LOT** OF TIME STUDYING. OUR DAD'S KINDA ALL ABOUT GOOD GRADES.

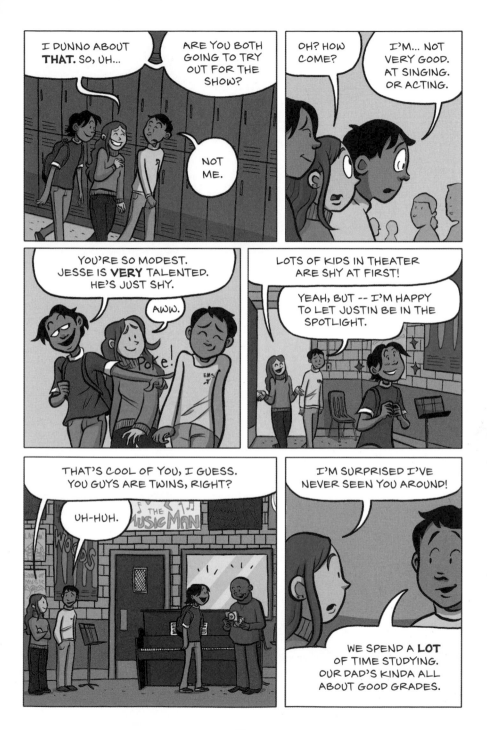

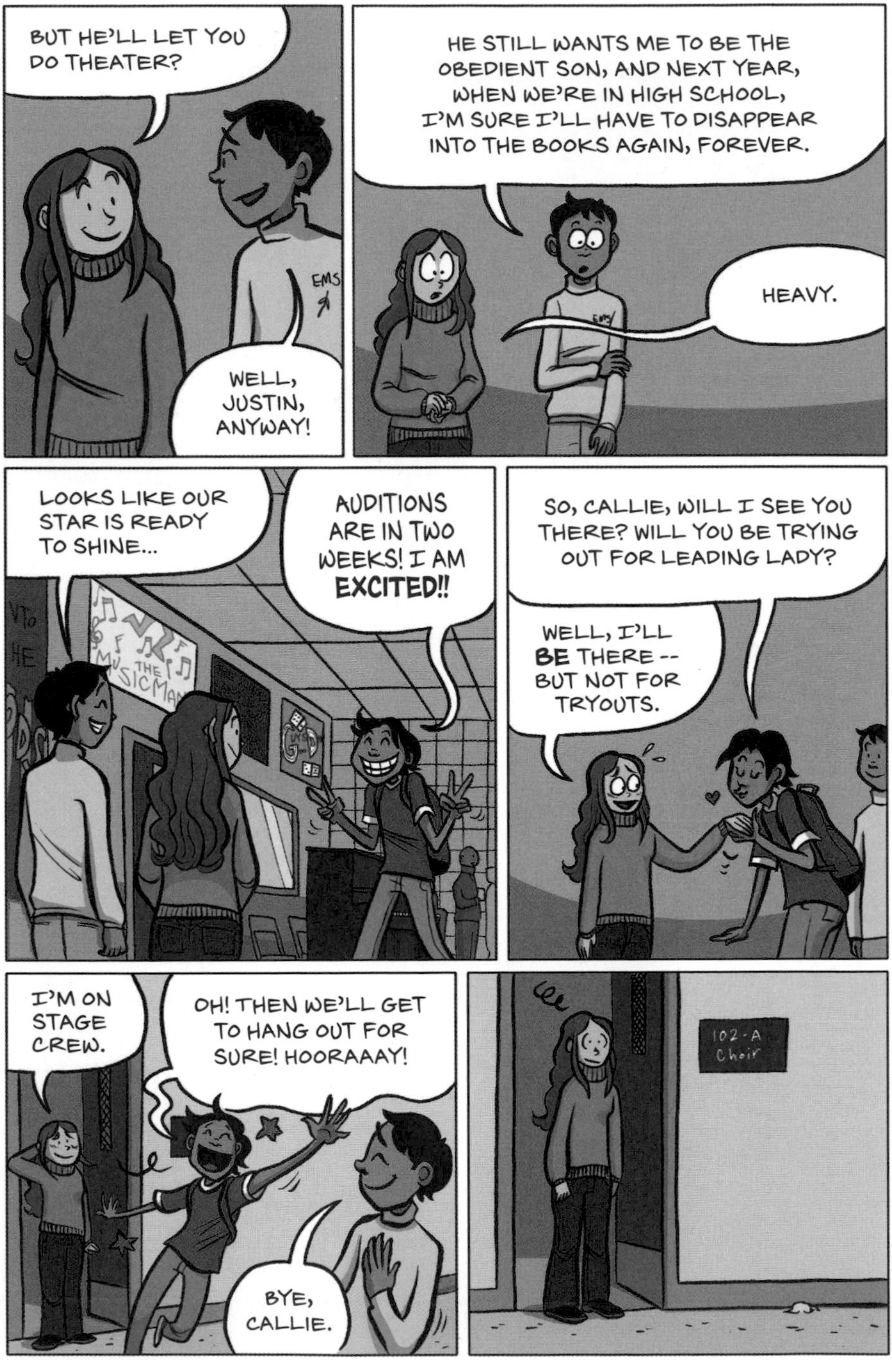
BUT HE'LL LET YOU DO THEATER?
WELL, JUSTIN, ANYWAY!
HE STILL WANTS ME TO BE THE OBEDIENT SON, AND NEXT YEAR, WHEN WE'RE IN HIGH SCHOOL, I'M SURE I'LL HAVE TO DISAPPEAR INTO THE BOOKS AGAIN, FOREVER.
HEAVY.
EMS
LOOKS LIKE OUR STAR IS READY TO SHINE...
AUDITIONS ARE IN TWO WEEKS! I AM **EXCITED!!**
THE MUSIC MAN
SO, CALLIE, WILL I SEE YOU THERE? WILL YOU BE TRYING OUT FOR LEADING LADY?
WELL, I'LL **BE** THERE -- BUT NOT FOR TRYOUTS.
I'M ON STAGE CREW.
OH! THEN WE'LL GET TO HANG OUT FOR SURE! HOORAAAY!
BYE, CALLIE.
102-A Choir

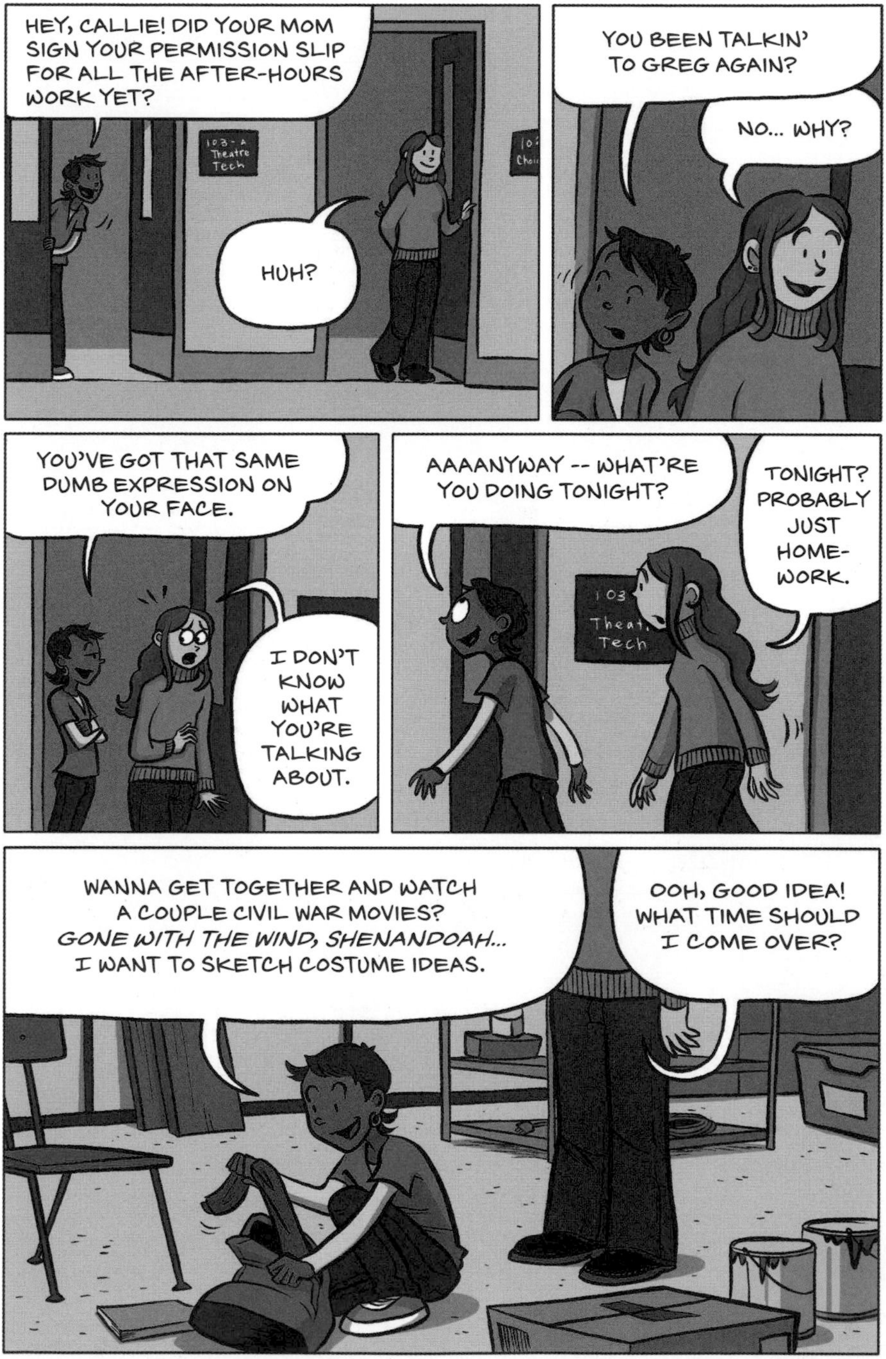
HEY, CALLIE! DID YOUR MOM SIGN YOUR PERMISSION SLIP FOR ALL THE AFTER-HOURS WORK YET?
103-A Theatre Tech
HUH?
YOU BEEN TALKIN' TO GREG AGAIN?
NO... WHY?
YOU'VE GOT THAT SAME DUMB EXPRESSION ON YOUR FACE.
I DON'T KNOW WHAT YOU'RE TALKING ABOUT.
AAAANYWAY -- WHAT'RE YOU DOING TONIGHT?
TONIGHT? PROBABLY JUST HOME-WORK.
WANNA GET TOGETHER AND WATCH A COUPLE CIVIL WAR MOVIES? *GONE WITH THE WIND*, *SHENANDOAH*... I WANT TO SKETCH COSTUME IDEAS.
OOH, GOOD IDEA! WHAT TIME SHOULD I COME OVER?

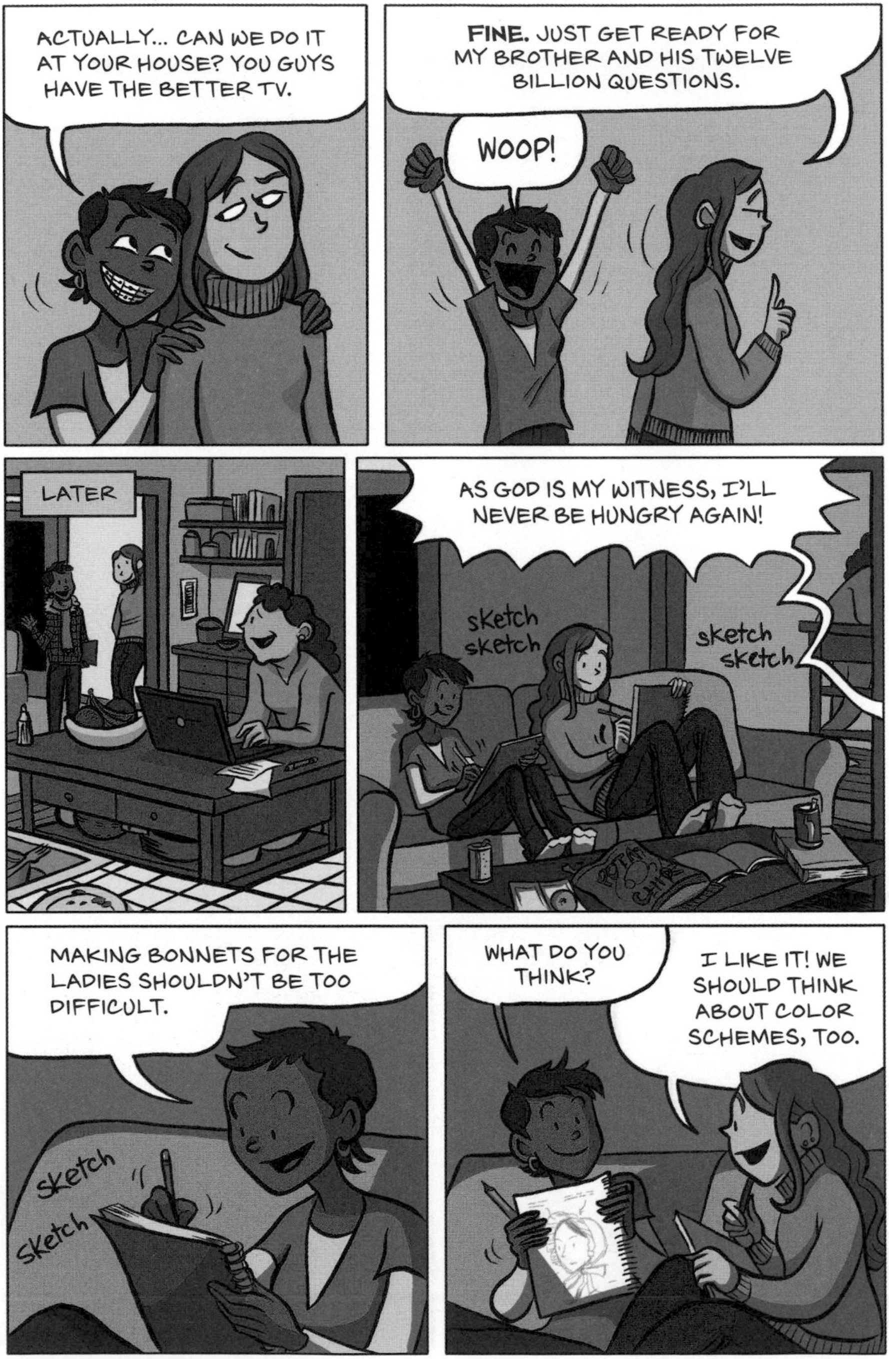
ACTUALLY... CAN WE DO IT AT YOUR HOUSE? YOU GUYS HAVE THE BETTER TV.
FINE. JUST GET READY FOR MY BROTHER AND HIS TWELVE BILLION QUESTIONS.
WOOP!
LATER
AS GOD IS MY WITNESS, I'LL NEVER BE HUNGRY AGAIN!
sketch sketch
sketch sketch
MAKING BONNETS FOR THE LADIES SHOULDN'T BE TOO DIFFICULT.
sketch
sketch
WHAT DO YOU THINK?
I LIKE IT! WE SHOULD THINK ABOUT COLOR SCHEMES, TOO.

LIKE, IF ALL THE SETS END UP BEING YELLOW AND ORANGE, THE COSTUMES SHOULD BE BLUES, GREENS, AND PURPLES SO THAT THEY STAND OUT.

OKAY, BUT YOU'RE MAKING A GARDEN SET TOO, RIGHT?

HMM, YEAH.

WHAT'S UP WITH THAT LADY'S DRESS? I LIKE HIS MUSTACHE! WHATCHA GUYS DRAWIN'? CAN I WATCH THIS MOVIE, TOO?

GREAT BALLS OF FIRE!

DID YOU KNOW CALLIE HAS A DRESS THAT I ▓▓▓▓ LIKE A ▓▓▓▓ ▓▓▓▓▓▓▓▓▓▓▓▓▓▓▓▓▓▓▓▓▓▓▓ F▓▓▓▓ PLAYER, BUT LAST YEAR MOM TOLD ME SHE DIDN'T HAVE TIME TO MAKE ME A FULL BASEBALL PLAYER OUTFIT, SO SHE ▓▓▓ ME TO THE STORE AND I ▓▓ TO CHOOSE A ▓▓▓▓D JERSEY...

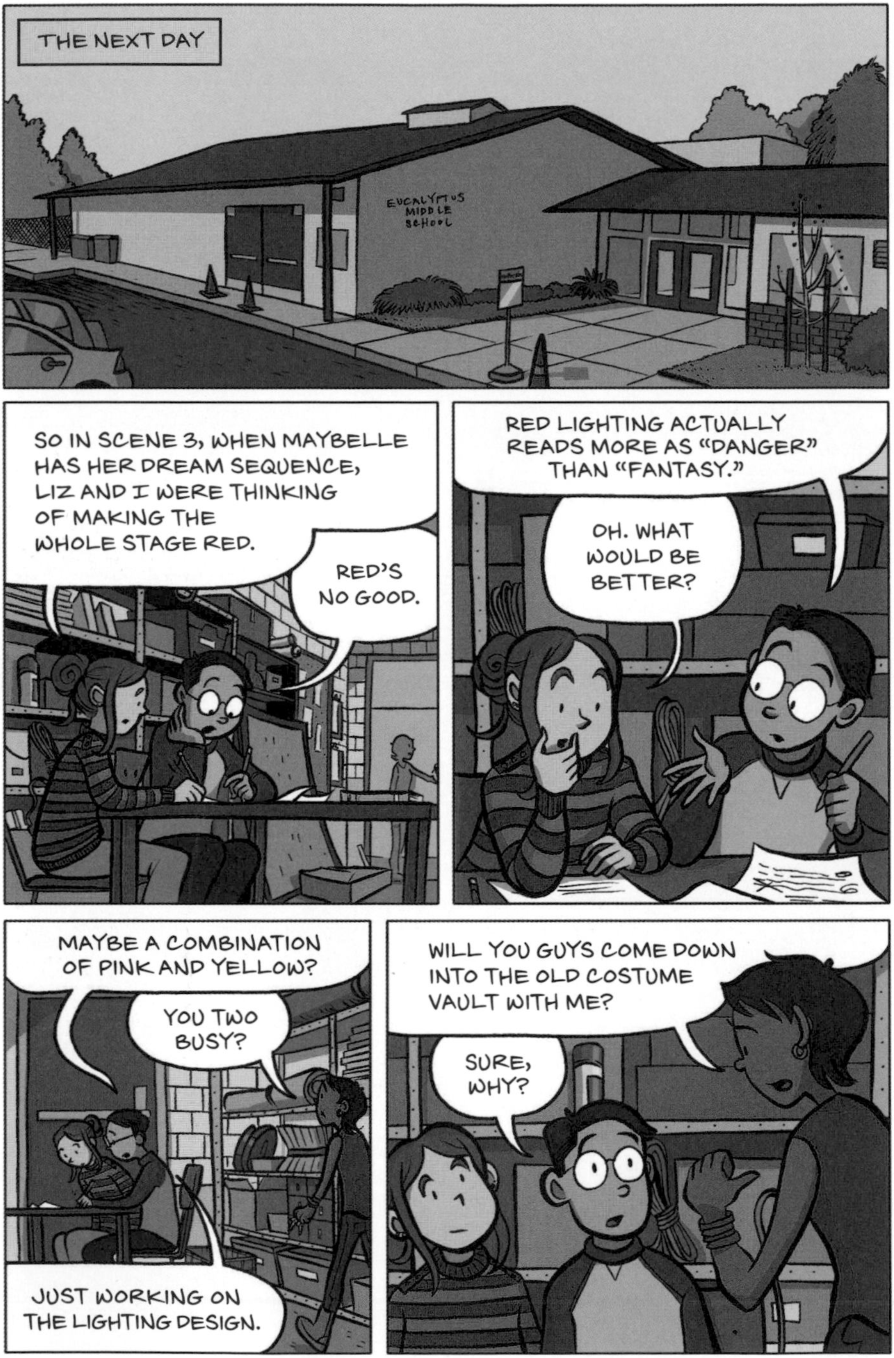
THE NEXT DAY
EUCALYPTUS MIDDLE SCHOOL
SO IN SCENE 3, WHEN MAYBELLE HAS HER DREAM SEQUENCE, LIZ AND I WERE THINKING OF MAKING THE WHOLE STAGE RED.
RED'S NO GOOD.
RED LIGHTING ACTUALLY READS MORE AS "DANGER" THAN "FANTASY."
OH. WHAT WOULD BE BETTER?
MAYBE A COMBINATION OF PINK AND YELLOW?
YOU TWO BUSY?
JUST WORKING ON THE LIGHTING DESIGN.
WILL YOU GUYS COME DOWN INTO THE OLD COSTUME VAULT WITH ME?
SURE, WHY?

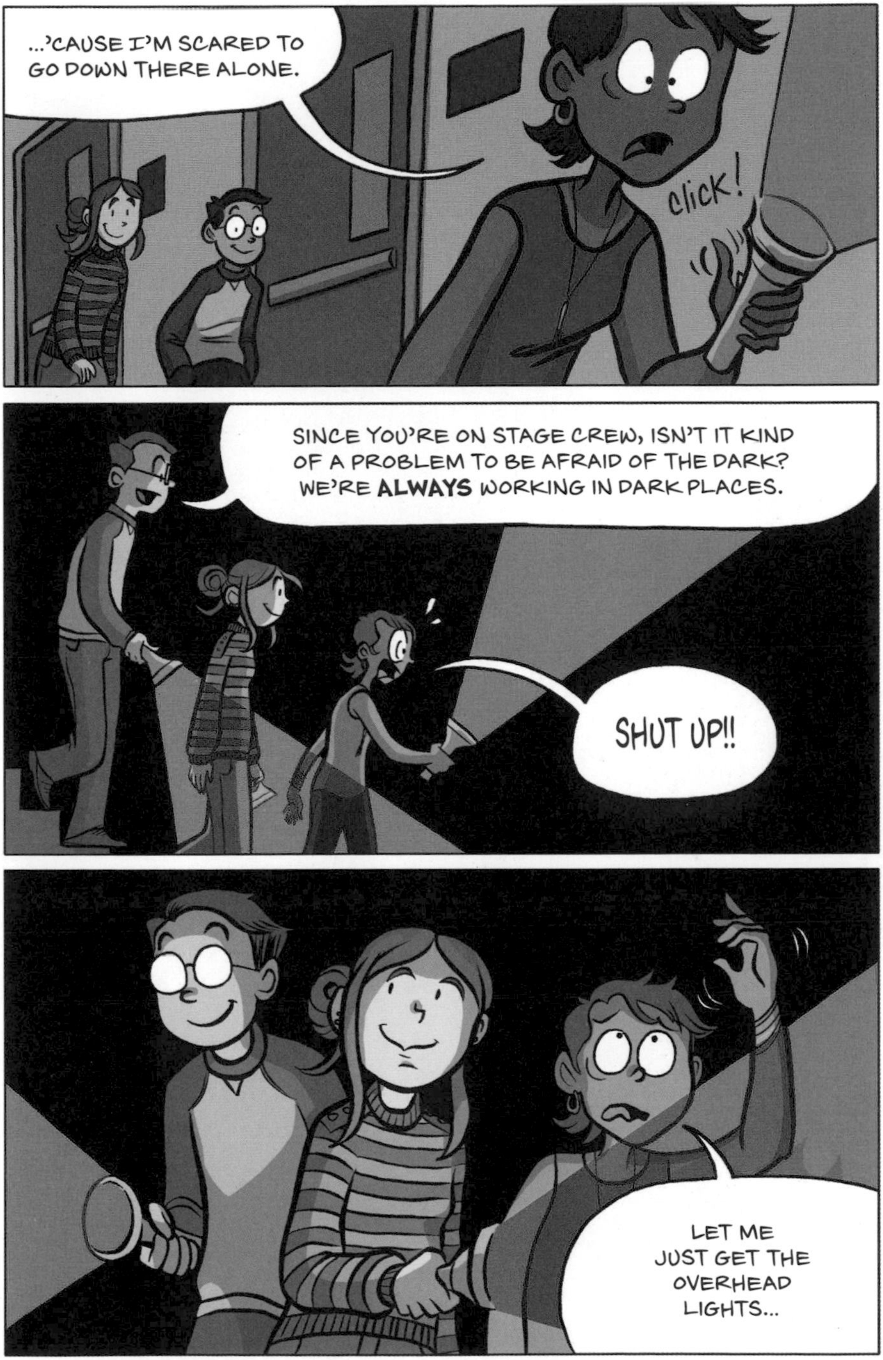
...'CAUSE I'M SCARED TO GO DOWN THERE ALONE.
CLICK!
SINCE YOU'RE ON STAGE CREW, ISN'T IT KIND OF A PROBLEM TO BE AFRAID OF THE DARK? WE'RE **ALWAYS** WORKING IN DARK PLACES.
SHUT UP!!
LET ME JUST GET THE OVERHEAD LIGHTS...

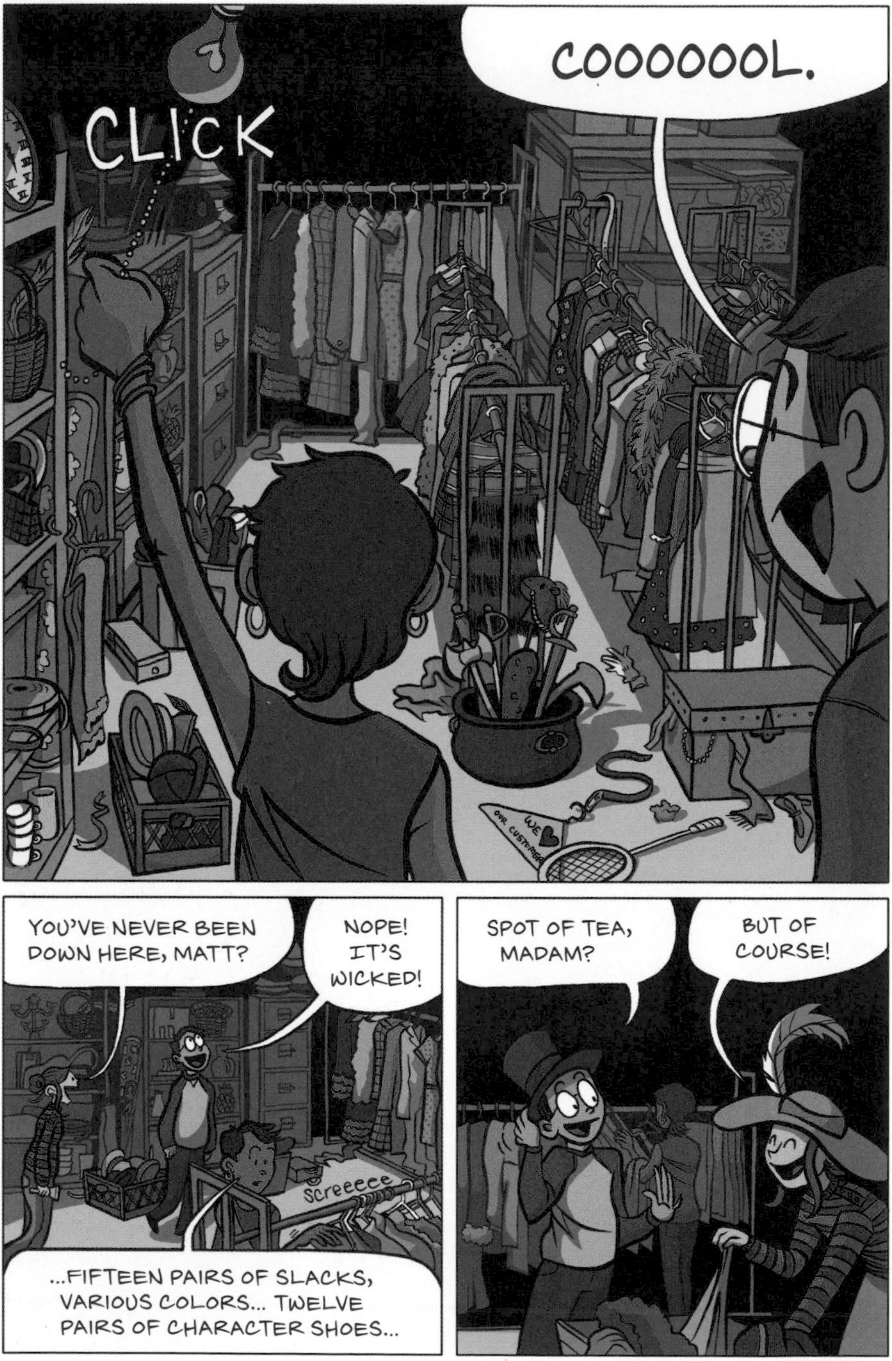
CLICK
COOOOOOL.
WE ♥ OUR CUSTOMERS
YOU'VE NEVER BEEN DOWN HERE, MATT?
NOPE! IT'S WICKED!
SCREEECE
...FIFTEEN PAIRS OF SLACKS, VARIOUS COLORS... TWELVE PAIRS OF CHARACTER SHOES...
SPOT OF TEA, MADAM?
BUT OF COURSE!

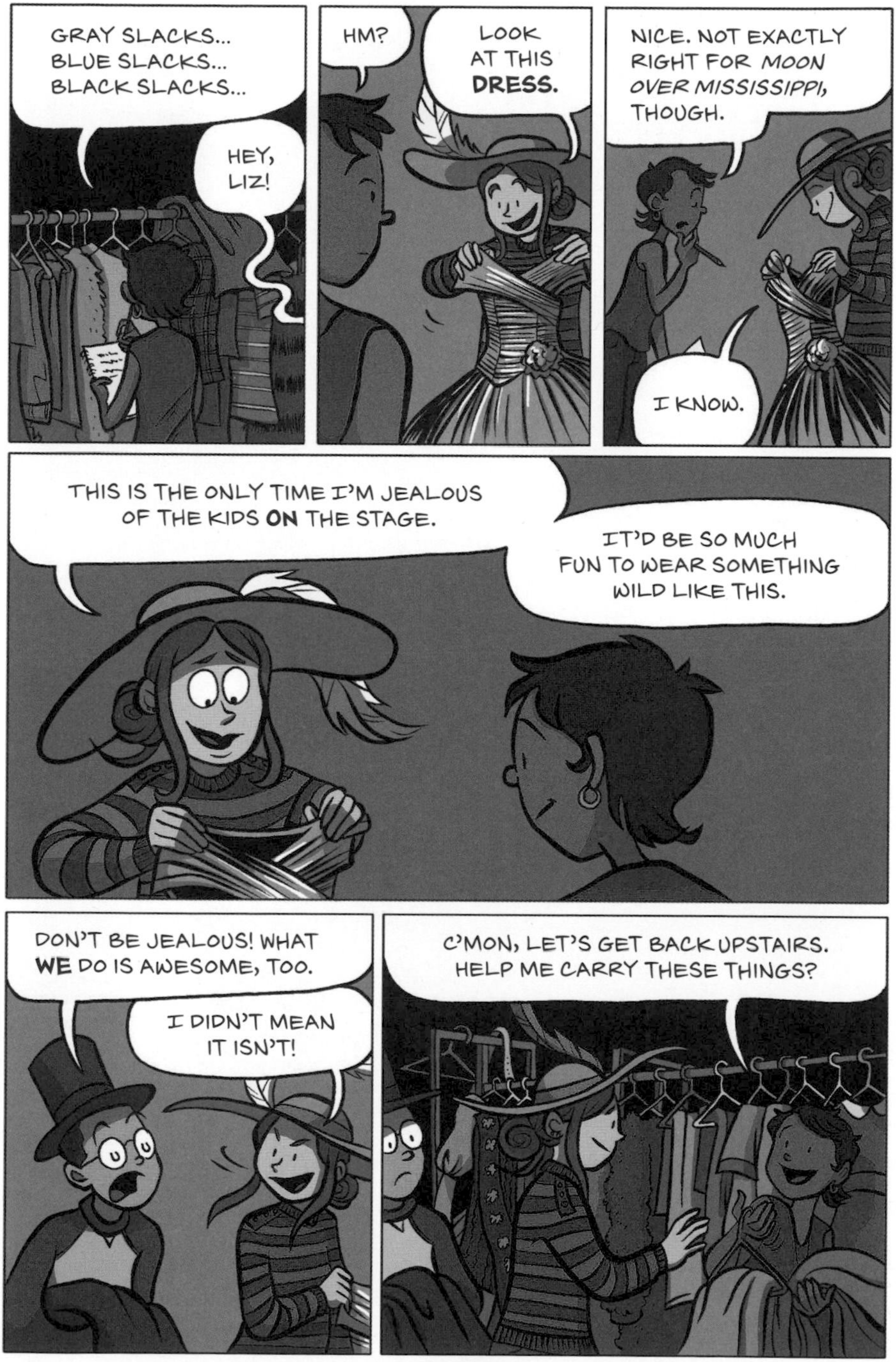
GRAY SLACKS... BLUE SLACKS... BLACK SLACKS...
HEY, LIZ!
HM?
LOOK AT THIS **DRESS.**
NICE. NOT EXACTLY RIGHT FOR *MOON OVER MISSISSIPPI,* THOUGH.
I KNOW.
THIS IS THE ONLY TIME I'M JEALOUS OF THE KIDS **ON** THE STAGE.
IT'D BE SO MUCH FUN TO WEAR SOMETHING WILD LIKE THIS.
DON'T BE JEALOUS! WHAT **WE** DO IS AWESOME, TOO.
I DIDN'T MEAN IT ISN'T!
C'MON, LET'S GET BACK UPSTAIRS. HELP ME CARRY THESE THINGS?

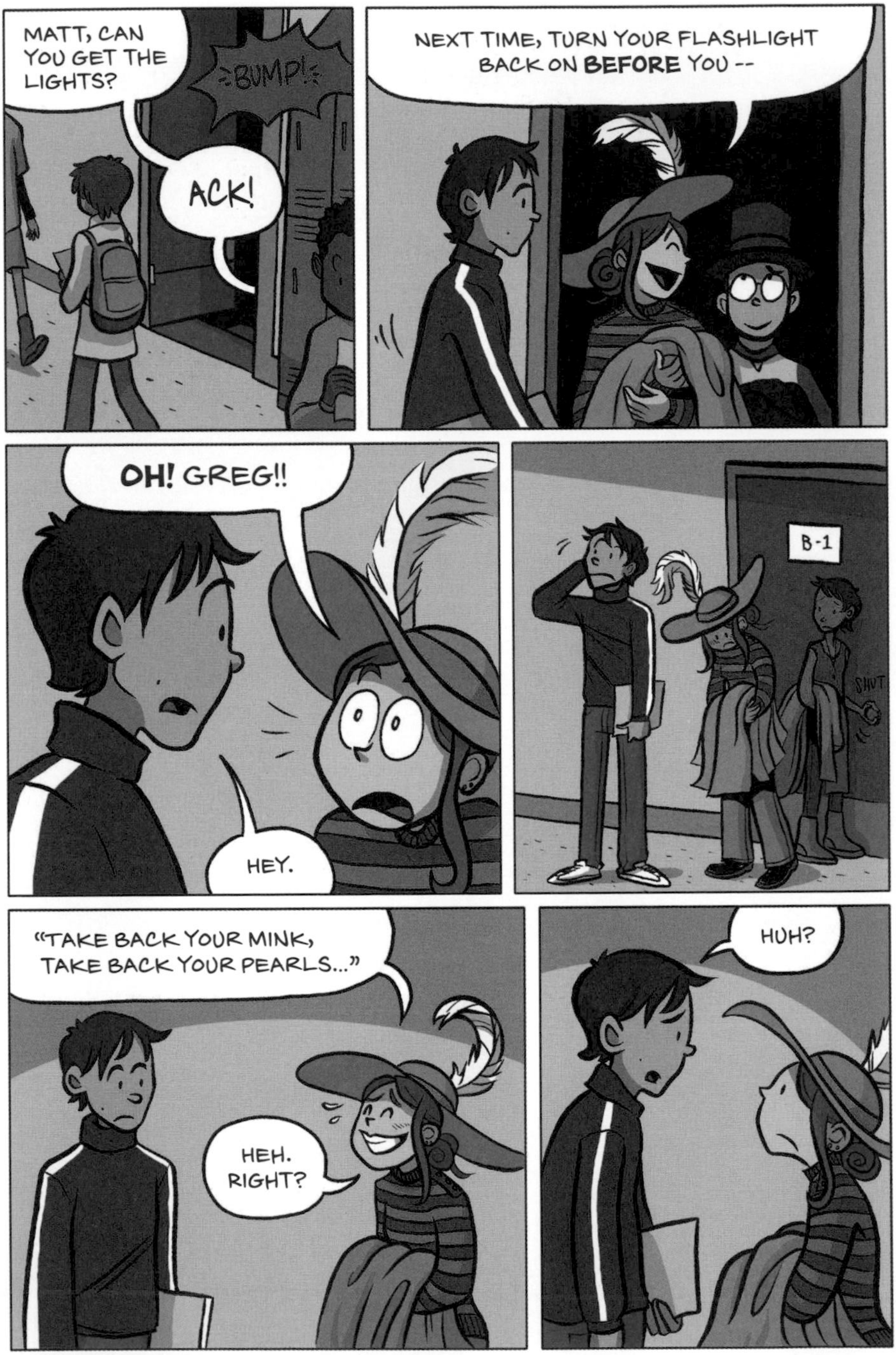
MATT, CAN YOU GET THE LIGHTS?
BUMP!
ACK!
NEXT TIME, TURN YOUR FLASHLIGHT BACK ON **BEFORE** YOU --
OH! GREG!!
HEY.
B-1
SHUT
"TAKE BACK YOUR MINK, TAKE BACK YOUR PEARLS..."
HEH. RIGHT?
HUH?

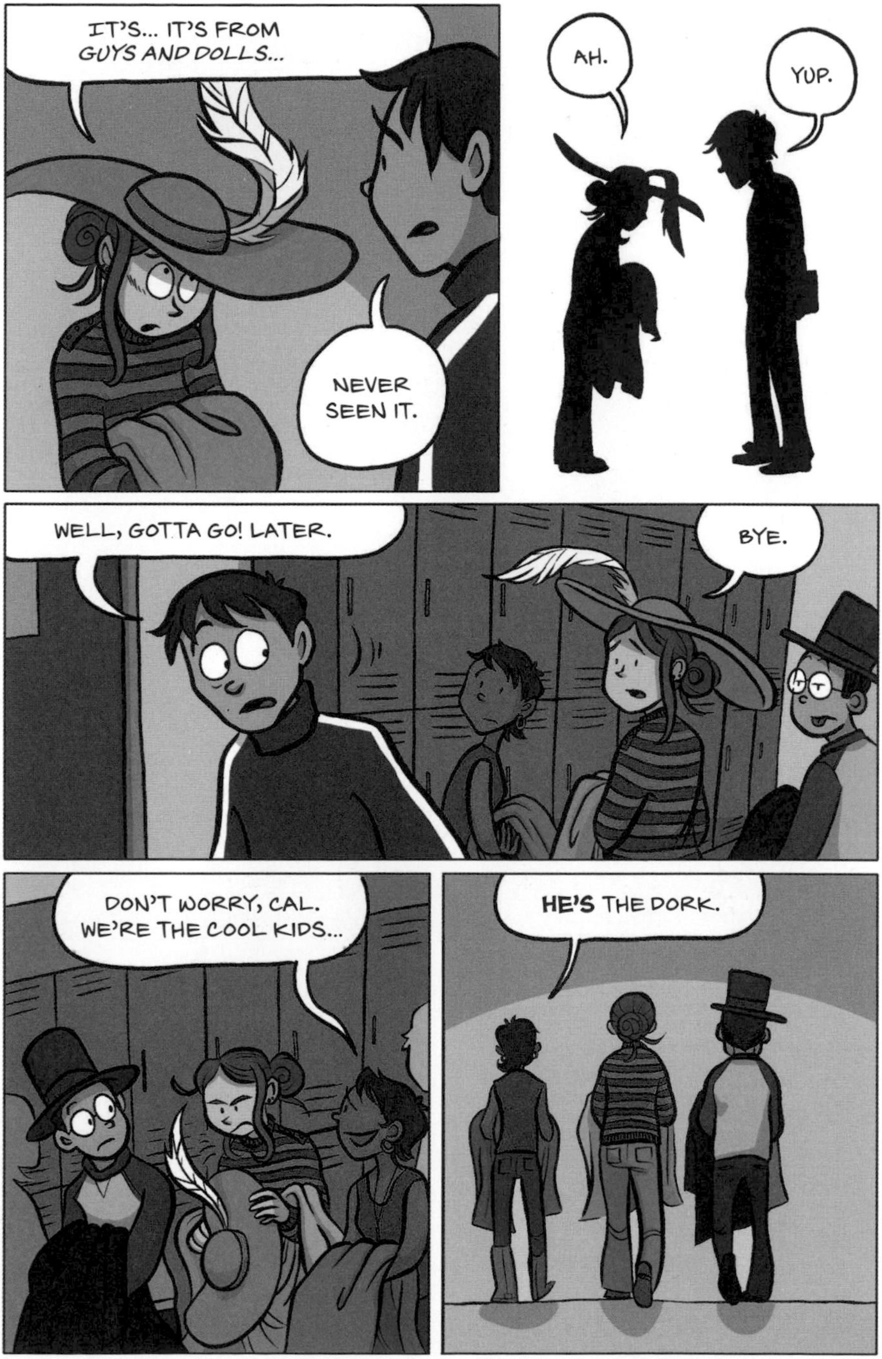
IT'S... IT'S FROM *GUYS AND DOLLS*...
NEVER SEEN IT.
AH.
YUP.
WELL, GOTTA GO! LATER.
BYE.
DON'T WORRY, CAL. WE'RE THE COOL KIDS...
HE'S THE DORK.

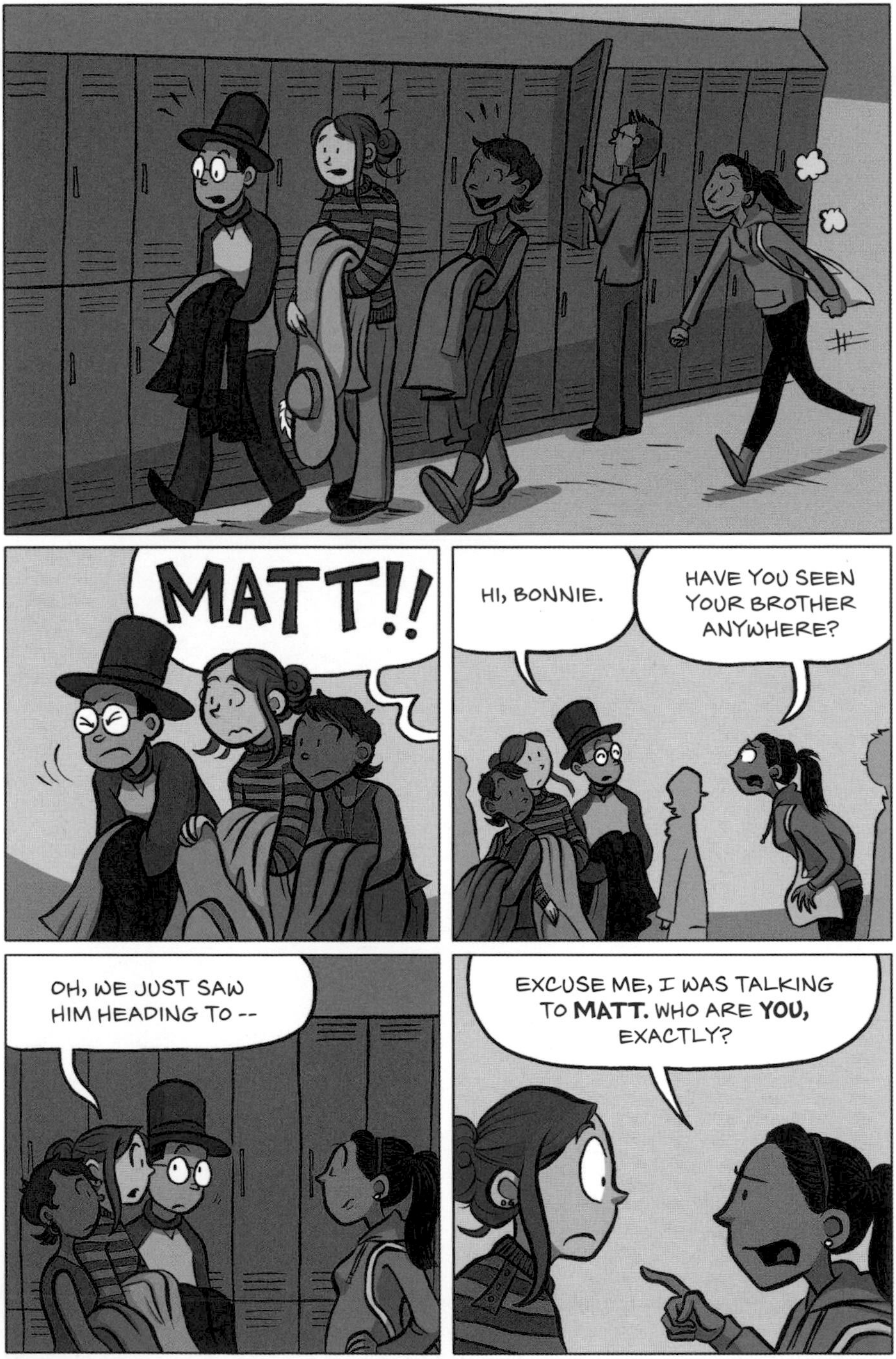
MATT!!
HI, BONNIE.
HAVE YOU SEEN YOUR BROTHER ANYWHERE?
OH, WE JUST SAW HIM HEADING TO --
EXCUSE ME, I WAS TALKING TO **MATT.** WHO ARE **YOU,** EXACTLY?

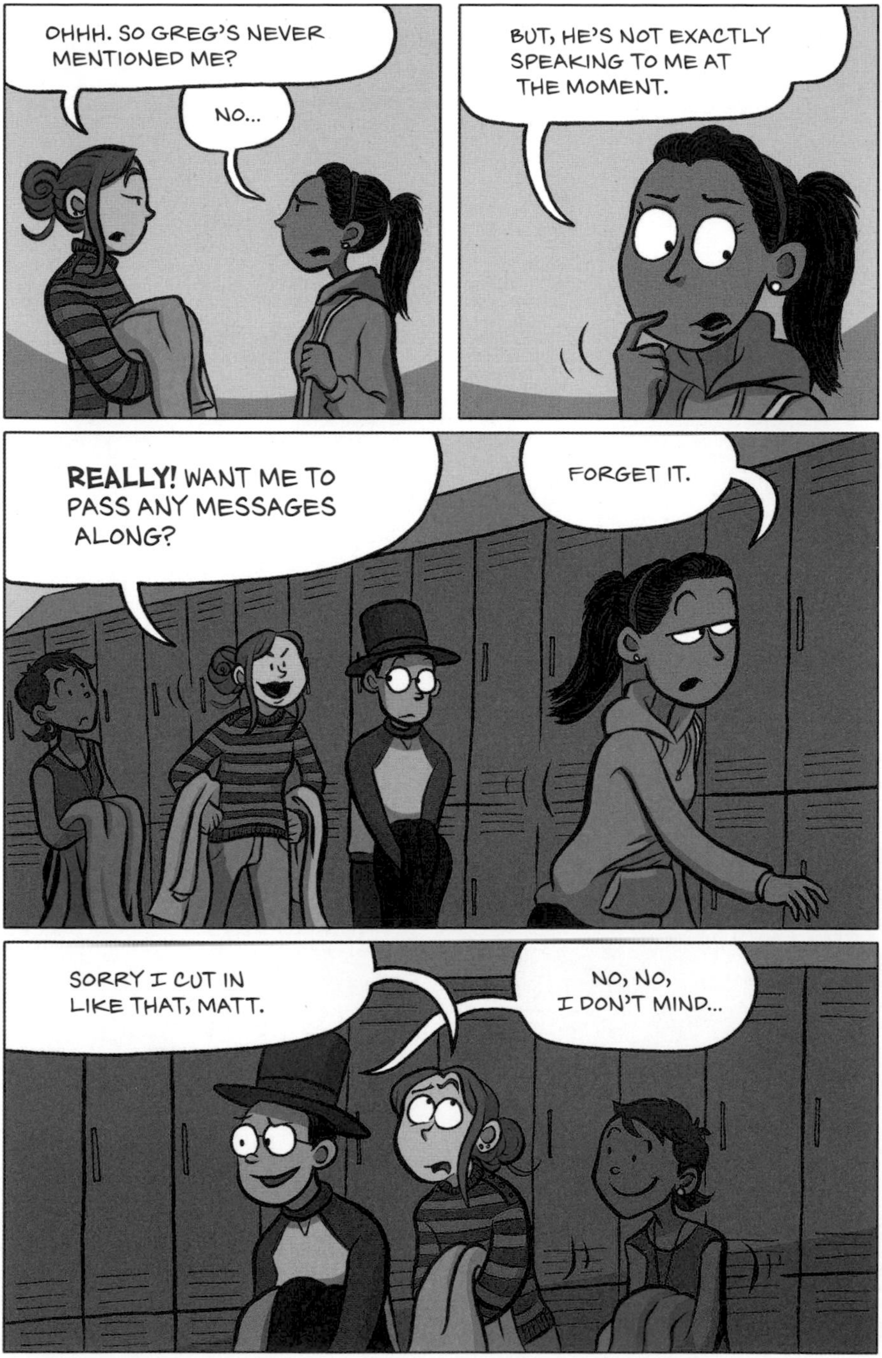
OHHH. SO GREG'S NEVER MENTIONED ME?
NO...
BUT, HE'S NOT EXACTLY SPEAKING TO ME AT THE MOMENT.
REALLY! WANT ME TO PASS ANY MESSAGES ALONG?
FORGET IT.
SORRY I CUT IN LIKE THAT, MATT.
NO, NO, I DON'T MIND...

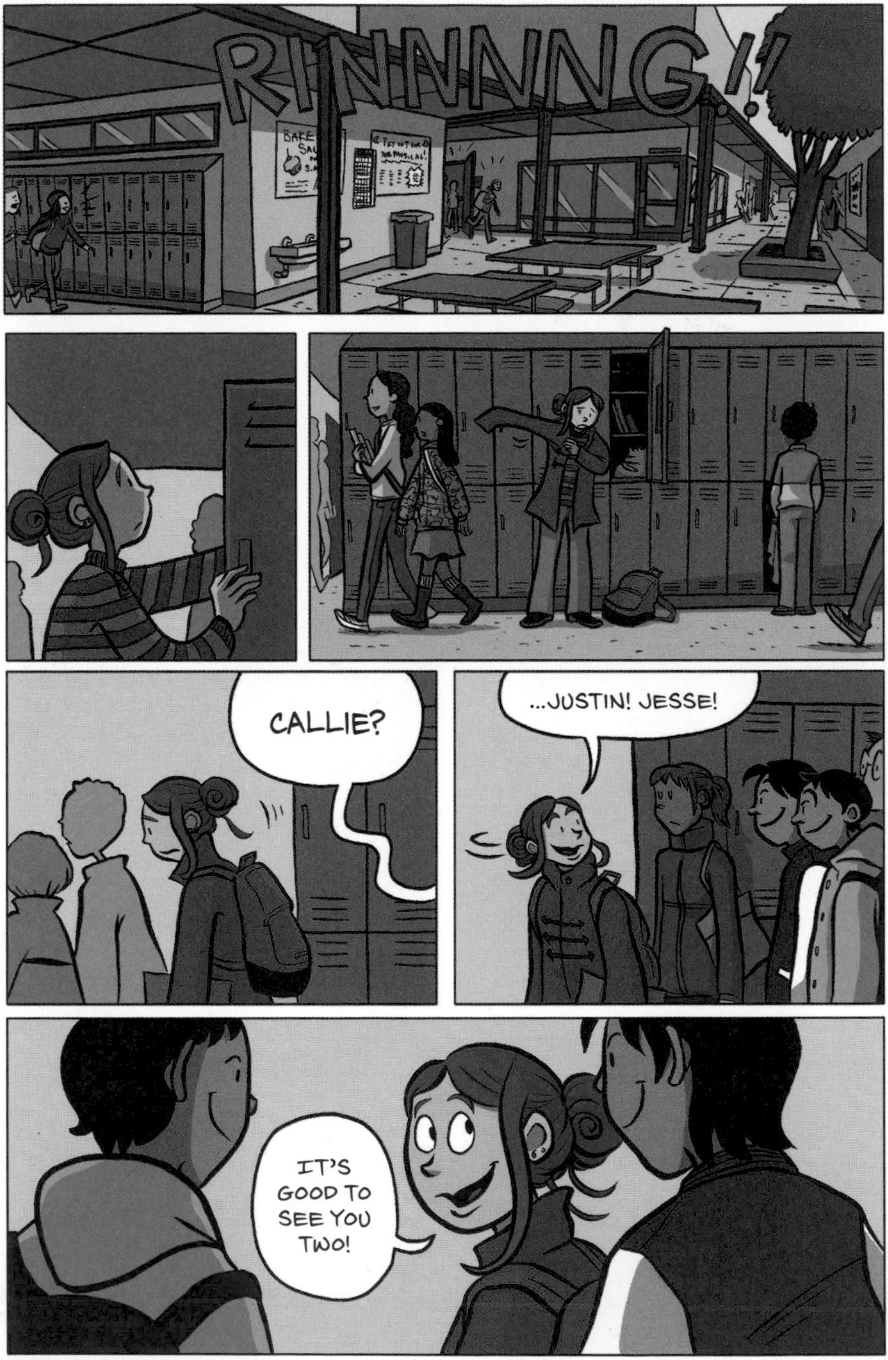
RINNNNG!!
TRY OUT FOR THE MUSICAL!
CALLIE?
...JUSTIN! JESSE!
IT'S GOOD TO SEE YOU TWO!

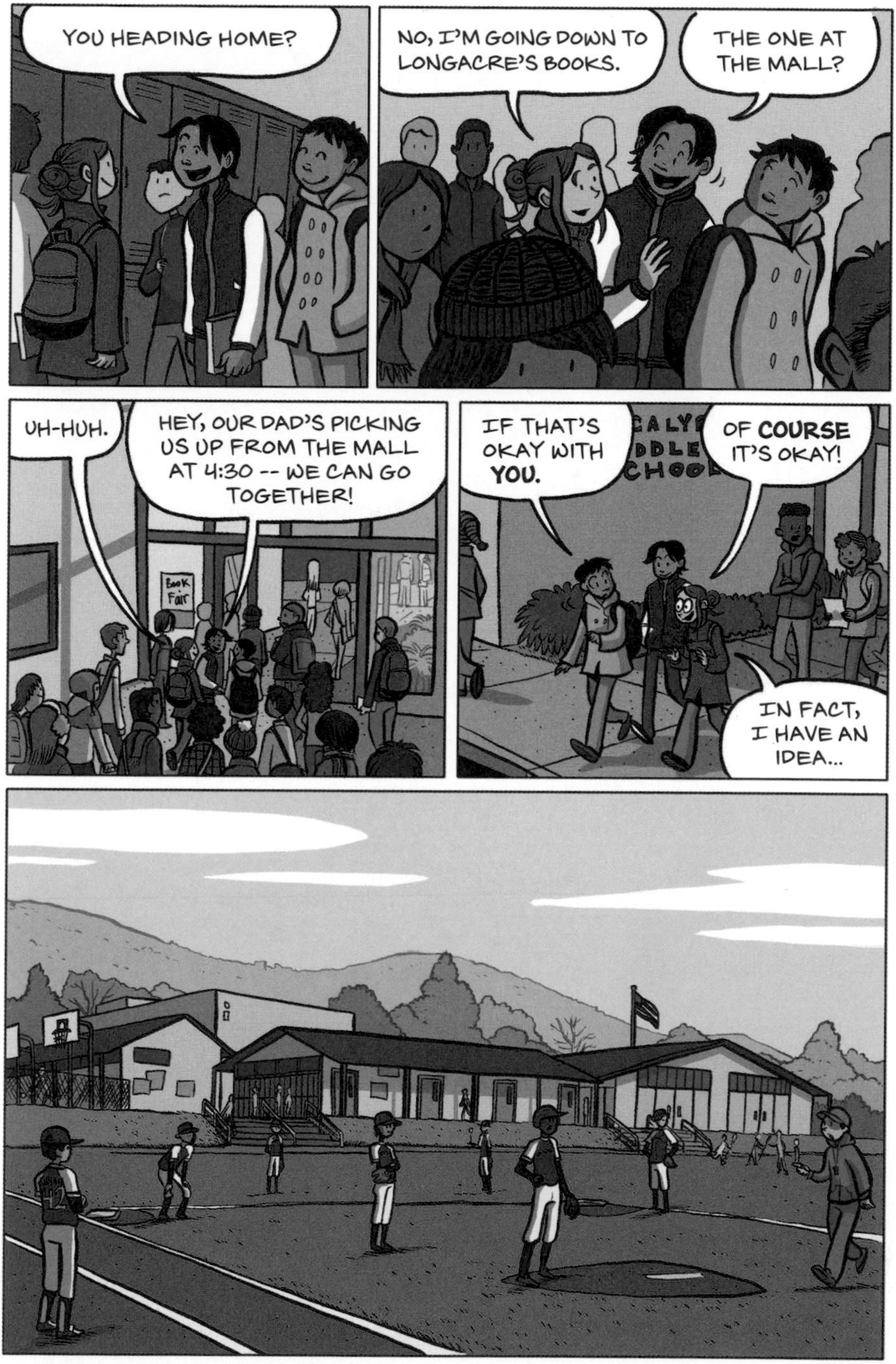
YOU HEADING HOME?
NO, I'M GOING DOWN TO LONGACRE'S BOOKS.
THE ONE AT THE MALL?
UH-HUH.
HEY, OUR DAD'S PICKING US UP FROM THE MALL AT 4:30 -- WE CAN GO TOGETHER!
Book Fair
IF THAT'S OKAY WITH **YOU.**
OF **COURSE** IT'S OKAY!
IN FACT, I HAVE AN IDEA...

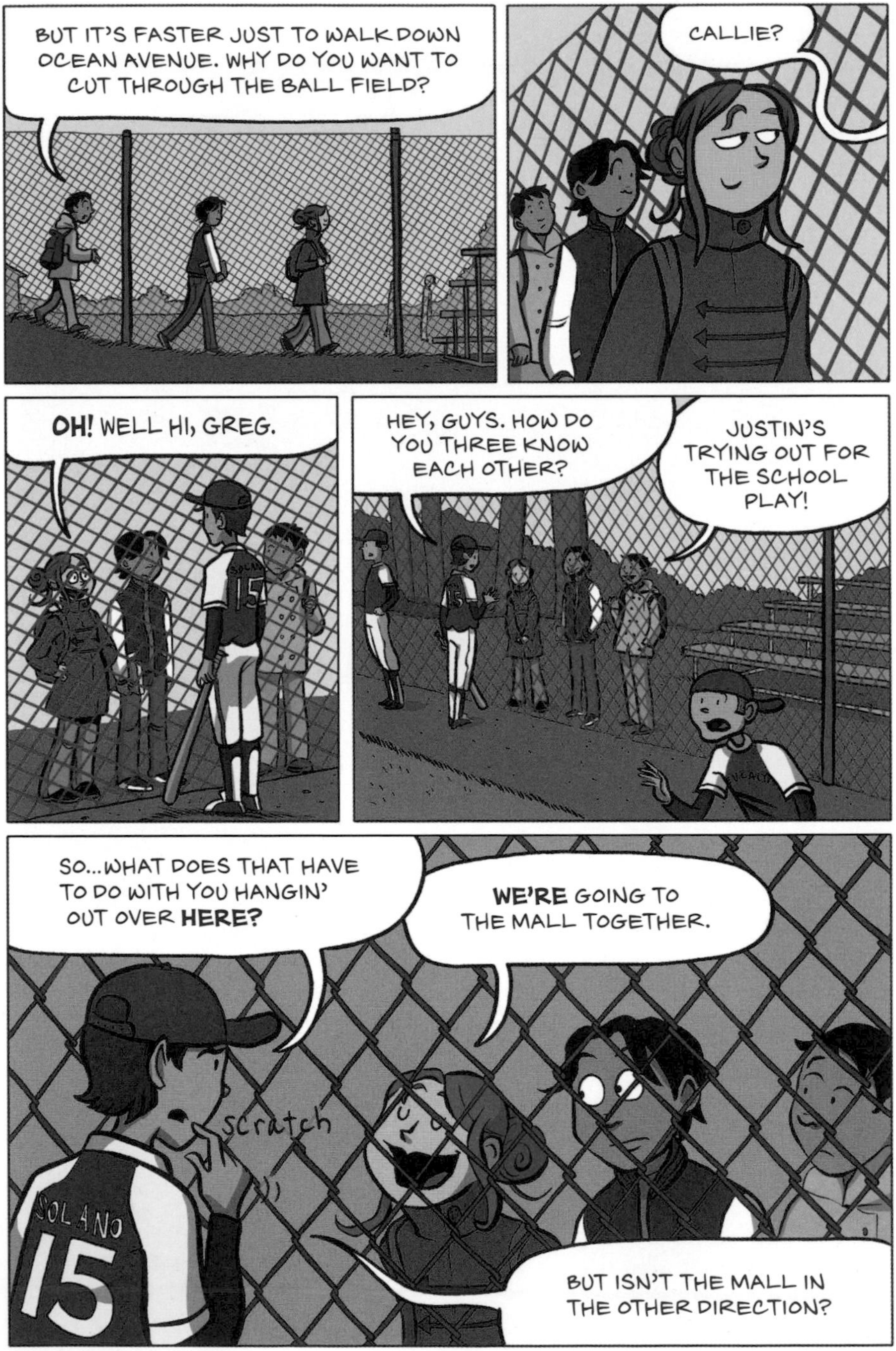

BUT IT'S FASTER JUST TO WALK DOWN OCEAN AVENUE. WHY DO YOU WANT TO CUT THROUGH THE BALL FIELD?
CALLIE?
OH! WELL HI, GREG.
HEY, GUYS. HOW DO YOU THREE KNOW EACH OTHER?
JUSTIN'S TRYING OUT FOR THE SCHOOL PLAY!
SO...WHAT DOES THAT HAVE TO DO WITH YOU HANGIN' OUT OVER HERE?
WE'RE GOING TO THE MALL TOGETHER.
scratch
SOLANO
15
BUT ISN'T THE MALL IN THE OTHER DIRECTION?

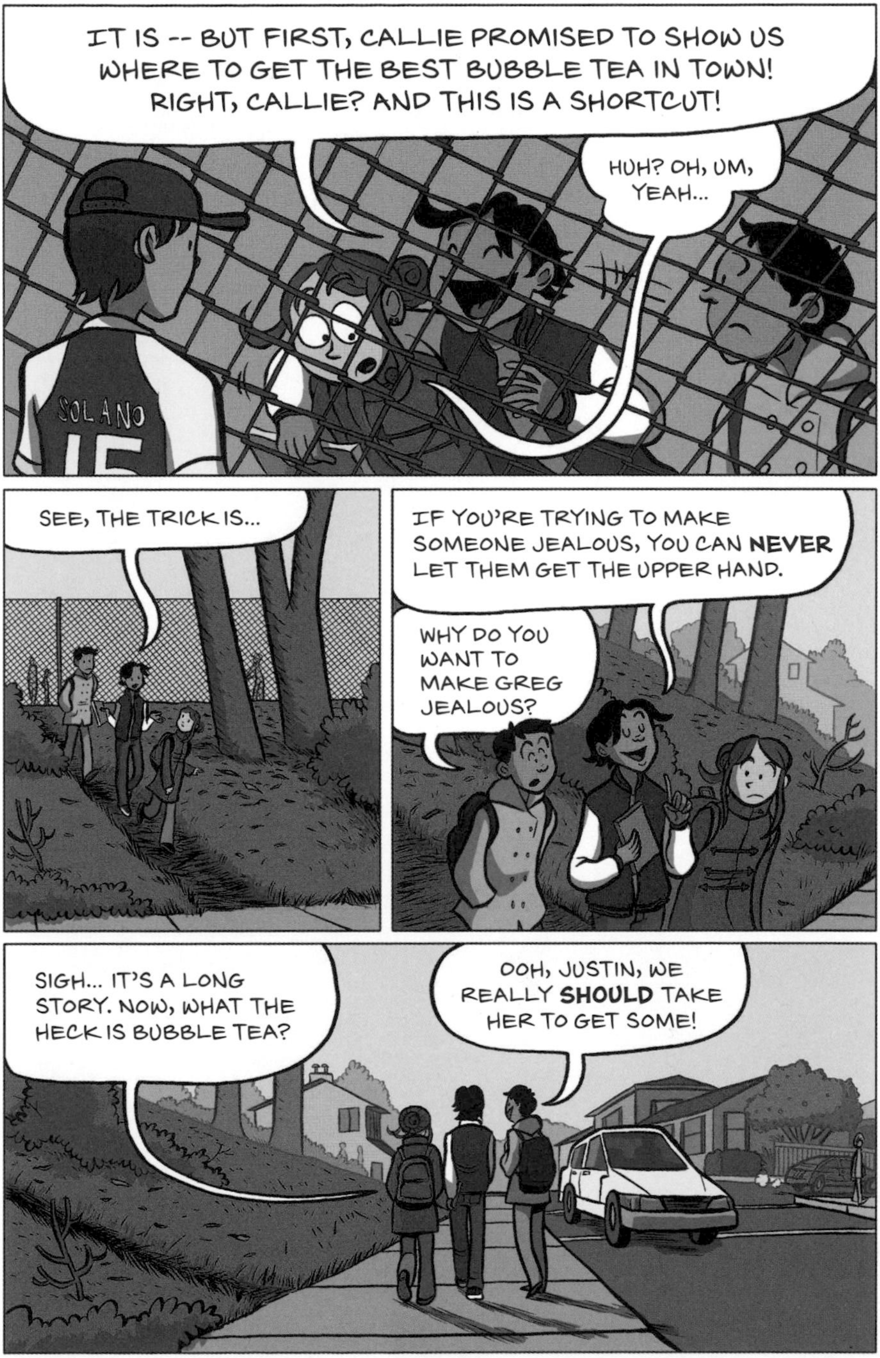
IT IS -- BUT FIRST, CALLIE PROMISED TO SHOW US WHERE TO GET THE BEST BUBBLE TEA IN TOWN! RIGHT, CALLIE? AND THIS IS A SHORTCUT!
HUH? OH, UM, YEAH...
SOLANO
15
SEE, THE TRICK IS...
IF YOU'RE TRYING TO MAKE SOMEONE JEALOUS, YOU CAN **NEVER** LET THEM GET THE UPPER HAND.
WHY DO YOU WANT TO MAKE GREG JEALOUS?
SIGH... IT'S A LONG STORY. NOW, WHAT THE HECK IS BUBBLE TEA?
OOH, JUSTIN, WE REALLY **SHOULD** TAKE HER TO GET SOME!

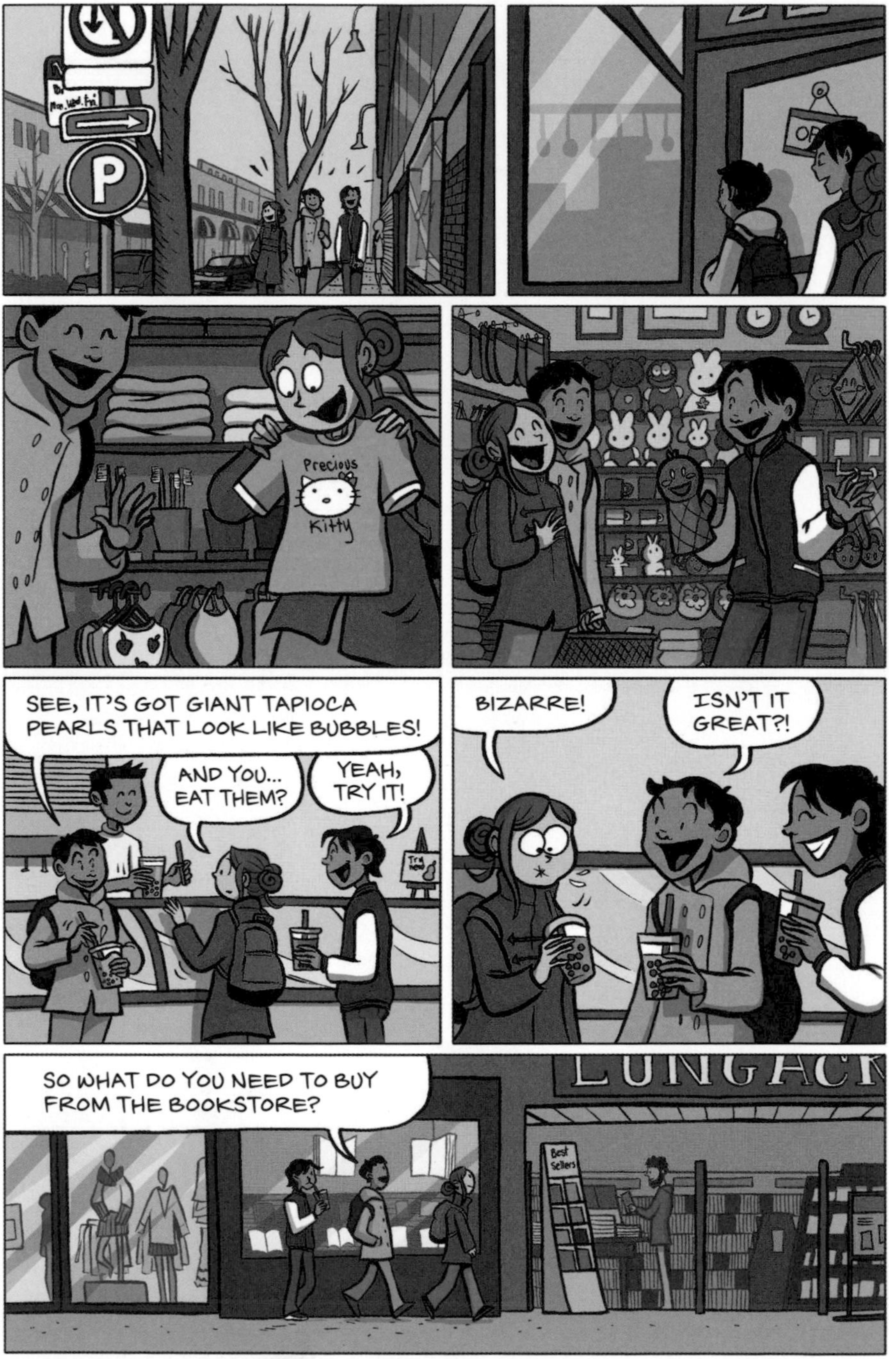
Precious Kitty
SEE, IT'S GOT GIANT TAPIOCA PEARLS THAT LOOK LIKE BUBBLES!
AND YOU... EAT THEM?
YEAH, TRY IT!
BIZARRE!
ISN'T IT GREAT?!
SO WHAT DO YOU NEED TO BUY FROM THE BOOKSTORE?
Best Sellers

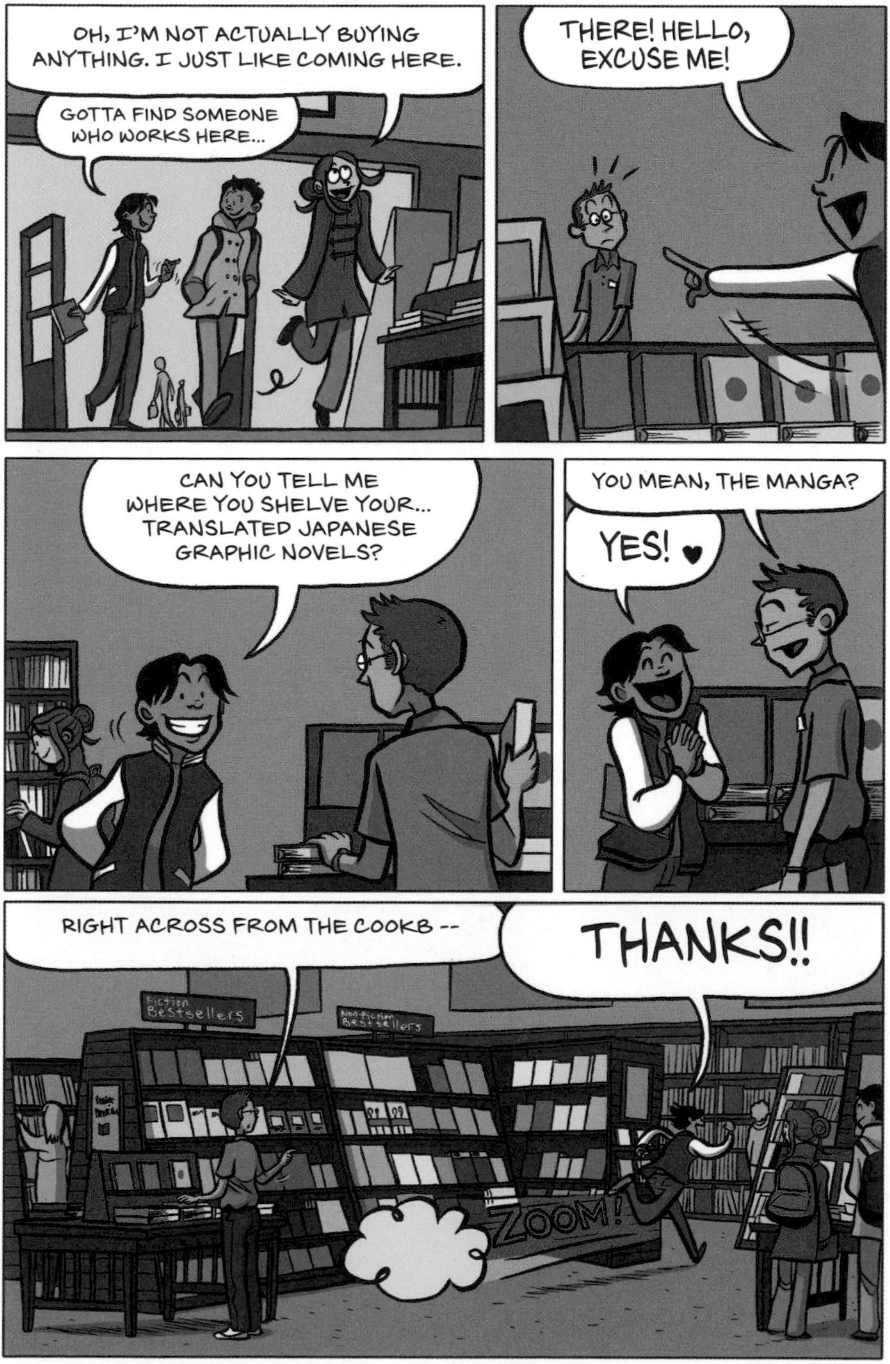

OH, I'M NOT ACTUALLY BUYING ANYTHING. I JUST LIKE COMING HERE.
GOTTA FIND SOMEONE WHO WORKS HERE...
THERE! HELLO, EXCUSE ME!
CAN YOU TELL ME WHERE YOU SHELVE YOUR... TRANSLATED JAPANESE GRAPHIC NOVELS?
YOU MEAN, THE MANGA?
YES! ♥
RIGHT ACROSS FROM THE COOKB --
THANKS!!
Fiction Bestsellers
ZOOM!

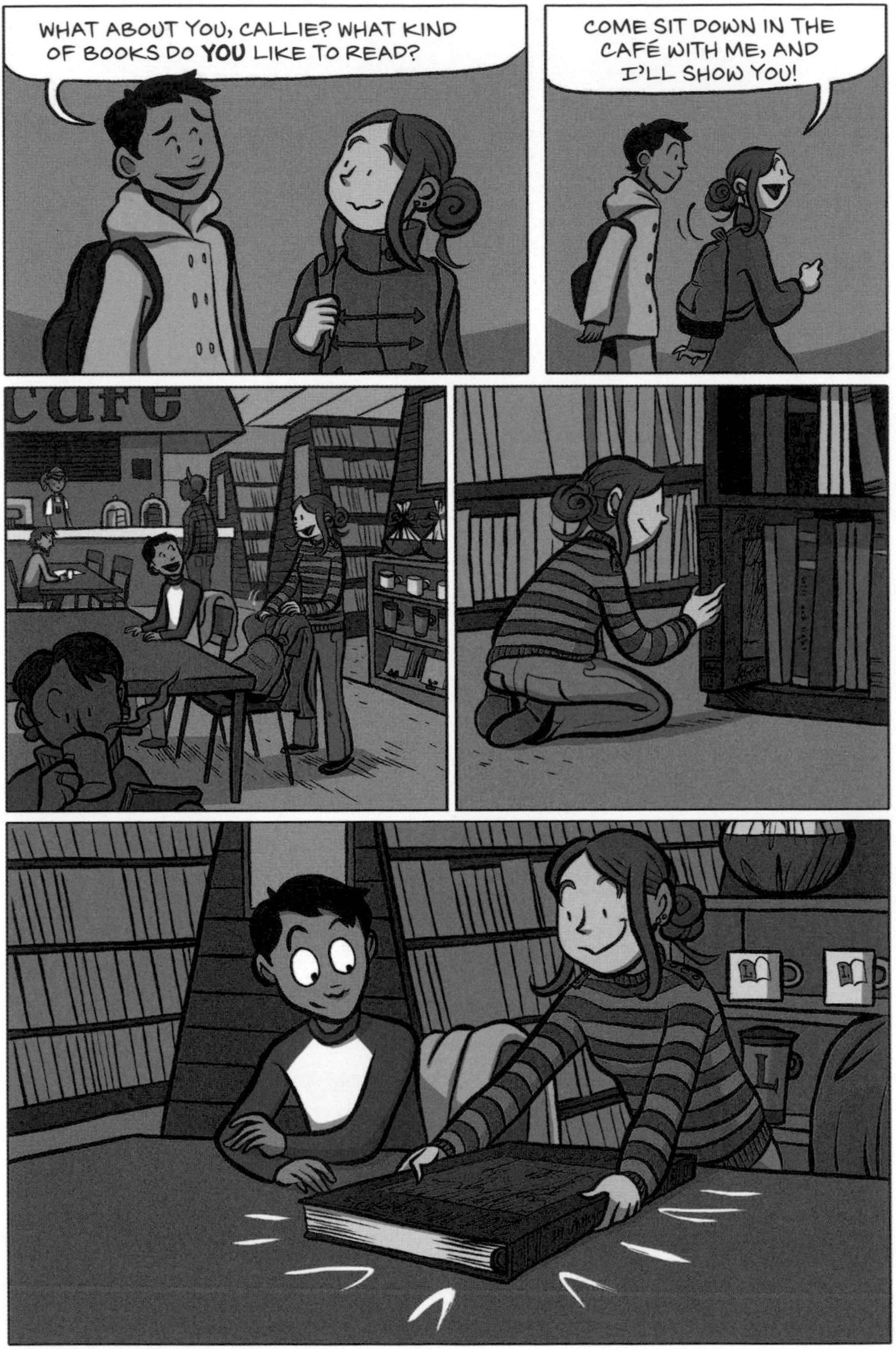
WHAT ABOUT YOU, CALLIE? WHAT KIND OF BOOKS DO **YOU** LIKE TO READ?
COME SIT DOWN IN THE CAFÉ WITH ME, AND I'LL SHOW YOU!
CAFE

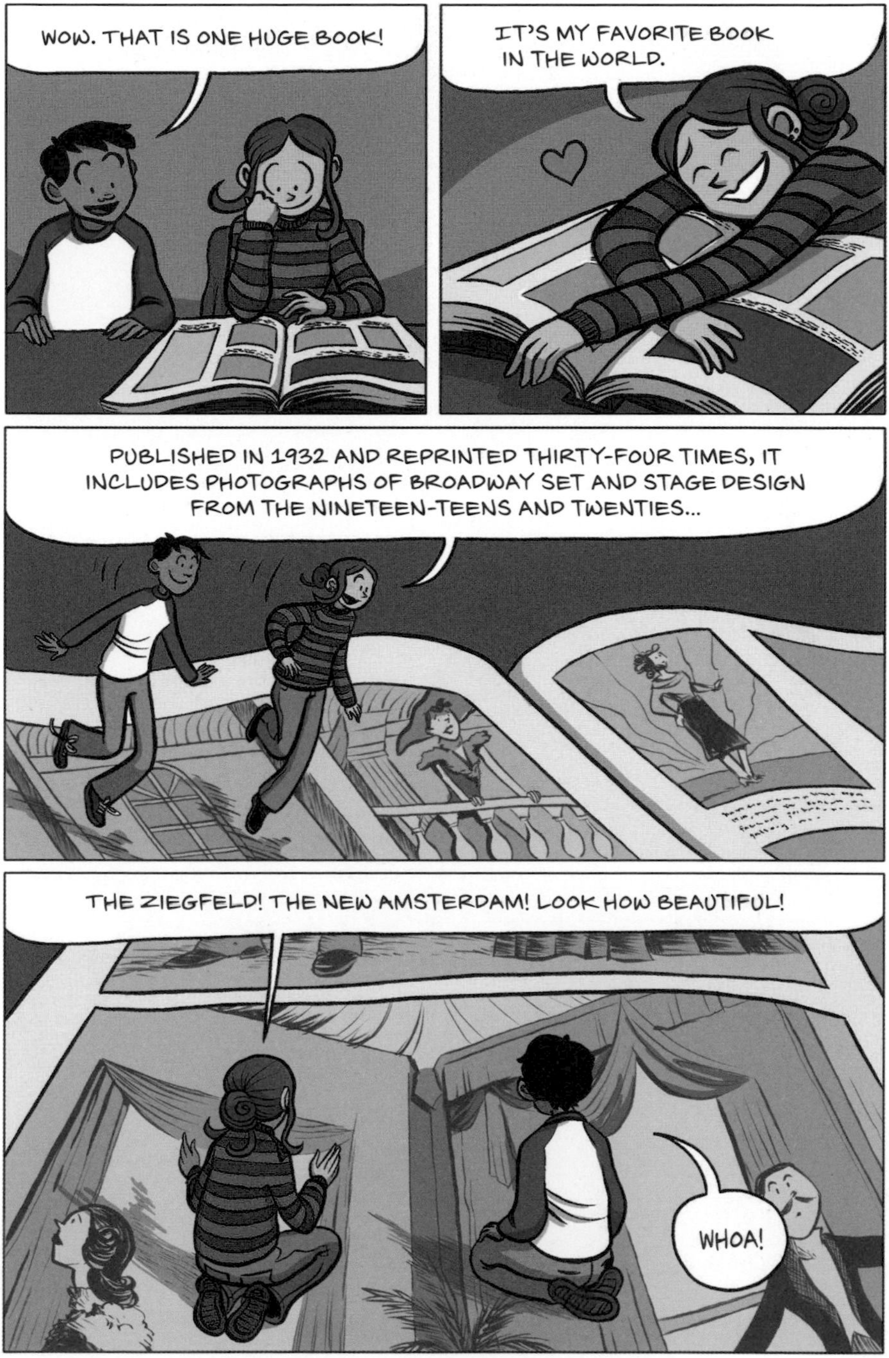
WOW. THAT IS ONE HUGE BOOK!
IT'S MY FAVORITE BOOK IN THE WORLD.
PUBLISHED IN 1932 AND REPRINTED THIRTY-FOUR TIMES, IT INCLUDES PHOTOGRAPHS OF BROADWAY SET AND STAGE DESIGN FROM THE NINETEEN-TEENS AND TWENTIES...
THE ZIEGFELD! THE NEW AMSTERDAM! LOOK HOW BEAUTIFUL!
WHOA!

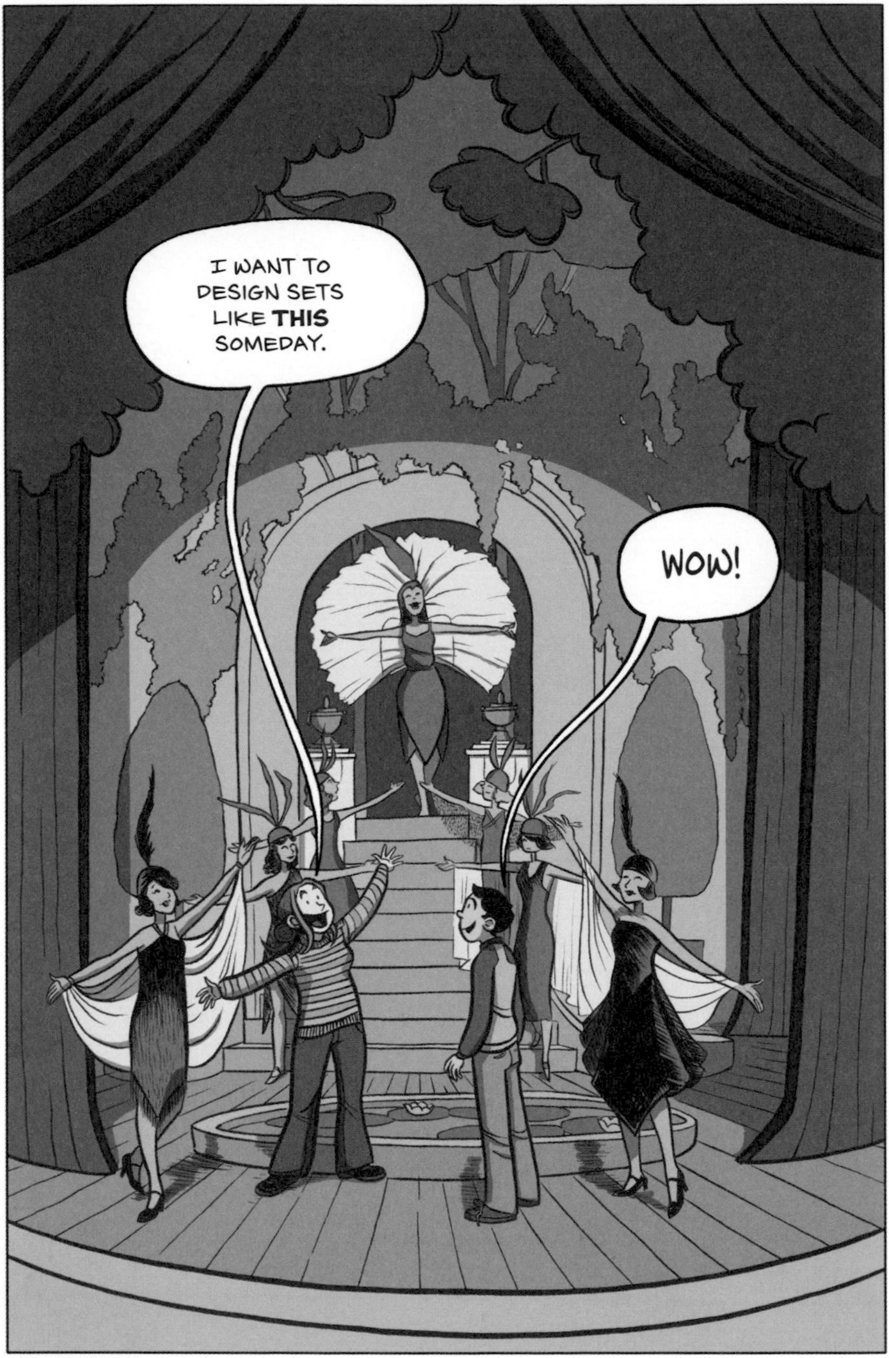
I WANT TO DESIGN SETS LIKE **THIS** SOMEDAY.
WOW!

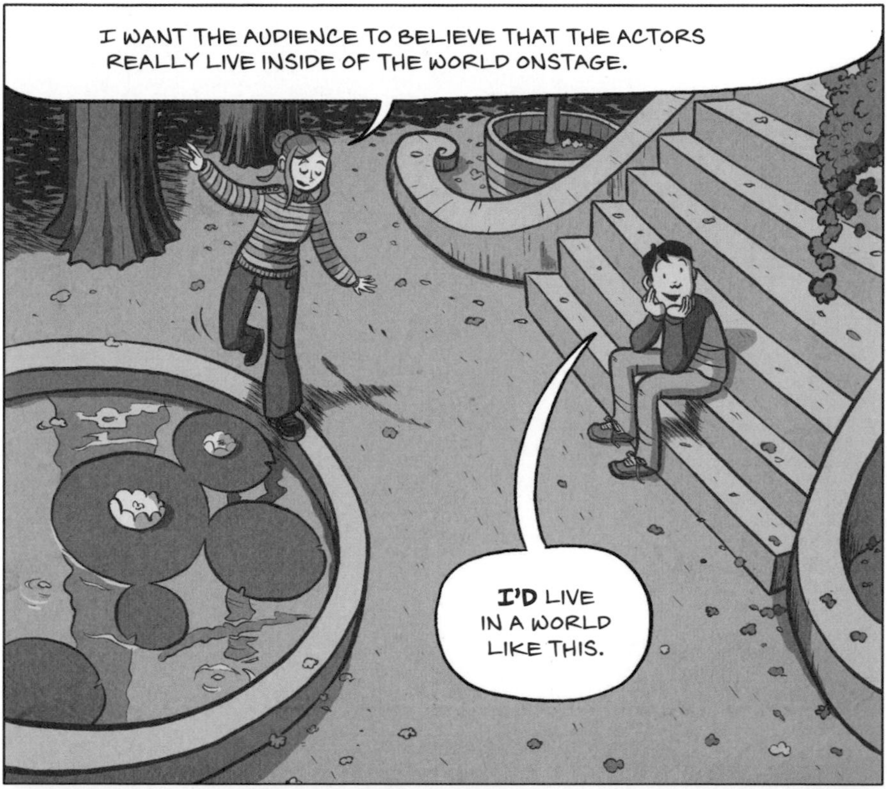
I WANT THE AUDIENCE TO BELIEVE THAT THE ACTORS REALLY LIVE INSIDE OF THE WORLD ONSTAGE.
I'D LIVE IN A WORLD LIKE THIS.

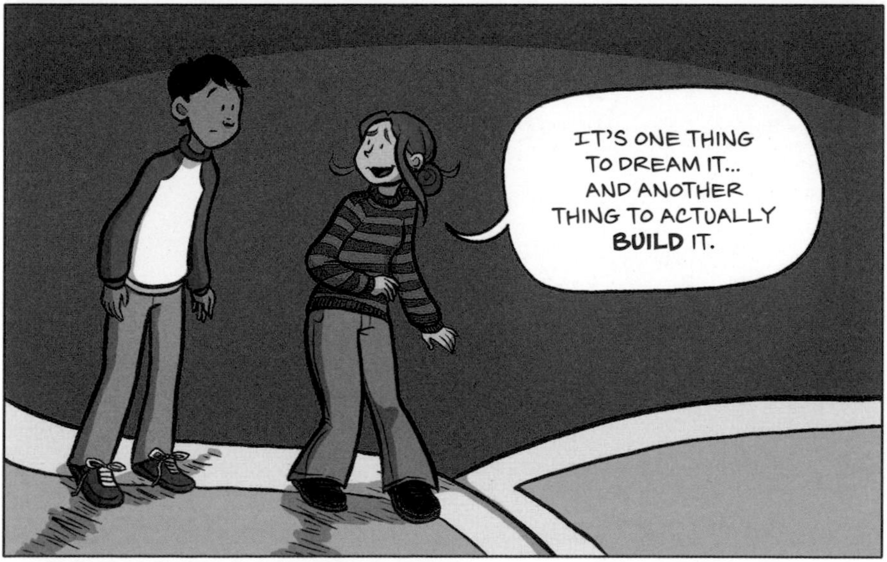
IT'S ONE THING TO DREAM IT... AND ANOTHER THING TO ACTUALLY BUILD IT.

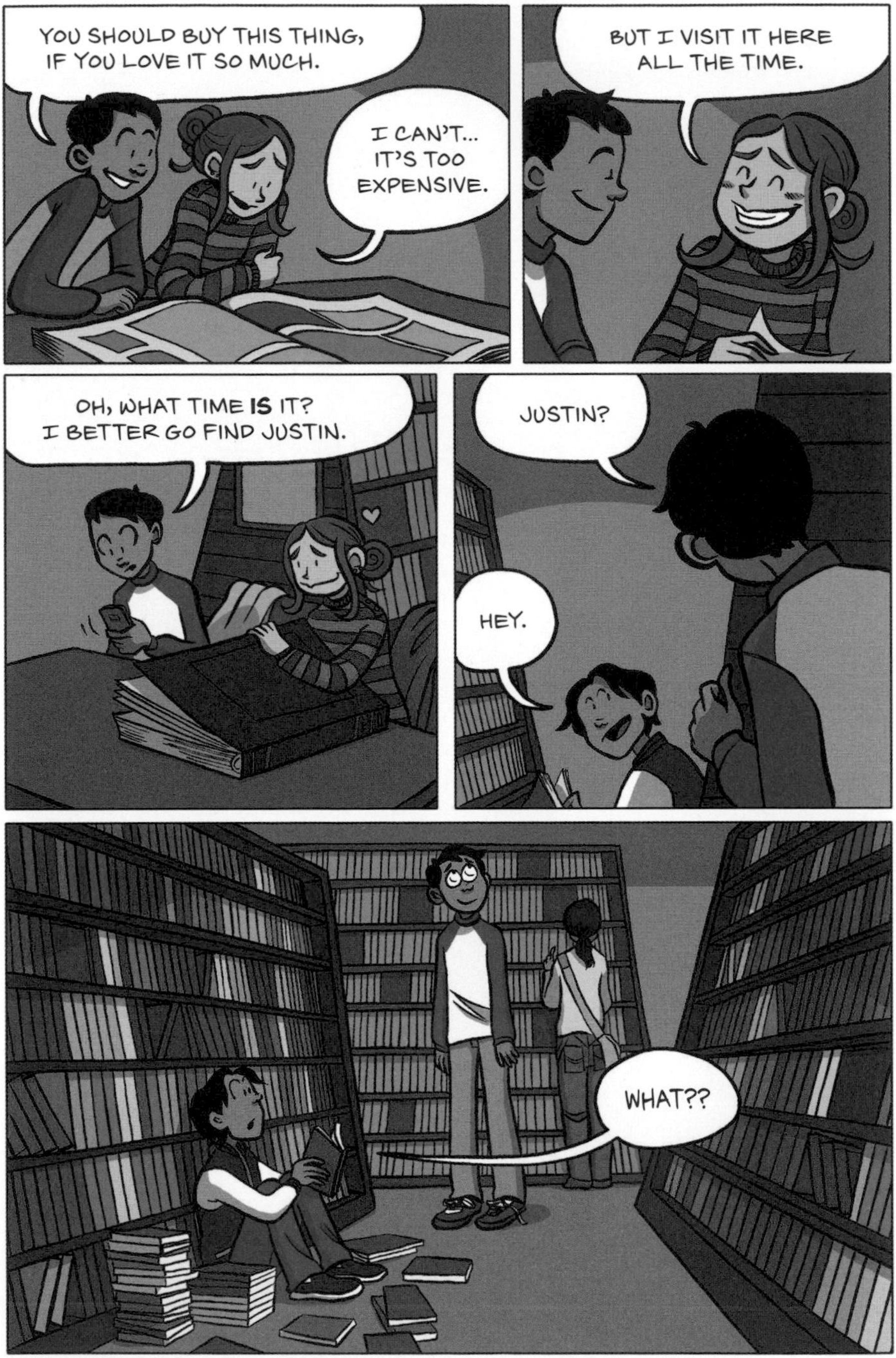
YOU SHOULD BUY THIS THING, IF YOU LOVE IT SO MUCH.
I CAN'T... IT'S TOO EXPENSIVE.
BUT I VISIT IT HERE ALL THE TIME.
OH, WHAT TIME **IS** IT? I BETTER GO FIND JUSTIN.
JUSTIN?
HEY.
WHAT??

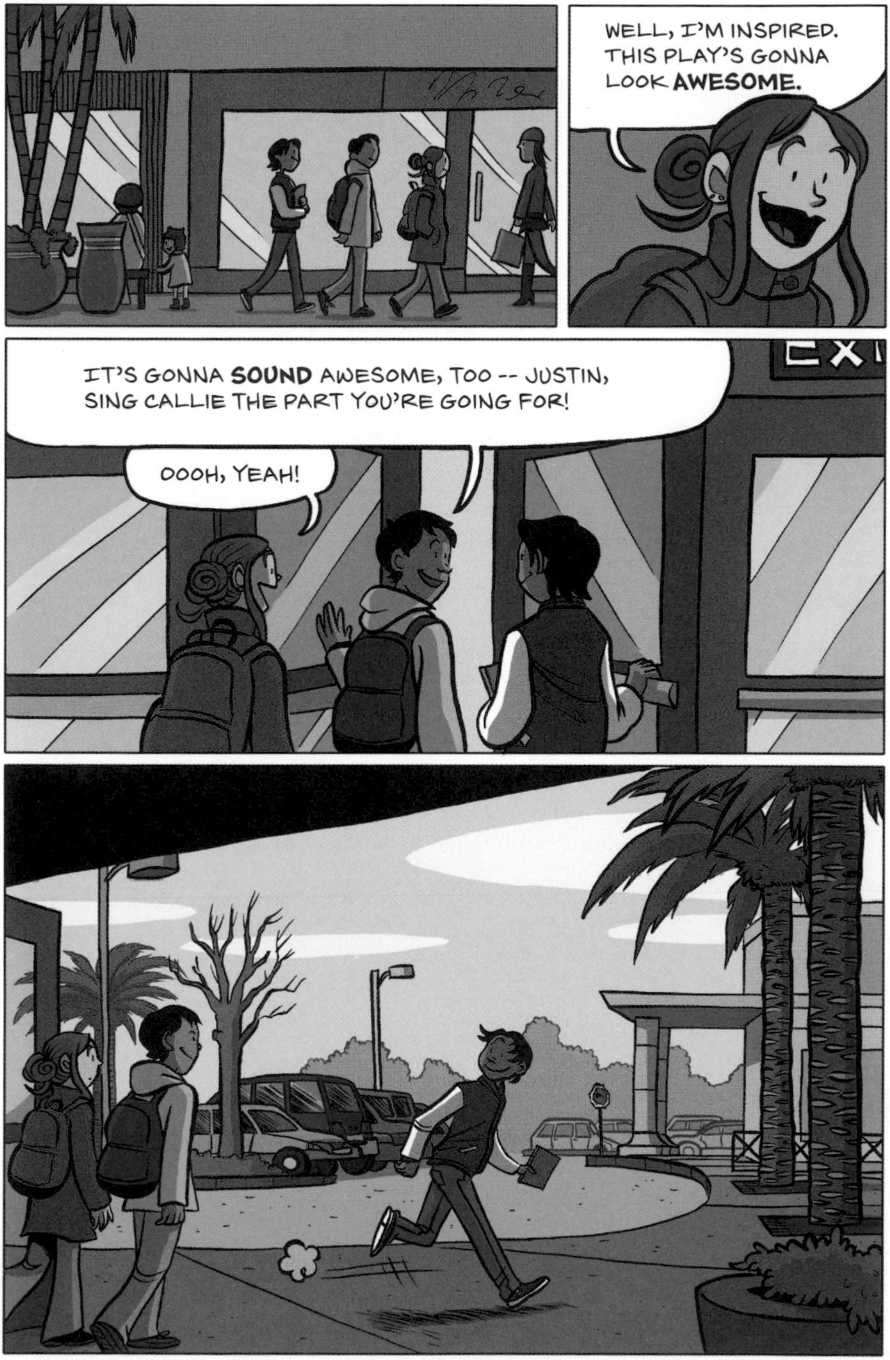
WELL, I'M INSPIRED. THIS PLAY'S GONNA LOOK **AWESOME.**
IT'S GONNA **SOUND** AWESOME, TOO -- JUSTIN, SING CALLIE THE PART YOU'RE GOING FOR!
OOOH, YEAH!

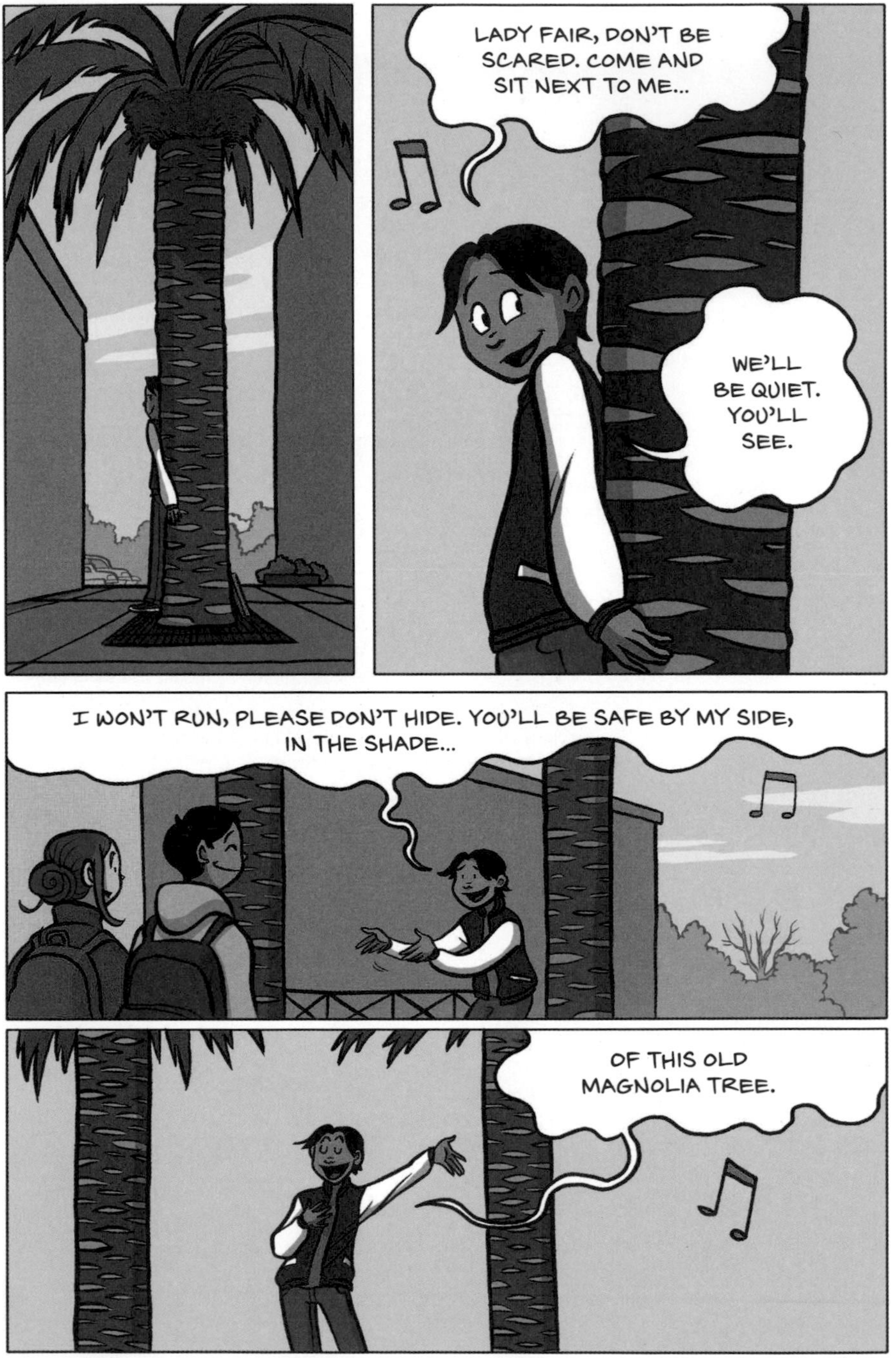
LADY FAIR, DON'T BE SCARED. COME AND SIT NEXT TO ME...
WE'LL BE QUIET. YOU'LL SEE.
I WON'T RUN, PLEASE DON'T HIDE. YOU'LL BE SAFE BY MY SIDE, IN THE SHADE...
OF THIS OLD MAGNOLIA TREE.

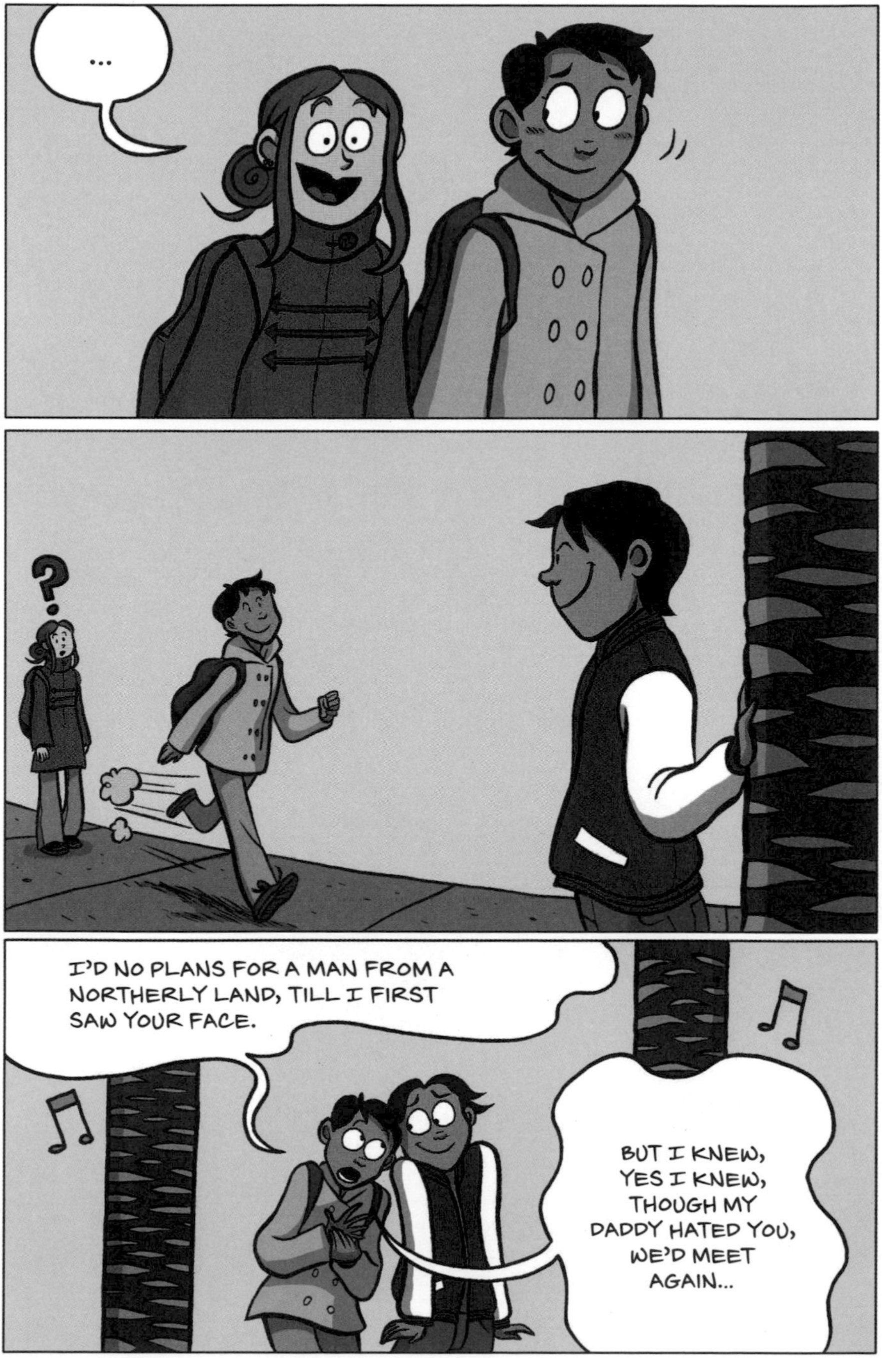
...
?
I'D NO PLANS FOR A MAN FROM A NORTHERLY LAND, TILL I FIRST SAW YOUR FACE.
BUT I KNEW, YES I KNEW, THOUGH MY DADDY HATED YOU, WE'D MEET AGAIN...

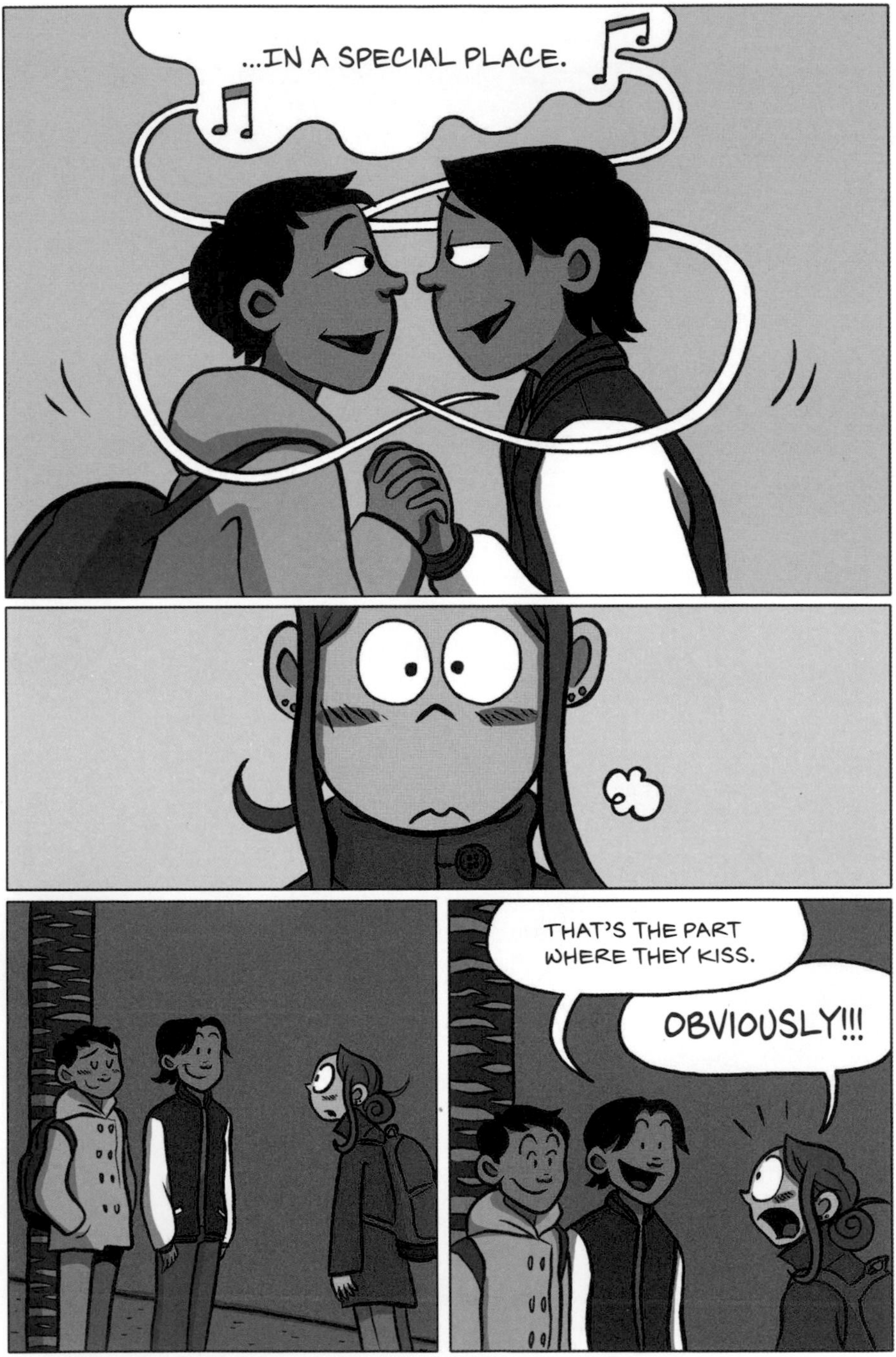
...IN A SPECIAL PLACE.
THAT'S THE PART WHERE THEY KISS.
OBVIOUSLY!!!

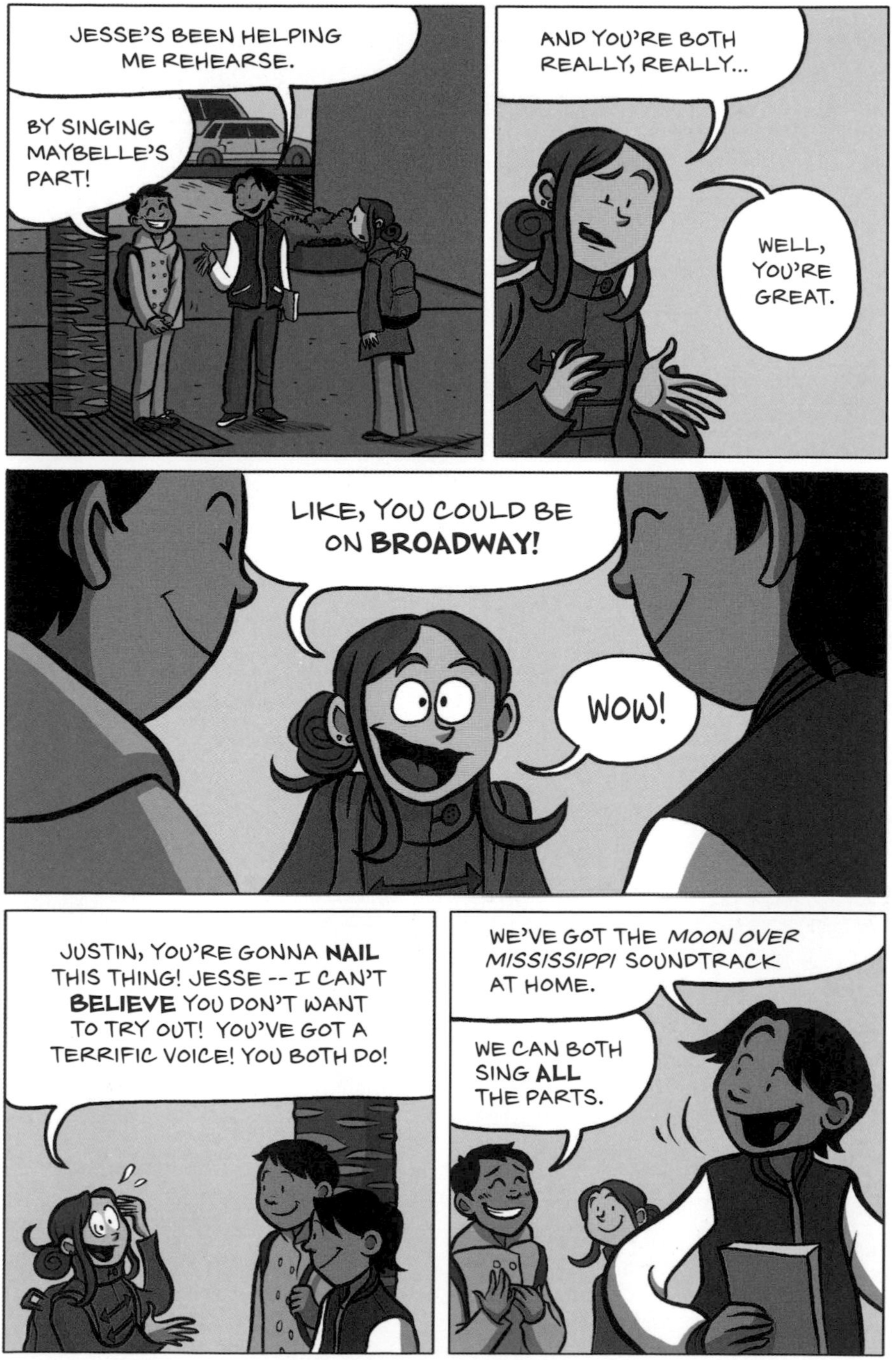
JESSE'S BEEN HELPING ME REHEARSE.
BY SINGING MAYBELLE'S PART!
AND YOU'RE BOTH REALLY, REALLY...
WELL, YOU'RE GREAT.
LIKE, YOU COULD BE ON **BROADWAY!**
WOW!
JUSTIN, YOU'RE GONNA **NAIL** THIS THING! JESSE -- I CAN'T **BELIEVE** YOU DON'T WANT TO TRY OUT! YOU'VE GOT A TERRIFIC VOICE! YOU BOTH DO!
WE'VE GOT THE *MOON OVER MISSISSIPPI* SOUNDTRACK AT HOME.
WE CAN BOTH SING **ALL** THE PARTS.

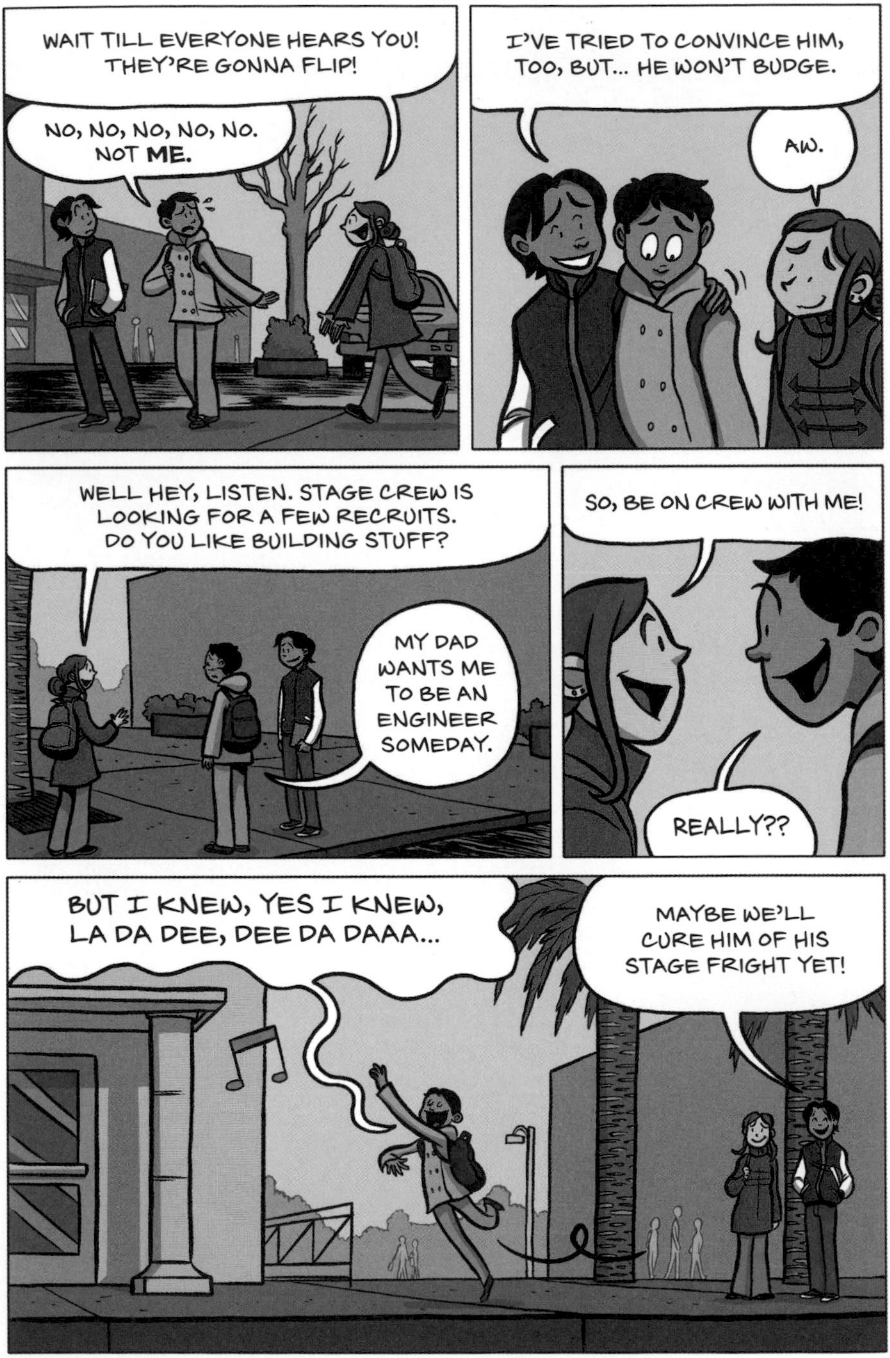
WAIT TILL EVERYONE HEARS YOU! THEY'RE GONNA FLIP!
NO, NO, NO, NO, NO. NOT **ME.**
I'VE TRIED TO CONVINCE HIM, TOO, BUT... HE WON'T BUDGE.
AW.
WELL HEY, LISTEN. STAGE CREW IS LOOKING FOR A FEW RECRUITS. DO YOU LIKE BUILDING STUFF?
MY DAD WANTS ME TO BE AN ENGINEER SOMEDAY.
SO, BE ON CREW WITH ME!
REALLY??
BUT I KNEW, YES I KNEW, LA DA DEE, DEE DA DAAA...
MAYBE WE'LL CURE HIM OF HIS STAGE FRIGHT YET!

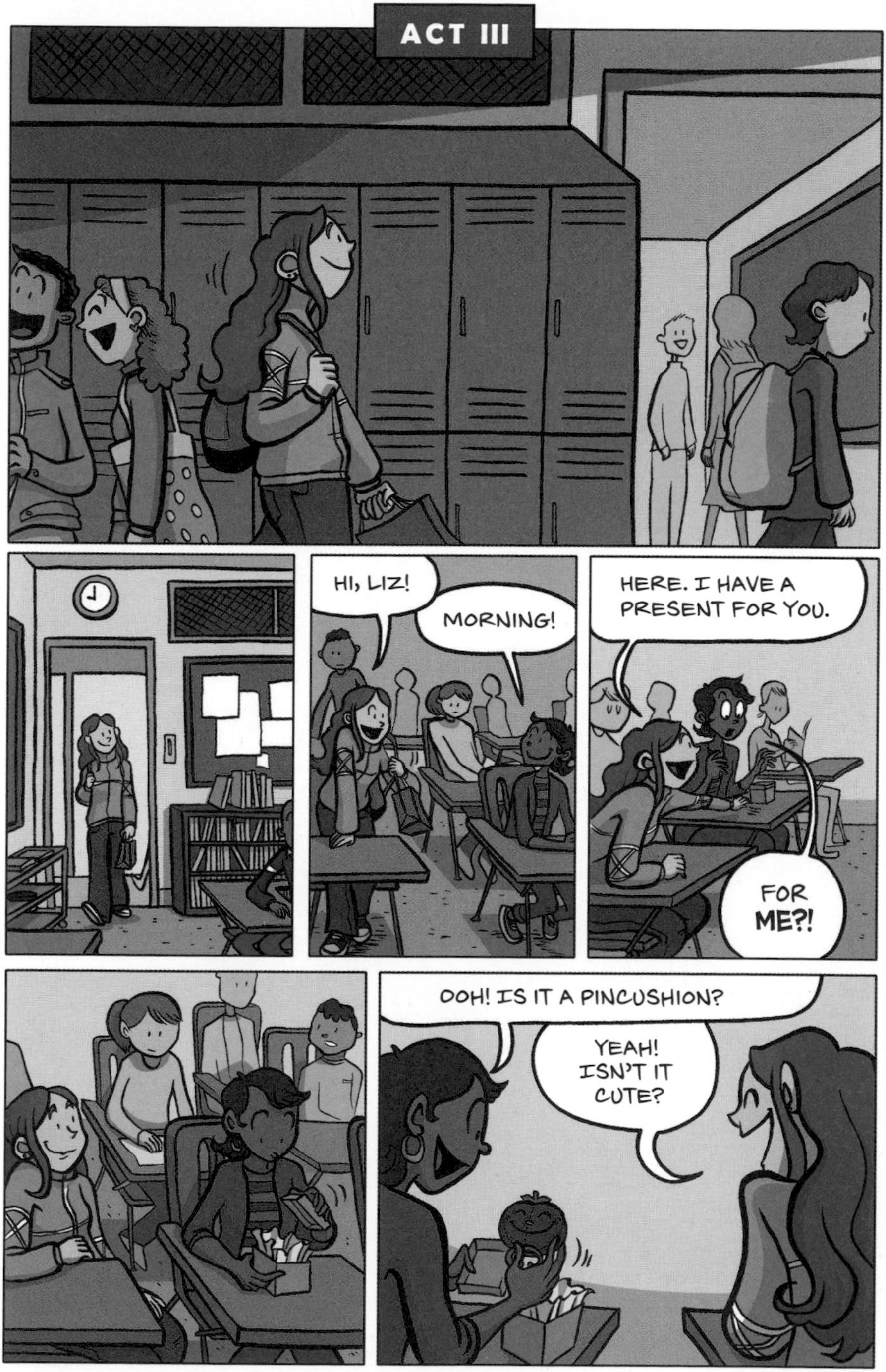
ACT III
HI, LIZ!
MORNING!
HERE. I HAVE A PRESENT FOR YOU.
FOR ME?!
OOH! IS IT A PINCUSHION?
YEAH! ISN'T IT CUTE?

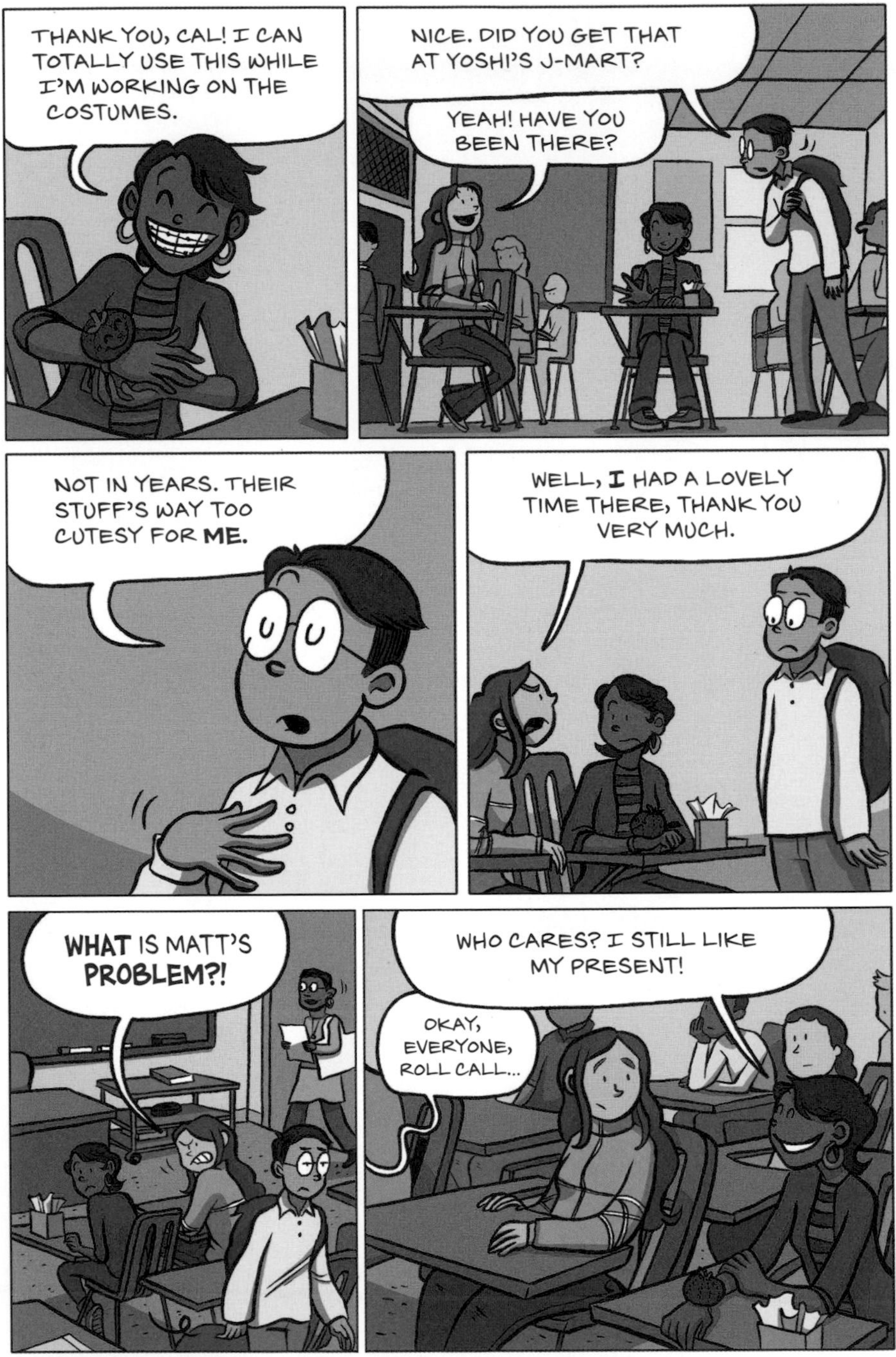
THANK YOU, CAL! I CAN TOTALLY USE THIS WHILE I'M WORKING ON THE COSTUMES.
NICE. DID YOU GET THAT AT YOSHI'S J-MART?
YEAH! HAVE YOU BEEN THERE?
NOT IN YEARS. THEIR STUFF'S WAY TOO CUTESY FOR **ME.**
WELL, **I** HAD A LOVELY TIME THERE, THANK YOU VERY MUCH.
WHAT IS MATT'S **PROBLEM?!**
WHO CARES? I STILL LIKE MY PRESENT!
OKAY, EVERYONE, ROLL CALL...

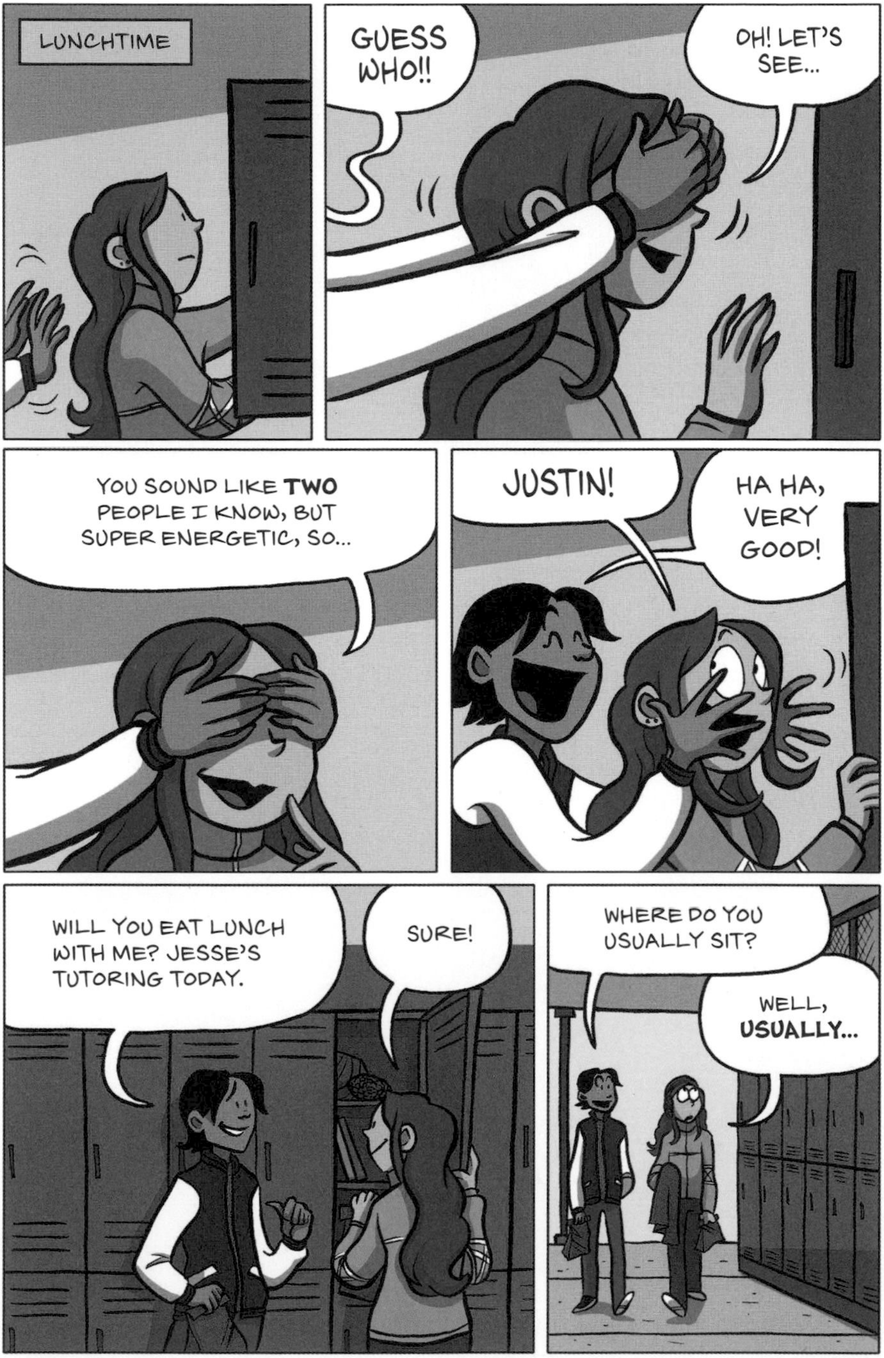
LUNCHTIME
GUESS WHO!!
OH! LET'S SEE...
YOU SOUND LIKE **TWO** PEOPLE I KNOW, BUT SUPER ENERGETIC, SO...
JUSTIN!
HA HA, VERY GOOD!
WILL YOU EAT LUNCH WITH ME? JESSE'S TUTORING TODAY.
SURE!
WHERE DO YOU USUALLY SIT?
WELL, **USUALLY...**

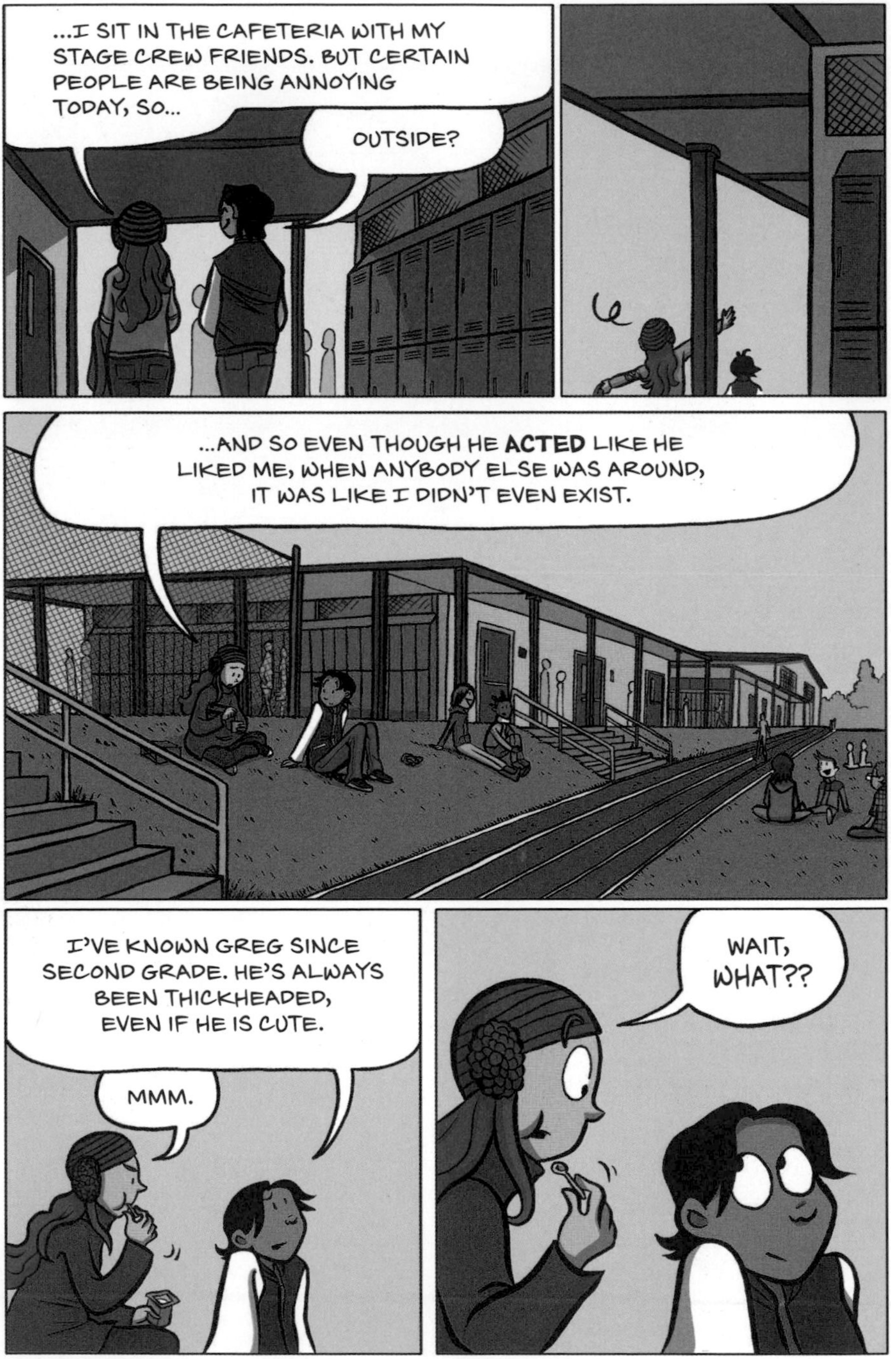
...I SIT IN THE CAFETERIA WITH MY STAGE CREW FRIENDS. BUT CERTAIN PEOPLE ARE BEING ANNOYING TODAY, SO...
OUTSIDE?
...AND SO EVEN THOUGH HE ACTED LIKE HE LIKED ME, WHEN ANYBODY ELSE WAS AROUND, IT WAS LIKE I DIDN'T EVEN EXIST.
I'VE KNOWN GREG SINCE SECOND GRADE. HE'S ALWAYS BEEN THICKHEADED, EVEN IF HE IS CUTE.
MMM.
WAIT, WHAT??

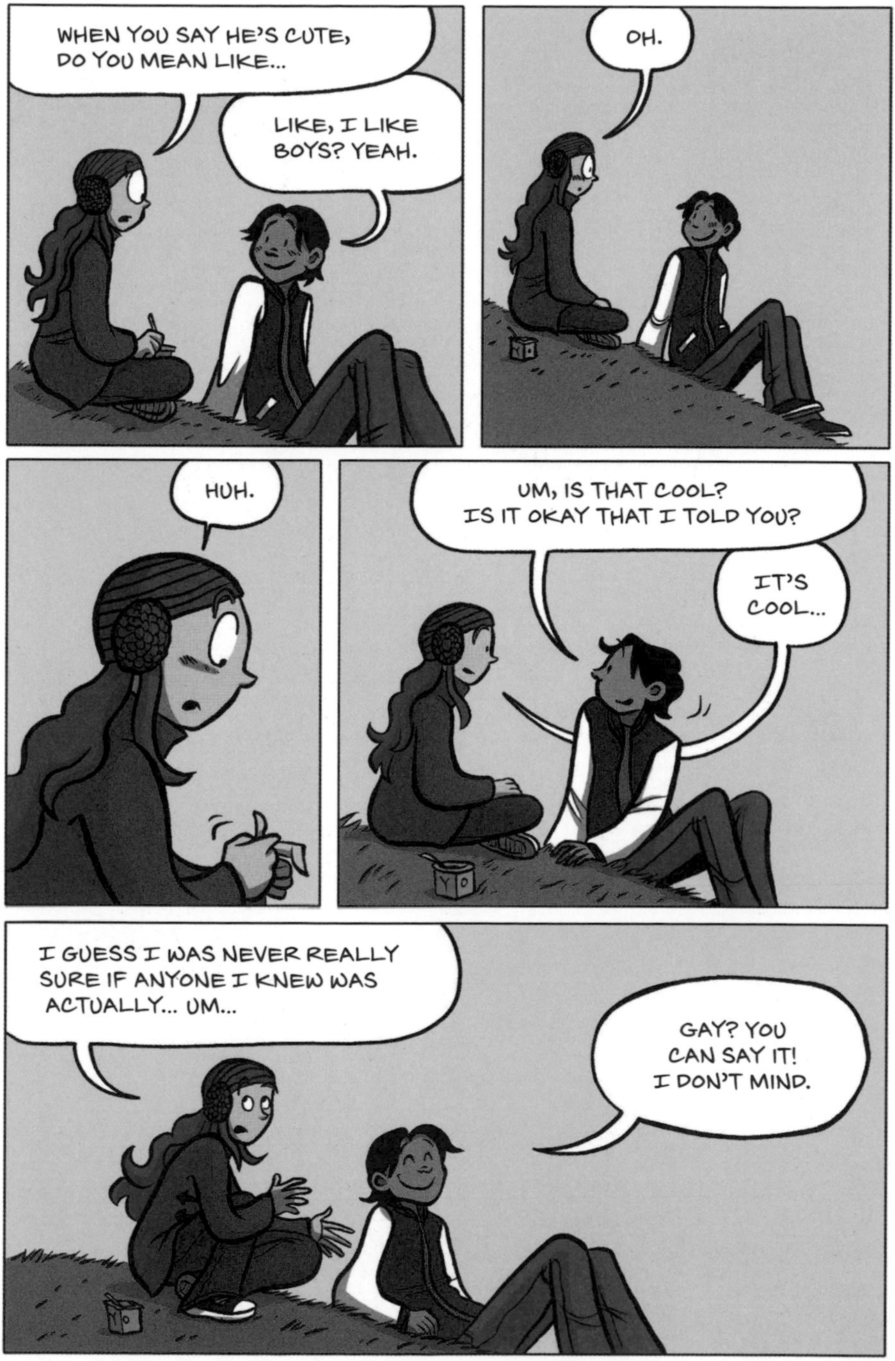
WHEN YOU SAY HE'S CUTE, DO YOU MEAN LIKE...
LIKE, I LIKE BOYS? YEAH.
OH.
HUH.
UM, IS THAT COOL? IS IT OKAY THAT I TOLD YOU?
IT'S COOL...
I GUESS I WAS NEVER REALLY SURE IF ANYONE I KNEW WAS ACTUALLY... UM...
GAY? YOU CAN SAY IT! I DON'T MIND.

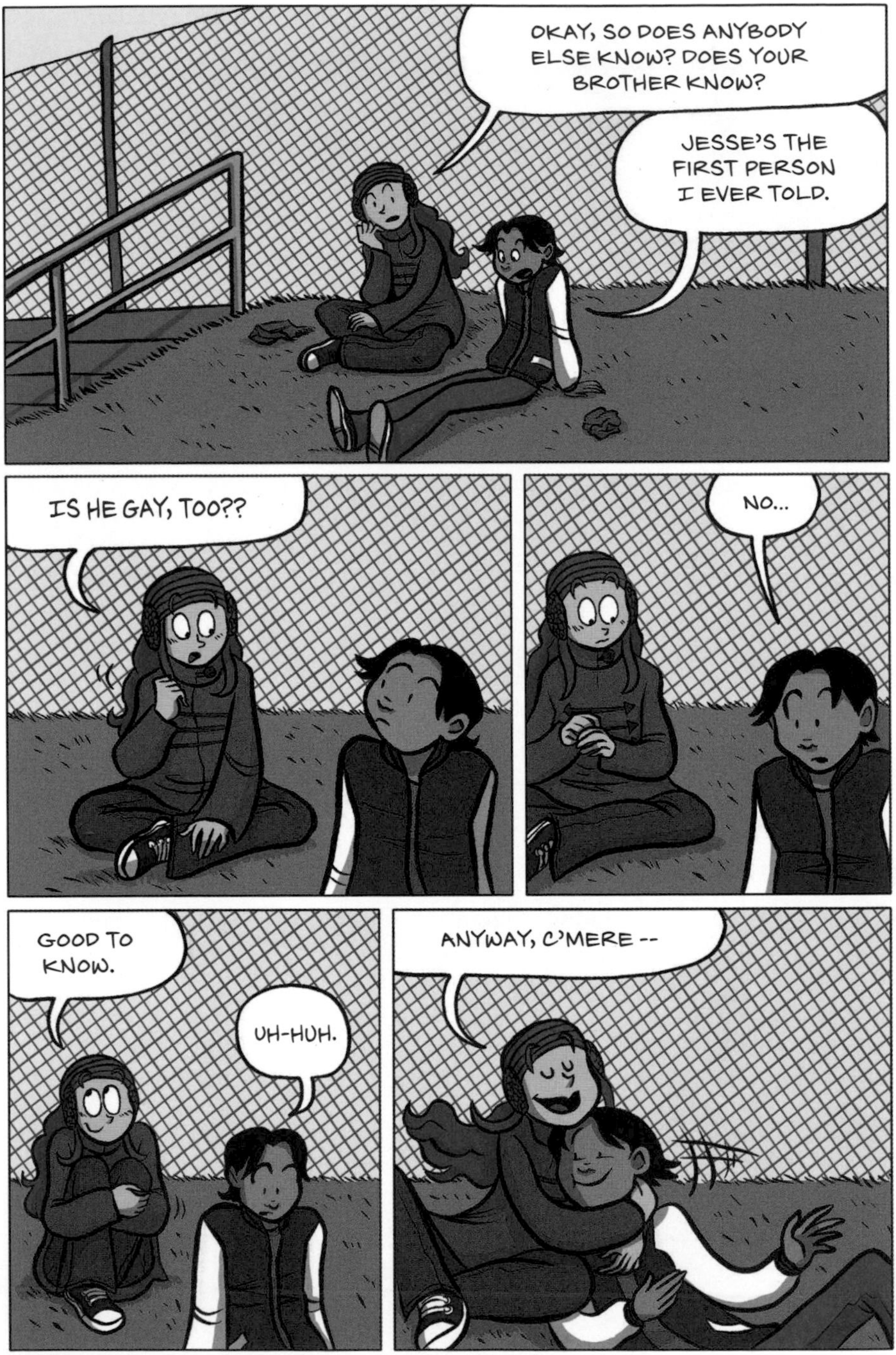
OKAY, SO DOES ANYBODY ELSE KNOW? DOES YOUR BROTHER KNOW?
JESSE'S THE FIRST PERSON I EVER TOLD.
IS HE GAY, TOO??
NO...
GOOD TO KNOW.
UH-HUH.
ANYWAY, C'MERE --

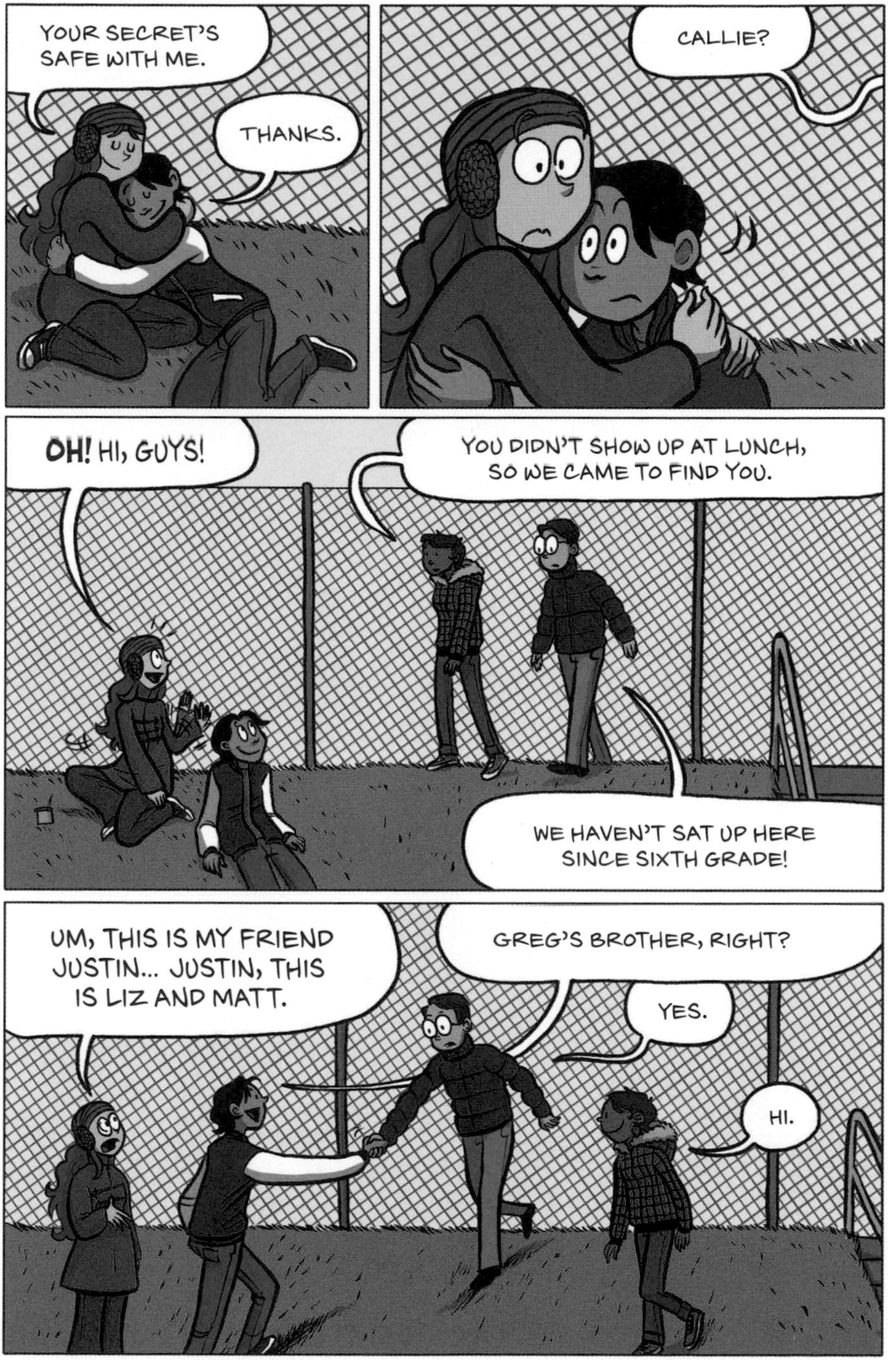
YOUR SECRET'S SAFE WITH ME.
THANKS.
CALLIE?
OH! HI, GUYS!
YOU DIDN'T SHOW UP AT LUNCH, SO WE CAME TO FIND YOU.
WE HAVEN'T SAT UP HERE SINCE SIXTH GRADE!
UM, THIS IS MY FRIEND JUSTIN... JUSTIN, THIS IS LIZ AND MATT.
GREG'S BROTHER, RIGHT?
YES.
HI.

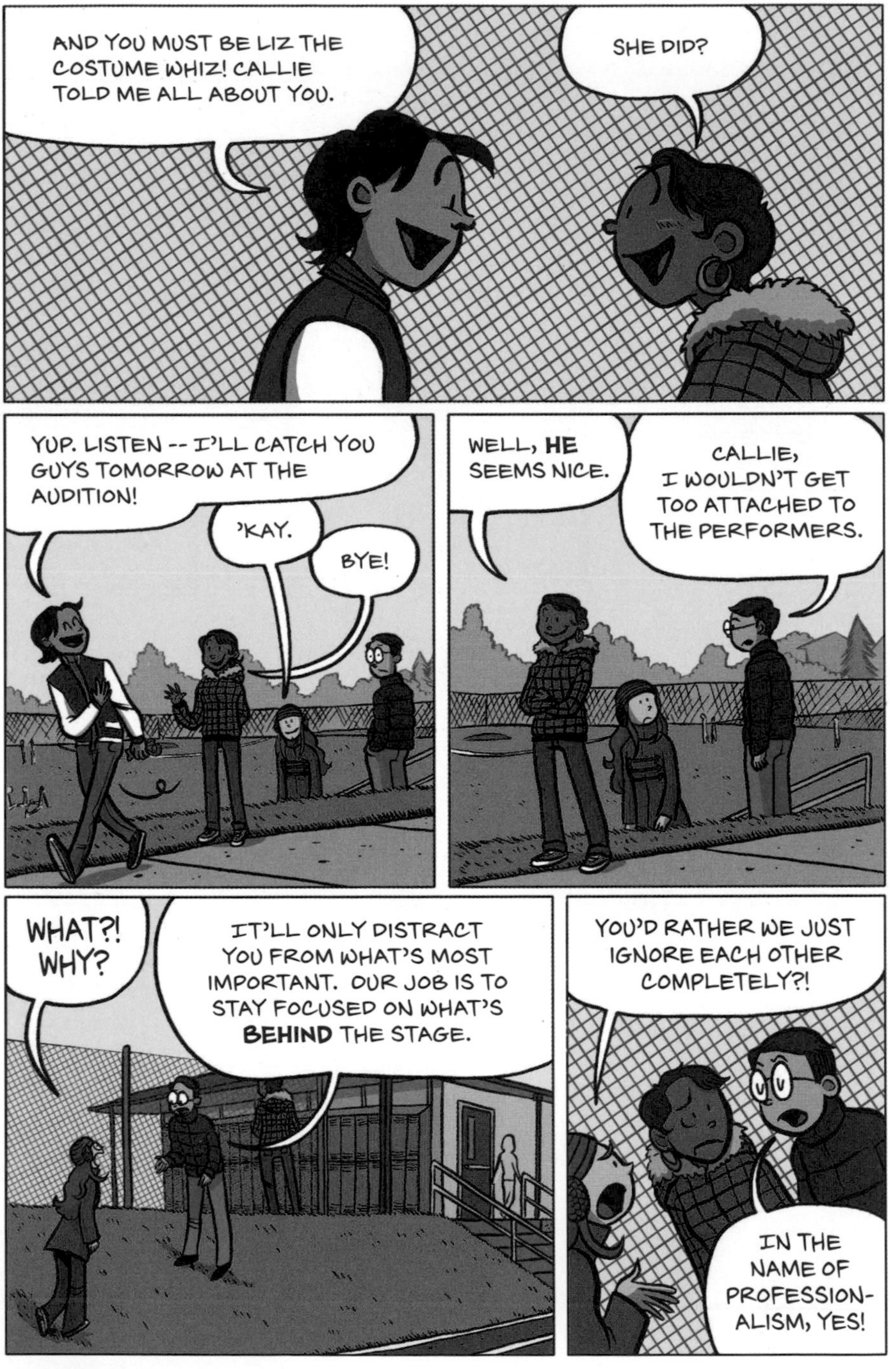
AND YOU MUST BE LIZ THE COSTUME WHIZ! CALLIE TOLD ME ALL ABOUT YOU.
SHE DID?
YUP. LISTEN -- I'LL CATCH YOU GUYS TOMORROW AT THE AUDITION!
'KAY.
BYE!
WELL, **HE** SEEMS NICE.
CALLIE, I WOULDN'T GET TOO ATTACHED TO THE PERFORMERS.
WHAT?! WHY?
IT'LL ONLY DISTRACT YOU FROM WHAT'S MOST IMPORTANT. OUR JOB IS TO STAY FOCUSED ON WHAT'S **BEHIND** THE STAGE.
YOU'D RATHER WE JUST IGNORE EACH OTHER COMPLETELY?!
IN THE NAME OF PROFESSION-ALISM, YES!

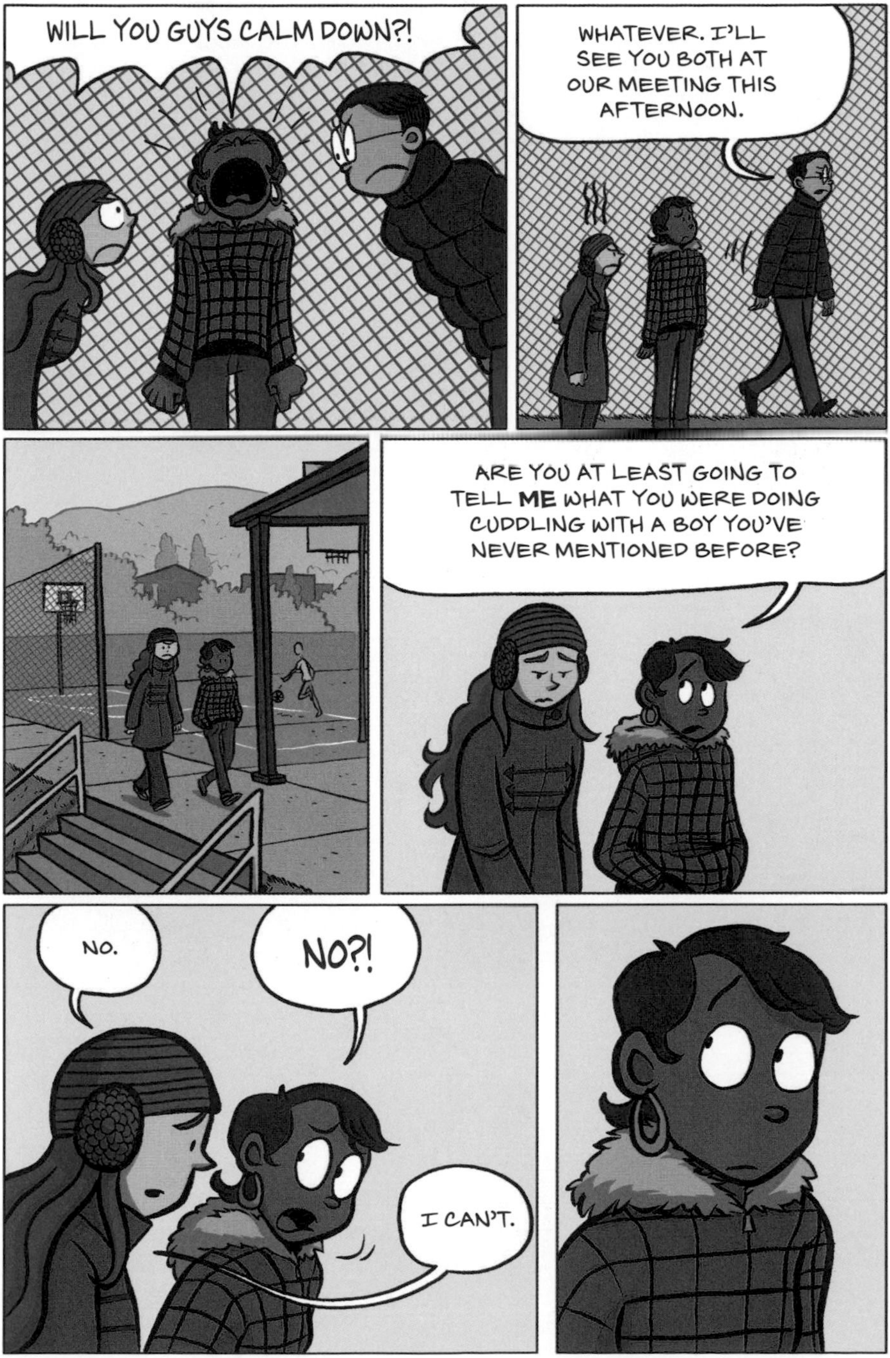
WILL YOU GUYS CALM DOWN?!
WHATEVER. I'LL SEE YOU BOTH AT OUR MEETING THIS AFTERNOON.
ARE YOU AT LEAST GOING TO TELL ME WHAT YOU WERE DOING CUDDLING WITH A BOY YOU'VE NEVER MENTIONED BEFORE?
NO.
NO?!
I CAN'T.

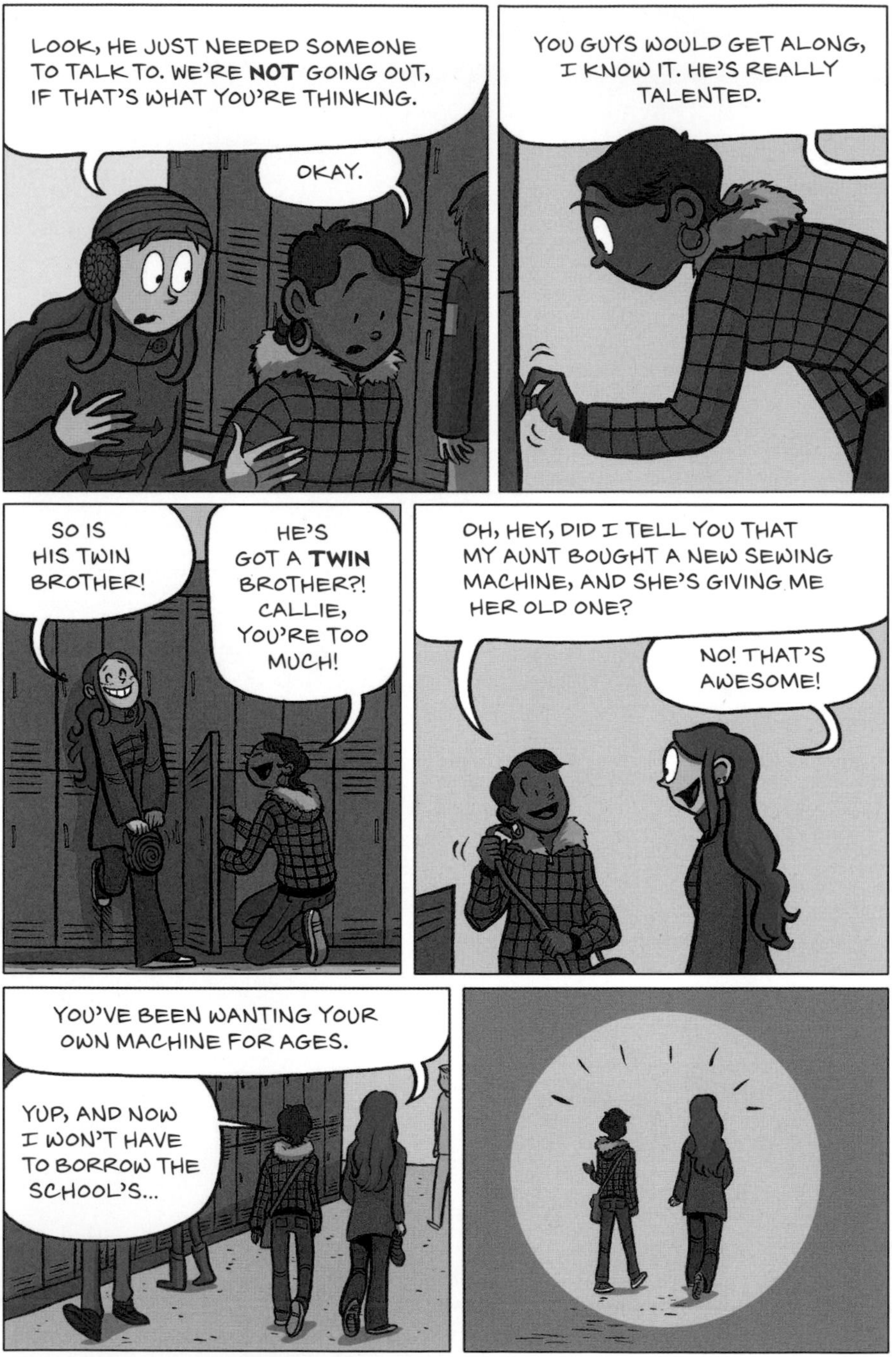
LOOK, HE JUST NEEDED SOMEONE TO TALK TO. WE'RE **NOT** GOING OUT, IF THAT'S WHAT YOU'RE THINKING.
OKAY.
YOU GUYS WOULD GET ALONG, I KNOW IT. HE'S REALLY TALENTED.
SO IS HIS TWIN BROTHER!
HE'S GOT A **TWIN** BROTHER?! CALLIE, YOU'RE TOO MUCH!
OH, HEY, DID I TELL YOU THAT MY AUNT BOUGHT A NEW SEWING MACHINE, AND SHE'S GIVING ME HER OLD ONE?
NO! THAT'S AWESOME!
YOU'VE BEEN WANTING YOUR OWN MACHINE FOR AGES.
YUP, AND NOW I WON'T HAVE TO BORROW THE SCHOOL'S...

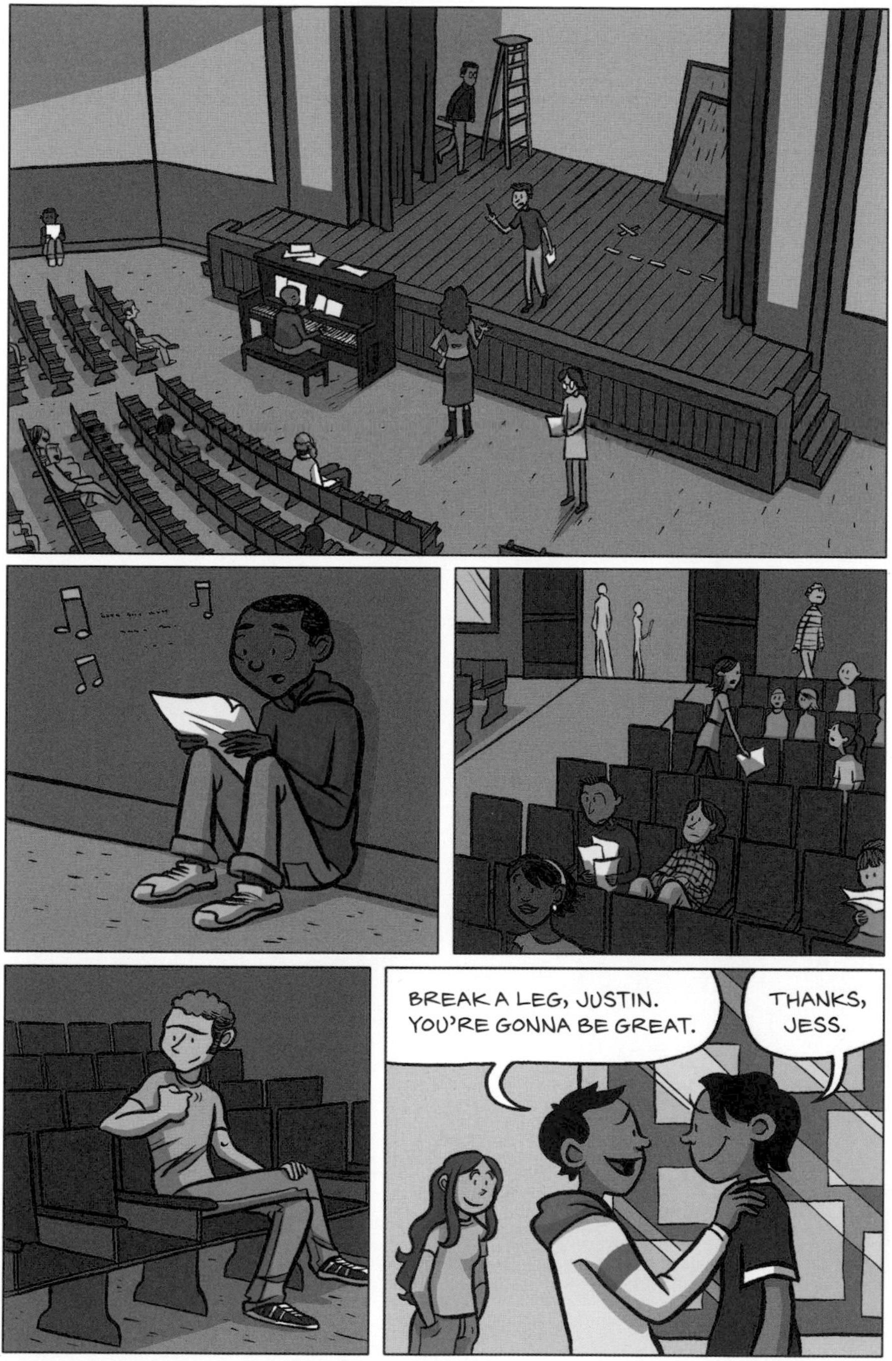
BREAK A LEG, JUSTIN.
YOU'RE GONNA BE GREAT.
THANKS,
JESS.

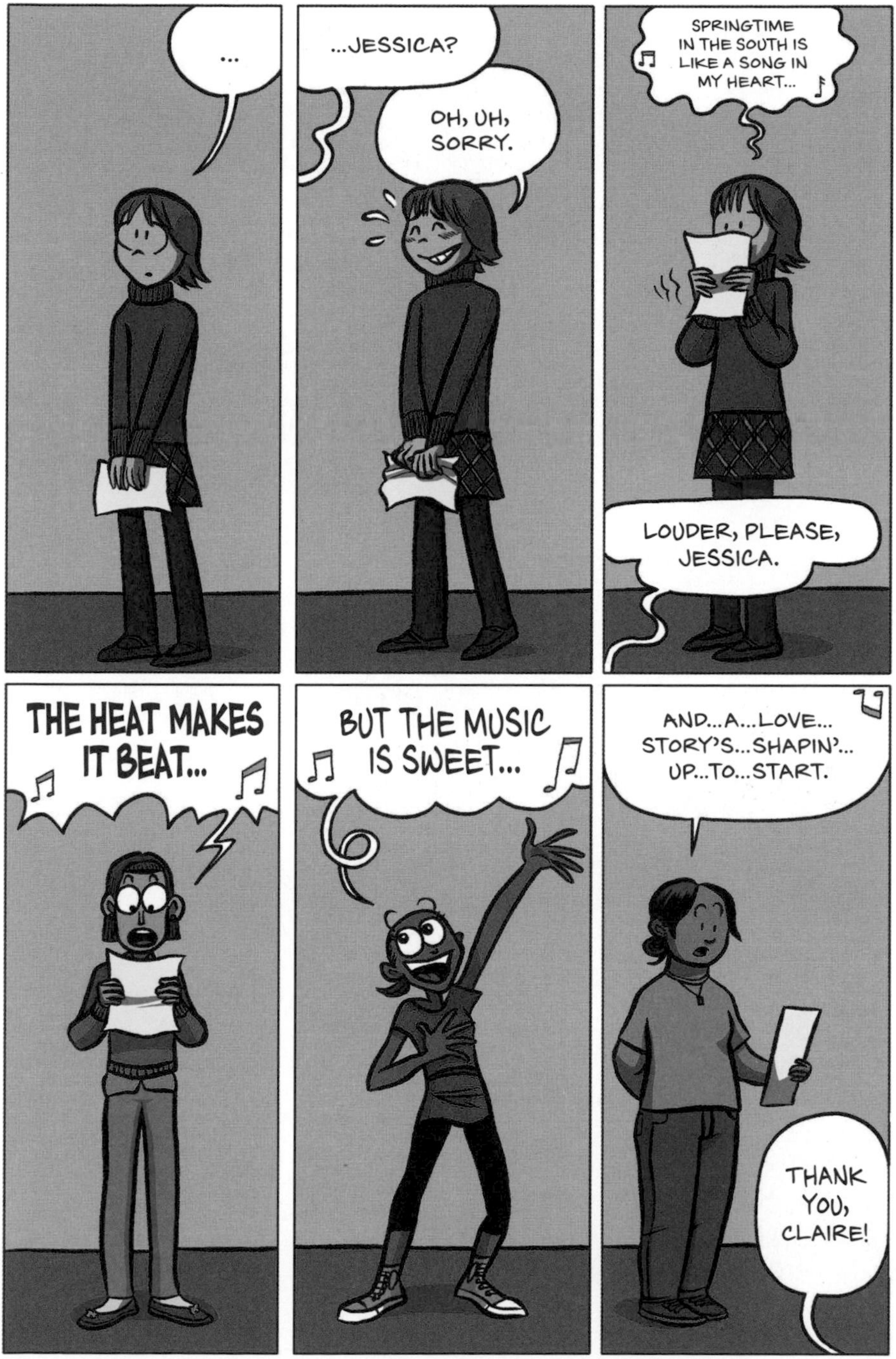
...
...JESSICA?
OH, UH, SORRY.
SPRINGTIME IN THE SOUTH IS LIKE A SONG IN MY HEART...
LOUDER, PLEASE, JESSICA.
THE HEAT MAKES IT BEAT...
BUT THE MUSIC IS SWEET...
AND...A...LOVE... STORY'S...SHAPIN'... UP...TO...START.
THANK YOU, CLAIRE!

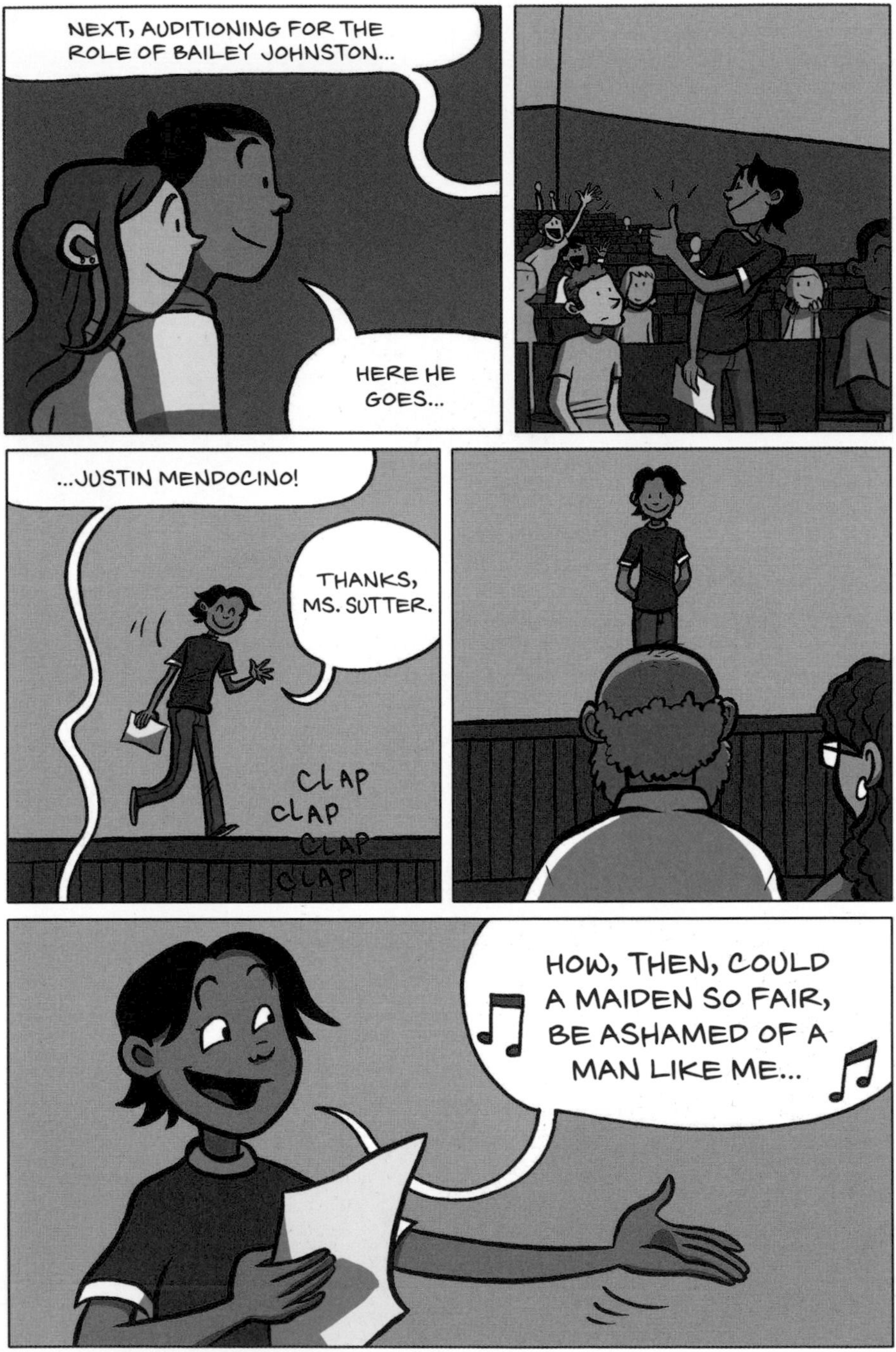
NEXT, AUDITIONING FOR THE ROLE OF BAILEY JOHNSTON...
HERE HE GOES...
...JUSTIN MENDOCINO!
THANKS, MS. SUTTER.
CLAP
CLAP
CLAP
CLAP
HOW, THEN, COULD A MAIDEN SO FAIR, BE ASHAMED OF A MAN LIKE ME...

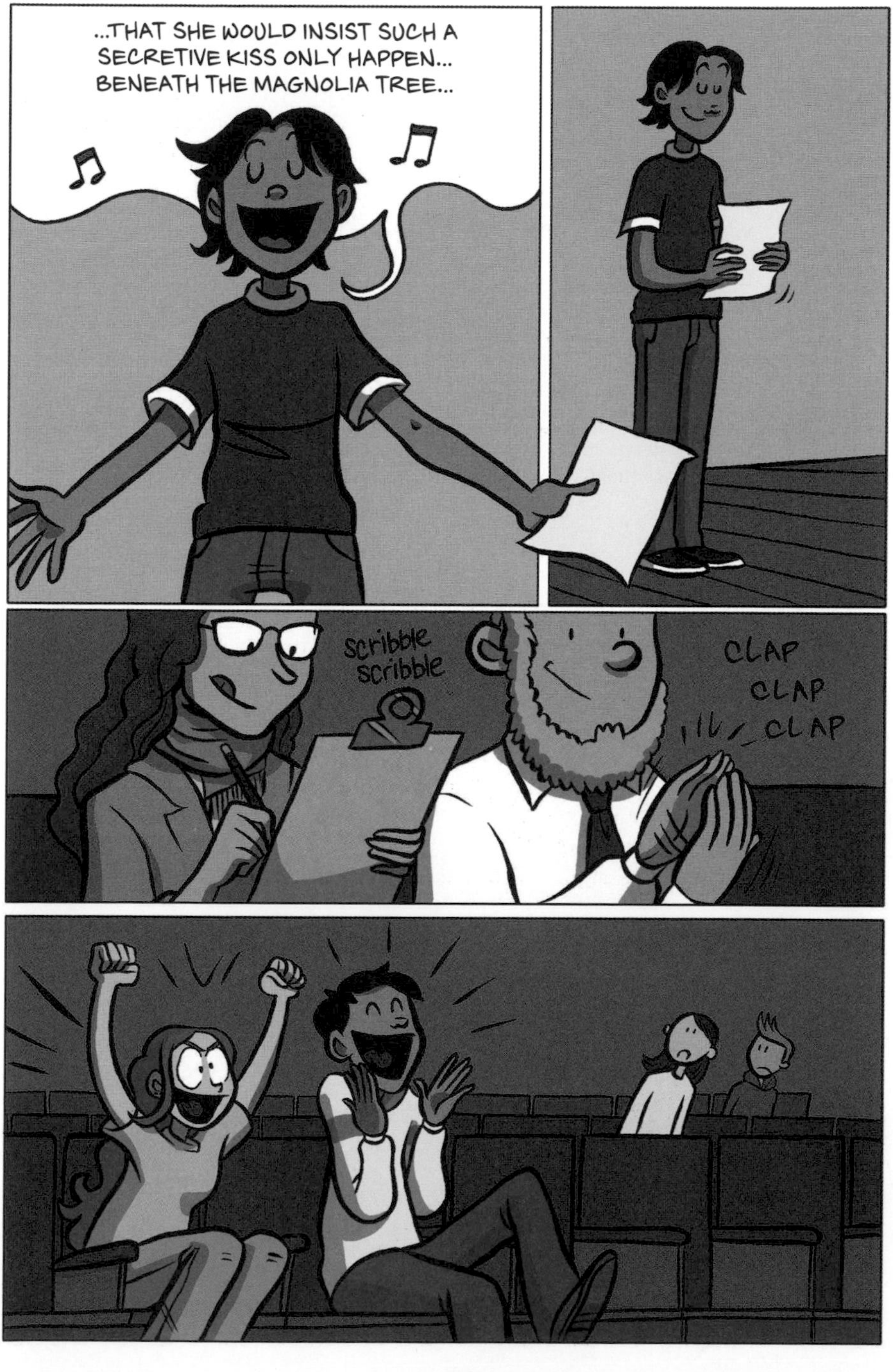

...THAT SHE WOULD INSIST SUCH A SECRETIVE KISS ONLY HAPPEN... BENEATH THE MAGNOLIA TREE...
scribble scribble
CLAP CLAP CLAP

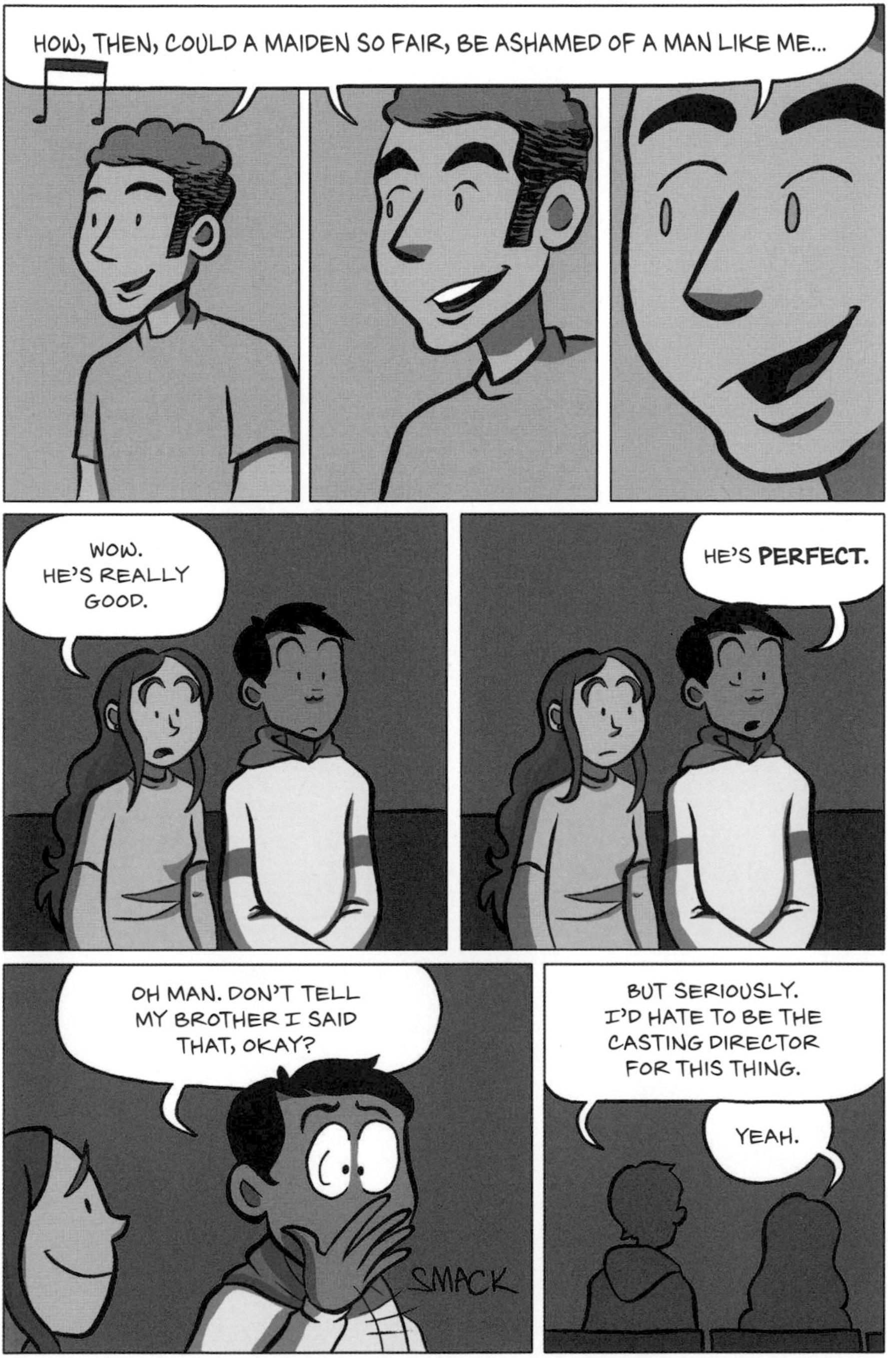
HOW, THEN, COULD A MAIDEN SO FAIR, BE ASHAMED OF A MAN LIKE ME...
WOW. HE'S REALLY GOOD.
HE'S **PERFECT.**
OH MAN. DON'T TELL MY BROTHER I SAID THAT, OKAY?
SMACK
BUT SERIOUSLY. I'D HATE TO BE THE CASTING DIRECTOR FOR THIS THING.
YEAH.

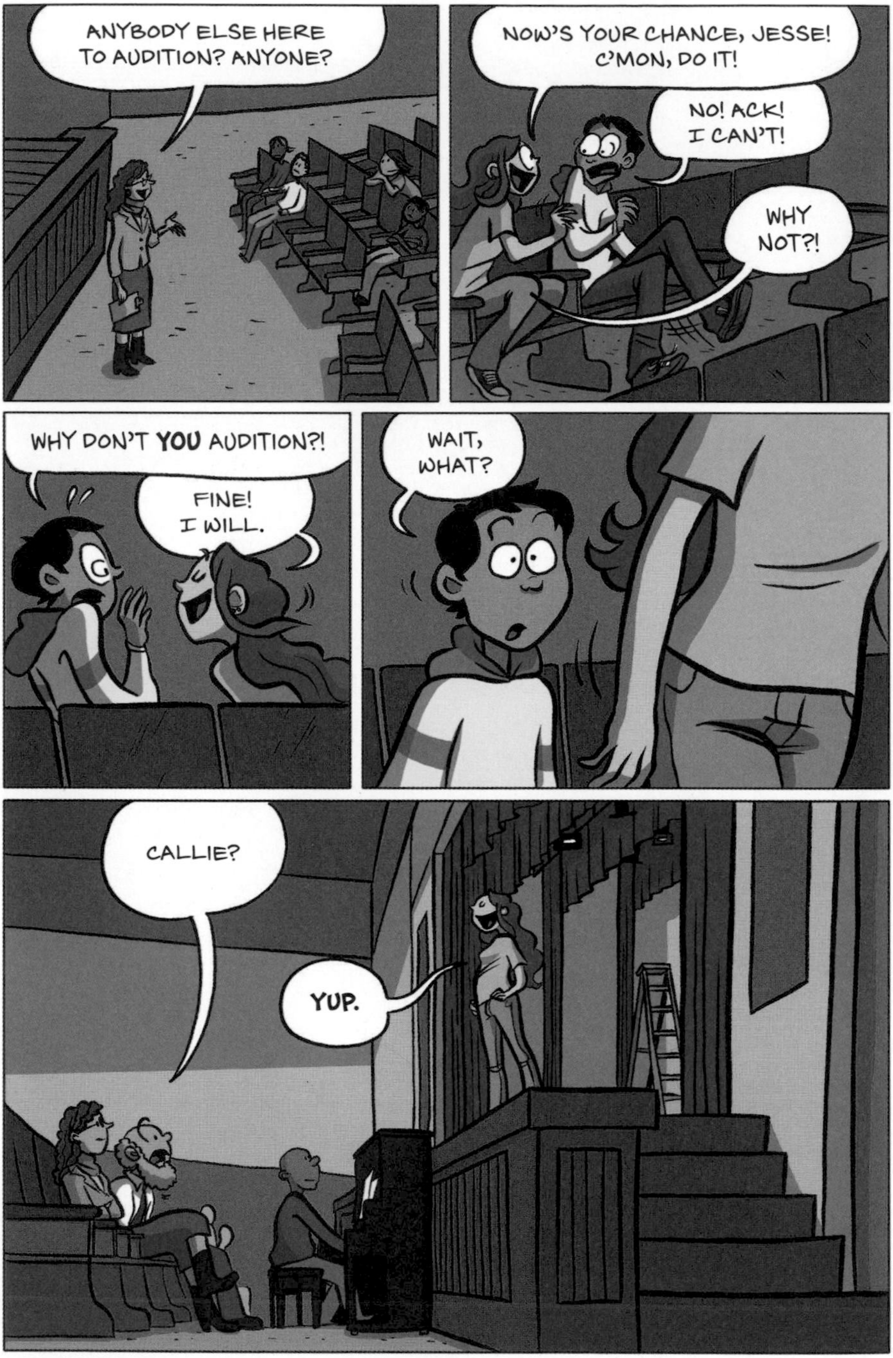
ANYBODY ELSE HERE TO AUDITION? ANYONE?
NOW'S YOUR CHANCE, JESSE! C'MON, DO IT!
NO! ACK! I CAN'T!
WHY NOT?!
WHY DON'T **YOU** AUDITION?!
FINE! I WILL.
WAIT, WHAT?
CALLIE?
YUP.

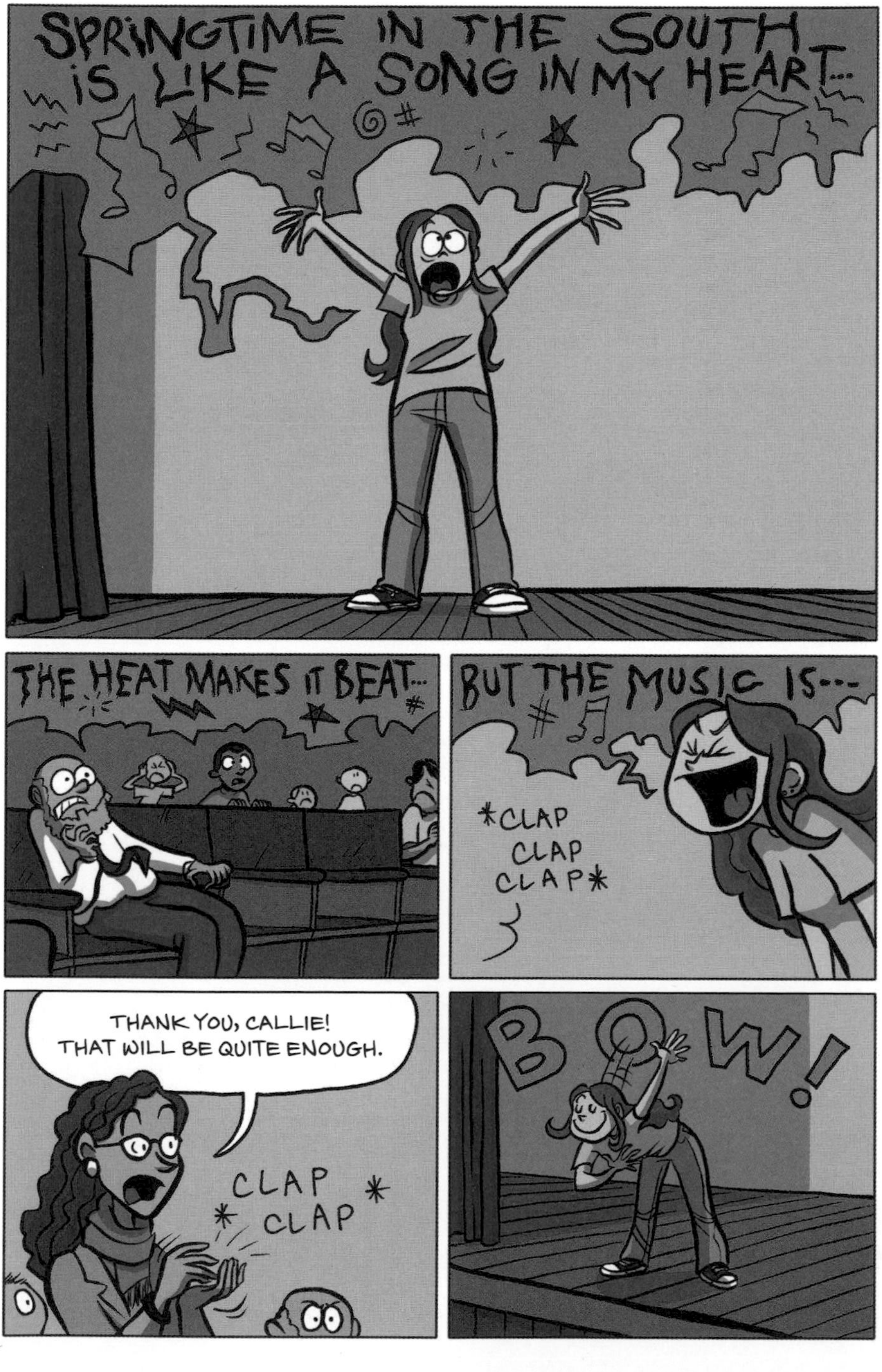
SPRINGTIME IN THE SOUTH IS LIKE A SONG IN MY HEART...
THE HEAT MAKES IT BEAT...
BUT THE MUSIC IS---
CLAP CLAP CLAP
THANK YOU, CALLIE! THAT WILL BE QUITE ENOUGH.
CLAP CLAP
BOW!

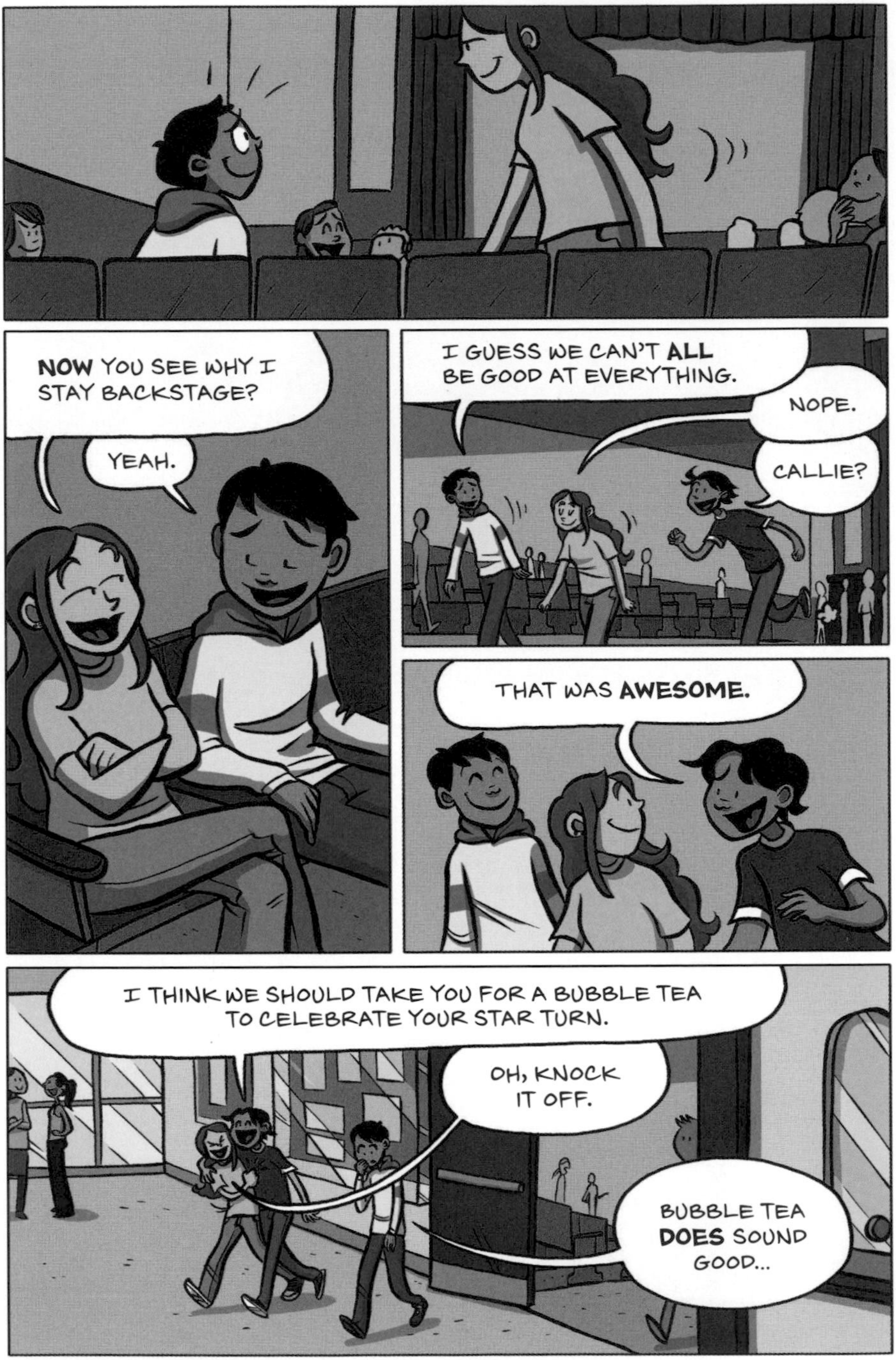

NOW YOU SEE WHY I STAY BACKSTAGE?
YEAH.
I GUESS WE CAN'T ALL BE GOOD AT EVERYTHING.
NOPE.
CALLIE?
THAT WAS AWESOME.
I THINK WE SHOULD TAKE YOU FOR A BUBBLE TEA TO CELEBRATE YOUR STAR TURN.
OH, KNOCK IT OFF.
BUBBLE TEA DOES SOUND GOOD...

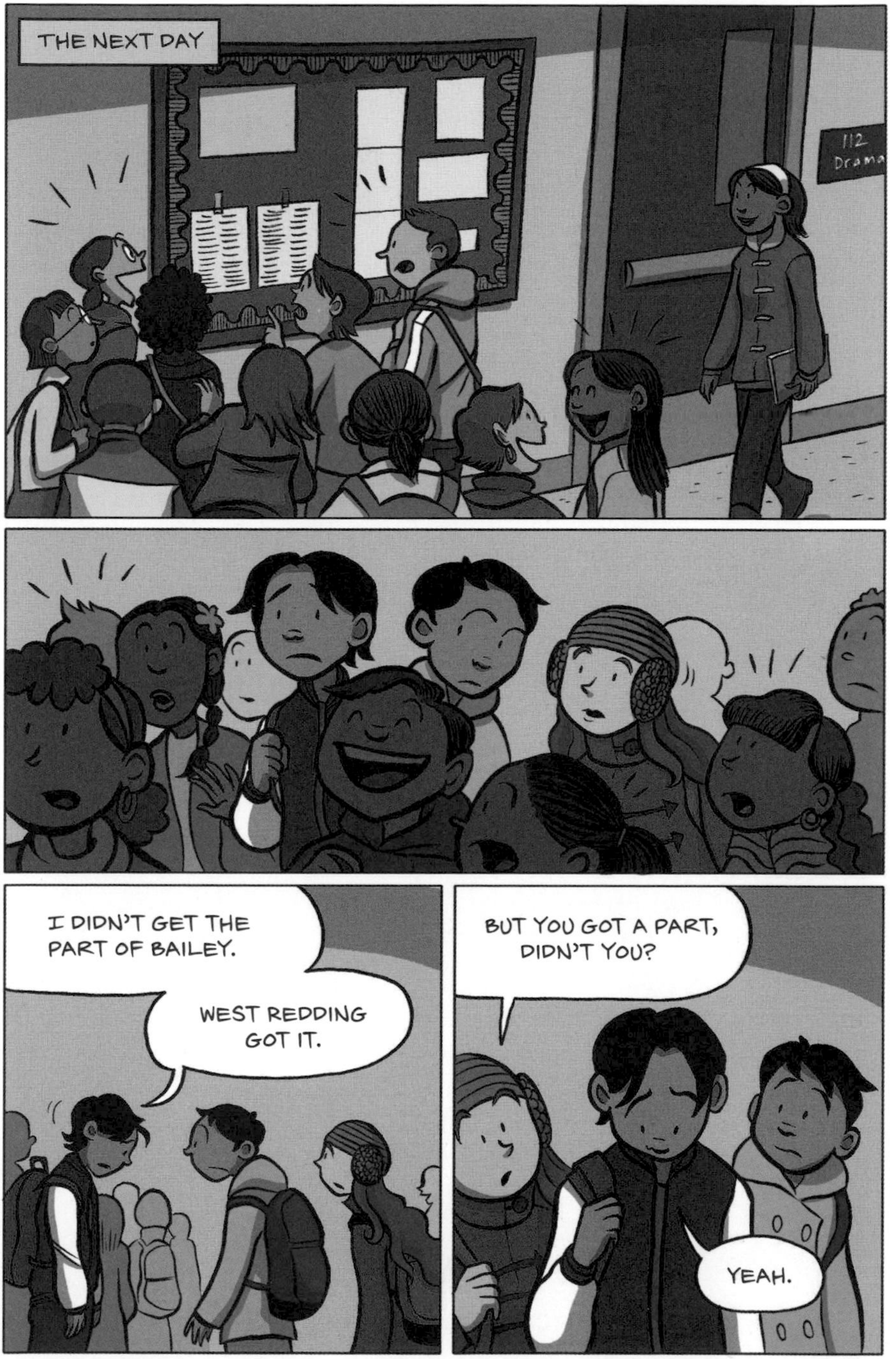
THE NEXT DAY
112 Drama
I DIDN'T GET THE PART OF BAILEY.
WEST REDDING GOT IT.
BUT YOU GOT A PART, DIDN'T YOU?
YEAH.

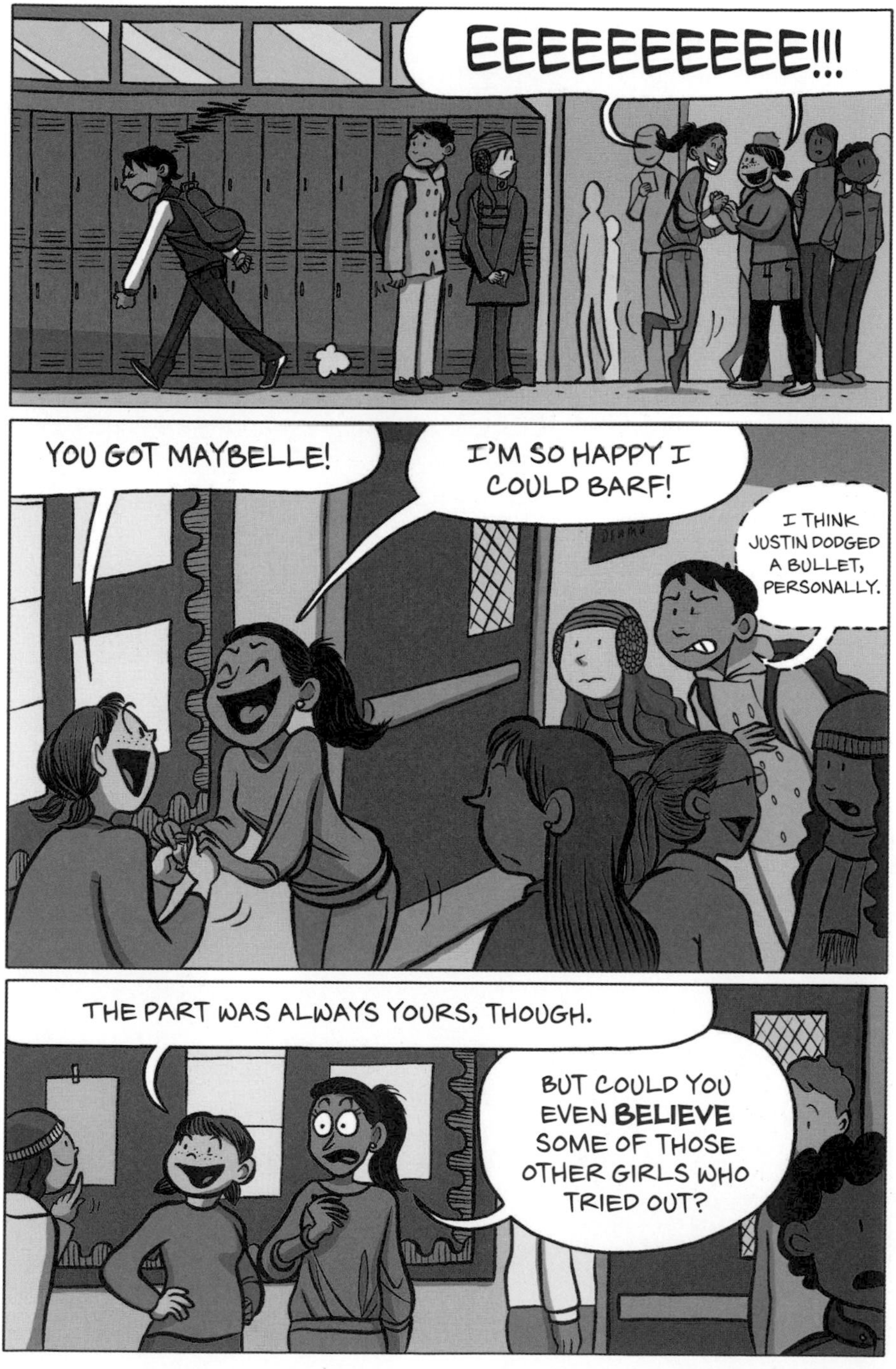
EEEEEEEEEEE!!!
YOU GOT MAYBELLE!
I'M SO HAPPY I COULD BARF!
I THINK JUSTIN DODGED A BULLET, PERSONALLY.
THE PART WAS ALWAYS YOURS, THOUGH.
BUT COULD YOU EVEN BELIEVE SOME OF THOSE OTHER GIRLS WHO TRIED OUT?

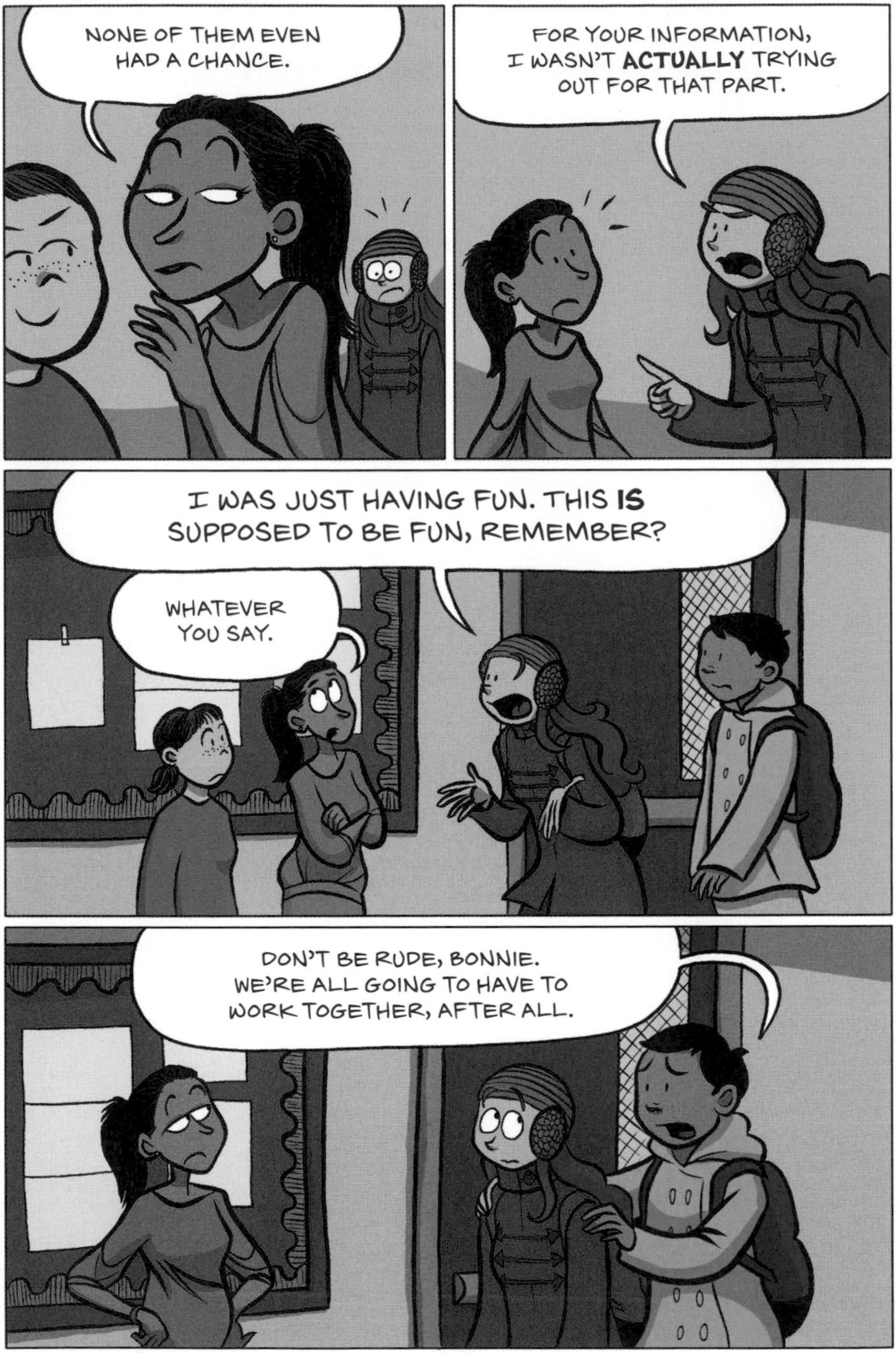
NONE OF THEM EVEN HAD A CHANCE.
FOR YOUR INFORMATION, I WASN'T **ACTUALLY** TRYING OUT FOR THAT PART.
I WAS JUST HAVING FUN. THIS **IS** SUPPOSED TO BE FUN, REMEMBER?
WHATEVER YOU SAY.
DON'T BE RUDE, BONNIE. WE'RE ALL GOING TO HAVE TO WORK TOGETHER, AFTER ALL.

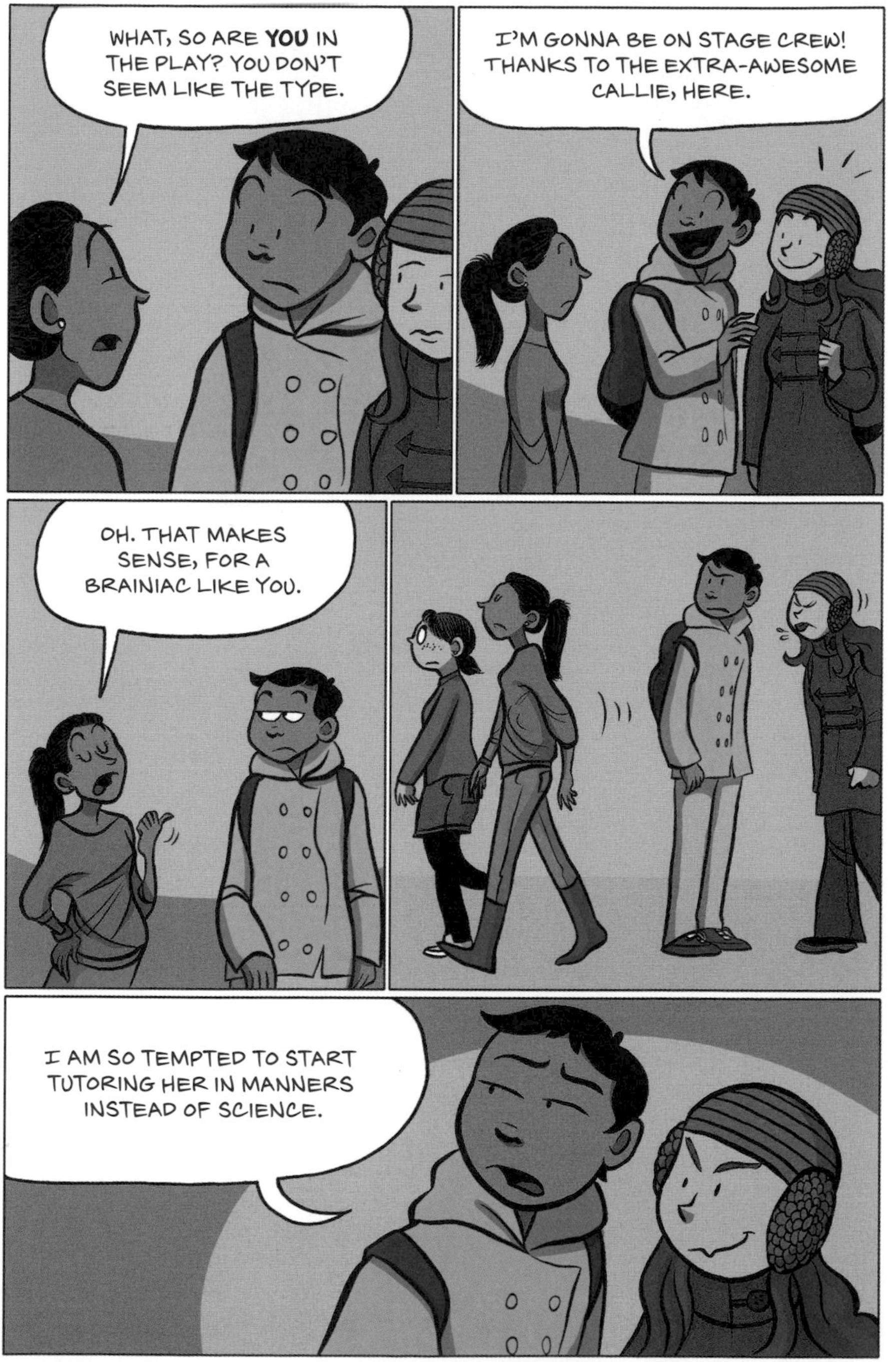
WHAT, SO ARE **YOU** IN THE PLAY? YOU DON'T SEEM LIKE THE TYPE.
I'M GONNA BE ON STAGE CREW! THANKS TO THE EXTRA-AWESOME CALLIE, HERE.
OH. THAT MAKES SENSE, FOR A BRAINIAC LIKE YOU.
I AM SO TEMPTED TO START TUTORING HER IN MANNERS INSTEAD OF SCIENCE.

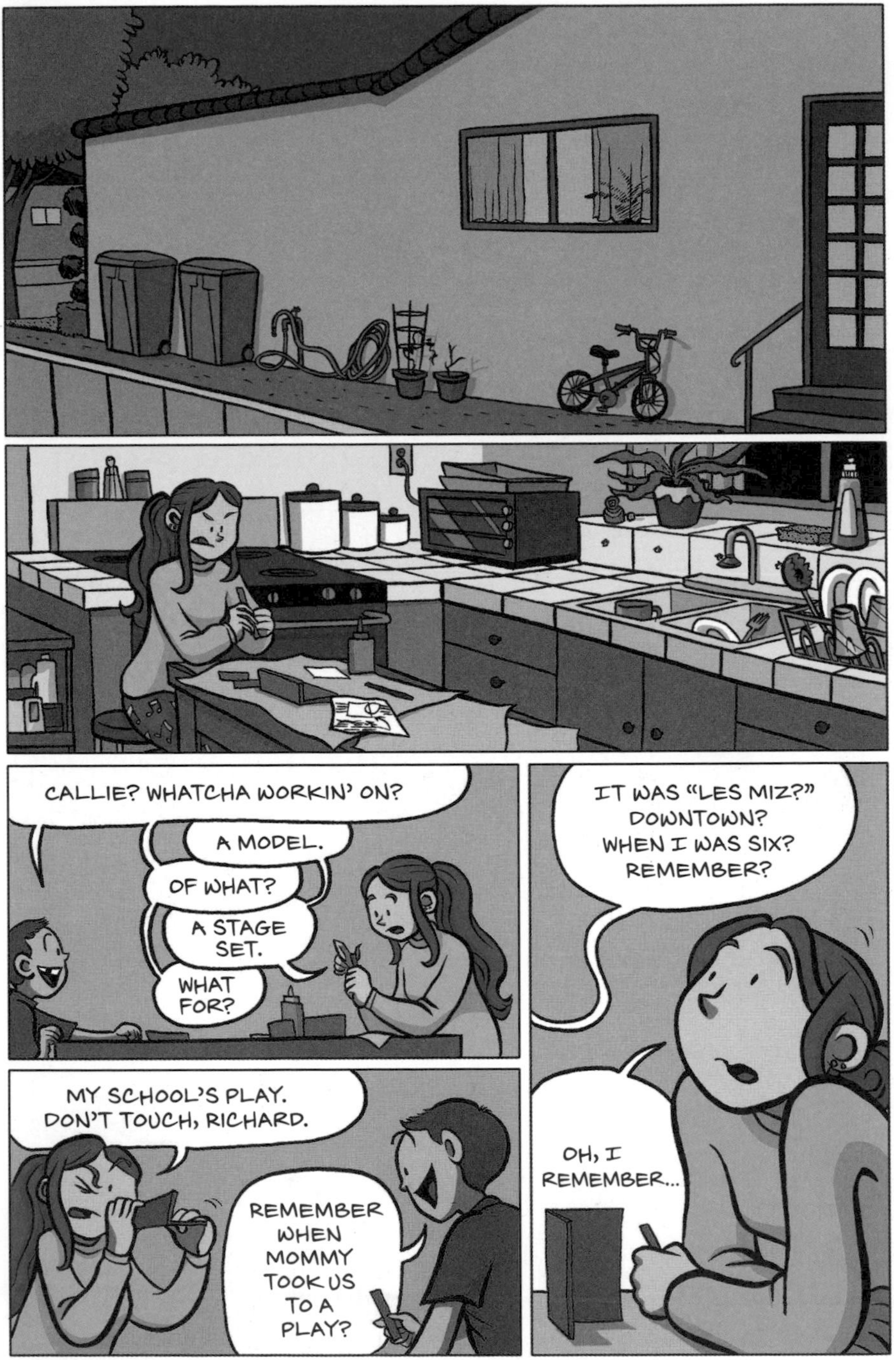
CALLIE? WHATCHA WORKIN' ON?
A MODEL.
OF WHAT?
A STAGE SET.
WHAT FOR?
MY SCHOOL'S PLAY. DON'T TOUCH, RICHARD.
REMEMBER WHEN MOMMY TOOK US TO A PLAY?
IT WAS "LES MIZ?" DOWNTOWN? WHEN I WAS SIX? REMEMBER?
OH, I REMEMBER...

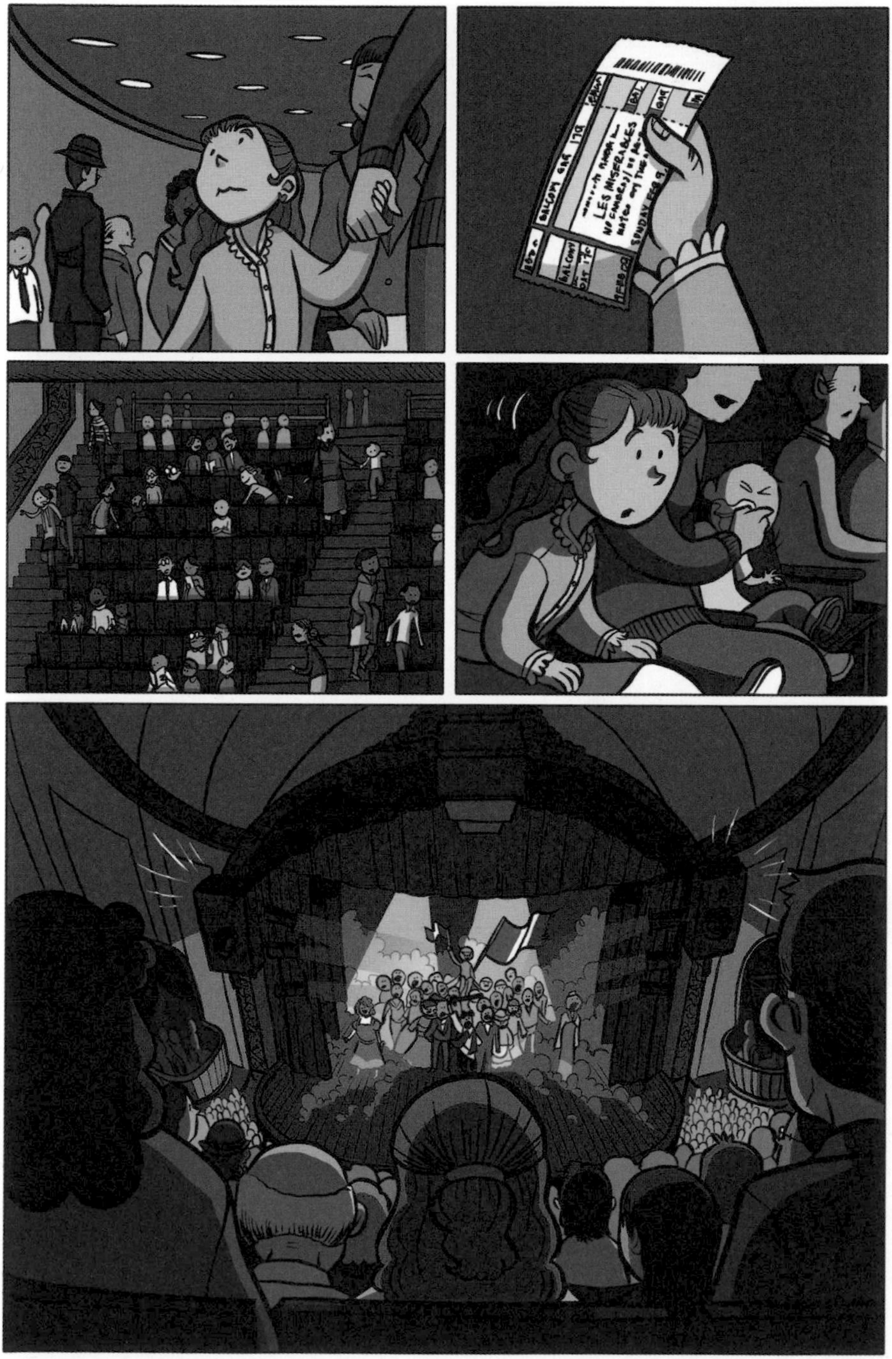
BALCONY
LES MISERABLES
SUNDAY FEB 9

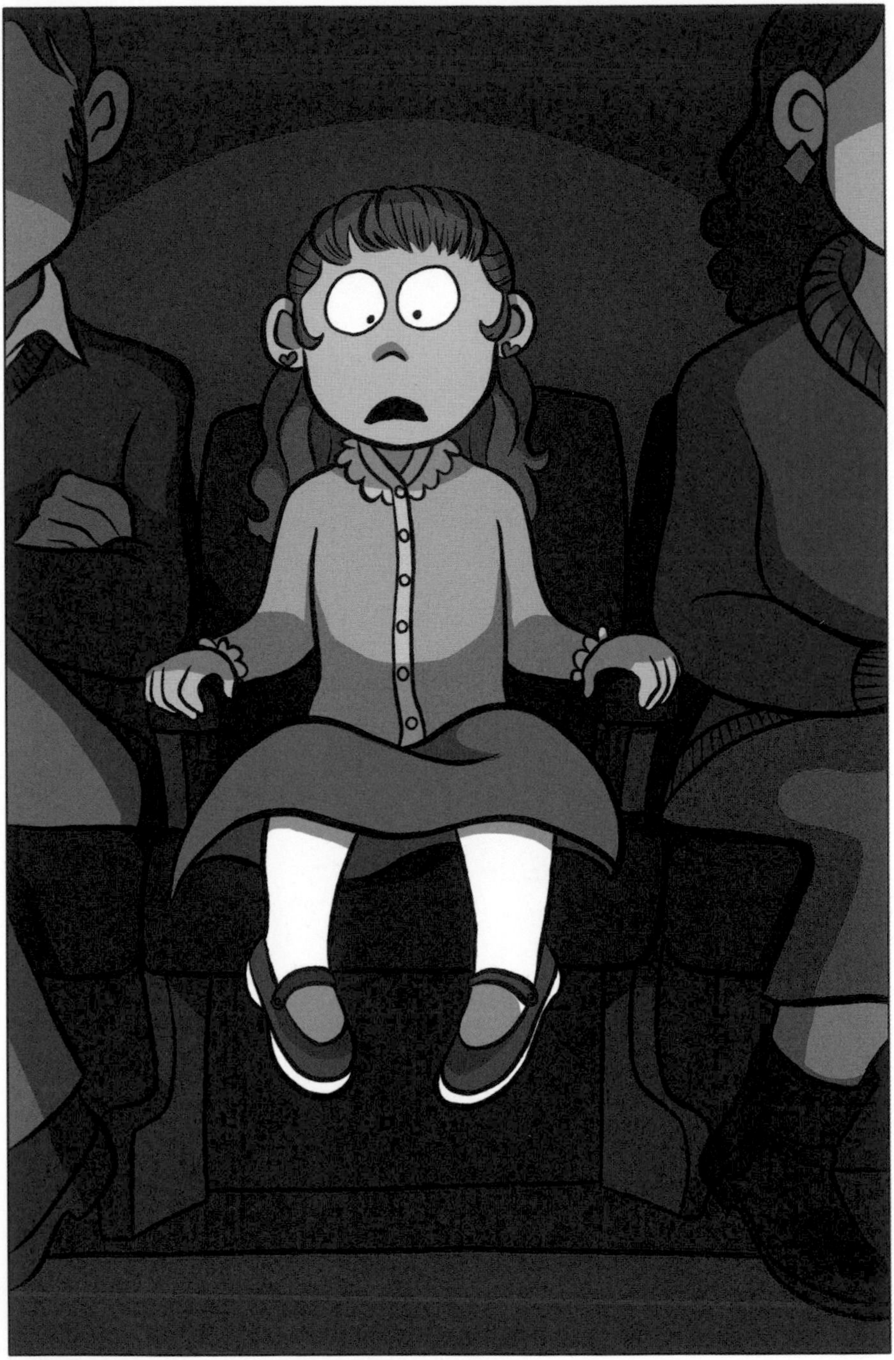

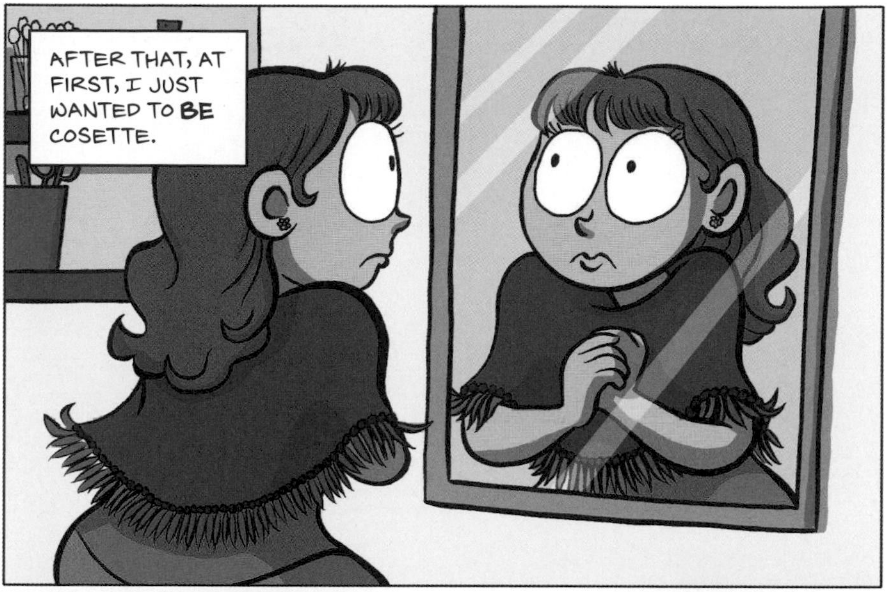
AFTER THAT, AT FIRST, I JUST WANTED TO **BE** COSETTE.

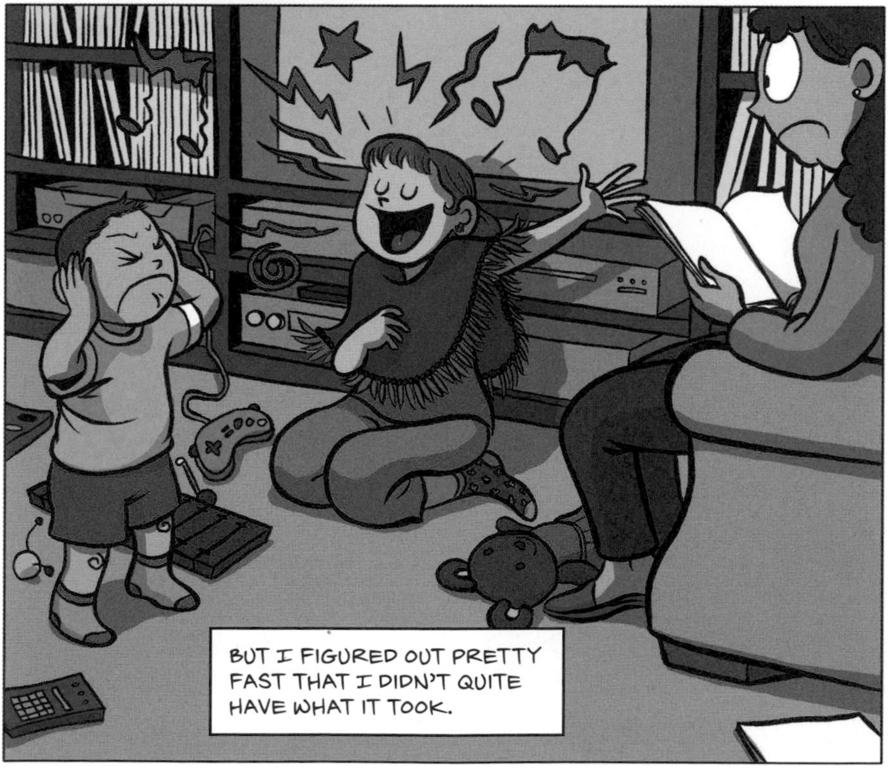
BUT I FIGURED OUT PRETTY FAST THAT I DIDN'T QUITE HAVE WHAT IT TOOK.

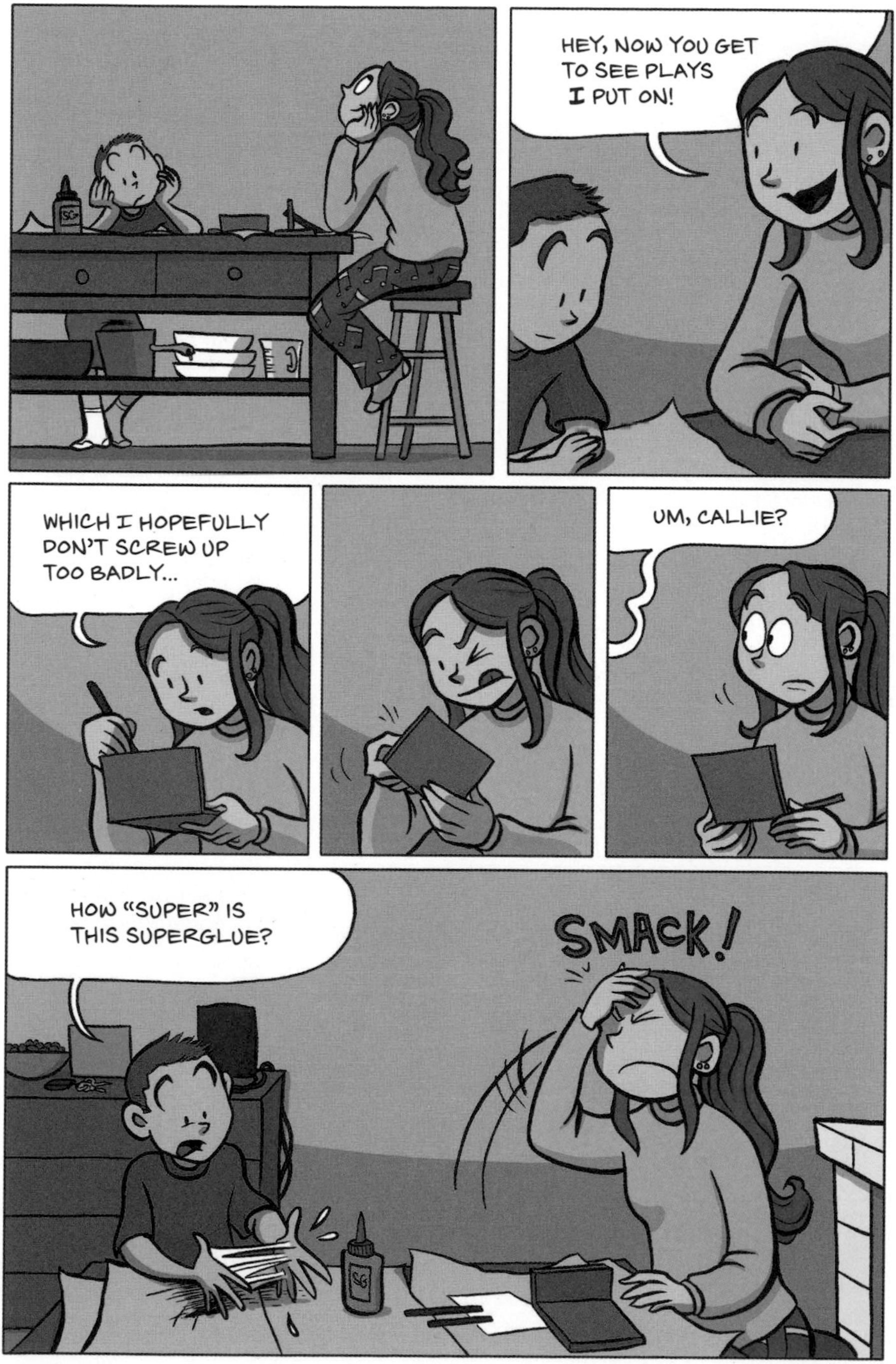
HEY, NOW YOU GET TO SEE PLAYS I PUT ON!
WHICH I HOPEFULLY DON'T SCREW UP TOO BADLY...
UM, CALLIE?
HOW "SUPER" IS THIS SUPERGLUE?
SMACK!

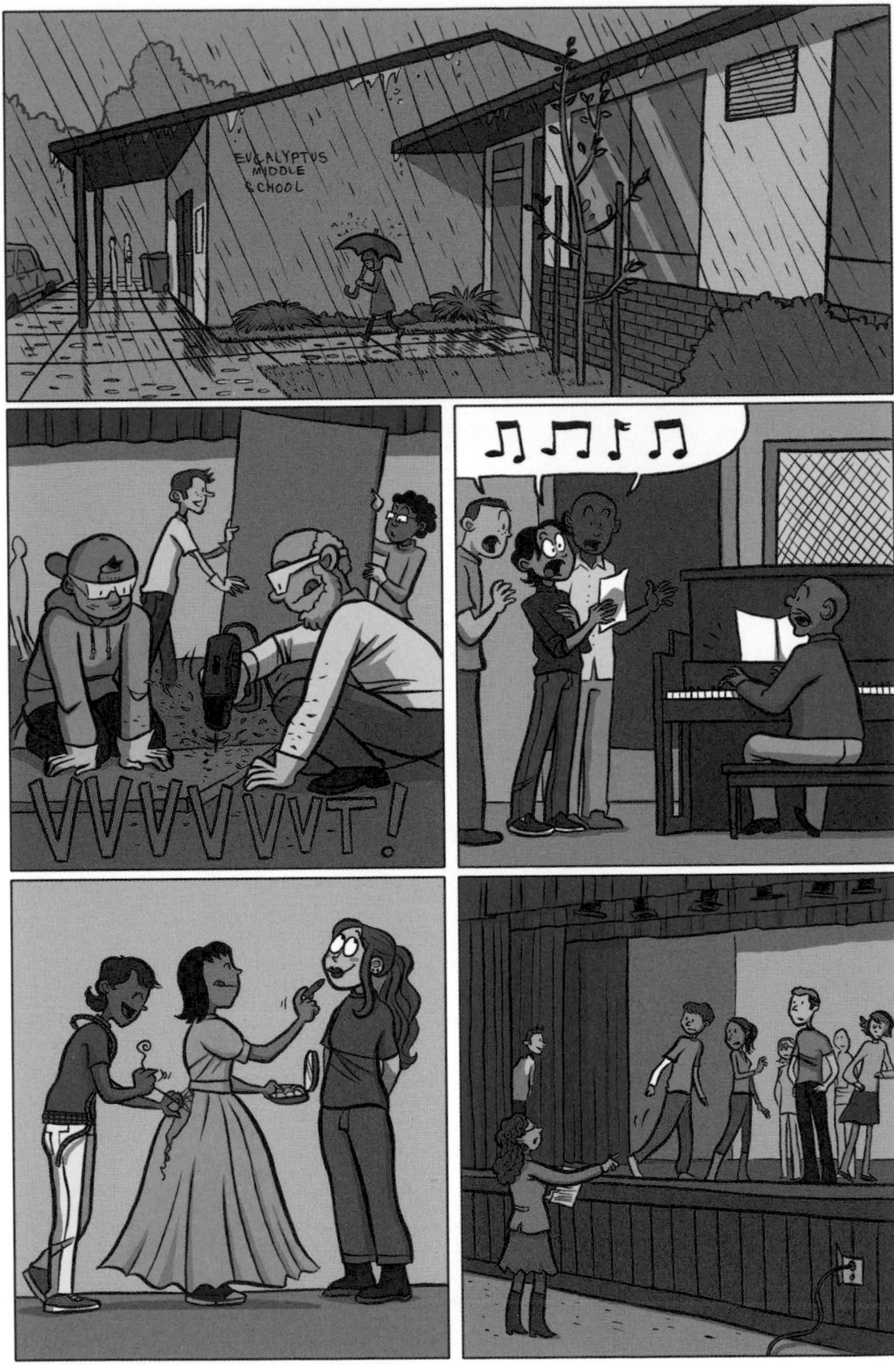
EUCALYPTUS
MIDDLE
SCHOOL
VVVVVVT!

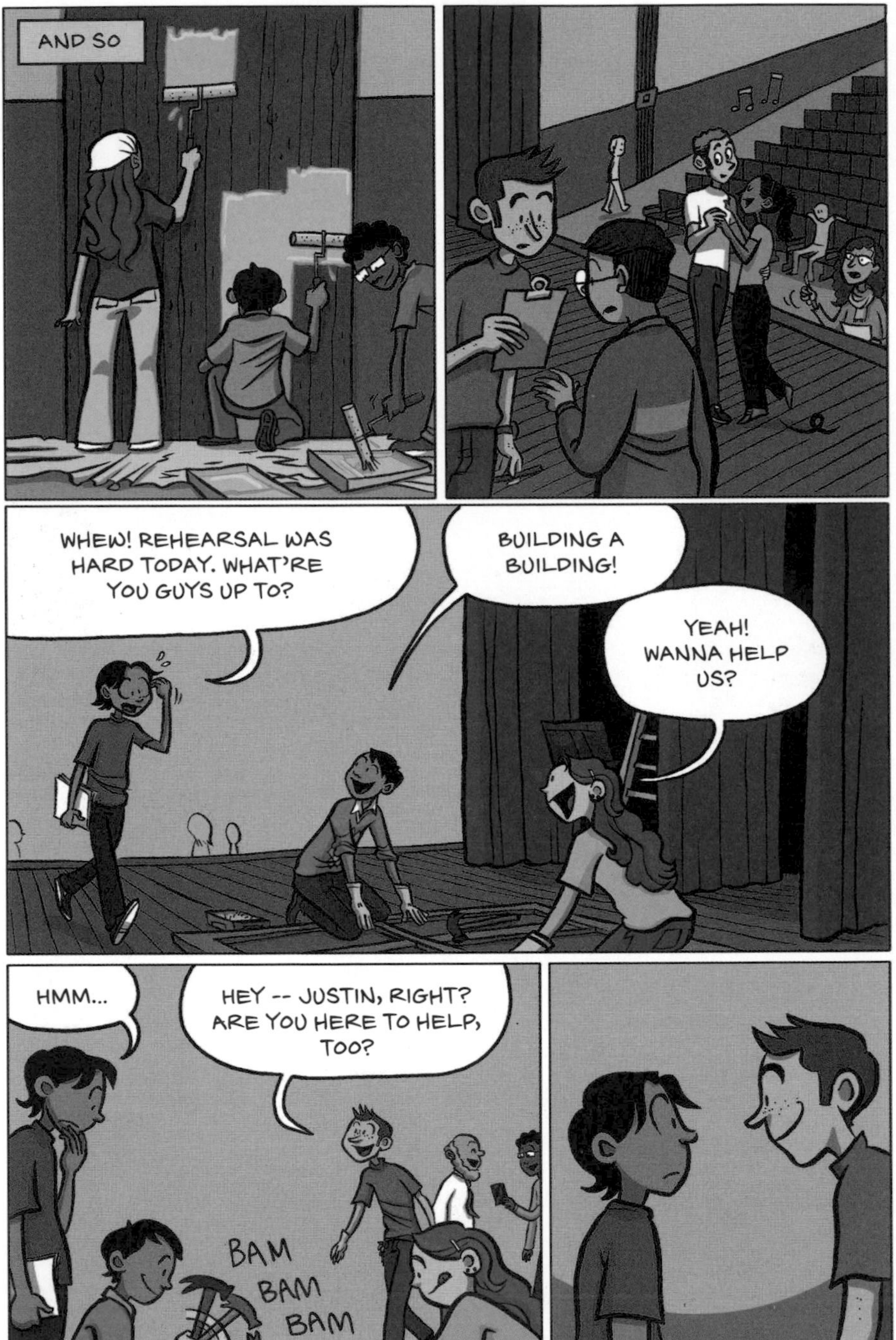
AND SO
WHEW! REHEARSAL WAS HARD TODAY. WHAT'RE YOU GUYS UP TO?
BUILDING A BUILDING!
YEAH! WANNA HELP US?
HMM...
HEY -- JUSTIN, RIGHT? ARE YOU HERE TO HELP, TOO?
BAM
BAM
BAM

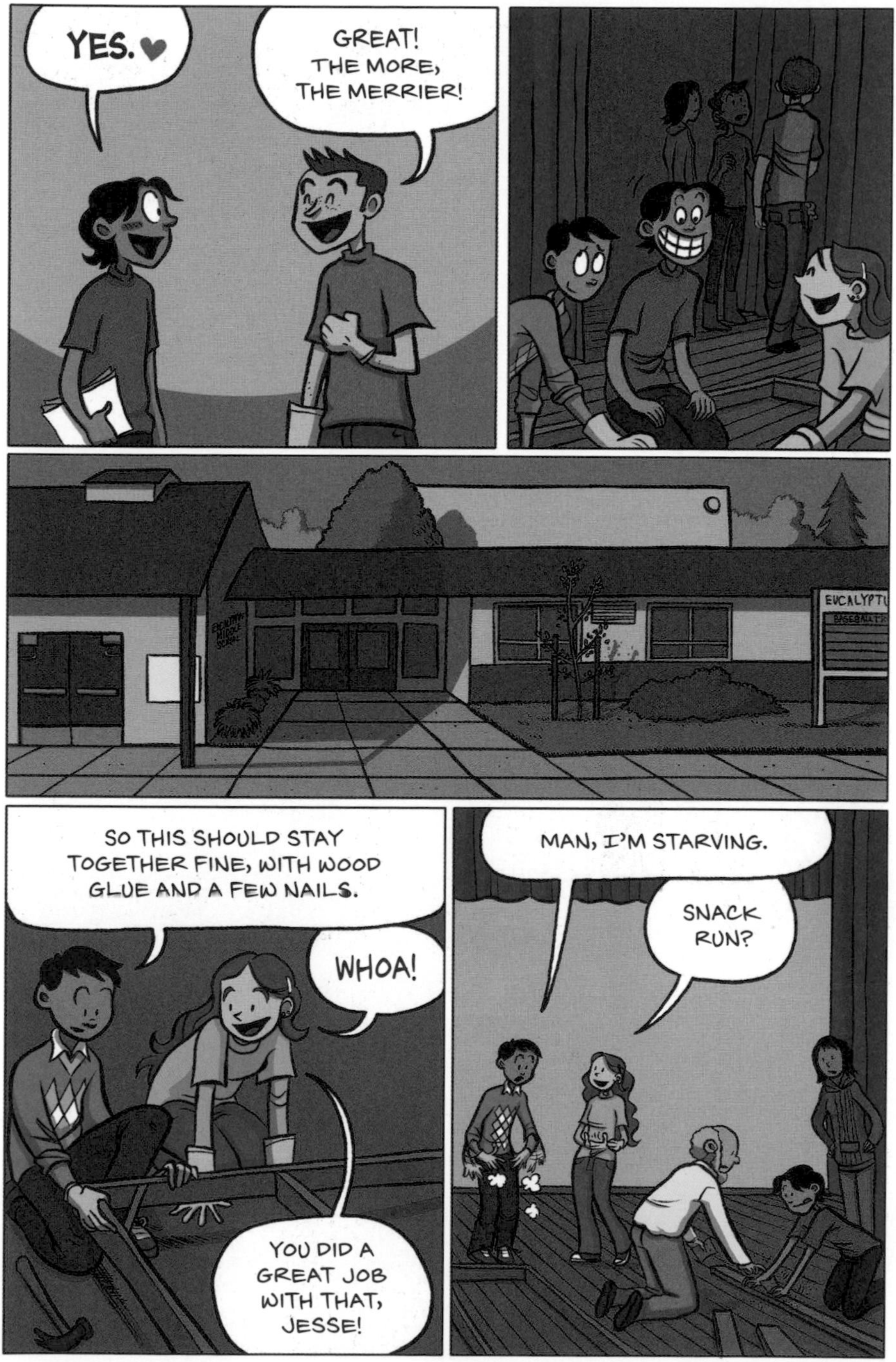
YES. ♥
GREAT! THE MORE, THE MERRIER!
SO THIS SHOULD STAY TOGETHER FINE, WITH WOOD GLUE AND A FEW NAILS.
WHOA!
YOU DID A GREAT JOB WITH THAT, JESSE!
MAN, I'M STARVING.
SNACK RUN?

Glick
Glick
Glick

Beep
Beep

LET'S SEE... JUSTIN WANTS CHEEZ DOODLES... LOREN GETS THE SNICKERS... THE SKITTLES ARE FOR MIRKO...

"LADY FAIR, DON'T BE SCARED, COME AND SIT NEXT TO ME..."

"WE'LL BE QUIET, YOU'LL SEE..."

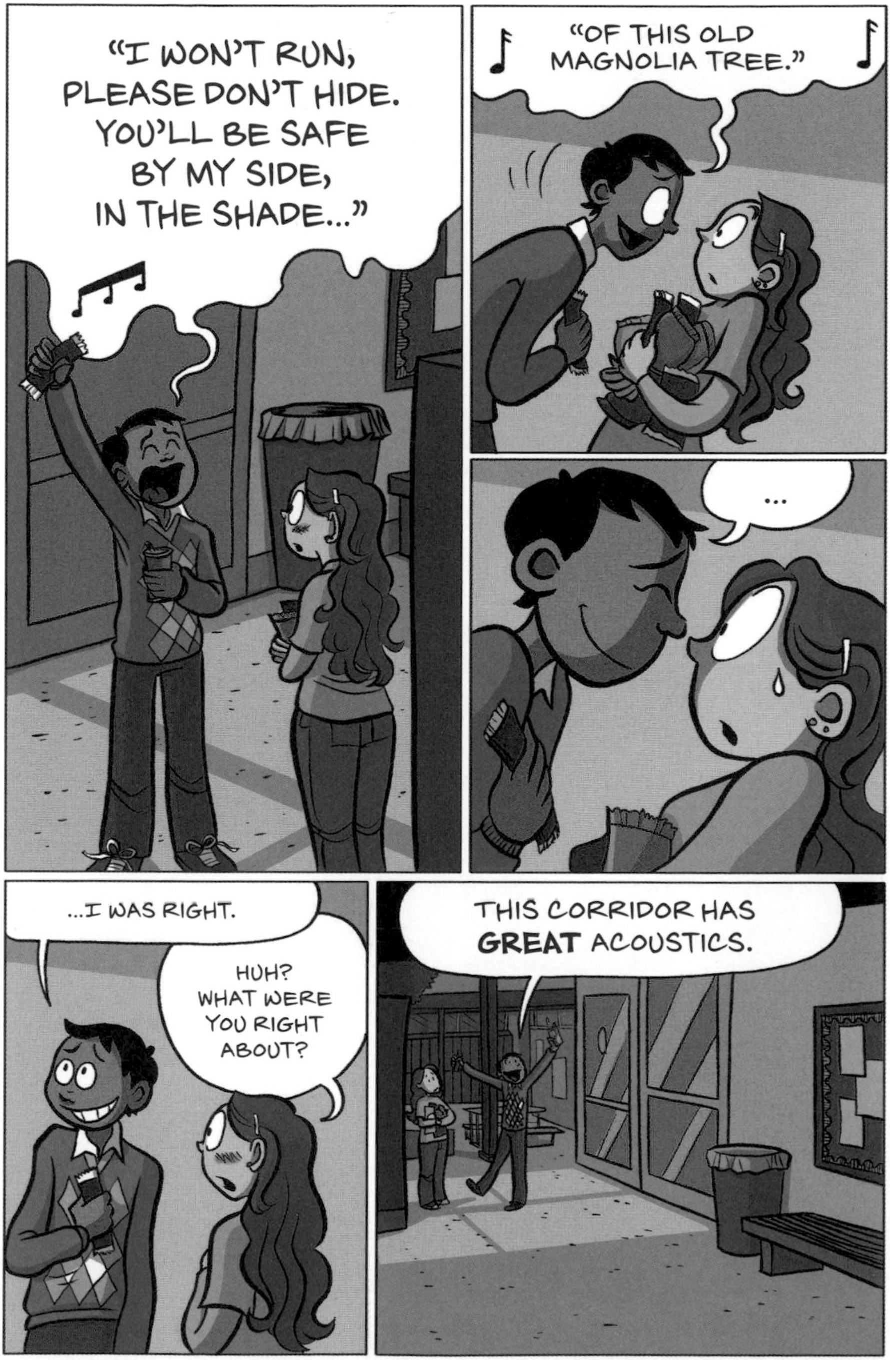
"I WON'T RUN, PLEASE DON'T HIDE. YOU'LL BE SAFE BY MY SIDE, IN THE SHADE..."
"OF THIS OLD MAGNOLIA TREE."
...
...I WAS RIGHT.
HUH? WHAT WERE YOU RIGHT ABOUT?
THIS CORRIDOR HAS **GREAT** ACOUSTICS.

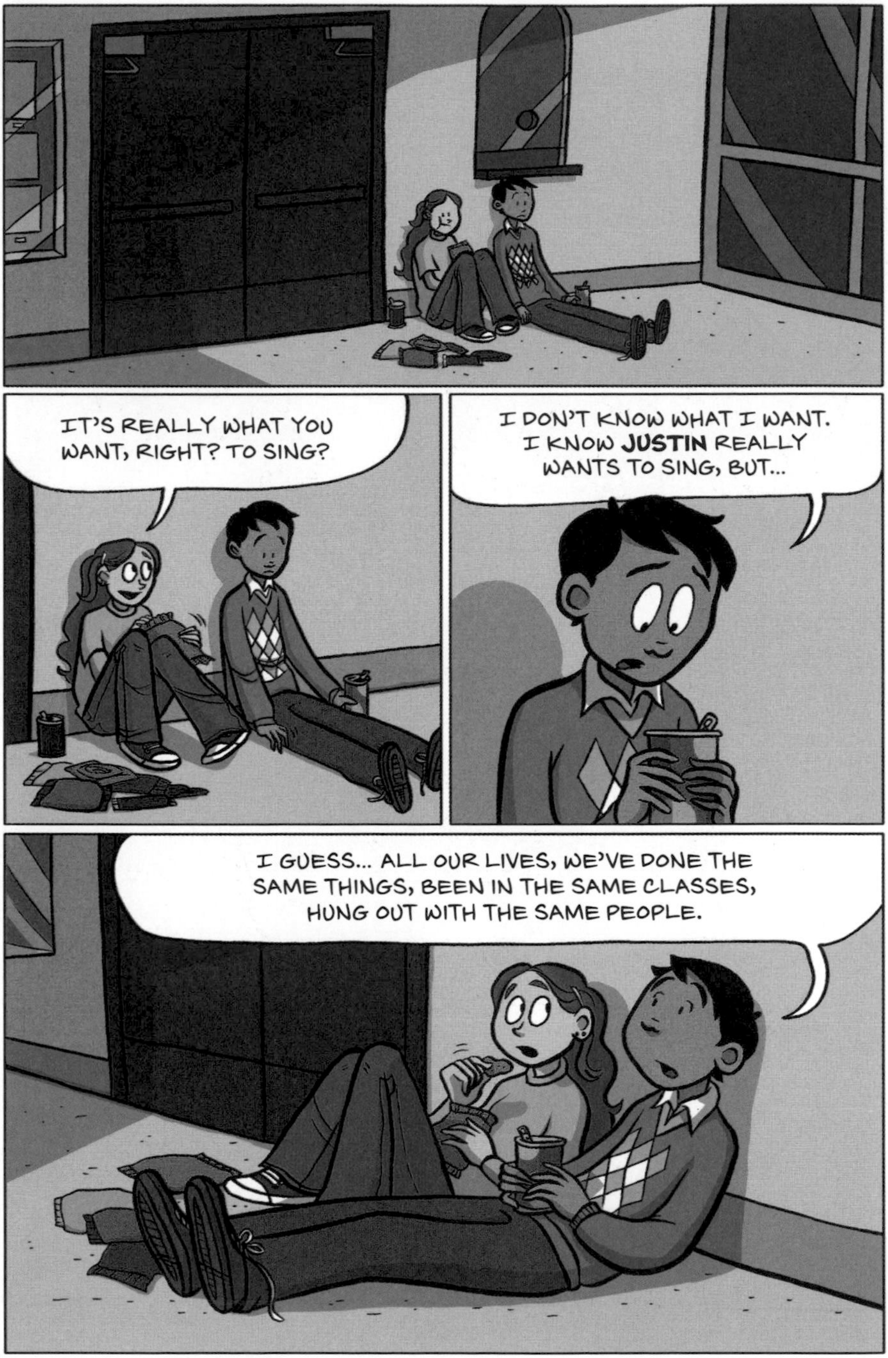
IT'S REALLY WHAT YOU WANT, RIGHT? TO SING?
I DON'T KNOW WHAT I WANT. I KNOW **JUSTIN** REALLY WANTS TO SING, BUT...
I GUESS... ALL OUR LIVES, WE'VE DONE THE SAME THINGS, BEEN IN THE SAME CLASSES, HUNG OUT WITH THE SAME PEOPLE.

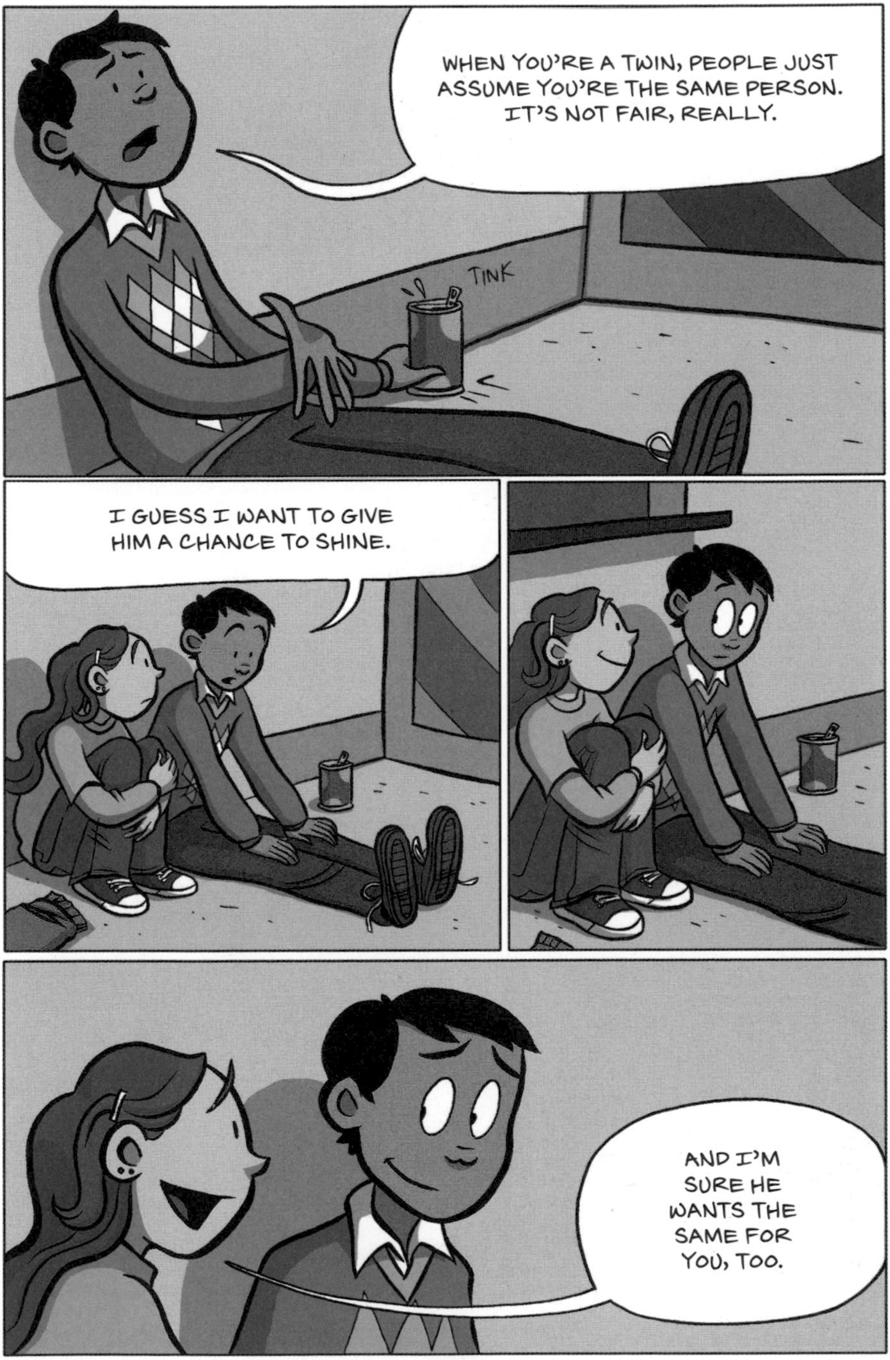
WHEN YOU'RE A TWIN, PEOPLE JUST ASSUME YOU'RE THE SAME PERSON. IT'S NOT FAIR, REALLY.
TINK
I GUESS I WANT TO GIVE HIM A CHANCE TO SHINE.
AND I'M SURE HE WANTS THE SAME FOR YOU, TOO.

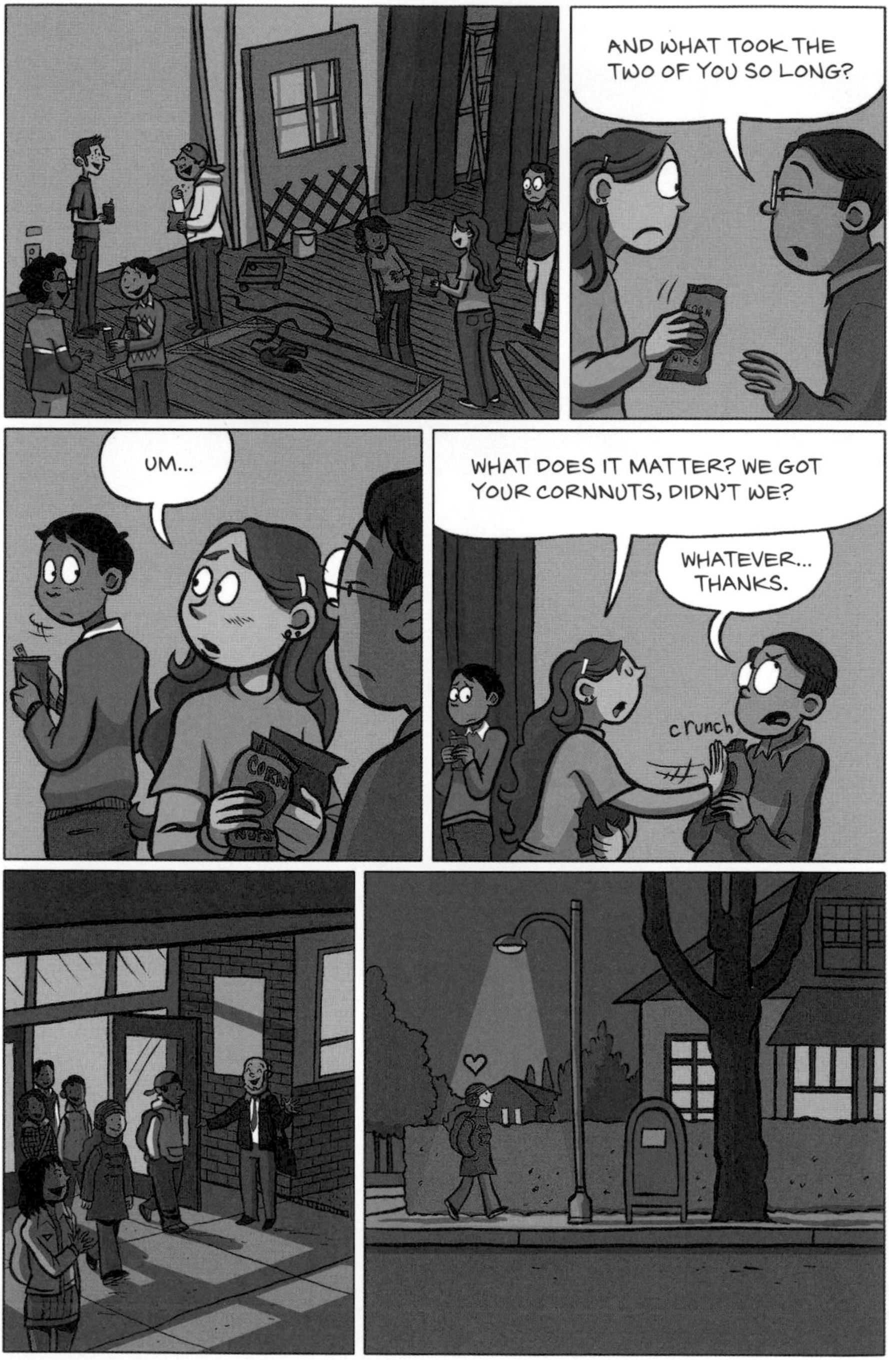
AND WHAT TOOK THE TWO OF YOU SO LONG?
CORN NUTS
UM...
CORN NUTS
WHAT DOES IT MATTER? WE GOT YOUR CORNNUTS, DIDN'T WE?
WHATEVER... THANKS.
crunch

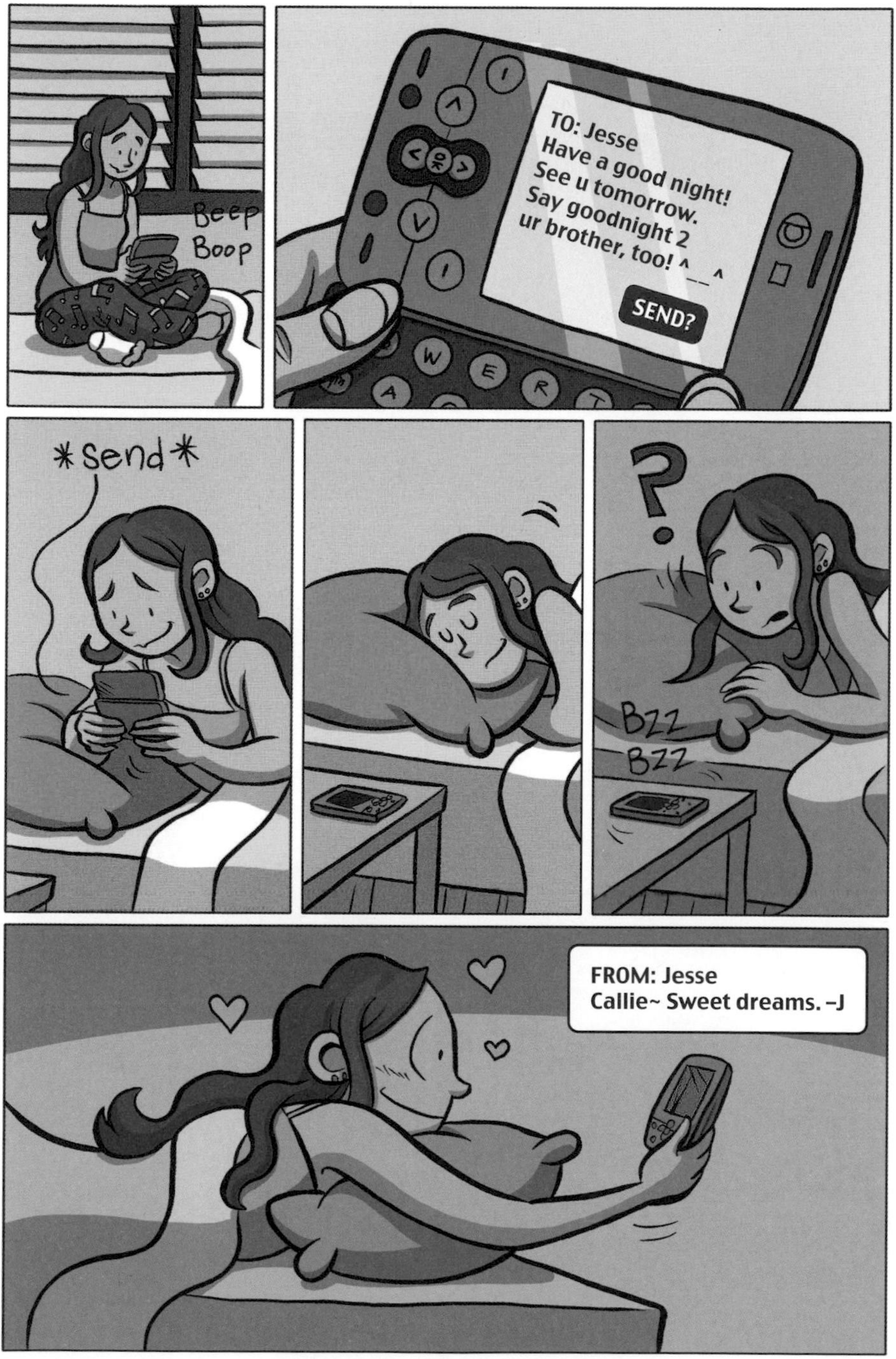
Beep
Boop
TO: Jesse
Have a good night!
See u tomorrow.
Say goodnight 2
ur brother, too! ^__^
SEND?
send
?
BZZ
BZZ
FROM: Jesse
Callie~ Sweet dreams. -J

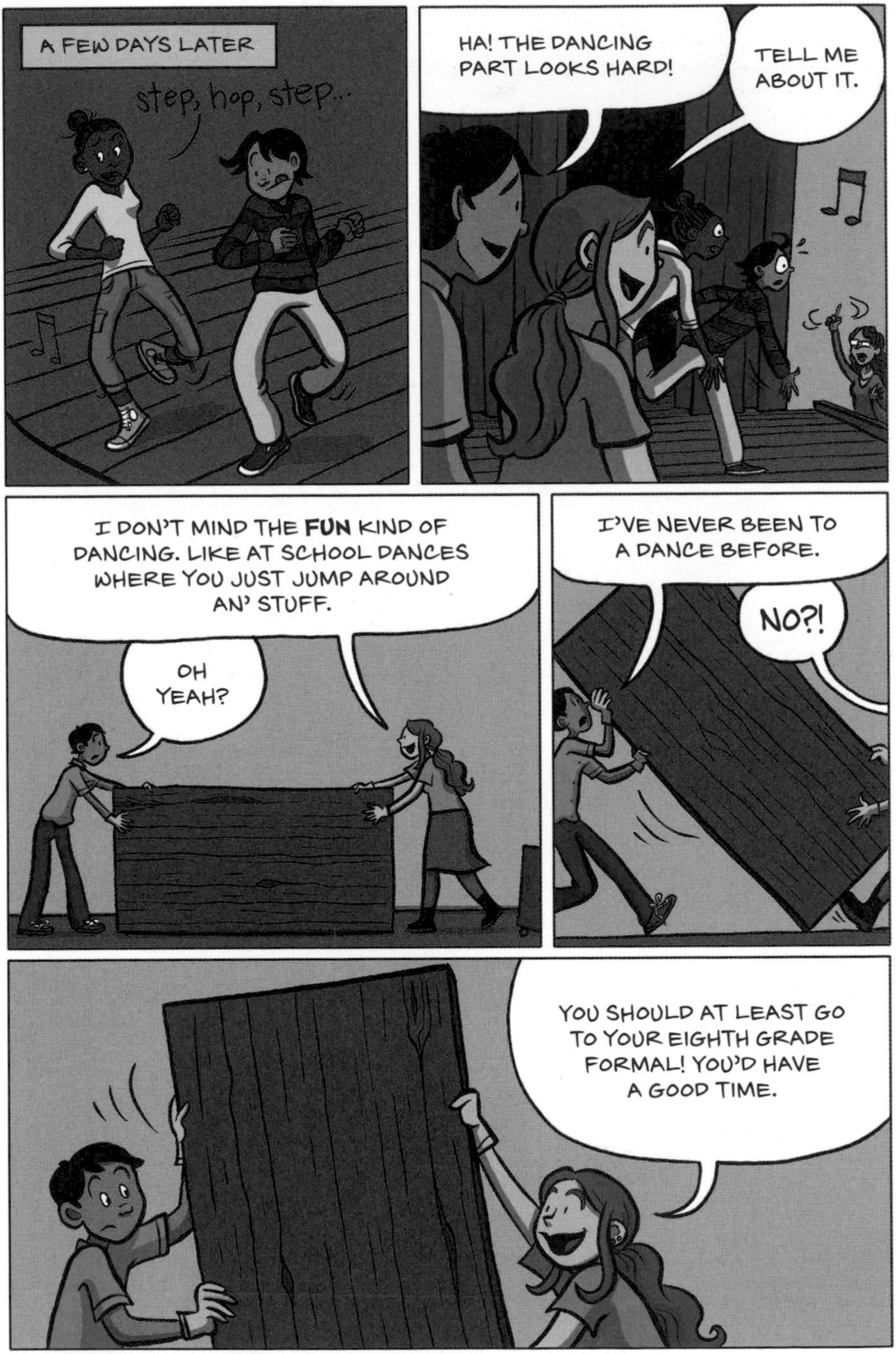
A FEW DAYS LATER
step, hop, step...
HA! THE DANCING PART LOOKS HARD!
TELL ME ABOUT IT.
I DON'T MIND THE **FUN** KIND OF DANCING. LIKE AT SCHOOL DANCES WHERE YOU JUST JUMP AROUND AN' STUFF.
OH YEAH?
I'VE NEVER BEEN TO A DANCE BEFORE.
NO?!
YOU SHOULD AT LEAST GO TO YOUR EIGHTH GRADE FORMAL! YOU'D HAVE A GOOD TIME.

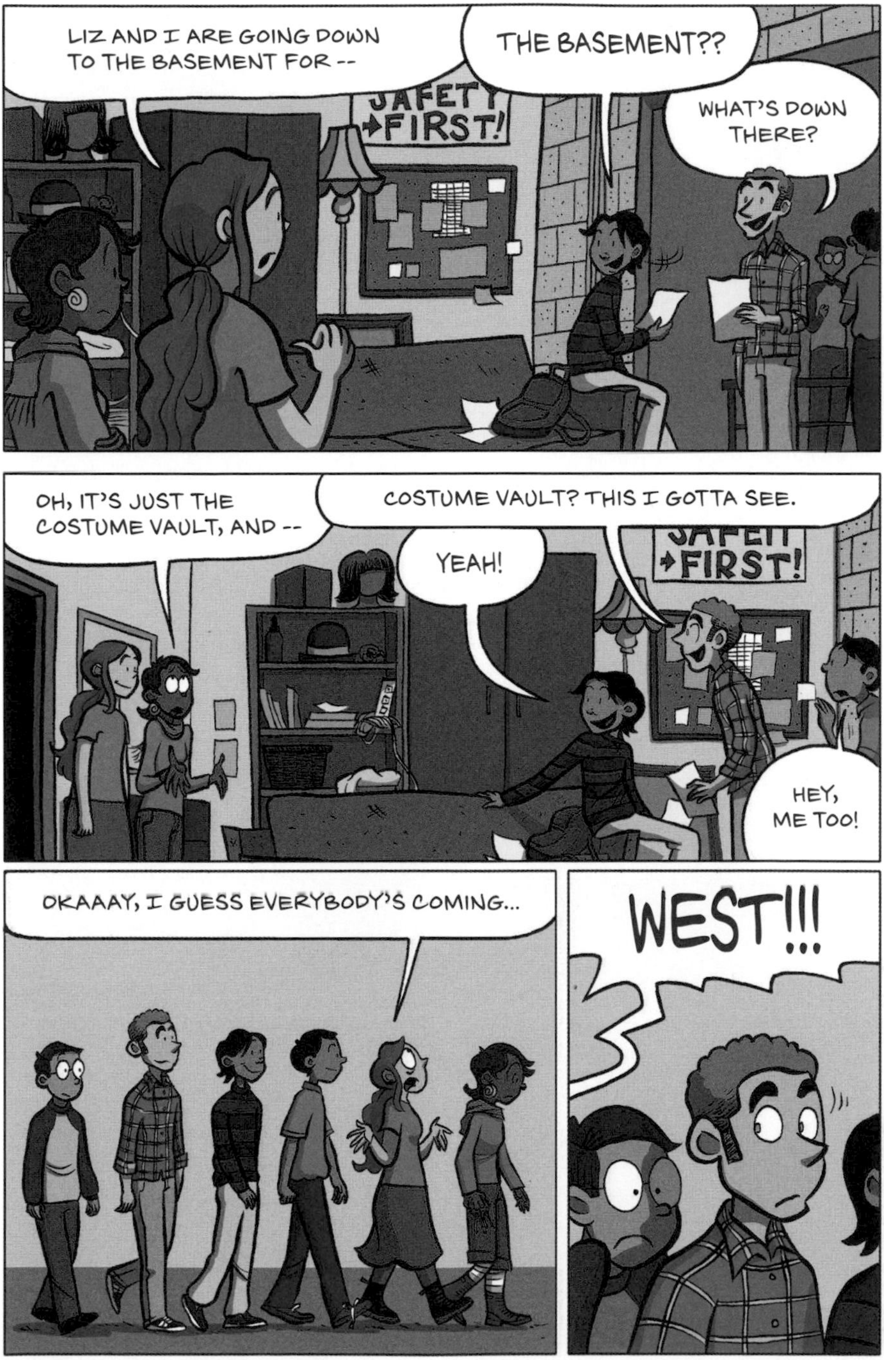
LIZ AND I ARE GOING DOWN TO THE BASEMENT FOR --
THE BASEMENT??
SAFETY FIRST!
WHAT'S DOWN THERE?
OH, IT'S JUST THE COSTUME VAULT, AND --
COSTUME VAULT? THIS I GOTTA SEE.
YEAH!
FIRST!
HEY, ME TOO!
OKAAAY, I GUESS EVERYBODY'S COMING...
WEST!!!

109

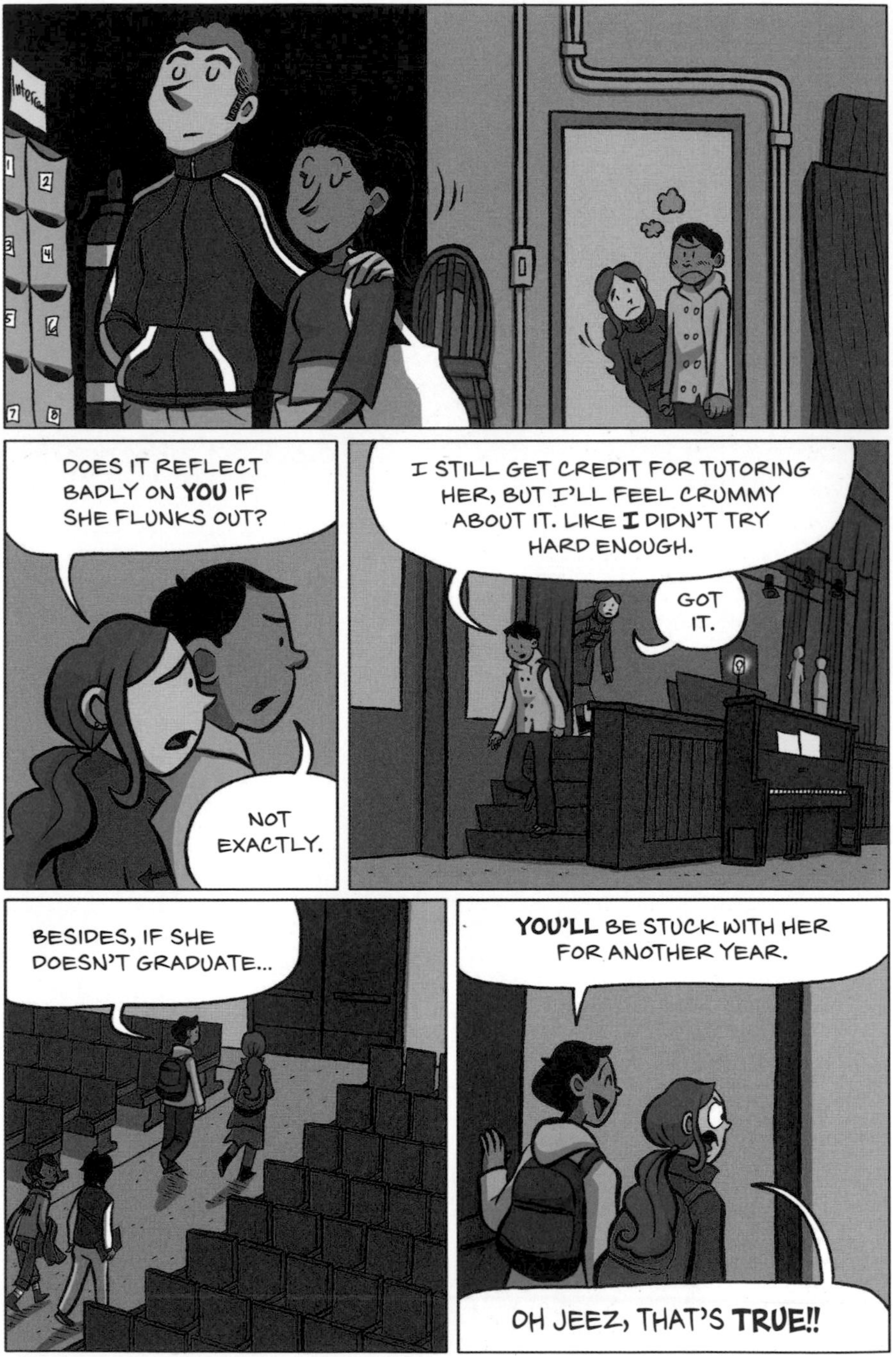
DOES IT REFLECT BADLY ON **YOU** IF SHE FLUNKS OUT?
NOT EXACTLY.
I STILL GET CREDIT FOR TUTORING HER, BUT I'LL FEEL CRUMMY ABOUT IT. LIKE **I** DIDN'T TRY HARD ENOUGH.
GOT IT.
BESIDES, IF SHE DOESN'T GRADUATE...
YOU'LL BE STUCK WITH HER FOR ANOTHER YEAR.
OH JEEZ, THAT'S **TRUE!!**

SORRY, CALLIE, WE'RE ALREADY WAY BEHIND SCHEDULE WITH THIS.

GOOD! I ALREADY MADE PHOTOCOPIES.

BUT THINK OF THE PEOPLE WHO **MIGHT** HAVE COME IF THEY KNEW THERE WAS A **CANNON** INVOLVED.

RINNNG!!

THANKS FOR HELPING ME FLYER THE SCHOOL, JUSTIN!

TOTALLY! I MET YOU BECAUSE OF A FLYER, SO THIS IS, LIKE, FULL CIRCLE.

115

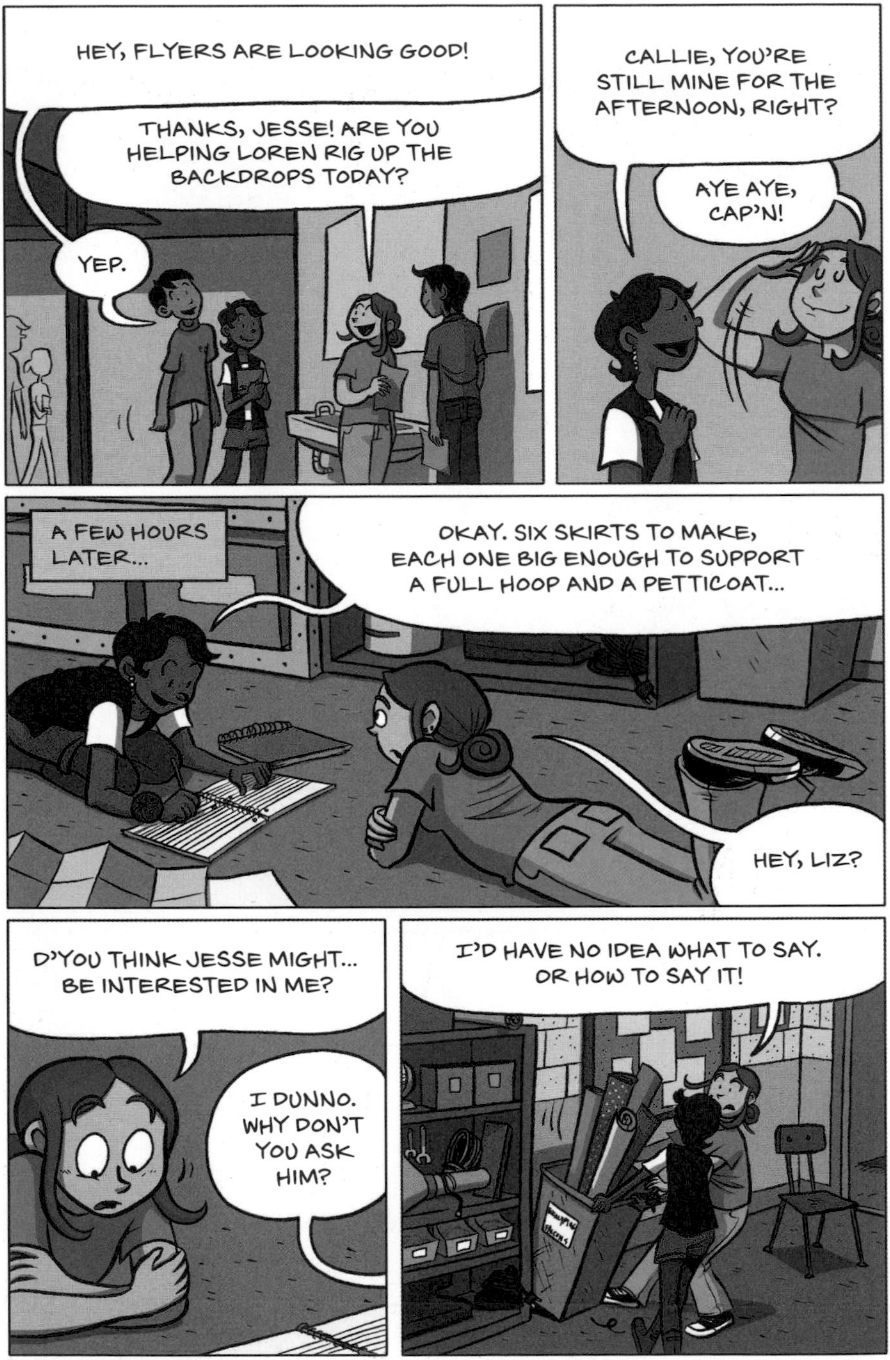
HEY, FLYERS ARE LOOKING GOOD!
THANKS, JESSE! ARE YOU HELPING LOREN RIG UP THE BACKDROPS TODAY?
YEP.
CALLIE, YOU'RE STILL MINE FOR THE AFTERNOON, RIGHT?
AYE AYE, CAP'N!
A FEW HOURS LATER...
OKAY. SIX SKIRTS TO MAKE, EACH ONE BIG ENOUGH TO SUPPORT A FULL HOOP AND A PETTICOAT...
HEY, LIZ?
D'YOU THINK JESSE MIGHT... BE INTERESTED IN ME?
I DUNNO. WHY DON'T YOU ASK HIM?
I'D HAVE NO IDEA WHAT TO SAY. OR HOW TO SAY IT!

117

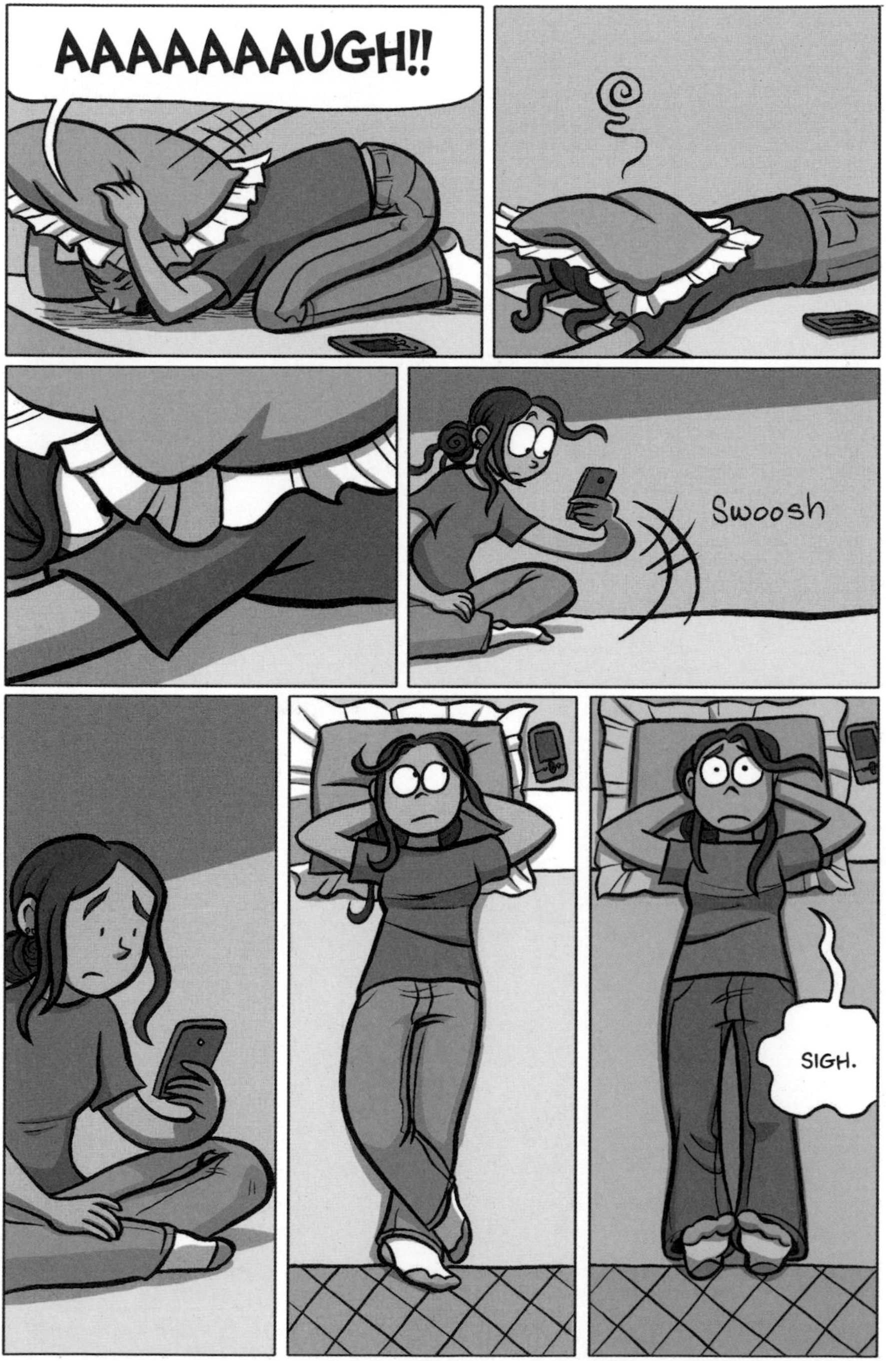
AAAAAAAUGH!!
Swoosh
SIGH.

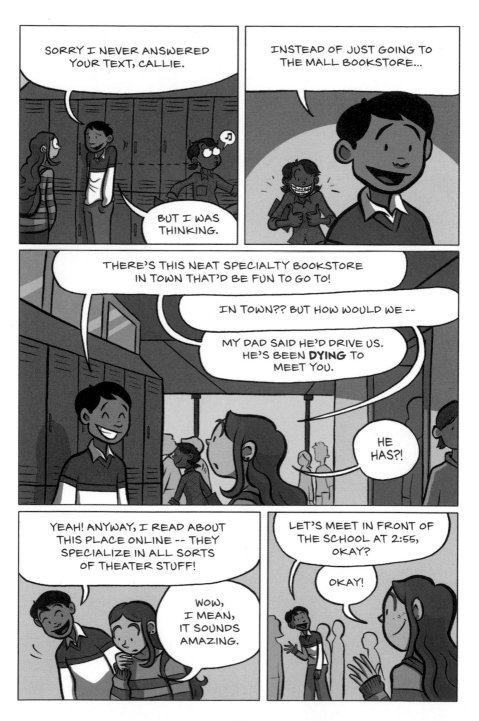

SORRY I NEVER ANSWERED YOUR TEXT, CALLIE.

INSTEAD OF JUST GOING TO THE MALL BOOKSTORE...

BUT I WAS THINKING.

THERE'S THIS NEAT SPECIALTY BOOKSTORE IN TOWN THAT'D BE FUN TO GO TO!

IN TOWN?? BUT HOW WOULD WE --

MY DAD SAID HE'D DRIVE US. HE'S BEEN **DYING** TO MEET YOU.

HE HAS?!

YEAH! ANYWAY, I READ ABOUT THIS PLACE ONLINE -- THEY SPECIALIZE IN ALL SORTS OF THEATER STUFF!

WOW, I MEAN, IT SOUNDS AMAZING.

LET'S MEET IN FRONT OF THE SCHOOL AT 2:55, OKAY?

OKAY!

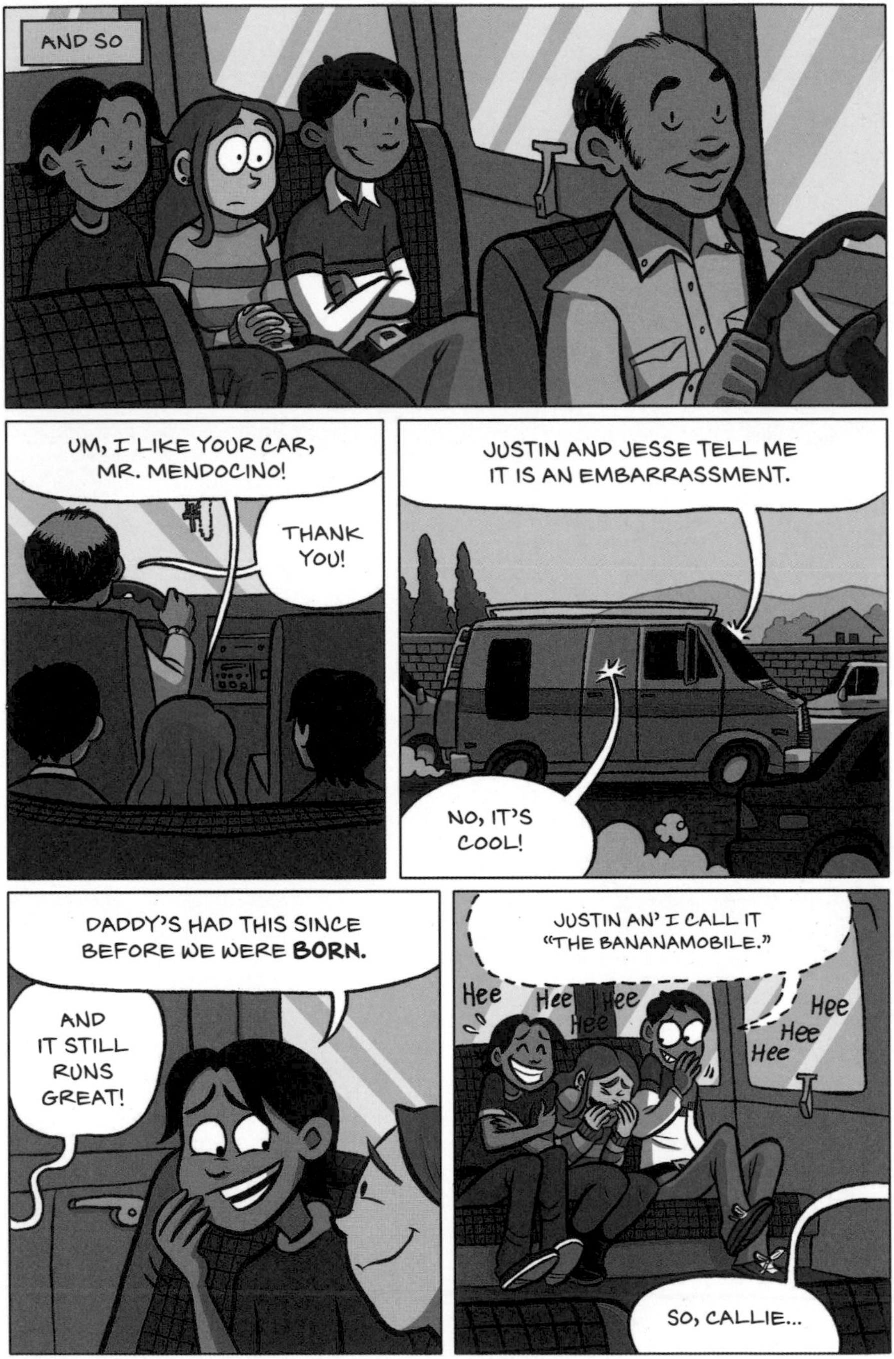

AND SO
UM, I LIKE YOUR CAR, MR. MENDOCINO!
THANK YOU!
JUSTIN AND JESSE TELL ME IT IS AN EMBARRASSMENT.
NO, IT'S COOL!
DADDY'S HAD THIS SINCE BEFORE WE WERE **BORN.**
AND IT STILL RUNS GREAT!
JUSTIN AN' I CALL IT "THE BANANAMOBILE."
Hee Hee Hee Hee Hee Hee Hee
SO, CALLIE...

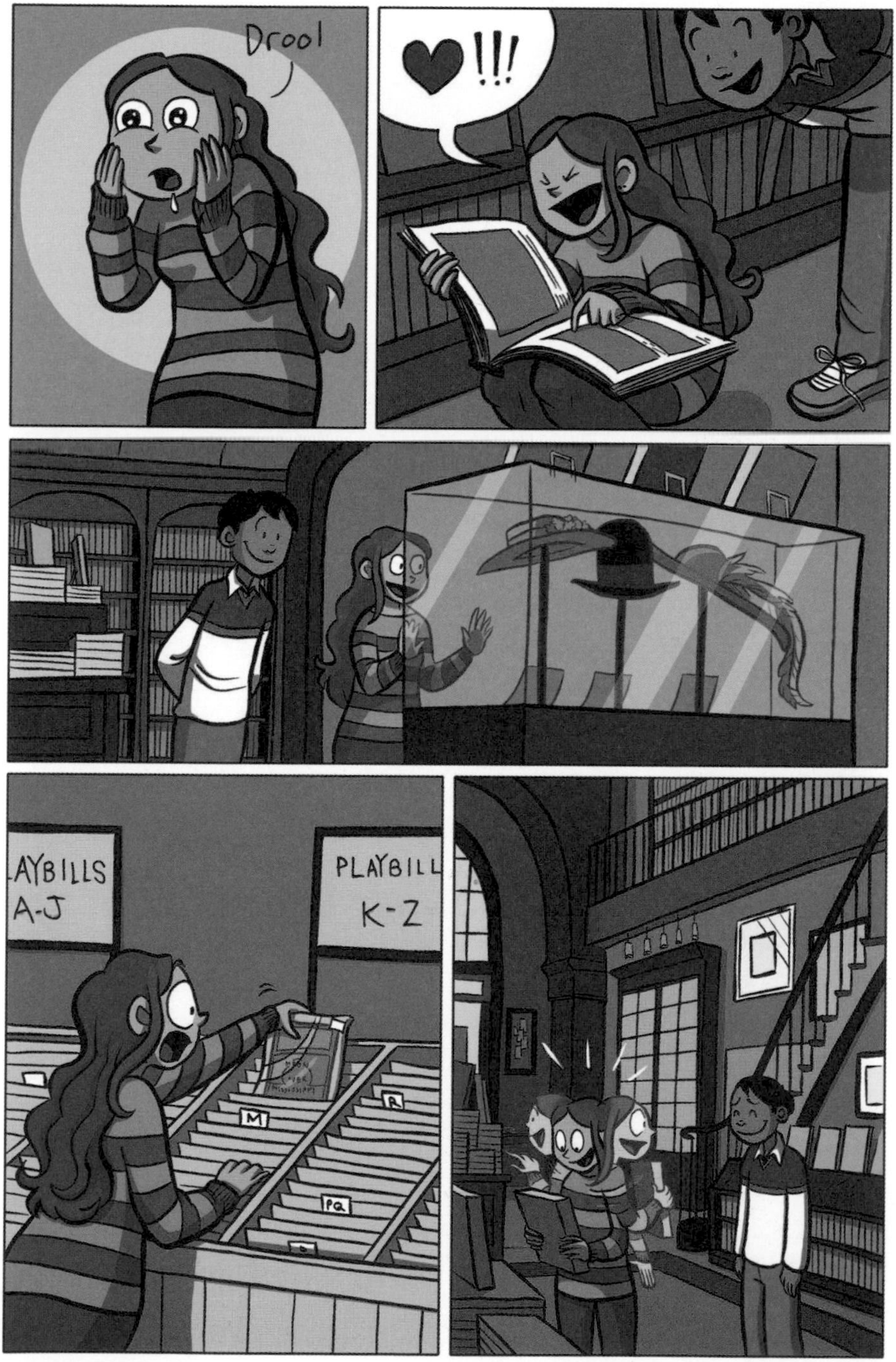
Drool
♥!!!
PLAYBILLS
A-J
PLAYBILL
K-Z
M
R
PQ

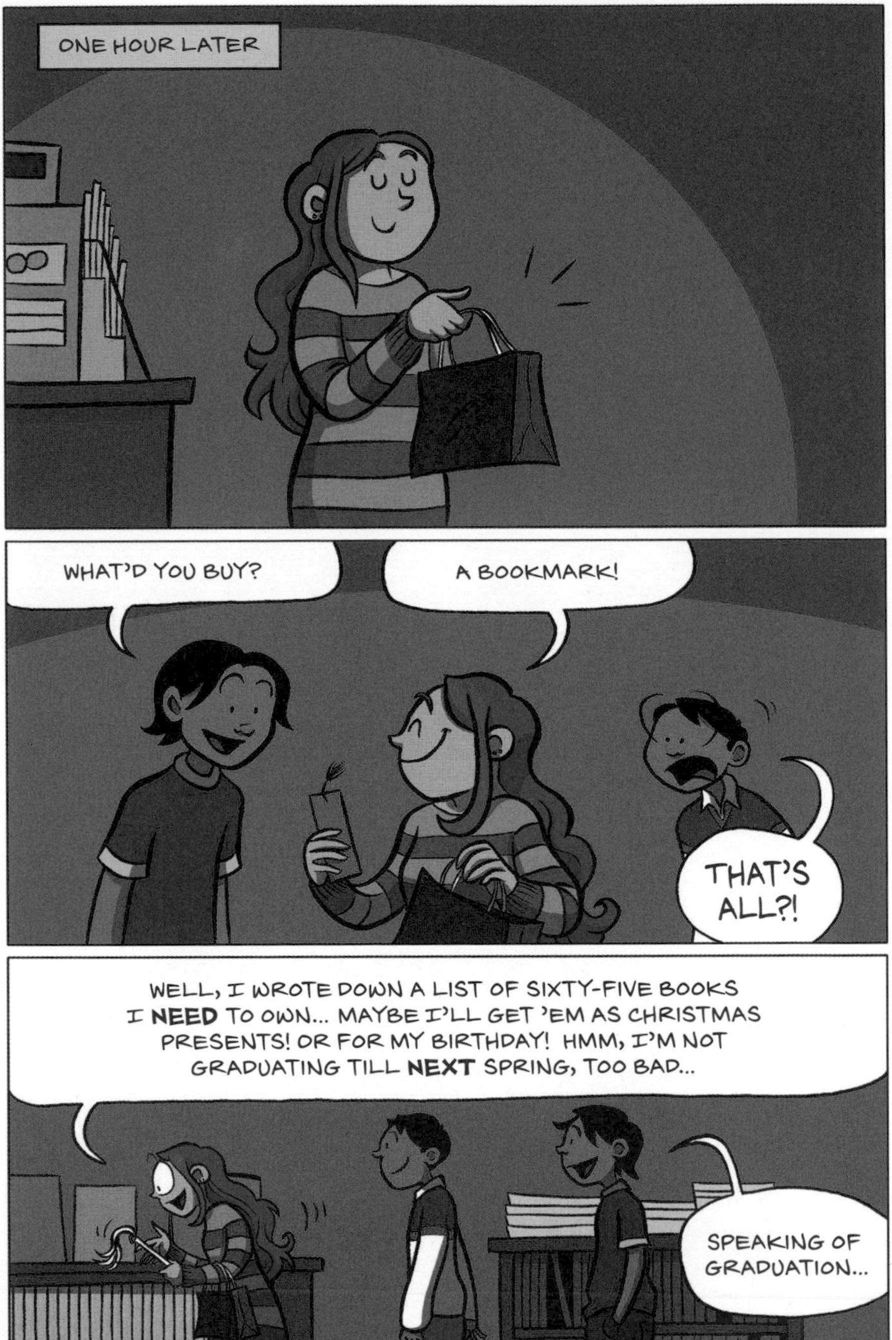
ONE HOUR LATER
WHAT'D YOU BUY?
A BOOKMARK!
THAT'S ALL?!
WELL, I WROTE DOWN A LIST OF SIXTY-FIVE BOOKS I **NEED** TO OWN... MAYBE I'LL GET 'EM AS CHRISTMAS PRESENTS! OR FOR MY BIRTHDAY! HMM, I'M NOT GRADUATING TILL **NEXT** SPRING, TOO BAD...
SPEAKING OF GRADUATION...

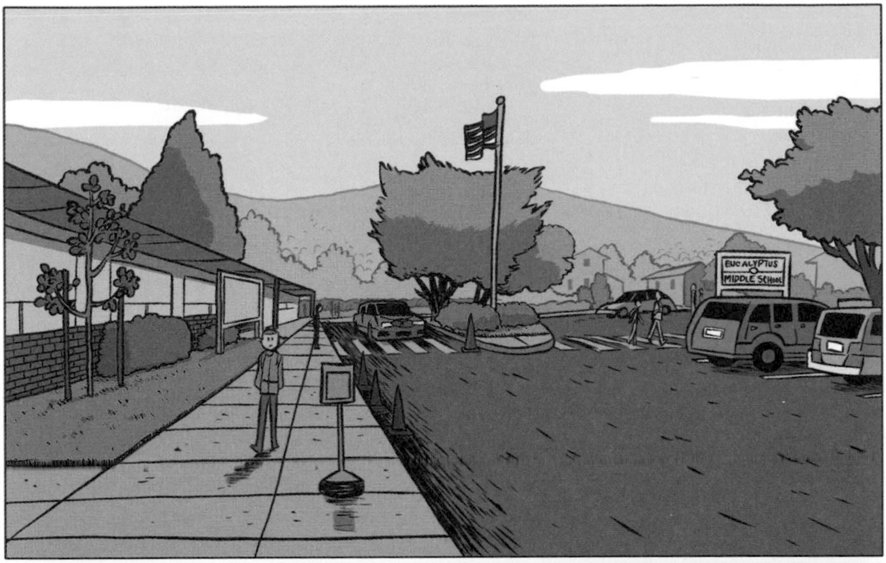
EUCALYPTUS MIDDLE SCHOOL

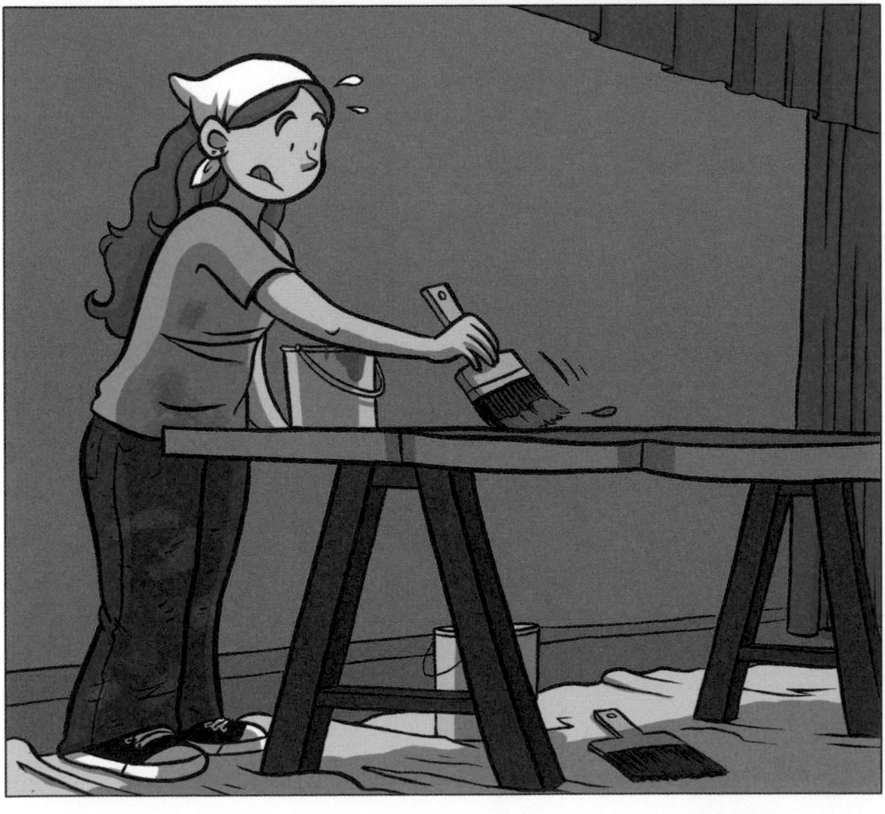

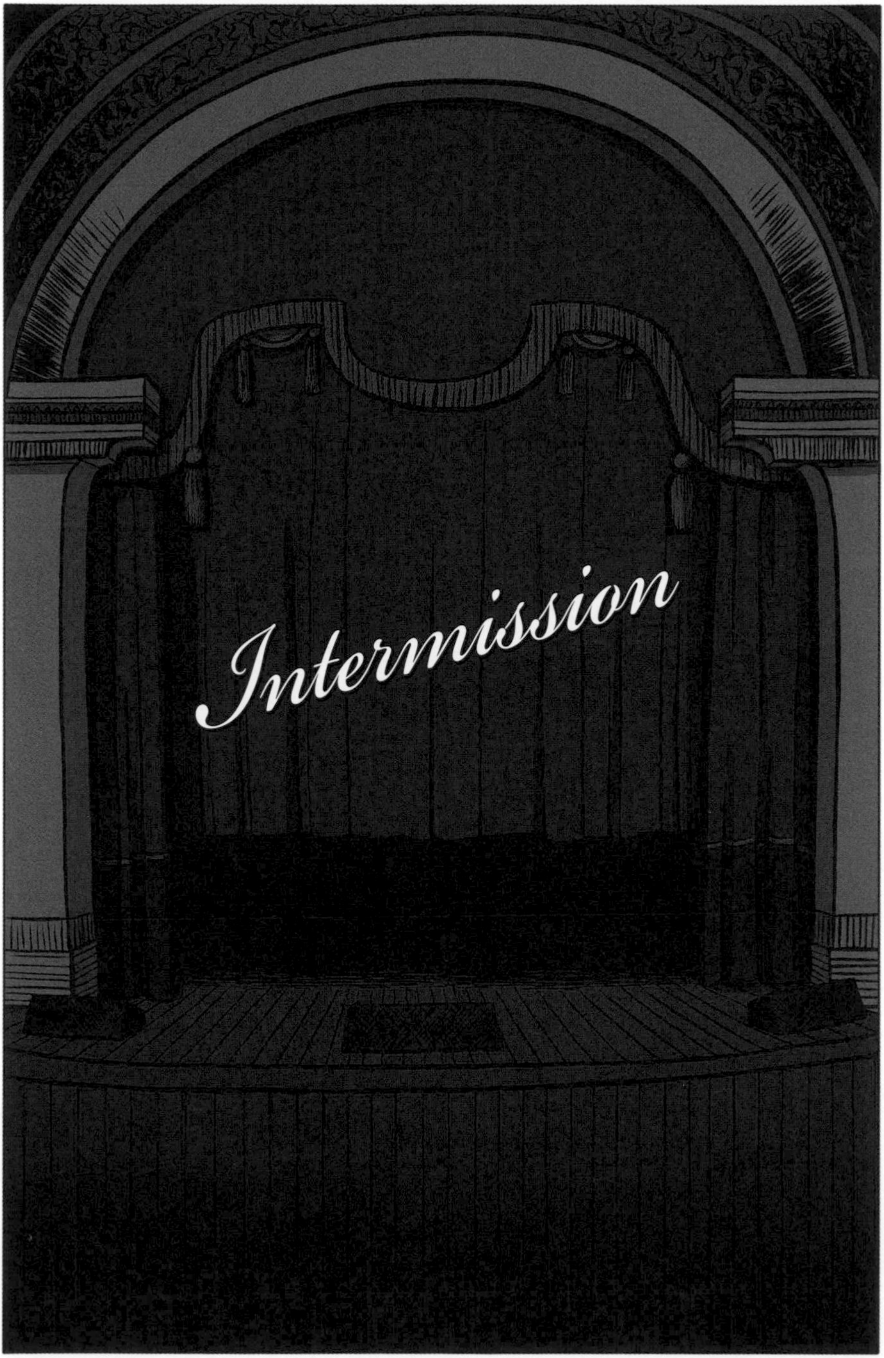
Intermission

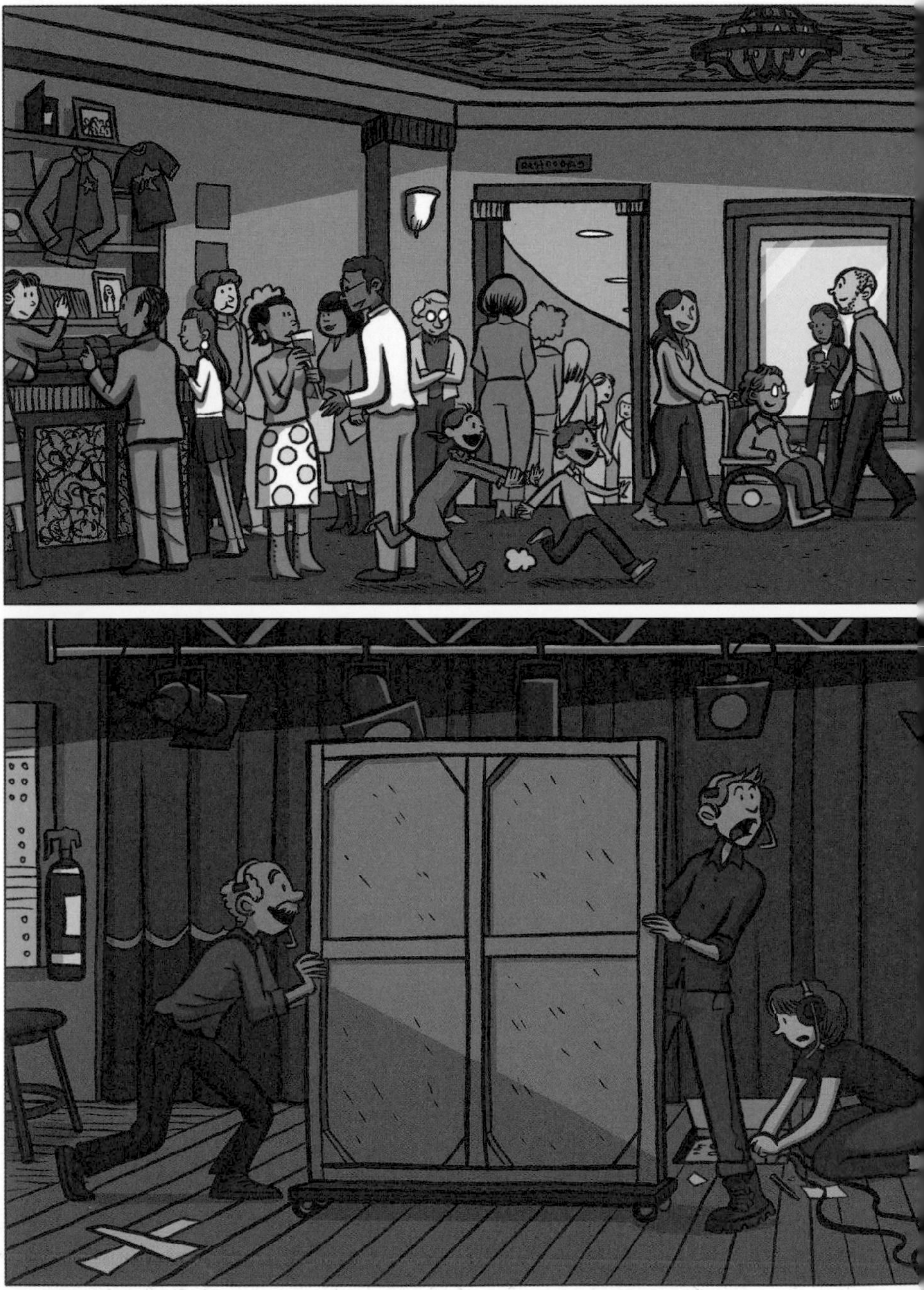

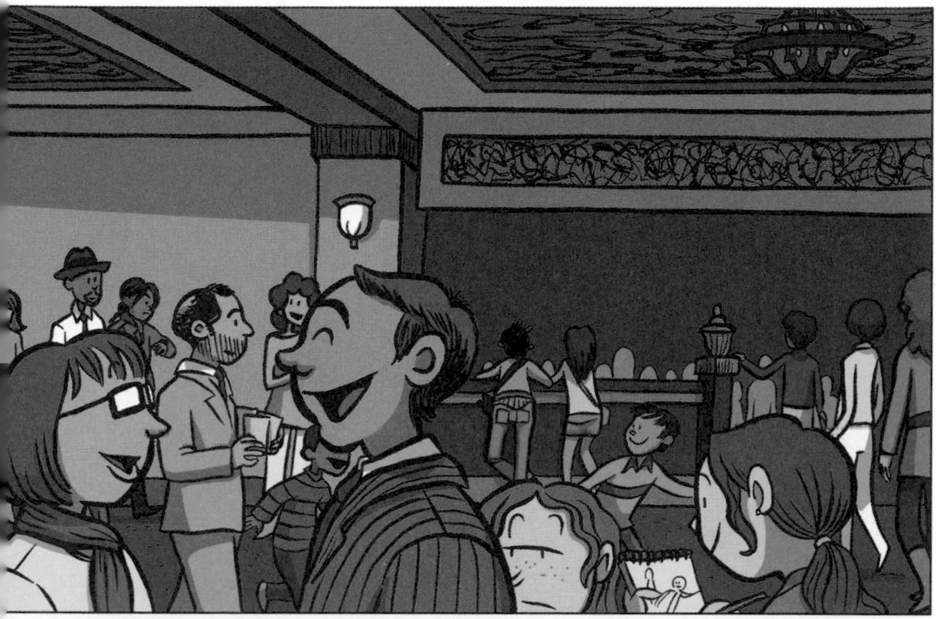

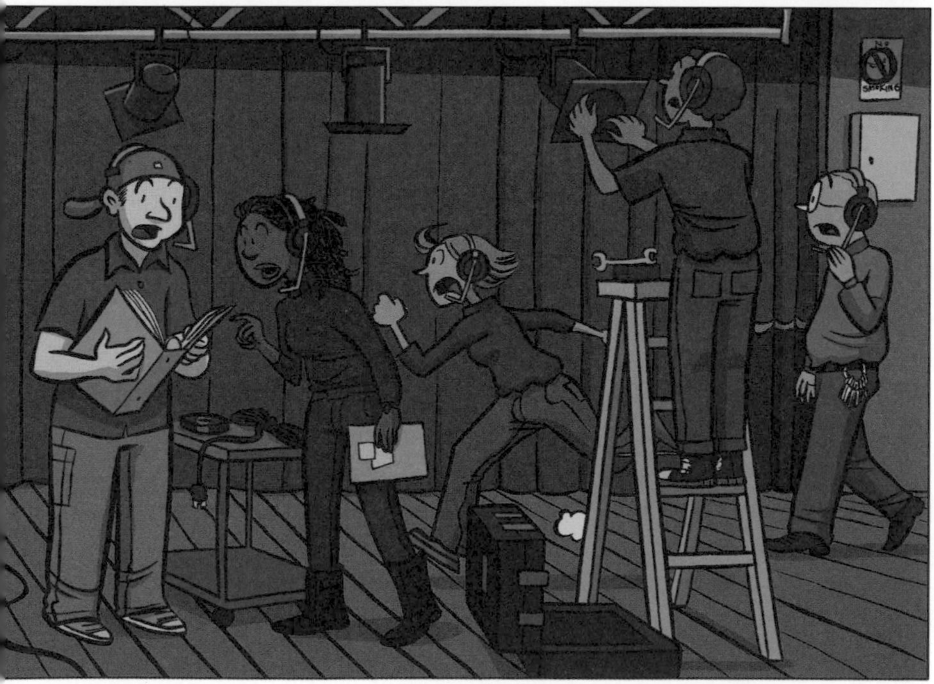

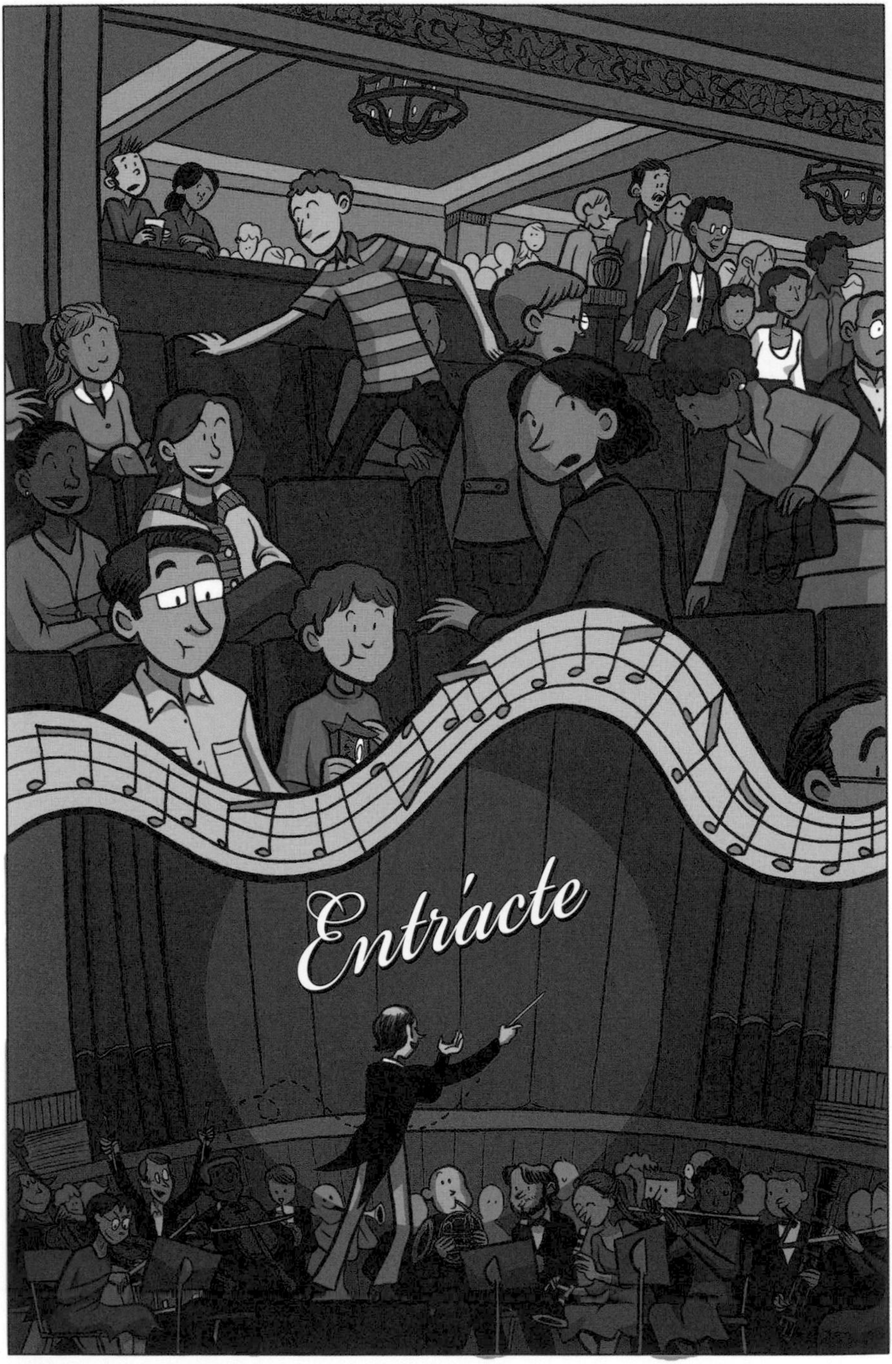
Entrácte

145

146

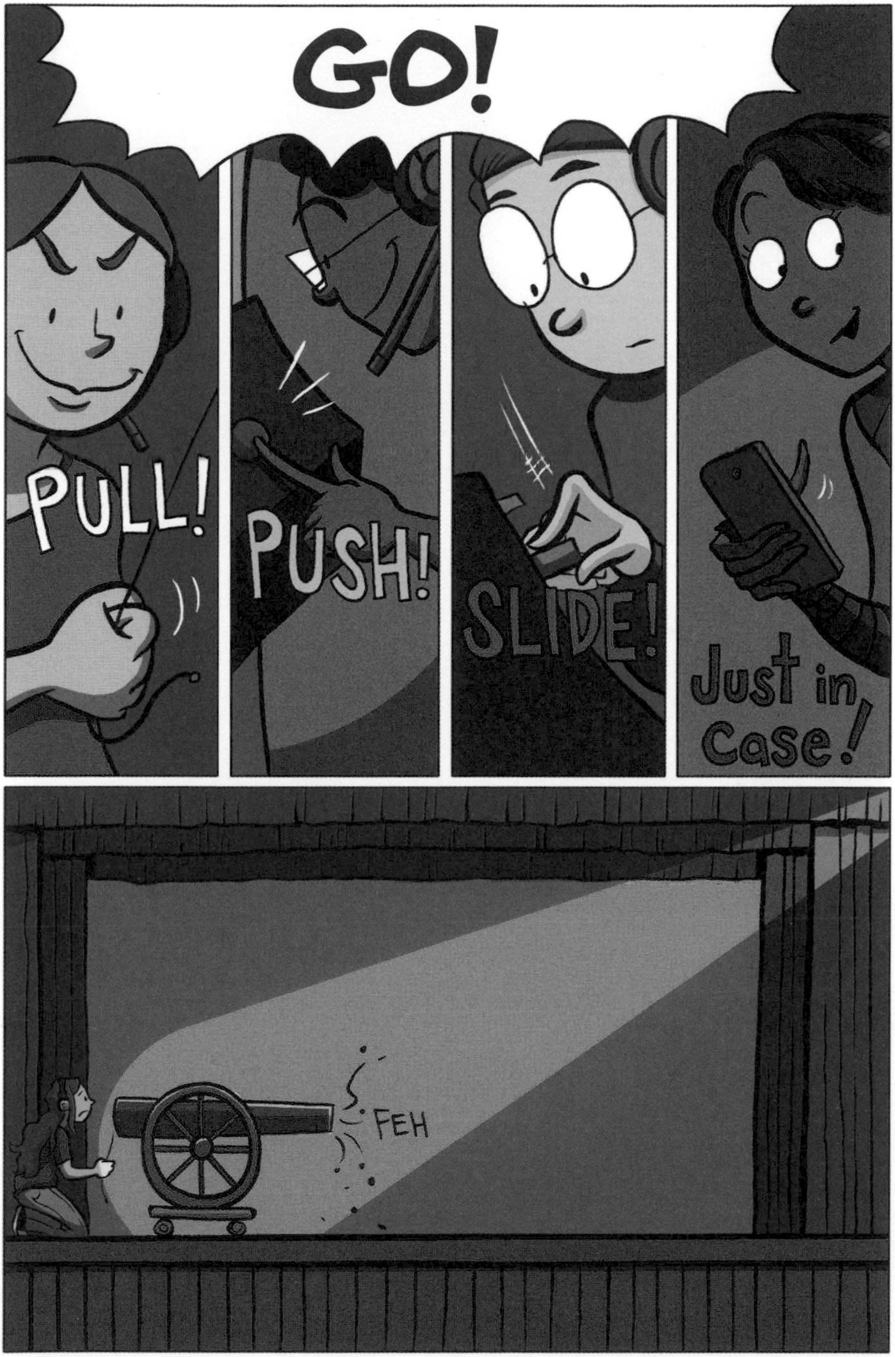
GO!
PULL!
PUSH!
SLIDE!
Just in Case!
FEH

154

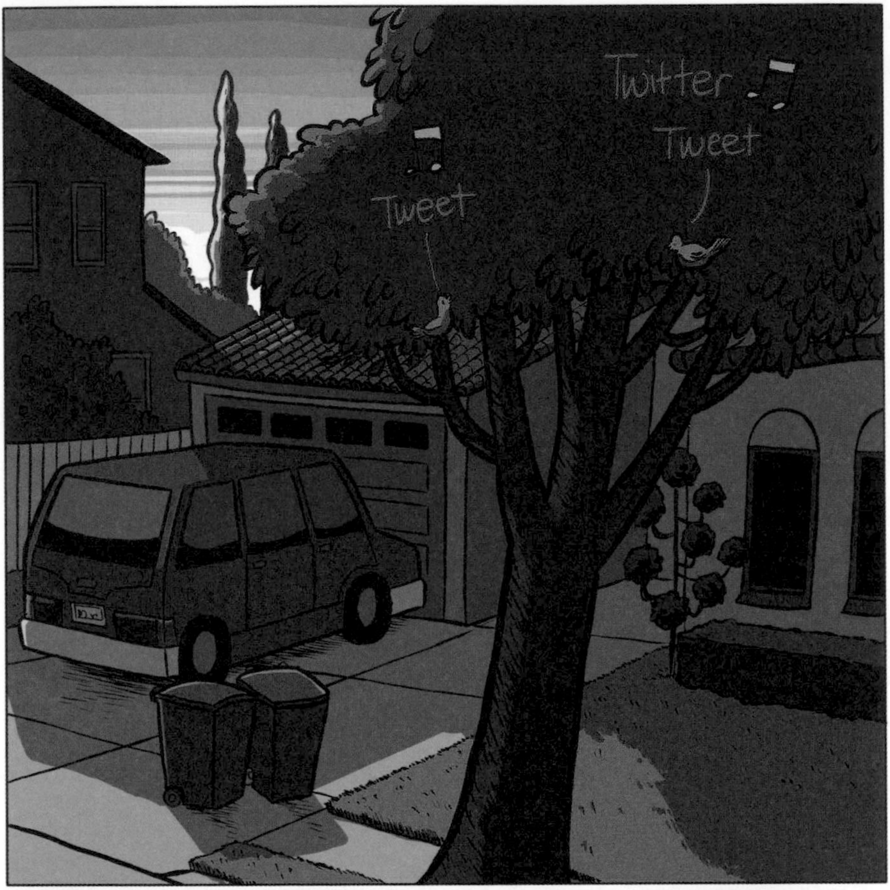
Twitter
Tweet
Tweet

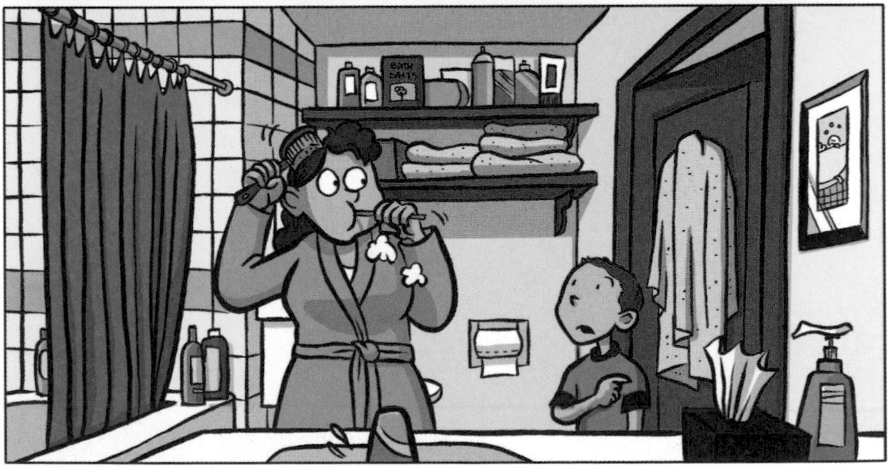

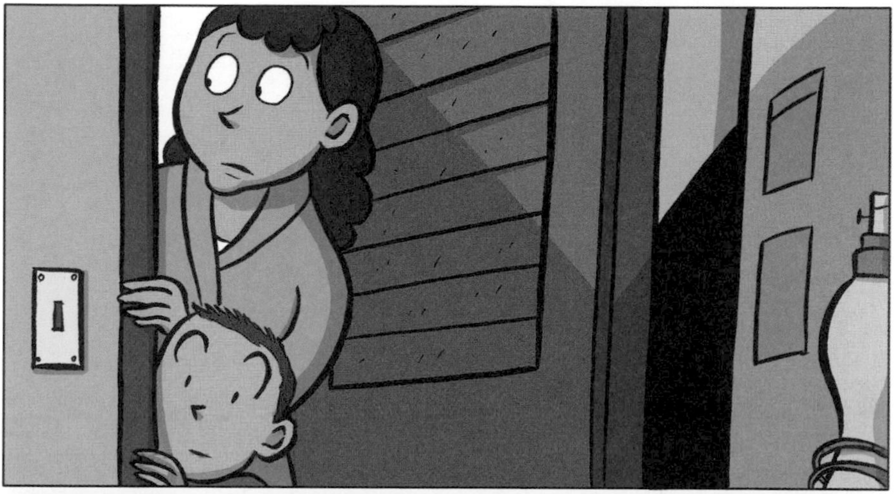

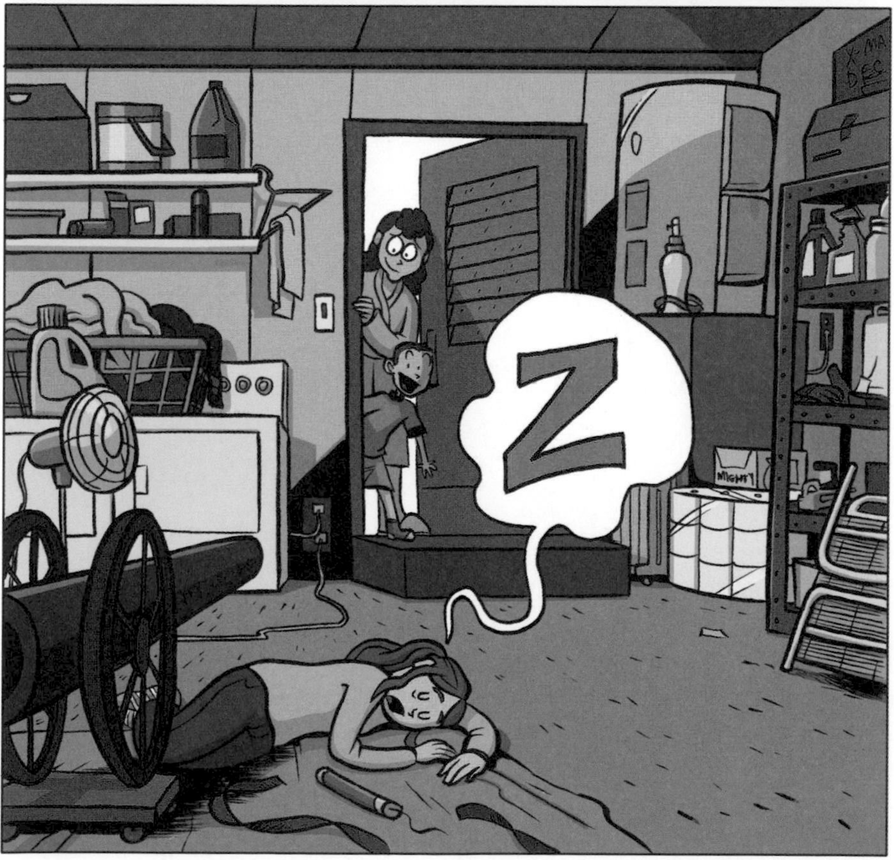
Z
MIGHTY

THREE DAYS (AND THREE LONG NIGHTS) LATER

≀AHEM≀... CAN I HAVE YOUR ATTENTION PLEASE, STUDENTS?

EUCALYPTUS MIDDLE SCHOOL'S STAGE CREW AND DRAMA CLUB ARE PROUD TO PRESENT YOU WITH A LUNCHTIME PREVIEW OF *MOON OVER MISSISSIPPI*...

...OPENING THURSDAY NIGHT IN THE SCHOOL AUDITORIUM! THREE NIGHTS ONLY! TICKETS ARE ON SALE NOW!

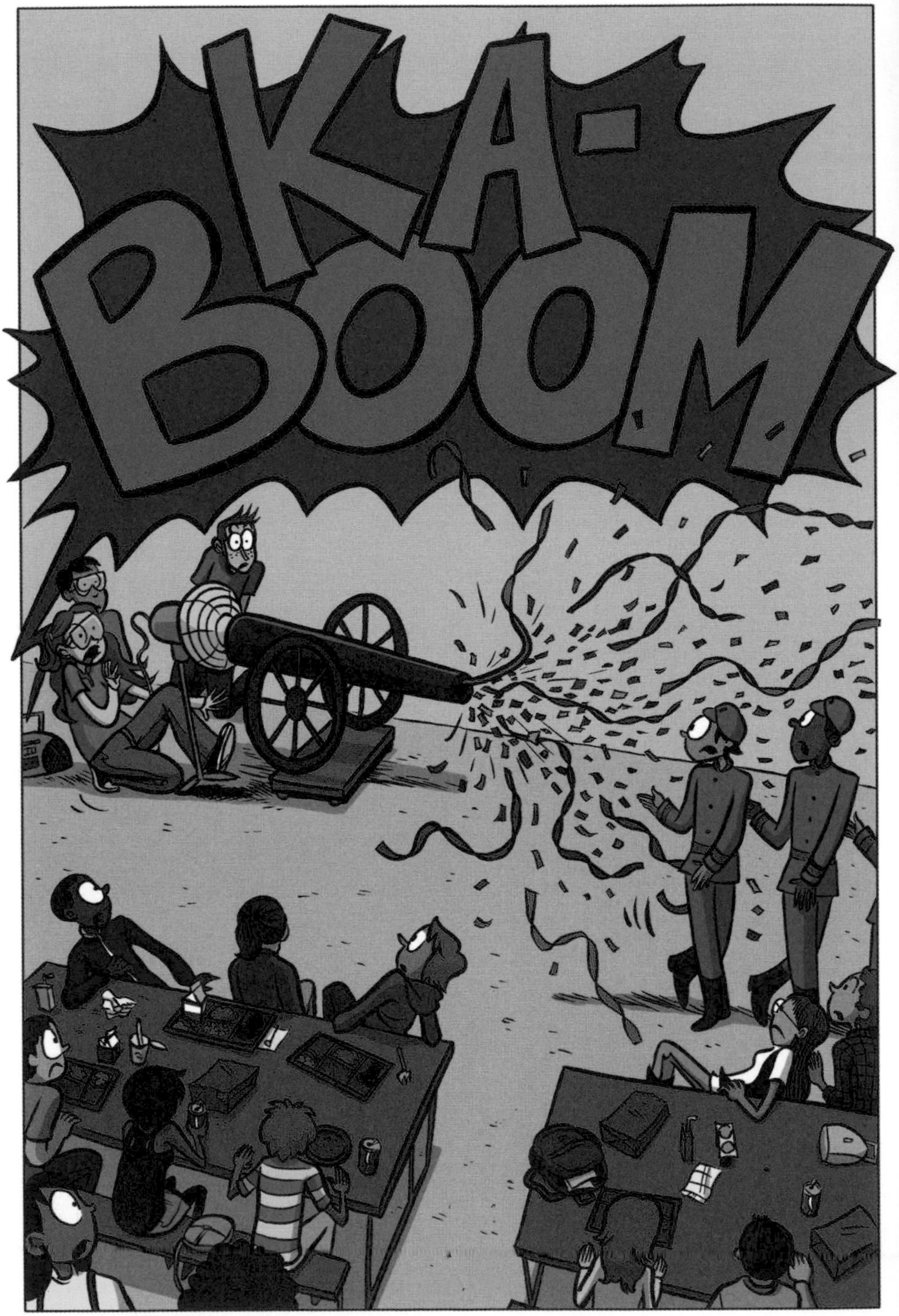
KA-BOOM

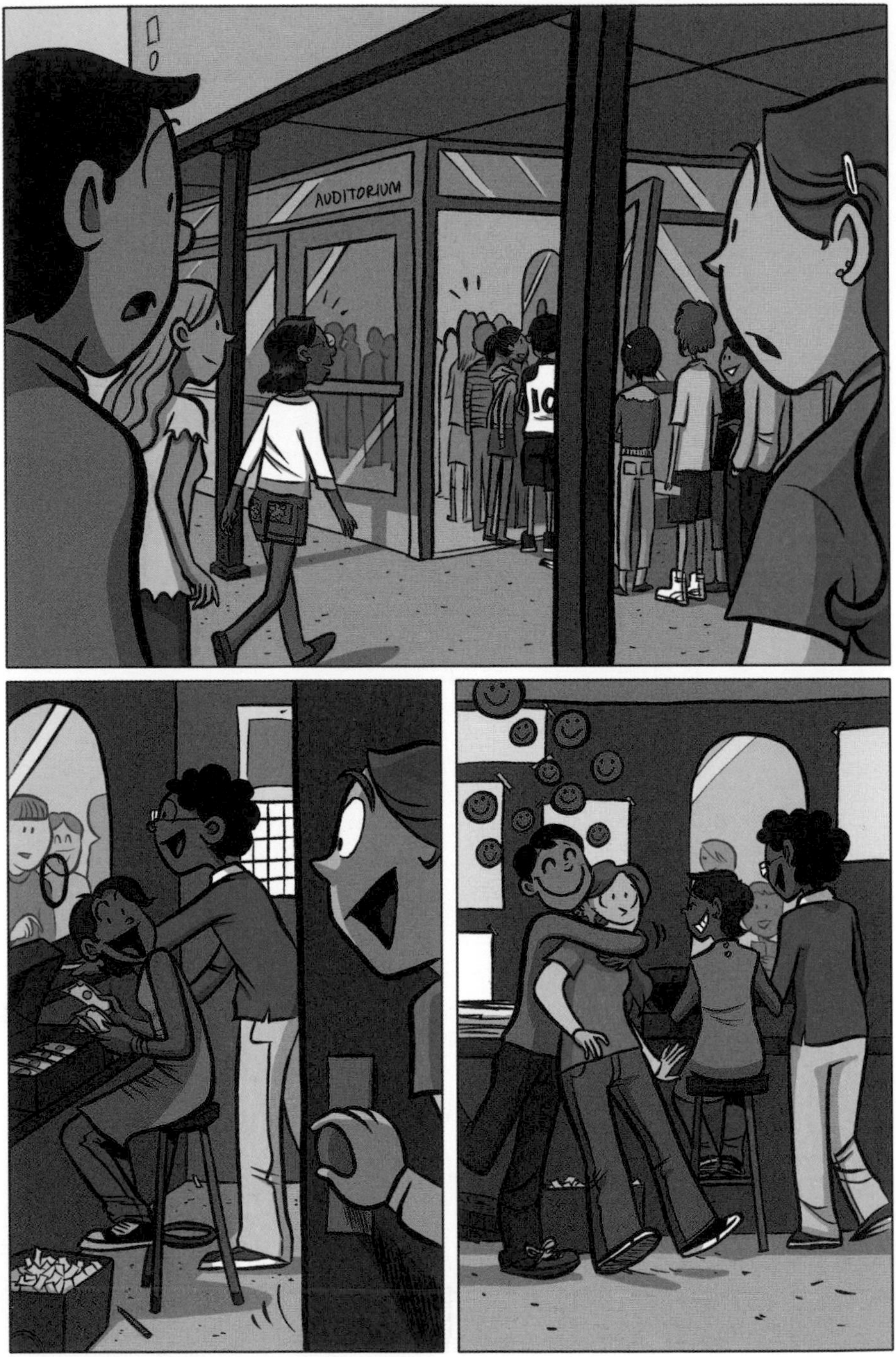
AUDITORIUM

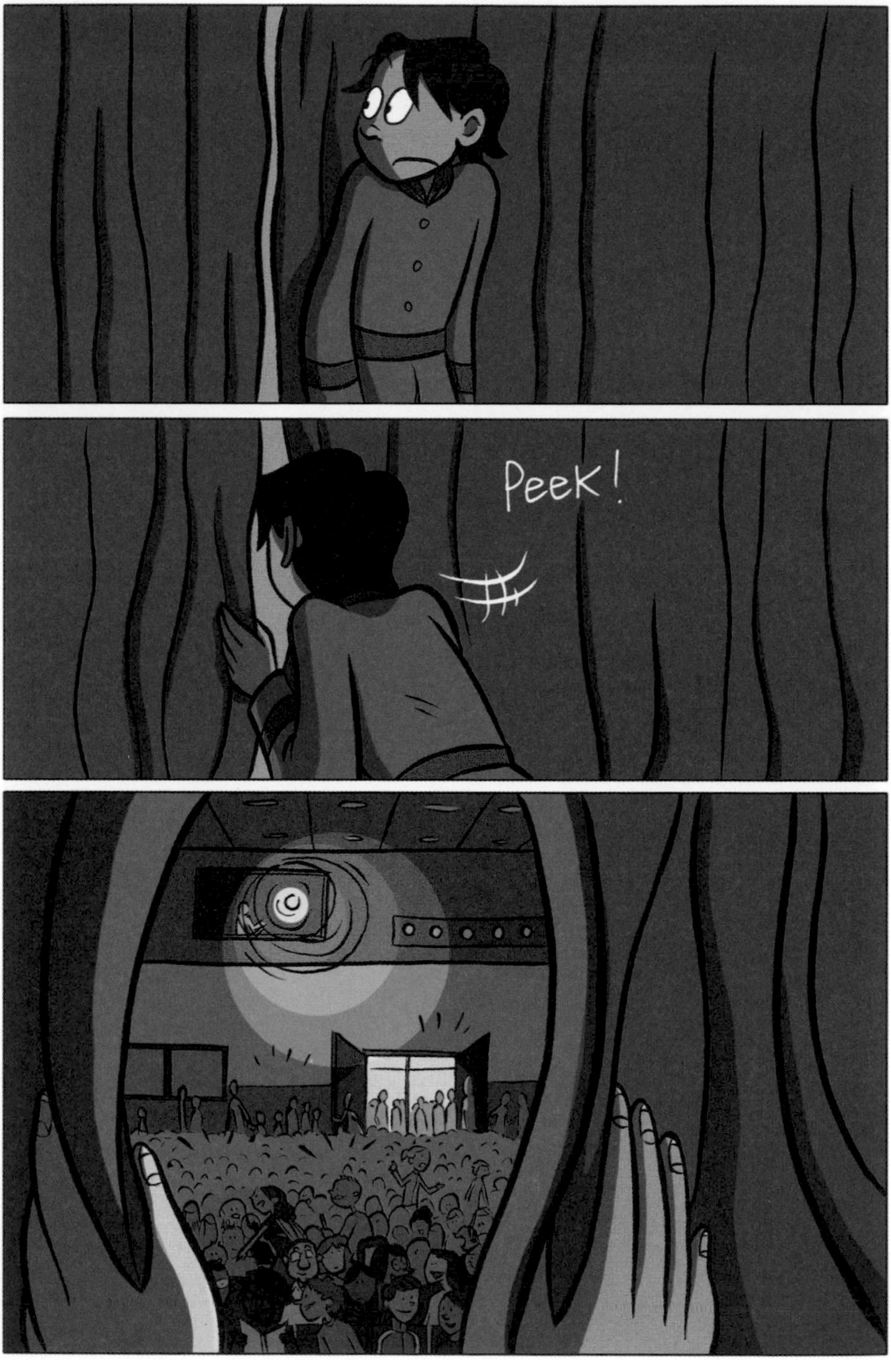
Peek!

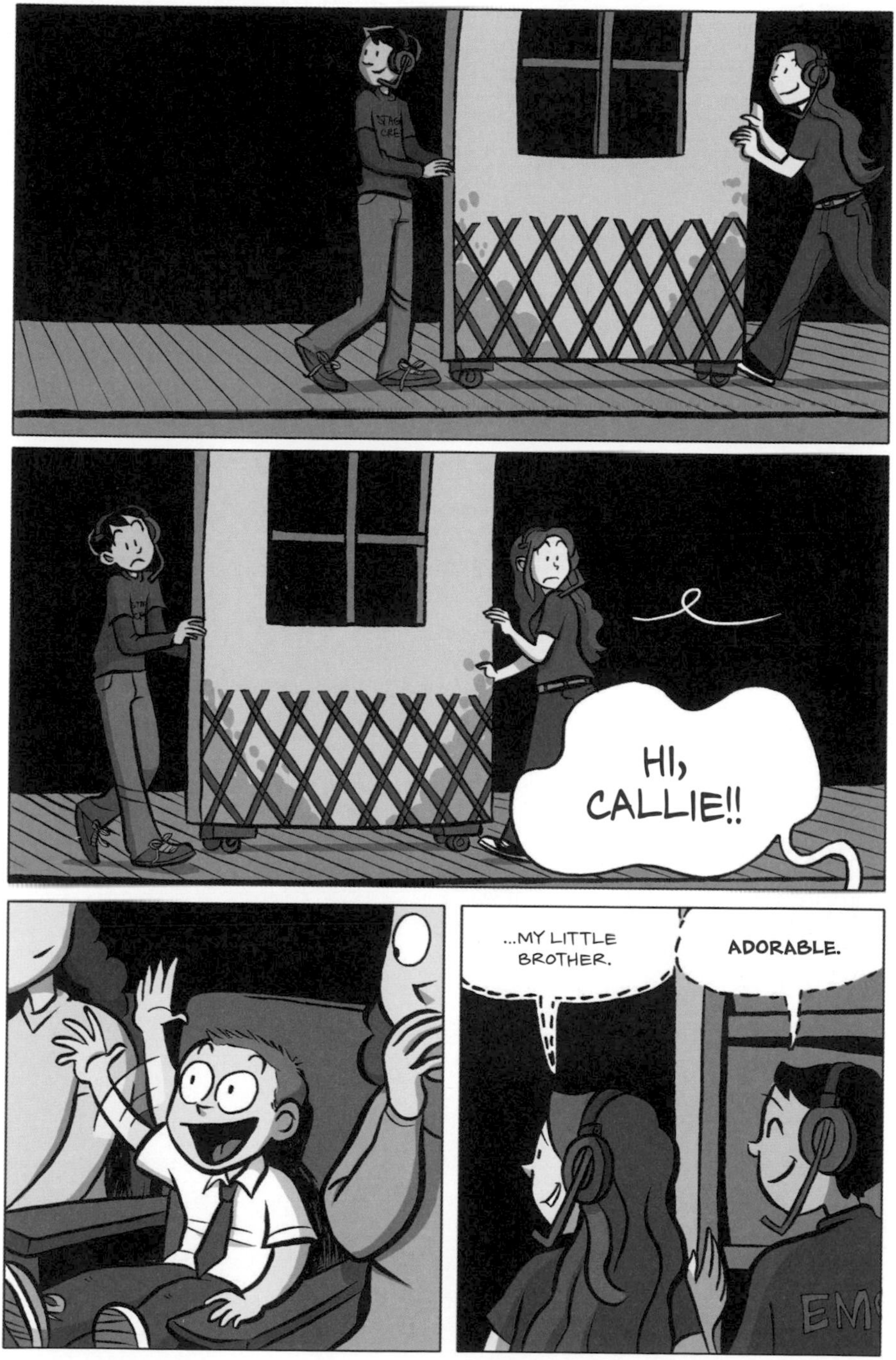
HI, CALLIE!!
...MY LITTLE BROTHER.
ADORABLE.

168

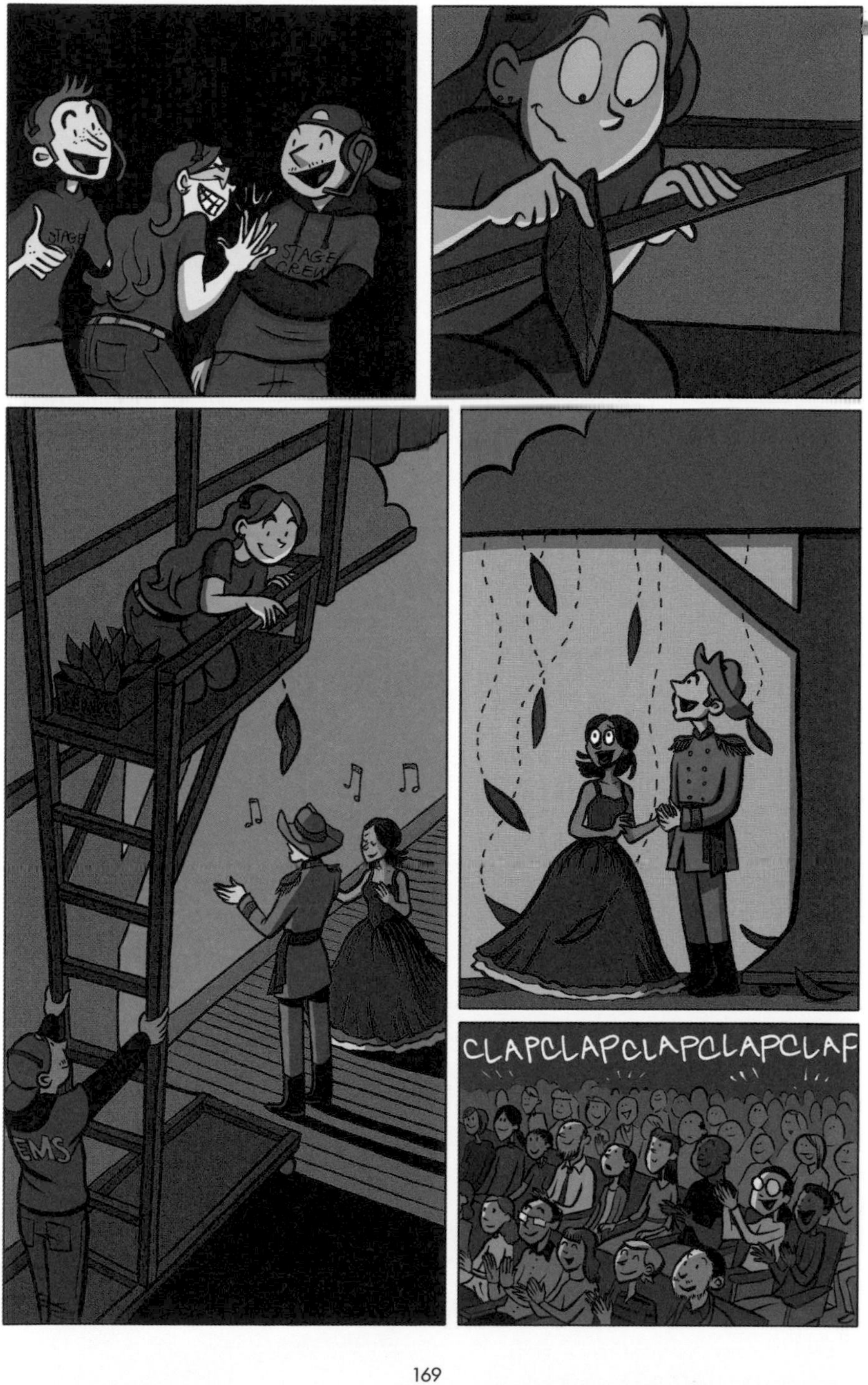
STAGE CREW
STAGE CREW
EMS
CLAPCLAPCLAPCLAPCLAP

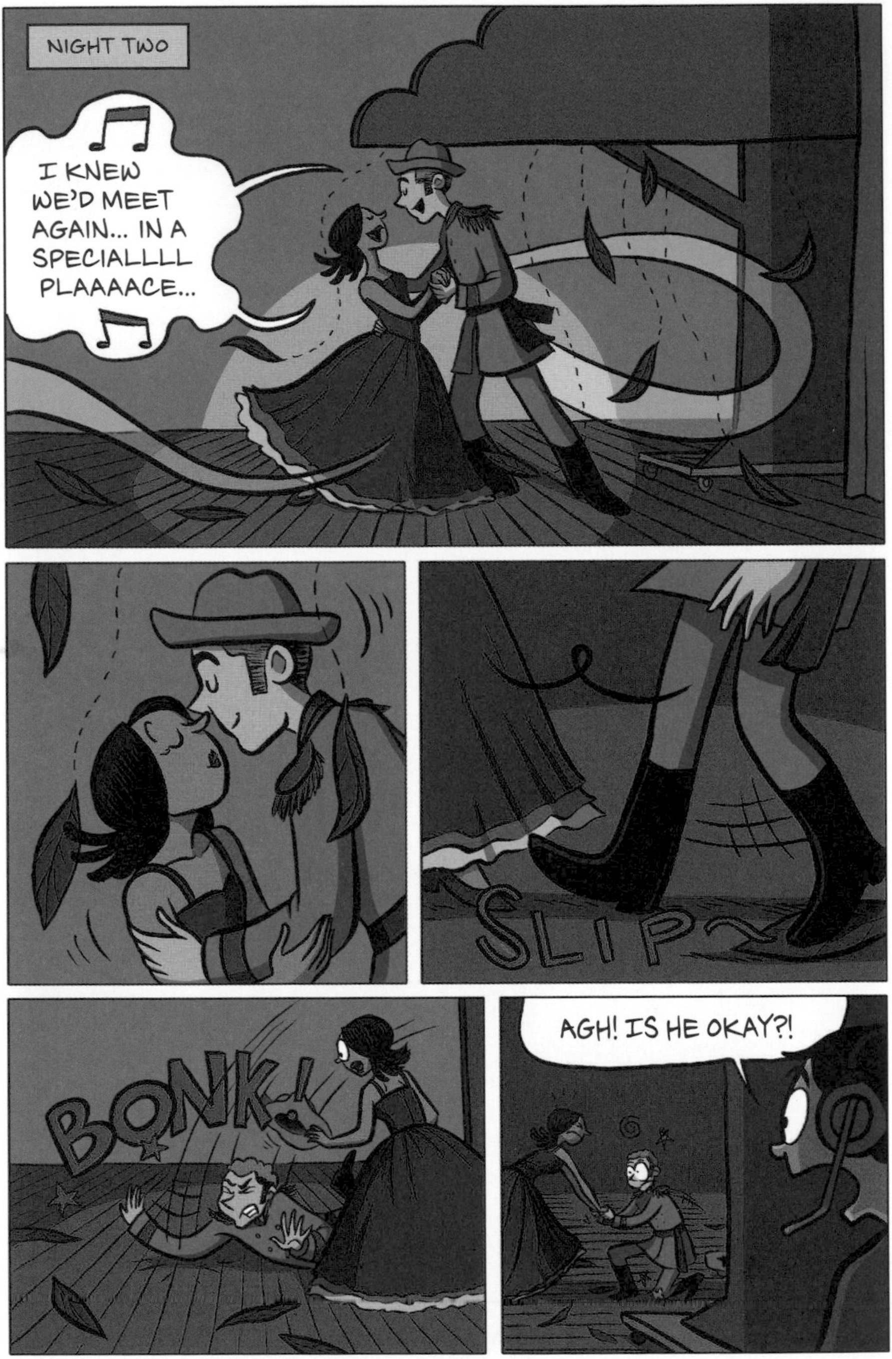
NIGHT TWO
I KNEW WE'D MEET AGAIN... IN A SPECIALLLL PLAAAACE...
SLIP~
BONK!
AGH! IS HE OKAY?!

173

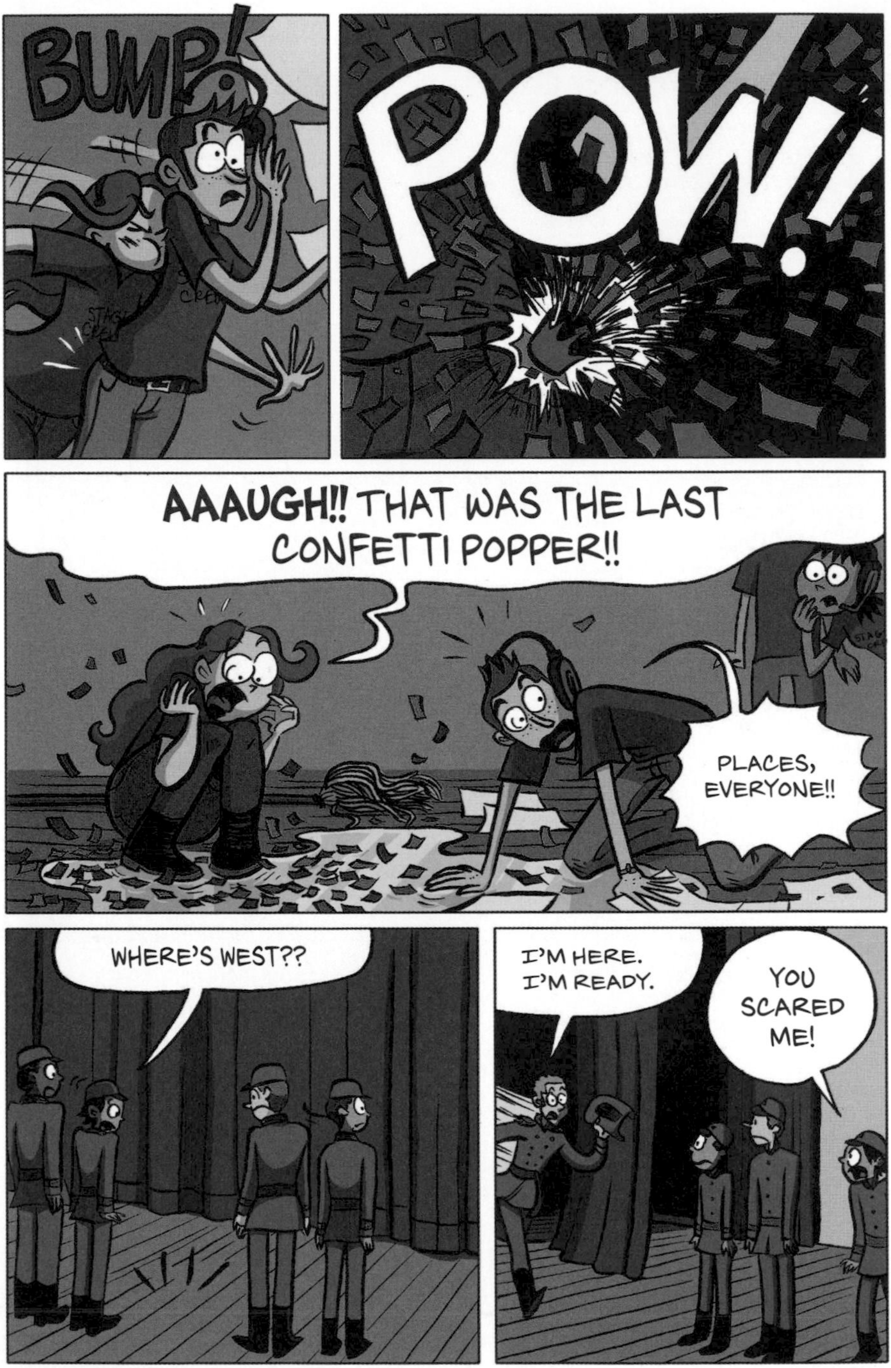
BUMP!
POW!!
AAAUGH!! THAT WAS THE LAST CONFETTI POPPER!!
PLACES, EVERYONE!!
WHERE'S WEST??
I'M HERE. I'M READY.
YOU SCARED ME!

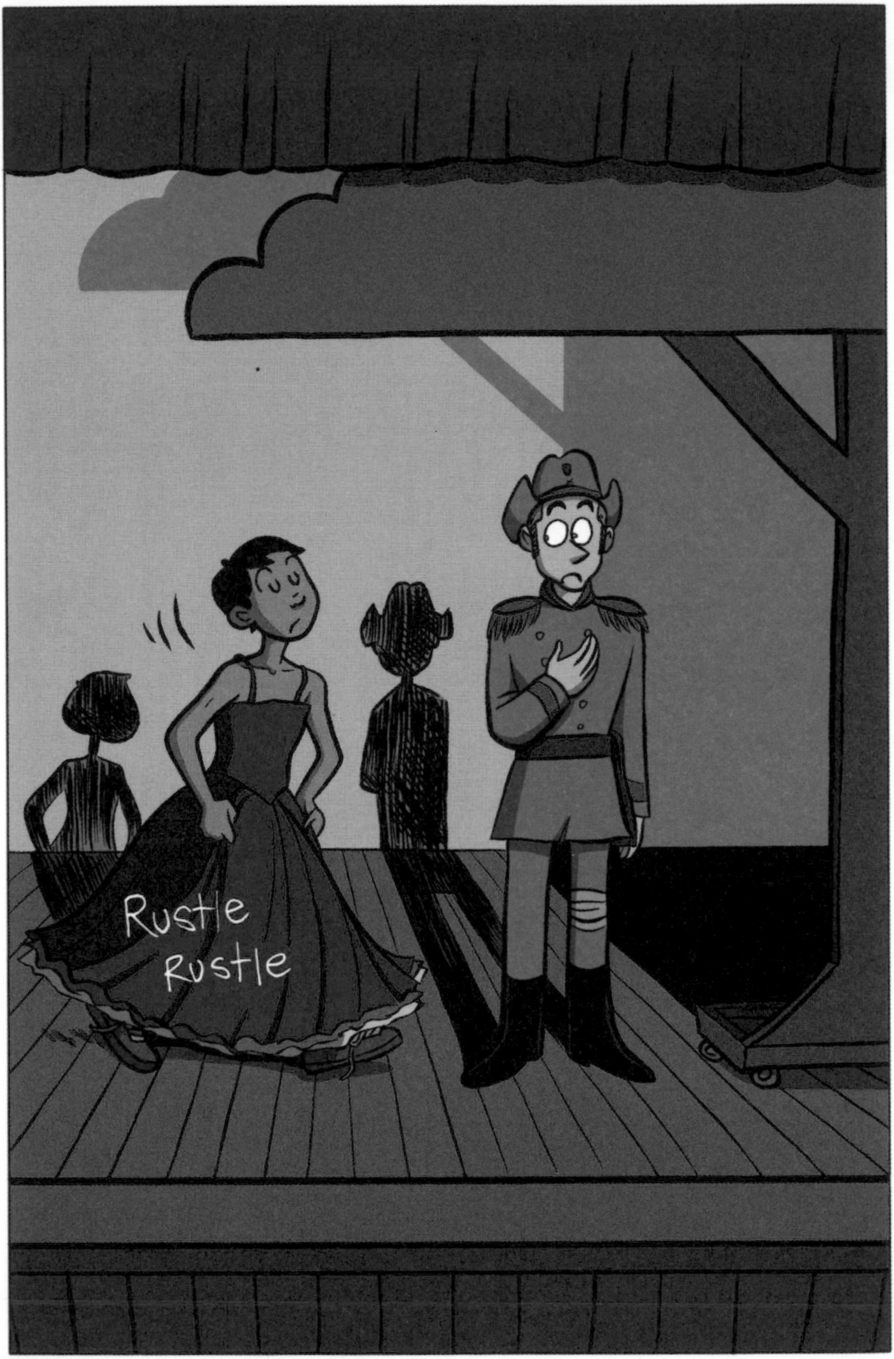
Rustle
Rustle

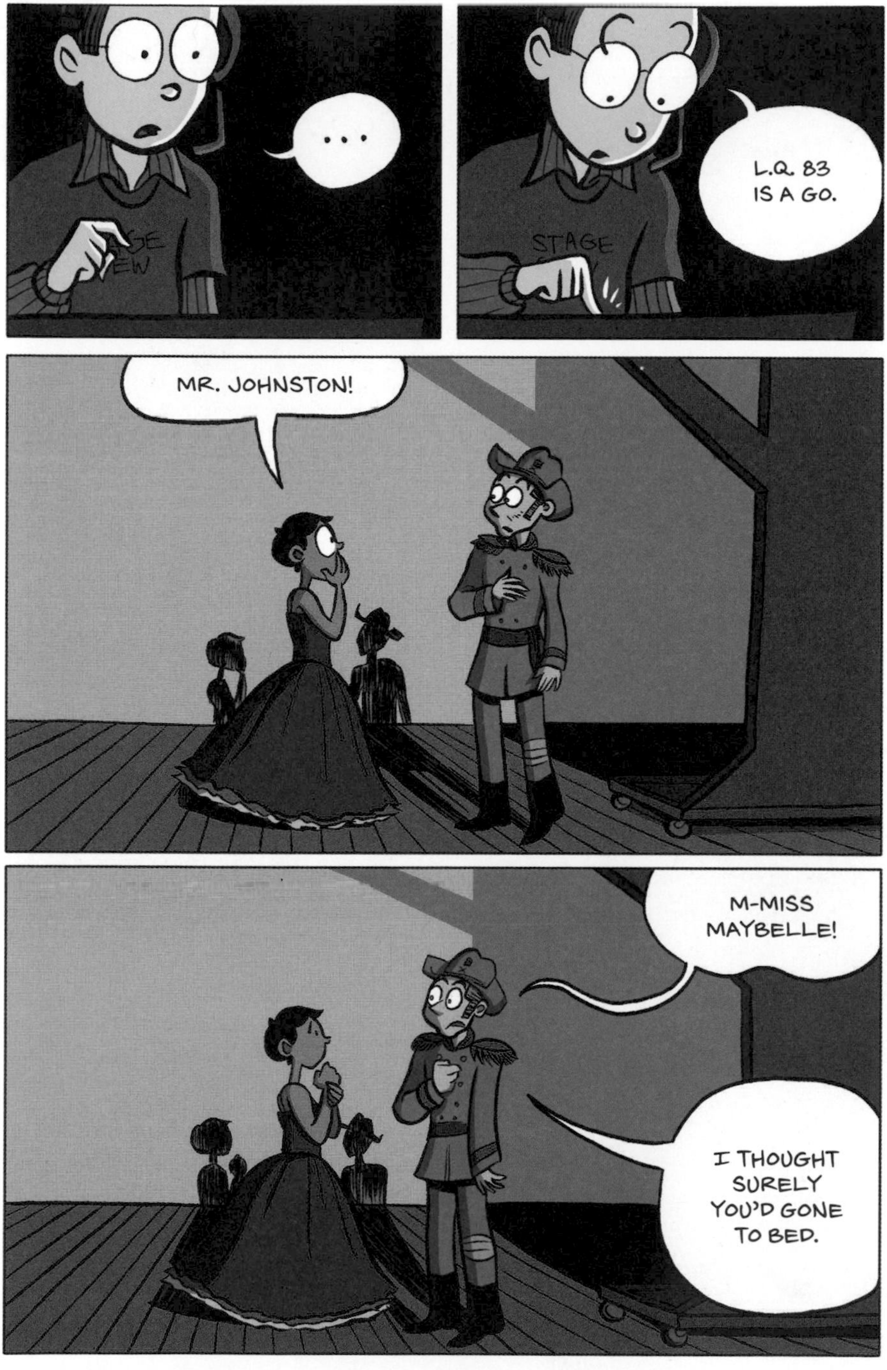
...
L.Q. 83
IS A GO.
STAGE
MR. JOHNSTON!
M-MISS MAYBELLE!
I THOUGHT SURELY YOU'D GONE TO BED.

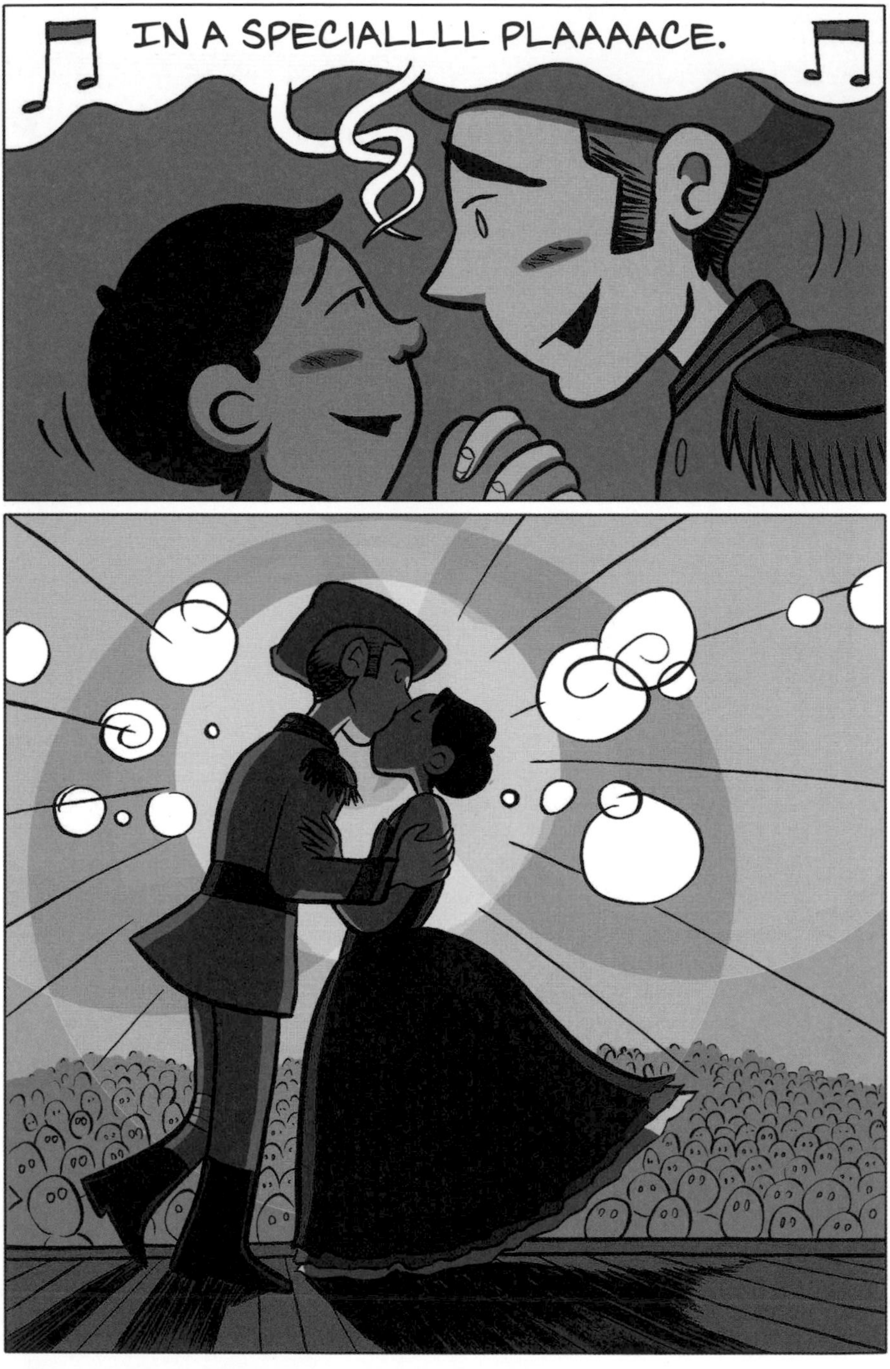
IN A SPECIALLLL PLAAAACE.

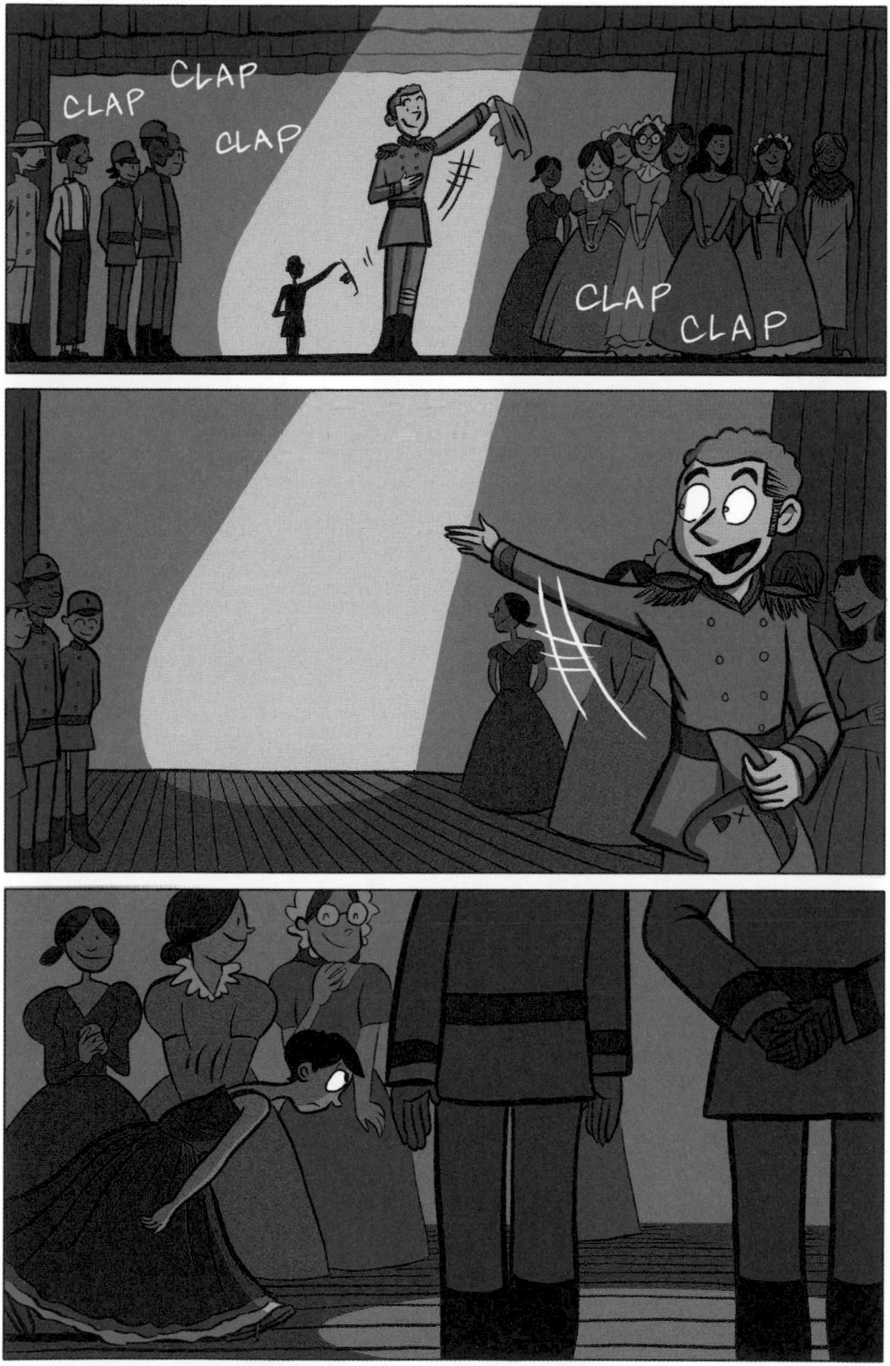
CLAP
CLAP
CLAP
CLAP
CLAP

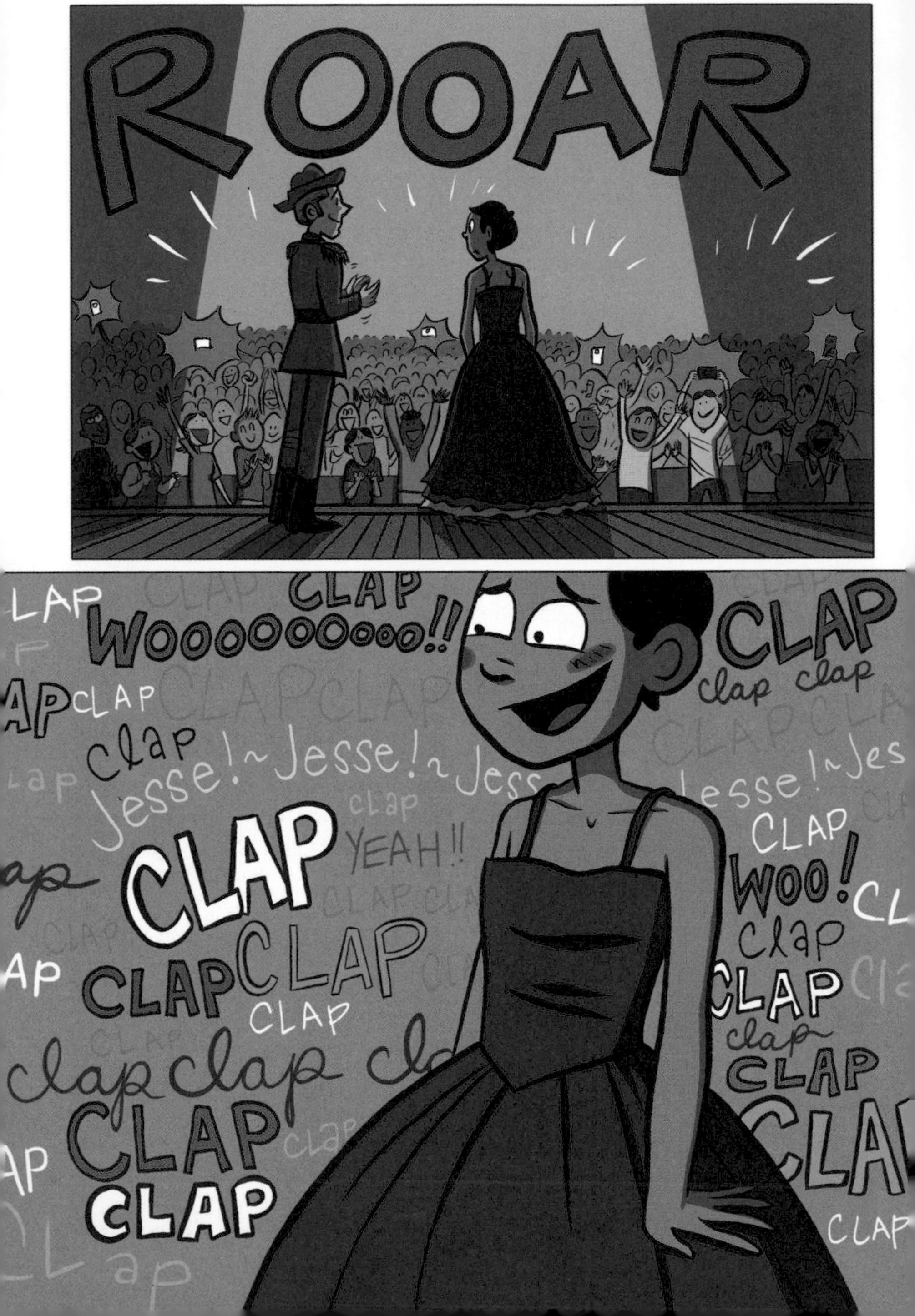
ROOAR
CLAP
WOOOOOOOOooo!!
CLAP
clap clap
CLAP
clap
Jesse!~Jesse!~
YEAH!!
CLAP
CLAP
WOO!
clap
CLAP
CLAP
CLAP
CLAP
clap clap
clap
CLAP
CLAP
CLAP
CLAP

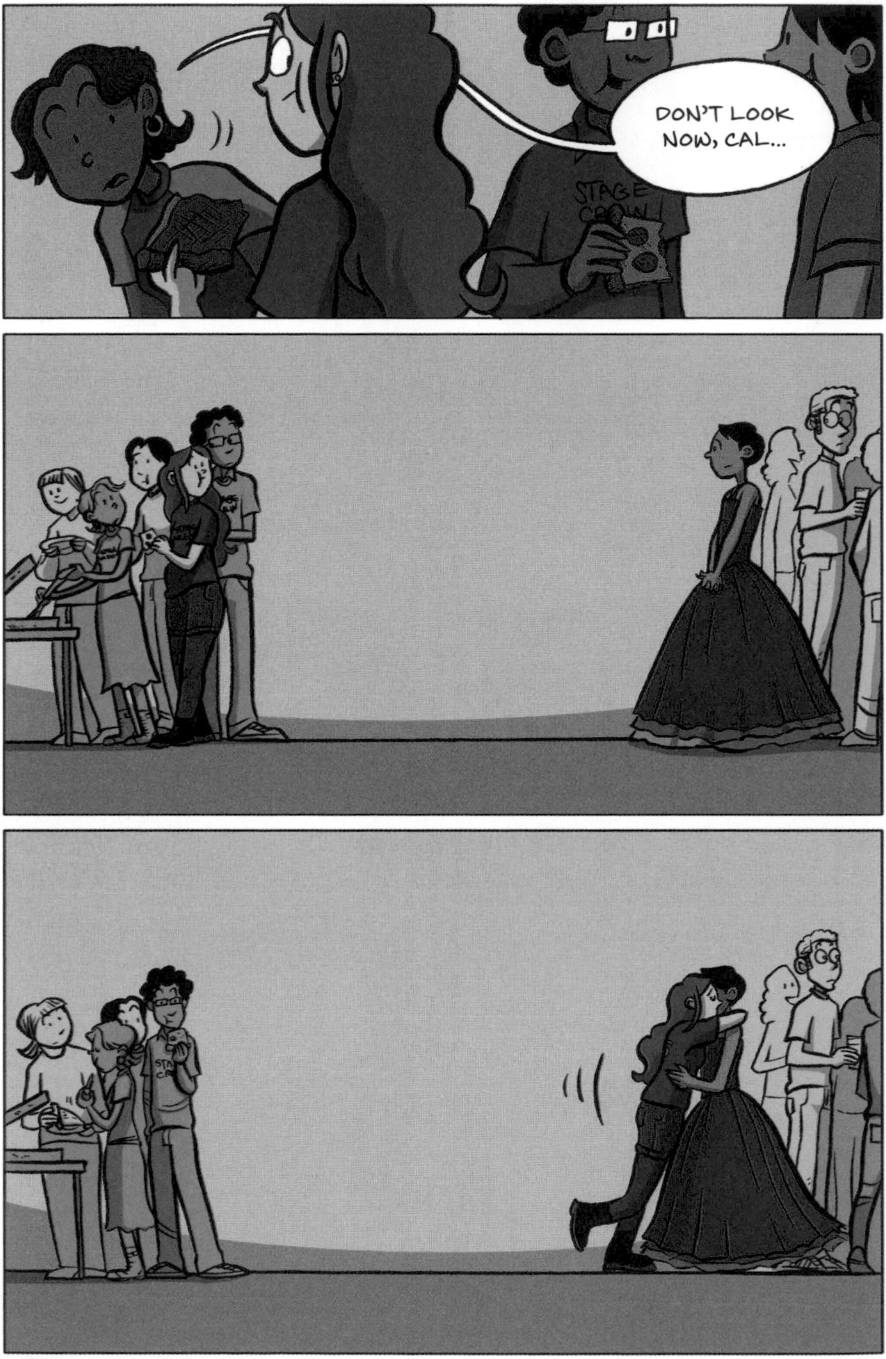
DON'T LOOK NOW, CAL...

197

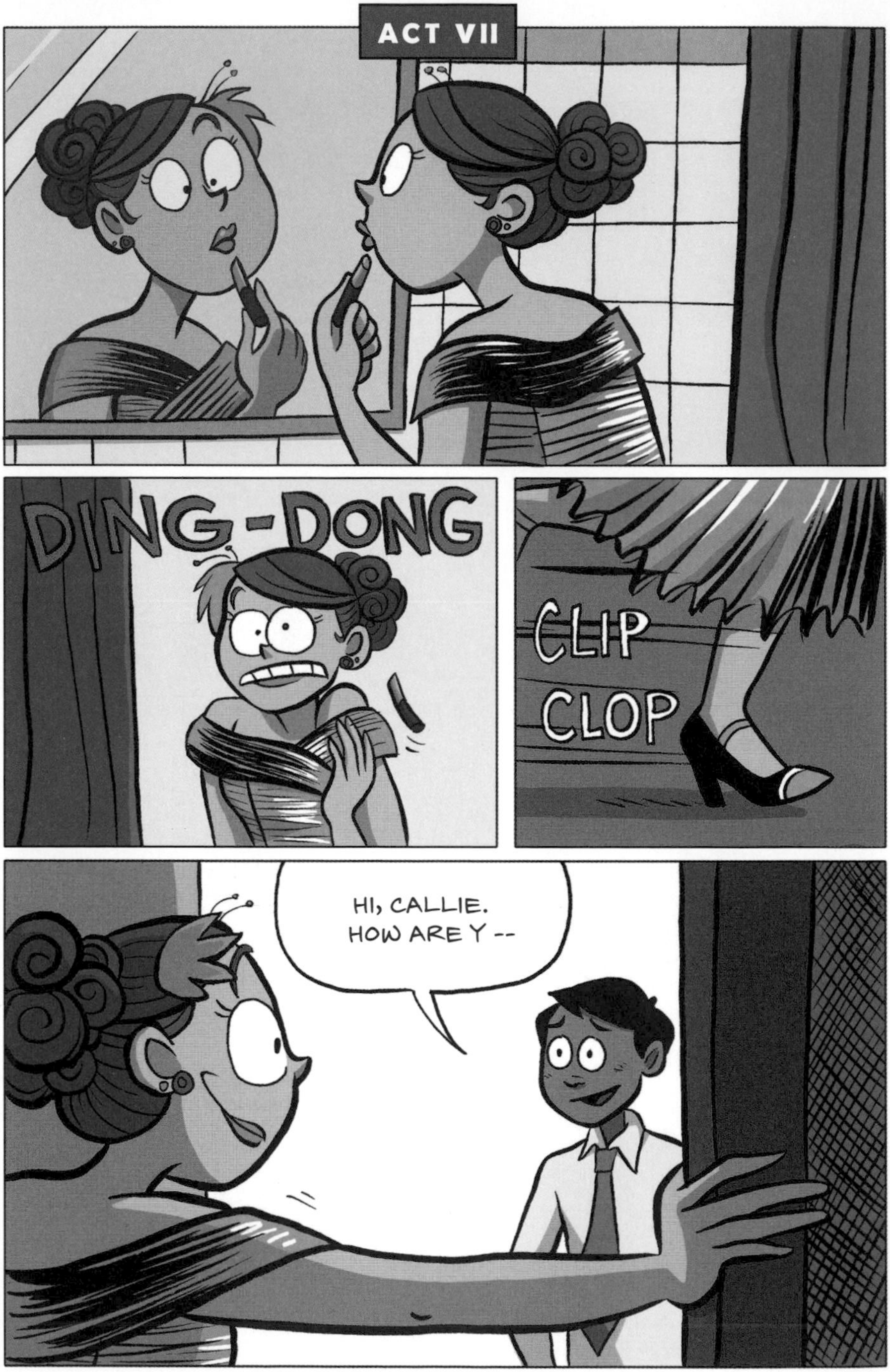
ACT VII
DING-DONG
CLIP
CLOP
HI, CALLIE.
HOW ARE Y --

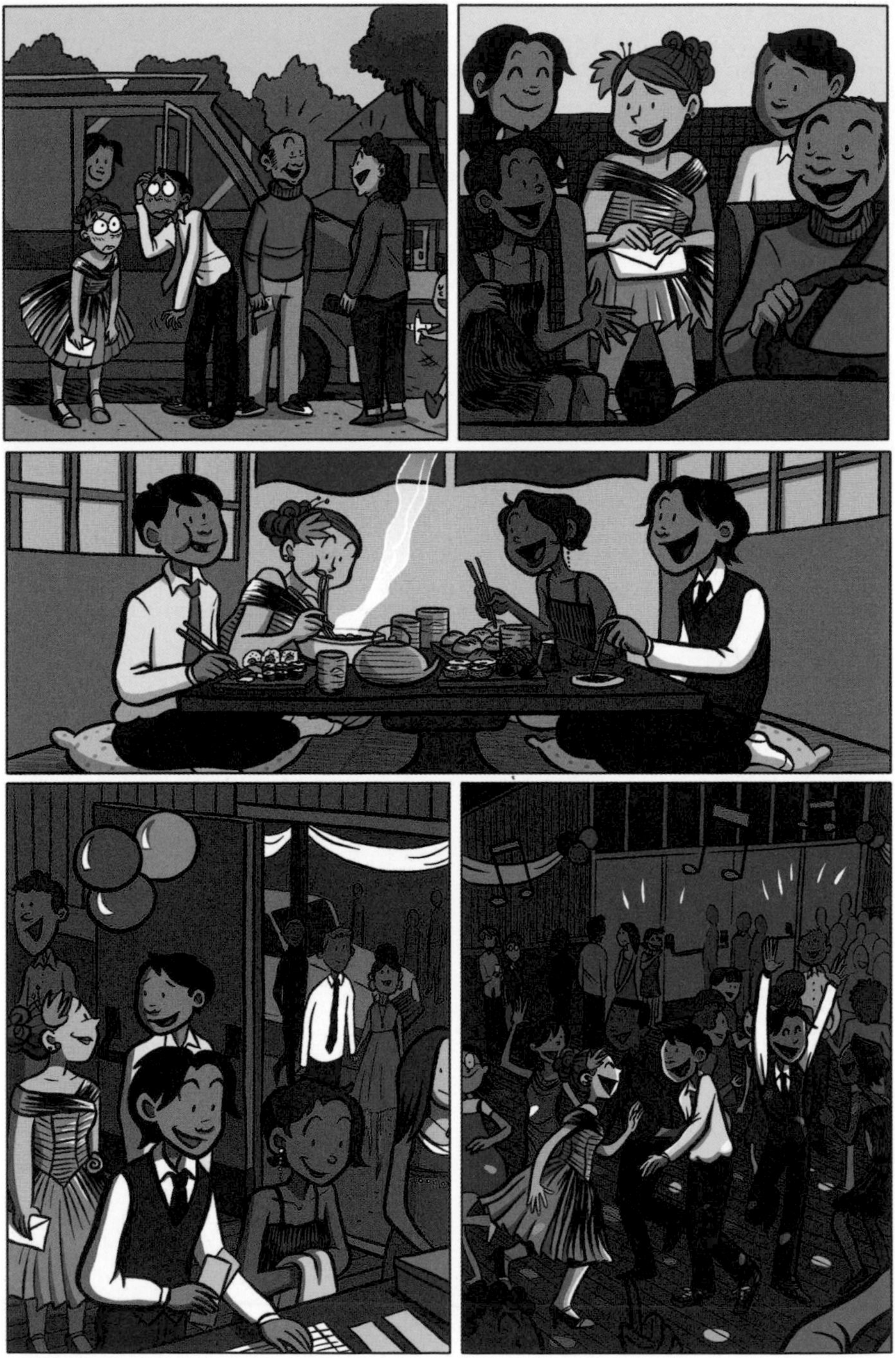

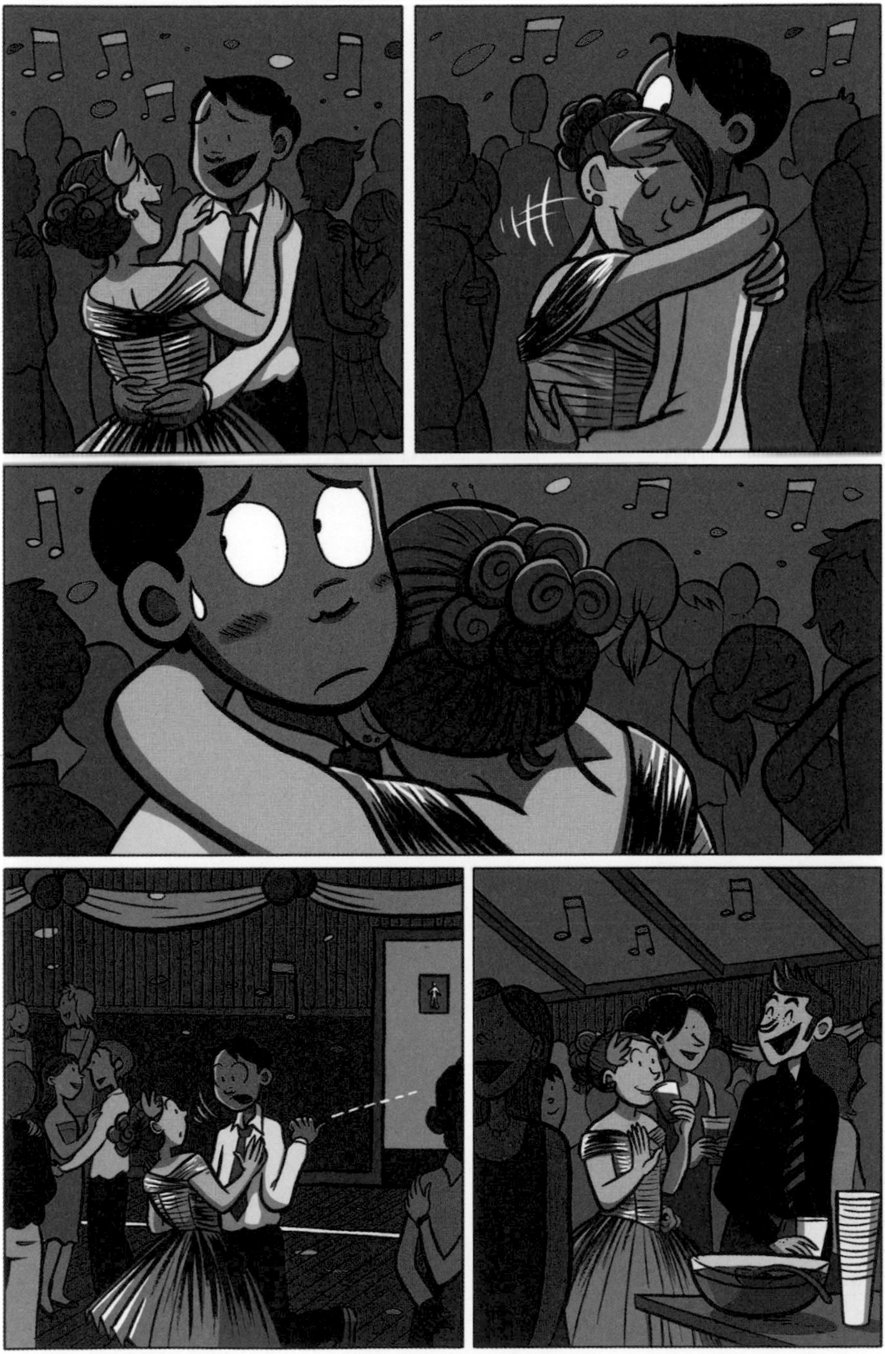

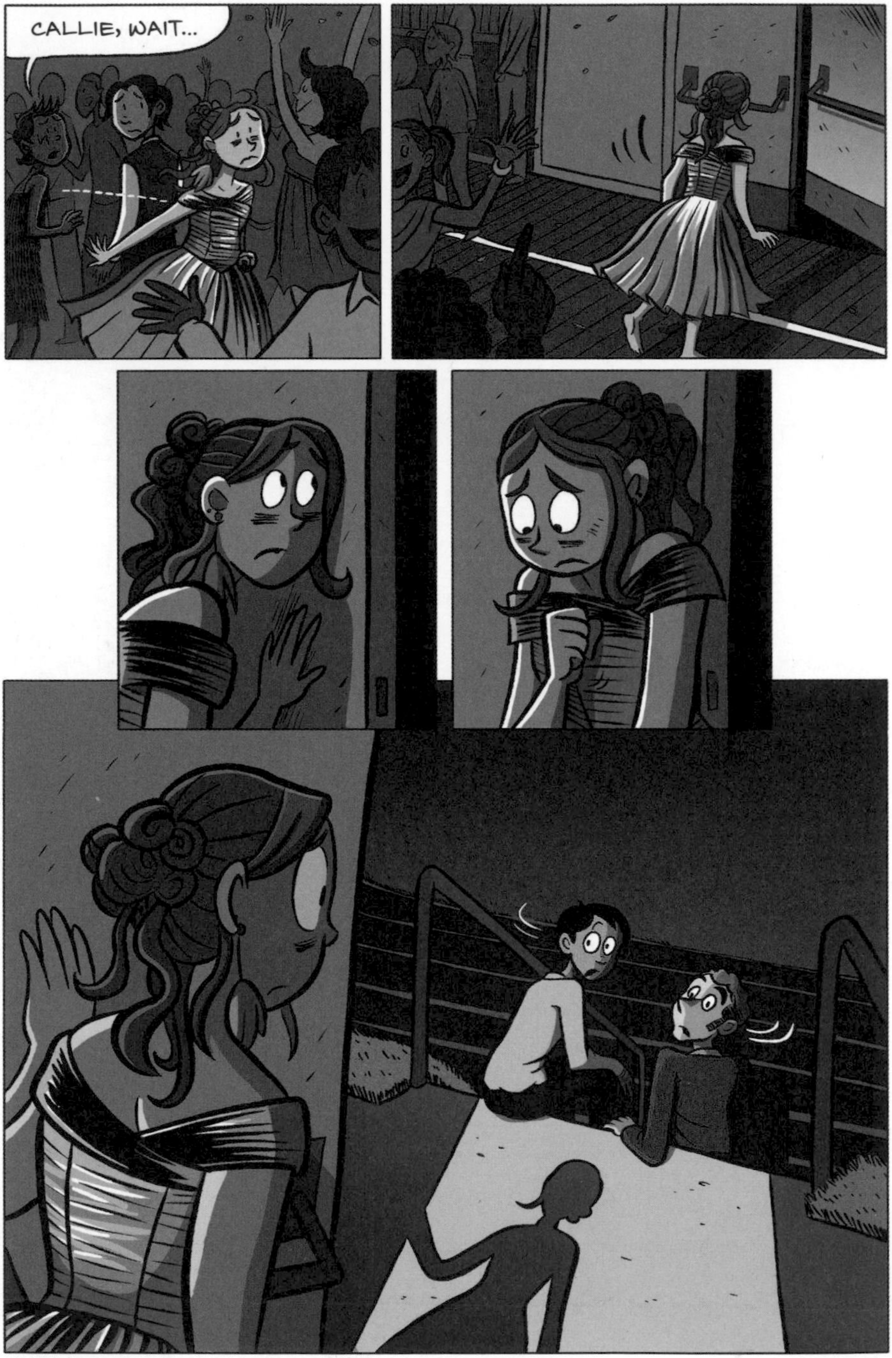
CALLIE, WAIT...

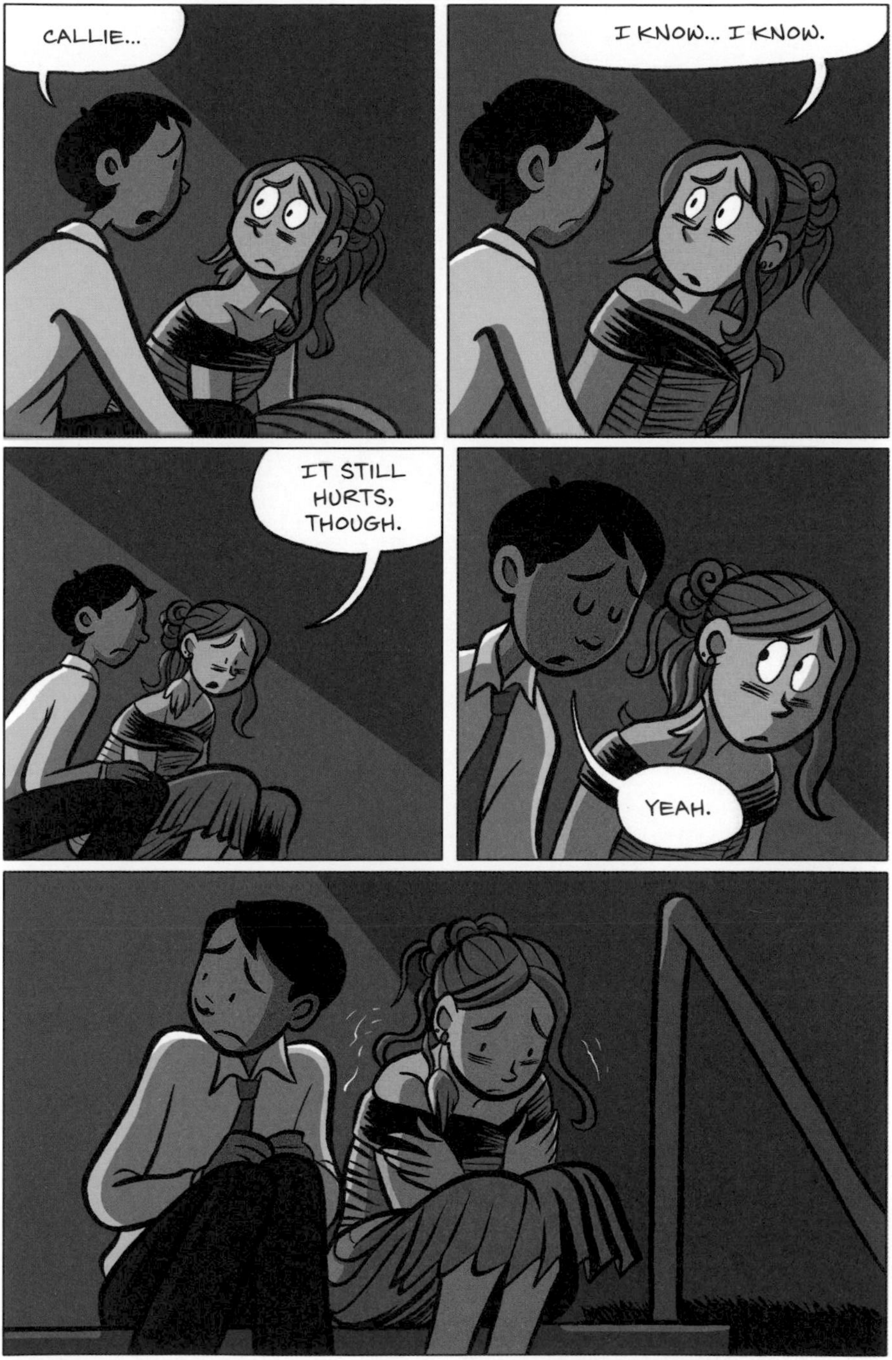
CALLIE...
I KNOW... I KNOW.
IT STILL HURTS, THOUGH.
YEAH.

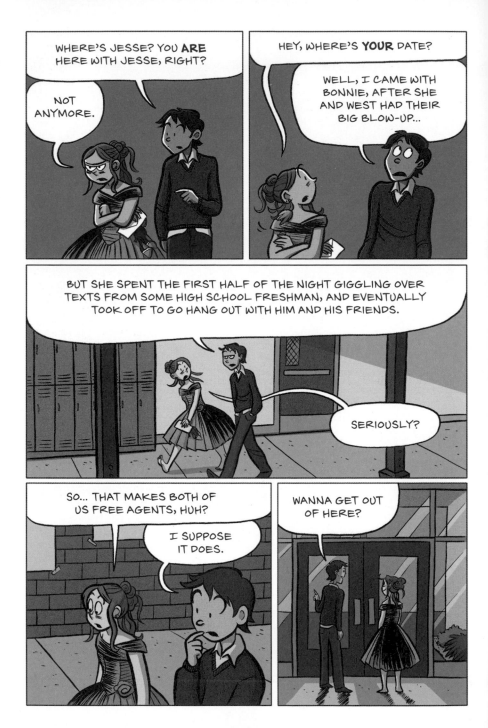

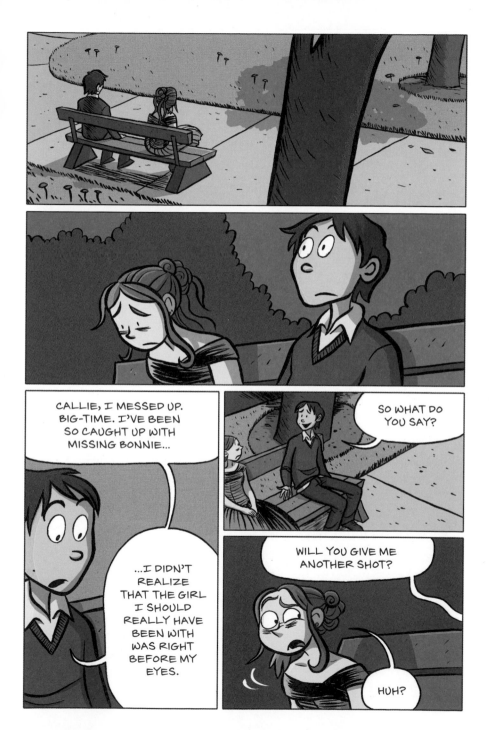

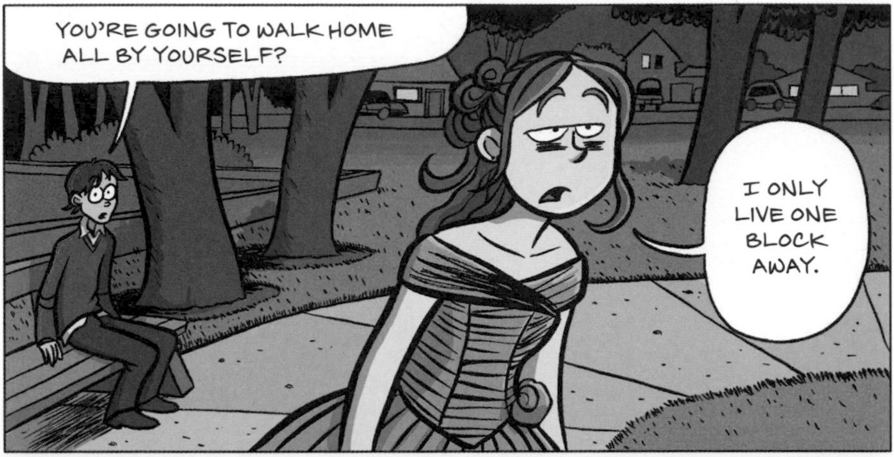
YOU'RE GOING TO WALK HOME ALL BY YOURSELF?
I ONLY LIVE ONE BLOCK AWAY.

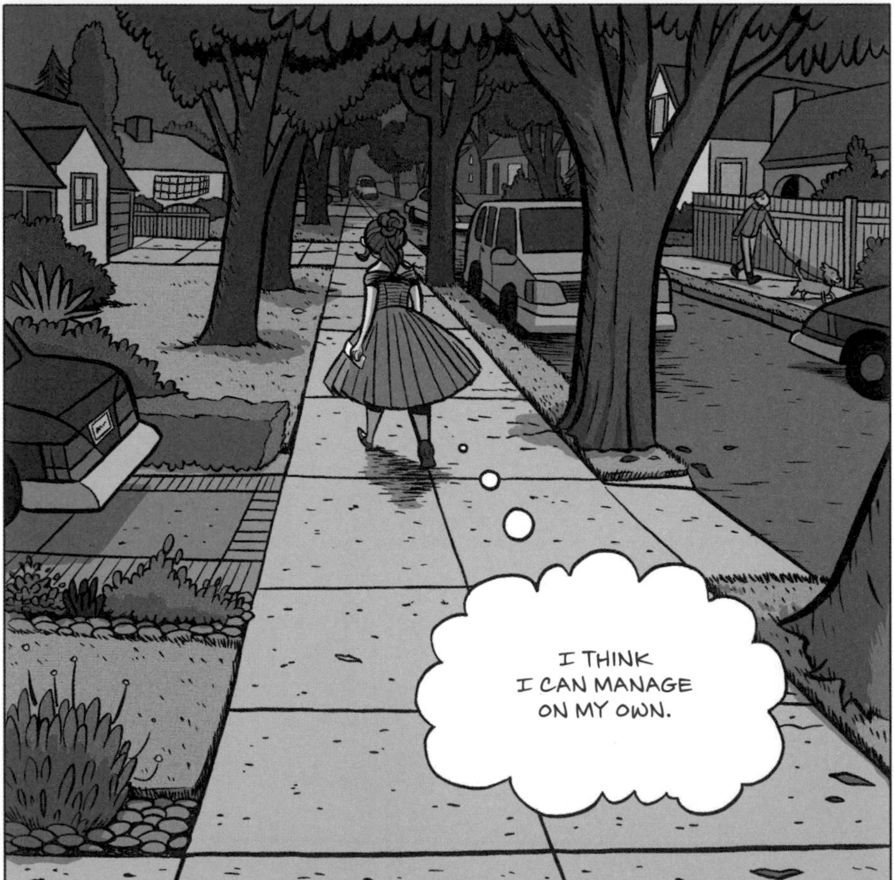
I THINK I CAN MANAGE ON MY OWN.

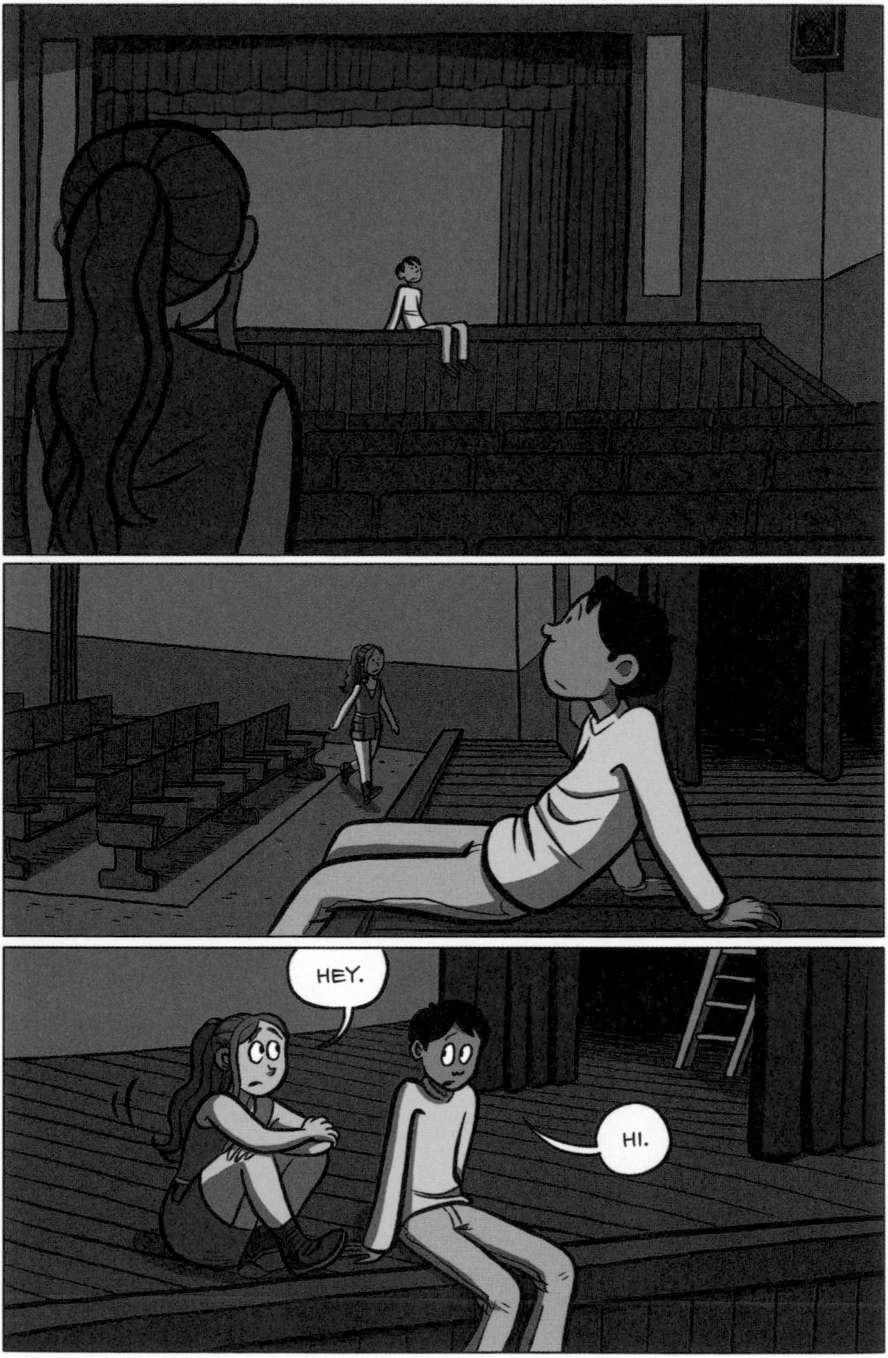
HEY.
HI.

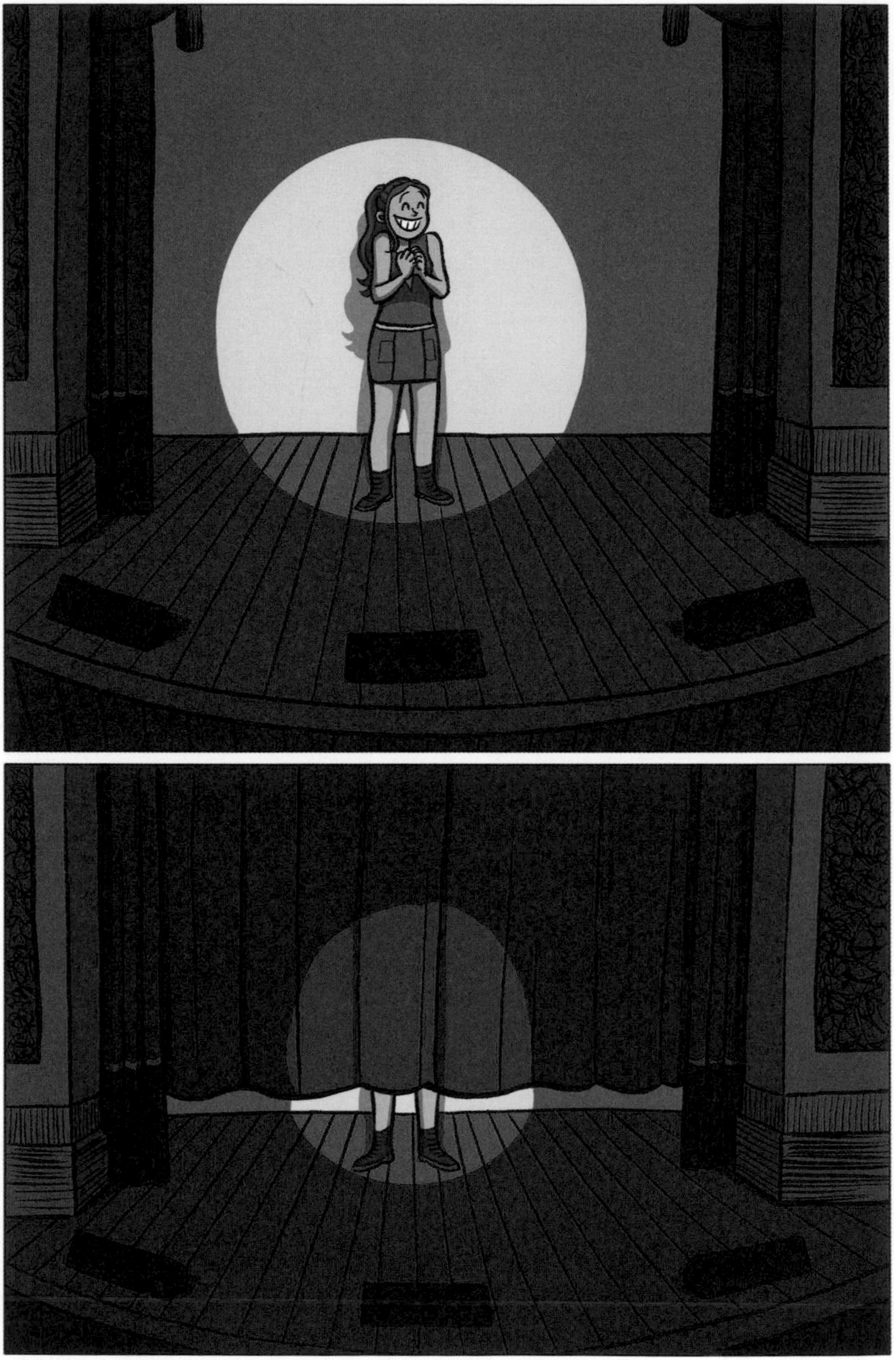

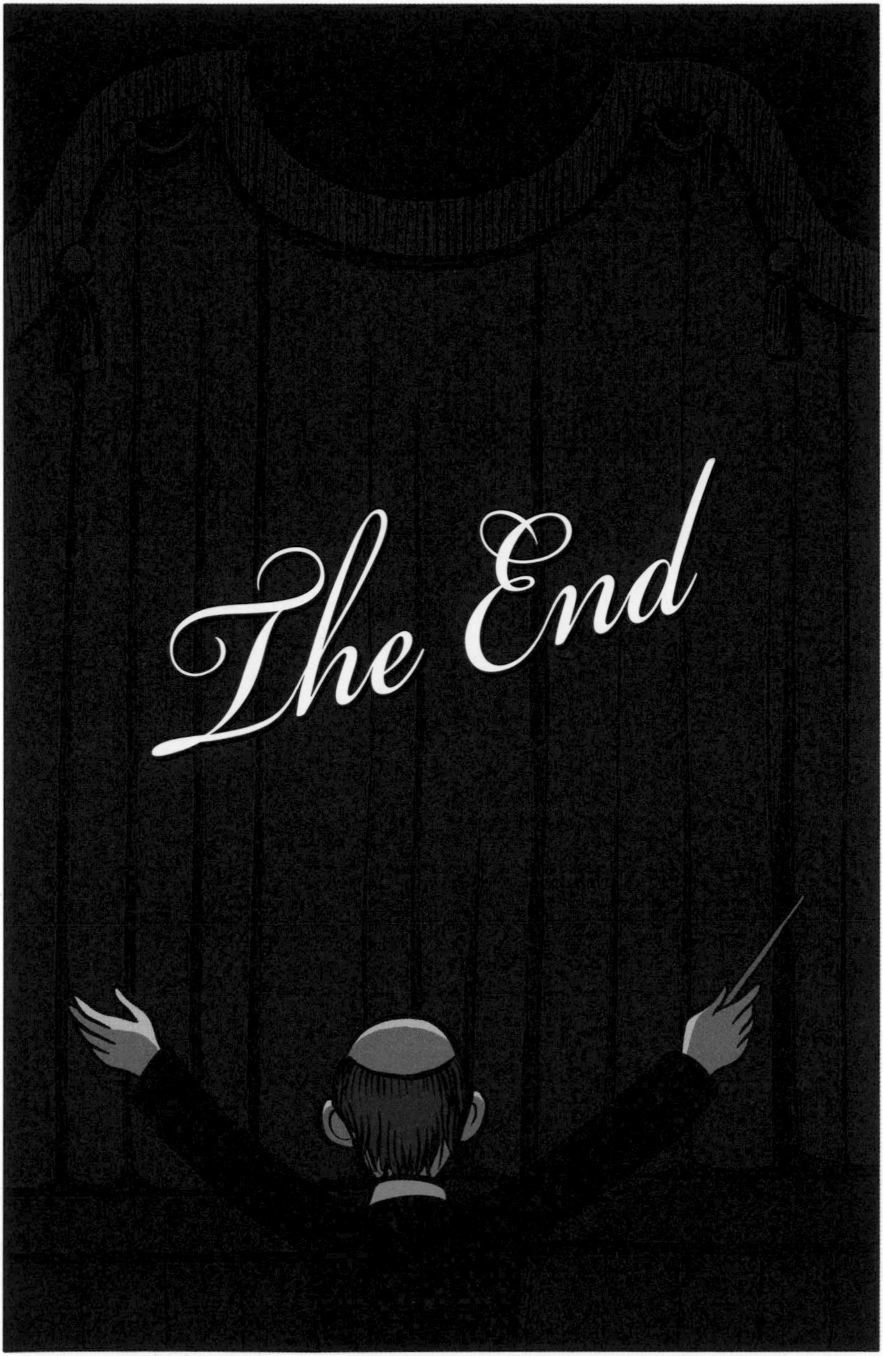
The End

AUTHOR'S NOTE

This book would not exist without my friends and instructors from the theater, choir, and stage crew communities in high school.

As a teenager, I took drama and choir classes, which led to small roles in school productions of *Guys and Dolls*, *Sweeney Todd*, *Evita*, and *City of Angels*. I sang exactly one solo line in my four years of high school, but enjoyed being part of the ensemble (singers who play lots of different characters, mostly in the background or crowd scenes) so much that I did it every chance I got.

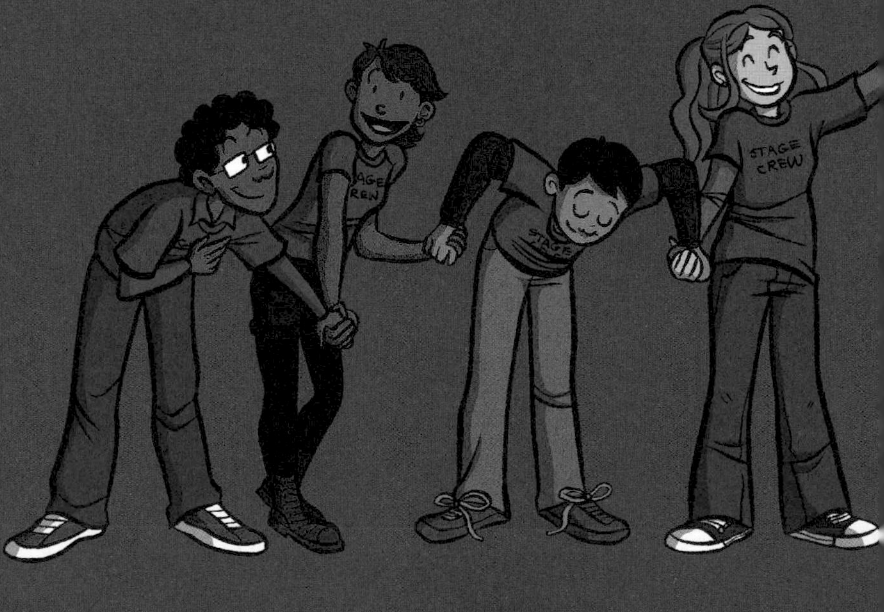
STAGE
CREW

More important than any of the parts I sang were the people I met: singers, dancers, actors — many of them surprisingly modest or shy! — set designers, stage managers, directors, band members . . . every person on or behind the stage had an important role to play, and pulling off a live show together was thrilling.

In a way, those years of my life helped me to find my voice and gave me a wealth of artistic material to draw from. Callie's experiences are different from my own, but many of the characters and events in this story are inspired by things I was a part of. And the talent, courage, and dedication of my friends continue to inspire me every single day.

—Raina

THANKS TO . . .

Jake and Jeff Manabat, for being two of my favorite people on the planet.

Cassandra Pelham, David Saylor, Phil Falco, Sheila Marie Everett, Lizette Serrano, Tracy van Straaten, Ed Masessa, and everyone at Scholastic. You are a joy to work with.

John Green, Gurihiru, and Aki Yanagi, my dedicated production team.

Megan Brennan and Gale Williams, my skilled production assistants.

The Riverdale Country School, who were kind enough to let me photograph their theater department.

Ivy Ratafia and Winter Mcleod, for their insightful notes on the manuscript.

Sara Ryan, Dylan Meconis, Faith Erin Hicks, Hope Larson, David Levithan, Kate Kubert Puls, Jerzy Drozd, Vera Brosgol, and Debbie Huey for their support, advice, and friendship during this book's creation.

Judy Hansen, my fabulous agent.

My family, who got me hooked on movie musicals when I was a kid.

And Dave Roman, who contributes so much of himself to my work, and cannot be thanked enough. I'm lucky to have him as my co-star.

BIBLIOGRAPHY

Appelbaum, Stanley, ed. *The New York Stage: Famous Productions in Photographs*. New York: Dover Publications, 1976.

Campbell, Drew. *Technical Theater for Nontechnical People*. New York: Allworth Press, 2004.

Carter, Paul. *Backstage Handbook: An Illustrated Almanac of Technical Information*. Louisville: Broadway Press, 1994.

RAINA TELGEMEIER is the #1 *New York Times* bestselling, multiple Eisner Award–winning creator of *Smile* and *Sisters*, which are both graphic memoirs based on her childhood. She is also the creator of *Drama*, which was named a Stonewall Honor Book and was selected for YALSA's Top Ten Great Graphic Novels for Teens. Raina lives in the San Francisco Bay Area. To learn more, visit her online at www.goRaina.com.

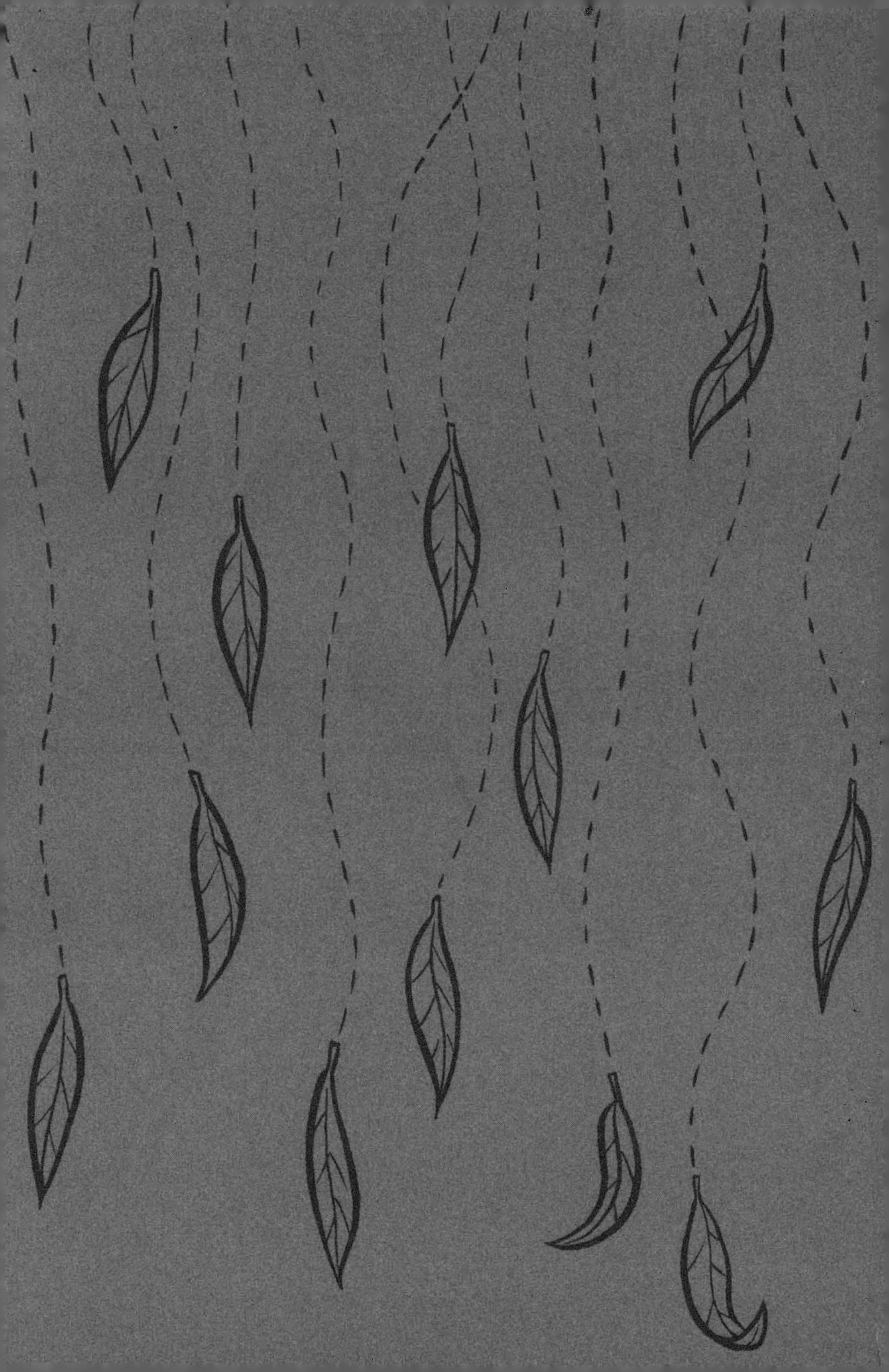